I0664431

JUSTICE

BOOK ONE OF THE GALILEE
FALLS TRILOGY

CHRONICLED BY JENNIFER HARLOW

Dedicated to anyone who saw injustice and had the strength to say, "Not on my watch."

ALSO BY JENNIFER HARLOW

Mind Over Monsters: A F.R.E.A.K.S. Squad Series 1

To Catch a Vampire: A F.R.E.A.K.S. Squad Series 2

What's A Witch To Do? A Midnight Magic Mystery 1

Death Takes A Holiday: A F.R.E.A.K.S. Squad Series 3 (8/13)

Werewolf Sings The Blues: A Midnight Magic Mystery 2 (3/14)

PRAISE FOR THE WORKS OF JENNIFER HARLOW

"Chills and laughter share equal time in Harlow's fresh and funny debut." – *The Library Journal*

"Funny, scary, and creepy, ridiculous amounts of fun!" –*Kat Richardson* The Greywalker Series

"Monstrously fun! Monstrously suspenseful! Monstrously good!" –*Victoria Laurie,* NYT Best Selling Author

"If Donald Westlake had ever gotten around to writing a paranormal mystery, it would have sounded like this." -*Kirkus*

"'Can you be so cruel?'

'Yes, I can be very cruel. I have been taught by masters.'"

-Paramount Picture's The Heiress (1949)

PROLOGUE

The wolves are at the gate.

I count thirty police officers on my security monitors, including SWAT, all armed to the gills led by him. *I always knew this day would come. It has been almost twenty years in the making, but now it's here...this must have been how Nero felt as he played that fiddle. My Rome is burning. Soon my freedom will be gone and yet I could still manage a tune. First things first.*

Waverly, one of my loyal employees these two years, runs into the study. His fear does not inspire confidence. "Sir, what are we supposed to do? The police and—"

"Stop sniveling for one," I say, taking a sip of my Scotch. I will miss this.

"Did Grace—"

The bullet I put between his eyes stops the rest of that sentence. I don't have time to answer a million questions. Company's coming. I down the rest of my drink as I run the electromagnet over my computer. Cleaner than the day I bought it. Must leave things tidy. I've already set the timers in the file cabinets. Thirty more seconds before, like Nero, all that remains of my empire is ashes.

The bombs detonate as I walk down the hall, no louder than gunshots but still rocking the walls sprinkling dust on my paintings. I wonder what will happen to my art. Probably sold for victim reparations. The Degas alone will cover the cost of the library we destroyed today. Smith and Rees are waiting in what is left of my living room. Just looking at it, especially what's left of Bradley under that bloody sheet, I feel embarrassed for myself. I never lose control like that. I don't know what I was thinking. I suppose I'm paying the price now.

"Sir, where do you want us?" Smith, a five year veteran of my service, asks.

I turn over the couch with a sigh. "Gentlemen, I want to thank you both for your loyal service through the years. You have both been invaluable. I wish things could have gone a different way. I apologize." I fire a single shot into Smith's forehead. Poor Rees is too shocked to even draw on me before he meets the same ending. The loose ends are no more. The rest is in the hands of the fates.

The last of my security doors fall, the sound of steel hitting marble echoing through the room. I cross my leg, wipe the speckles of dust off my costume, and put a smile on my face. The bane of my existence, the man I hate, who has consumed my life for years, super-speeds into my living room as if he owns it. And the press calls me arrogant.

"Alkaline," he says beneath that dark mask.

"Justice," I say with a nod. We stare at each other for a few seconds, even now locked in battle. "Grace?"

"She's safe. You can't hurt her or anyone else ever again." He pauses for dramatic effect, or to savor his victory. "Will this be easy or hard?"

For a moment, I consider an attack. It always gives me almost orgasmic pleasure when my fist hits his body and he cries out in pain. One last taste for the road? No, I quell this urge. My body has not completely healed from our fight a few hours ago and quite frankly, I need a break. Being the scourge of the city is exhausting. "You may take me to jail now."

As I'm led out past the frightened police and gawking bystanders, I keep that smile on my face. Not because I'm arrogant, not to save face, because…I may have lost this battle, but the war has just begun.

Then Rome will truly burn.

CHAPTER ONE
PERFECTION

THREE YEARS LATER...

Why did she have to be so perfect?

Glossy red hair, curves in all the right places, dimples when she smiles—which is all the time—and soulful green eyes. Even a perfect sparking personality. The woman spends all day saving sick children, then goes home to her equally perfect daughter to be Supermom. How the hell can I compete with that?

They are a sight to see, with him more breathtaking than her. Blonde hair, lean body, bright blue eyes, strong jaw, and cleft chin just ripe for caressing. The soon-to-be first Lord and Lady of Galilee Falls. In a month, I'll lose him to the most perfect woman who ever walked the earth. Perfect.

Dobbs, Justin's butler, pours me another flute of champagne, which I down with one gulp. It'll take about five more of these before this evening becomes manageable. I don't even know why I'm here. Like I want to meet Rebecca's mother. She's a brown haired version of her daughter, probably in her late fifties and nary a gray hair. Sure she has a few wrinkles near her eyes and laugh lines, but the age fairy has pretty much passed her by. If Mom's any indication, perfect Rebecca will probably be fucking perfect even in the grave. So unfair.

They sit on the eighteenth century blue French silk couch that once belonged to Marie Antoinette, royalty in their own right. They ignore the champagne in their hands, instead grinning as Rebecca's three-year-old daughter Daisy draws a duck or malformed tree or something. From the looks on the adults' faces, you'd think the kid was painting the Sistine Chapel.

We've gathered tonight to welcome Marnie, Rebecca's mother who will be staying until the wedding in a month. For the third time tonight I ask myself why I'm here. I can't come up with an answer. I've been up since two in the morning after working a triple homicide in Diablo's Ward. Half the time was in the field interviewing the usual pillars of the community like the junkie clients of the deceased, and the other half was in a cramped room grilling the dead dealer's supplier. My partner Cam and I finally broke him, but it took twice as long as I thought it would.

I considered flaking out but promised I'd be part of the welcoming committee. I try to be a woman of my word. Apparently Rebecca's been telling her mother *all* about me, and Marnie was just *dying* to meet me. The bride-to-be is under the impression that since I'm Justin's best friend, then I must be hers too. She even joked that they had a fight over if I would be the best man or the maid of honor. I didn't believe it for a second. They're too perfect to fight.

"Is that a duck?" Justin asks in that baritone voice that commands attention.

"Yep," Daisy answers. "It's Super-Duck!"

"Really? What are its superpowers?" Rebecca asks.

"It quacks!" Daisy answers.

"That is a very good power," Marnie says with a smile. She looks at me, and I plaster a fake smile that fools them every time. Lots of practice, thank you very much. Marnie saunters toward me. "So, you're a detective?"

"Youngest ever to work the Priority Homicide Squad," Justin says with pride.

"That must be difficult. All those dead bodies. I can't even imagine it," Marnie says.

"I have a strong stomach."

"And you two met as children?"

"Twenty years," Justin says.

"Jesus, that long?" I say with a fake sneer.

"How did you two meet?" Marnie asks.

I swig the once again full champagne. "I was trying to kill myself on his bridge, and he stopped me."

Marine's face falls. "Oh. I'm sorry I—"

"Oh, don't worry. I got over it."

"Jo…" Justin says reproachfully.

"Well, we all go through our rough times," Marnie says, patting my hand. "What matters is you made it through it. And much stronger I bet. You were so young, though."

"Twelve, but I've always been precocious."

"Do you mind if I ask why?"

"Mom," Rebecca warns.

"It's okay. My father had just been murdered. It seemed like a good idea at the time." I smile at Justin, who smiles back. "And I got a best friend out of it, so there you go."

"They've been inseparable ever since," Rebecca adds.

The fake smile resurfaces. They've known each other all of a year, and she's talking like we've been the Three Musketeers forever. Was she there when he swam out too far and almost drowned? Was she there when he was accused of cheating in Algebra and was suspended? Was she there when Pendergast Industries was sued for tax fraud and almost went under? No, she wasn't. I was. I called the ambulance, I ditched school those three days and played video games with him, and I listened to hours of boring financial crap while he tried to figure out what happened. *Me*. I'd point this out, but I'd sound bratty. God, I need more booze.

I'm out of the hot seat as the three adults begin talking about the wedding, and I tune out, slowly inching myself to the back wall and hopefully out of their attention. I really want another drink, but three glasses is my limit when I have to drive home. I could go to town and crash in one of the seven guest rooms, but I'm sure they're staying here tonight and I can only take so much perfection before my head explodes.

I didn't give Rebecca much thought when he introduced us twelve months ago. Sure she was gorgeous and a talented doctor, but Justin always dated the talented gorgeous. He'd done the billionaire playboy thing since he was seventeen, with the usual models and actresses or a lawyer or businesswoman thrown in for good measure. I'd met a lot of them, so I just assumed he'd keep his MO of three months, just enough time for them to fall in love before he'd give them the polite boot. The jerk even complained about how hard it was having all those women fall head over heels for him. If only he knew. It took all my strength not to sock him in the jaw.

Then they passed the three month mark. The fourth. We didn't see each other for weeks at a time, and when we did she'd be there. At the shooting range. At dinner. Instead of sailing, we'd meet at a playground and watch Daisy swing. No more bars, only restaurants with mechanical mice singing. No more jetting off to see a football game on a moment's notice. Then she called me. And called again, insisting we meet for lunch. Shopping. Facials. The best and only advice my mother gave me years before rang in my ears.

"Never make him choose. Remember, he's a man and he's fucking *her*. Who do you think he'll pick?"

It was important to Justin, *she* was important to Justin, so I agreed. Even attended Daisy's ballet recital with them.

I could feel it coming, and I did my best to prepare for it. The engagement. But when he called me to the house, and they were both grinning like mental patients, not so subtly pointing to the diamond on her finger, I had no idea my reaction would be so severe. I saw that ring, and it was as if all the joy and peace I ever had or ever would feel was sucked out of every one of my cells.

I have no idea how I got through the following ten minutes of congratulations and champagne, but I managed to smile and hold off the tears until I got off the property. Then I got drunk. *Very* drunk. It was a miracle I didn't end up in the hospital with charcoal in my stomach. That miracle came in the form of my boss Harry, who the bartender at Neptune's called and then saw me home. Another man saving me from myself.

I know I'm a horrible friend, I *know* this. When your best friend finds the love of his life, and is blissfully happy, and you're trying to figure out the best way to frame his bride for drug possession, this becomes abundantly clear. Mind you, I do get some points for not actually doing it, but just the thought makes me feel better. It's me. It's all me. I am the asshole in this situation, I am fully aware of that. If I gave her half a chance I'm sure I'd love her just like everyone else on planet earth. The green-eyed monster who lives inside me just won't allow it. And I don't have the energy or strength to kill the fucker.

Not that they'd ever guess my ire. A combination of that ecstasy bubble, and my stellar lying skills, have shielded me from any awkward questions or situations. Except in the case of Justin's Aunt Lucy. She cornered me in the hall one day and threatened to have me killed if I did anything to ruin the wedding. I very politely told her where to shove her threat. We've never been best friends.

Lucy sits on the other side of the room, her nose in a book. *She's* allowed to be anti-social. The first moment I saw her on that bridge I was reminded of a strict nun who wouldn't hesitate to smack me with a ruler for sneezing during prayer. She's in her late fifties with short salt and pepper hair, face stretched across sharp cheekbones and pointed nose, and gaunt body always in chic black. She hasn't changed much in twenty years. Still just tolerates me. She's not even trying tonight.

"Isn't that right, Joanna?" Rebecca asks, pulling me out of my head.

"I'm sorry. What?"

"You've met Justice, haven't you?"

"I've had an encounter or two," I say, not hiding my distaste.

"He helped you on the Corona case, right?" Rebecca asks.

"How frightening," Marnie says. "I can't imagine having to be near, let alone chasing after a super. It must be so dangerous."

"It happens less often than the press would have you believe," I say. "Most of the time I deal with the usual. Gangs, domestic violence, drugs. When supers fight, it's usually just with other supers. We, sadly, just handle the collateral damage."

"Isn't Galilee one of the only cities that passed a law giving some supers latitude in pursuing criminals?" Marnie asks.

"Yes. It allows certain supers the ability to be deputized as a Marshal to catch other supers," Justin says.

"And how great that's been," I say sarcastically. "We have the biggest concentration of superheroes in the country, and with them comes the biggest number of villains. We also have the highest property insurance and taxes in the world because of all the buildings these people destroy. Not to mention several times a year I have to tell some poor kid their idiot father put some suction cups all over his body and tried to fight crime but instead was shot to death in Diablo's Ward."

"Joanna, your prejudice is showing," Justin chides.

"I'm not prejudiced. People with powers have been around forever, and it's not like they can help being born like they are. Just because you can run really fast or move a car with your mind doesn't mean you should put on a costume and beat people up. I've just seen the reality and all the lives messed up because people take the law into their own hands instead of leaving it to the trained professionals. It's gotten worse over the years with the media coverage and fandemonium. Vigilantism is illegal for a reason, and these people just ignore that fact."

"You'd rather they squander their god-given gift?" Justin asks.

"I'd rather they leave the hero business to those of us trained to do it."

Justin and Rebecca share an uncomfortable glance, but quickly recover their smiles. "You make some good points," Rebecca says, "but I personally feel safer knowing there are men like Justice who have the ability to stop others like Stinger. It evens the playing field."

"Forget it darling," Justin says, "I've been trying to convince her for twenty years that supers aren't all bad. Even after Justice saved her from Corona she didn't change her tune."

"He didn't save me," I say, "he just pushed me out of the way when Corona shot out an energy blast. I would have *arrested* him if Justice hadn't sped in."

It was a good bust, the one that got me my spot in Priority. Reginald Fairweather, AKA Corona, was the latest baddie to hit the scene, using his solar flares to burn through buildings. He caught our attention when he used this skill to burn through the mayor's mansion. After that a task force, which I happened to worm my way onto, went about trying to locate him. Through some of my lowlife connections, and I have quite a few growing up where I did, I tracked down a henchman who led me straight to Corona. SWAT and I stormed in, and I was about to slap the cuffs on him, when Justice super-sped in, distracting me. Corona used that and almost blasted me to hell. After Justice subdued the villain, he handed him over to me. I was arresting officer of record and Justice made sure to let everyone know, including the brass and Mayor. Still don't like him.

Justice. Everyone's *favorite* superhero. Songs have been written about the man, but they seem to forget that villains like Hellion and Alkaline specifically donned their masks in Galilee to prove themselves against one of the foremost superheroes in America, injuring or killing dozens just to get his attention. Maybe if he didn't make himself so conspicuous with the press conferences, public appearances, cereals, or clothing line things might die down. Sure, all the money goes to the Restoration Society or Victim Assistance, but still. Gauche.

The department considers him a necessary evil. Rebecca's right about one thing—they do level the playing field. I'm not suicidal—well, anymore—enough to face off against a woman who creates tornados at will or blinds me with a look. I just wish they'd all go away. Even the good ones. They give us false hope that when a mugger approaches, Justice or Olympia will swoop in and save the day. People should know the only person who can really save them is themselves. I learned that at twelve, forty-year-olds should know better.

I didn't always hate supers. At first I worshiped Justice. His merchandise was all over my room. I'd been obsessed with him since he took down Dr. Phantom and his cyborgs on live TV. Even made a scrapbook of all his clippings. He'd saved thousands of people through the last thirty years, but then two months before Pop died, he just vanished. No word, no warning, nothing. Reports had him in Genevaville or Moscow, but not where he was really needed. When my Pop really needed him. I lost two heroes and my faith all in a month. So yeah, I'm a little prejudiced.

"Well, I like him," the always chipper Rebecca says. "I think he's cute."

"Should I be jealous?" Justin asks in a cutesy tone he caught from her.

Rebecca smirks and leans in to kiss him right on the cleft in his chin. "Never."

Cue projectile vomit.

"He must be about a hundred years old," I point out to stop the public display of affection. I wasn't kidding about the vomit.

"Who?" Marnie asks.

"Justice. He's been around since the thirties."

"Maybe when one retires another takes his place," Rebecca says.

"Then why not be original?" I ask.

"He's a symbol," she says. "One we've always had and looked up to. Like God or Jesus."

"Maybe we'd all be better off if we relied less on the abstract and more on reality," I say.

"You both make valid points," Justin says, "but I'm not that cynical, Jo. He serves a purpose. Hope is never a bad thing."

He always sides with her. Always and forever. I've lost him.

Before he says another word, my cell phone chirps on my belt. I didn't bother to change out of my suit, so the phone is right next to the gun. I've never been a fashion plate like Rebecca, who is dressed in a vintage Chanel dress with primroses imprinted up and down its loose fit. No, I stick to jeans and pantsuits in either gray or black, my colors. I flip open the phone. "Detective Fallon."

Everyone in the room but Justin seems impressed. He just stares at me. He can be a tad overprotective. Whenever I take a work call he moves closer to listen as his lips purse in disapproval. When I told him I was joining the force, he spent days trying to convince me that it was too dangerous. Too hard. He even offered me a cushy job at his company in the security department. He was worried about me, and I can't begin to describe how good that made me feel, but I'd known since I was thirteen I wanted to be a police officer. All that authority. All that power. Helping people. The gun doesn't hurt either. I got my AA in Criminal Justice at Galilee Community College and signed up the day after I graduated. Haven't regretted it to this day.

"Hey, Jo," my partner Terrance Cameron says. "I hope you're not too tired."

I press my finger against the receiver. "Excuse me," I say before stepping out of the library into the ginormous hallway. Every floor, except in the bedrooms, is covered with Corinthian marble the color of bone. The walls of the hallway are filled with paintings of landscapes and old soldiers or landowners in their red or brown uniforms. Every generation of Pendergast watching me from their oil canvas as I talk to my partner.

"Why? What happened?"

"I just got a call from ADA White. Janus Manx's attorney called him. She says Manx wants to talk to us about the rest of his victims."

"What? Tonight?"

Justin walks out, his usual look of concern plastered on his face. He's as nosy as I am.

"We have to be at the prison promptly at 7:30. Can you make it?"

I check my watch. "Just."

"See you there." He hangs up.

"What's going on?" Justin asks.

"The usual. Rape. Murder."

"You shouldn't joke like that," Justin chides.

I roll my eyes. "I'm a homicide detective. Gallows humor keeps me sane."

Rebecca pokes her head out, all smiles. "Hi. Is everything okay?"

"Yeah. I just have to go to work," I say.

She steps toward me, the smile falling. "Oh, no." She quickly glances at Justin. "Is everything okay?"

"Yeah, just the usual. Sorry to dash but duty calls and all."

Rebecca reaches out and squeezes my arm. There are precious few I let into my personal space, and those are usually the result of too much alcohol. I keep my mouth shut though. "I understand," Rebecca says. "You just be careful, okay?"

"Careful is my middle name. Tell your mom and Daisy good-bye for me."

"Of course. And if you can't make it to the engagement party, we'll understand."

I may not have to dress up and schmooze with high society. Silver lining. "I'll do what I can to make it."

"We know you will," Justin says. "Call me tomorrow, okay? So I know you're safe?"

He's always done this since I've been on the job. I have to call every morning just to tell him I'm alive with all my limbs still attached. It should annoy me, what with me being an independent butt kicking woman who doesn't need any man to look after her, but instead it warms my heart that he cares so much.

One time I was drowning in a case and barely ate, let alone had time to call anyone, and Justin showed up in the squad room demanding to see me. I was out in the field, but Harry assured him I was fine. I called right away when I heard. Not many people would do that, certainly not for me. I can count them on one hand.

"Don't I always?' I say with a smirk. "You guys have a good night." With my best fake smile, I turn around and walk out.

Another perfect end to another perfect night with the perfect lovebirds. I prefer a conversation with a serial killer any day of the damn week.

CHAPTER TWO
ESCAPE

I leave Galilee Gardens with its million dollar homes up and down the coast with suburbs and strip malls filling in the rest until the state park begins. As I drive over the infamous mile long Pendergast Bridge, a steel structure whose pylons undulate like the Andalucía River waves below, I feel nothing. Not even when I pass the spot right in the middle where I stopped that night twenty years ago.

Now, I was never one to believe in anything higher than the top of my head. I'm practical to a fault, or so I've been told. So the fact that the two of us ended up on that bridge at the same time, to me, is just a random, happy occurrence. Justin gives the credit to the universe. I will admit that the fact two sort-of orphans the same age, who had no cause to meet, both arriving on a deserted bridge at two in the morning is odd. If I believed in fate then that's what I'd call it. But I don't, so I'll just chalk it up to blind luck.

I chose that spot for the view. I wanted the last thing I'd ever see to be the best of my city, Galilee Falls, the fifth largest in the nation. I love my city. I wouldn't live anywhere else. Whenever I think about it, I swell with pride. Like now. To the north, glass and concrete fill the sky for what seems like the end of the world. The biggest is Pendergast Pavilion, seventy-seven stories topped with a silver spire off a church salvaged from the Dark Ages adding five more stories to it. But my favorite building is the hospital right at the edge of the river facing The Falls on the other side of the bridge. It's the biggest hospital in the country at thirty stories. The best too, at least according to every major magazine. Know where they first isolated the Uber-Gene? Our Lady of Perpetual Sorrow in my home town, that's where.

With the good always comes the bad. The beauty fades as I continue driving into the heart of darkness known as Diablo's Ward, my old neighborhood. Vagrants, corner kids, junkies, and hookers litter the streets surrounded by boarded up, graffittied buildings that are barely standing. Gunshots and shouting are commonplace. Ever since I've been on the job I've spent more time here than when I was a kid.

I drive through the Ward toward the ocean where the road to the Xavier Bridge is. Two miles offshore with only the drawbridge for access is Xavier Maximum Security Prison, home to the worst of the worst: Hellion, Wolfsbane, Belladonna, and the man I'm making the trip for, Janus Manx, a serial killer responsible for killing ten prostitutes a year ago. Xavier is smaller than a normal prison, housing only two hundred inmates, three psychiatrists, seventy-five guards, and a partridge in a pear tree. The cells are encased in lead, the inmates get an hour of rec time a day, followed by some of the strongest tranquilizers this side of the zoo. Drooling idiots, just how I like my murderers.

I cross the small, two-lane metal bridge over the ocean, the water sparking with an orange tint as the sun sets above. I'm soon back on dry land. As I approach the three-story building, the huge electrified fence looms with twirling lights above barbwire. Men in brown uniforms toting shotguns stand like centurions on either side of the gate. The one on my side approaches as I flash my shield. He signals to his partner and the gate slides open. I add my car to the rest in the small lot and walk up the steps to the double doors. I'm right on time.

Cam, my man on the front lines, waits for me right near the overweight guard standing by the metal detector. Cam's in his very late forties with a boxer's build, which he compliments with a bald head, almost true black skin, and a problem matching his clothes. I'm no fashion plate by any standards, but any member of normal society should know that bowties and suspenders went out in the fifties. He towers over me at 6"1' with enough muscle that my thigh is the exact size of his arm. We know because on a stake-out we measured. We look ridiculous standing next to each other. I'm 5"2', so petite my clothes from middle school still fit, pale as a ghost with freckles on my nose, long curly jet black hair, and wide bright blue eyes. Shortest person on the force.

If his size intimidates, his face makes you fall in love with him. Not a wrinkle, with a black and gray goatee. If his wife Tawny didn't feed me every other week, I'd entertain the thought of seducing him. Her pork chops are *that* good.

We've been partners since I started at Priority Homicide for almost two years. He was hesitant at first as his partner of five years had just retired, but after one week when I tackled a drugged-out man double my size, he started to warm a little. A month after that, I was practically part of the family. I've lost count of how many blind dates that family's tried to set me up on. If they only knew.

"I hope this guy isn't just jerking us around," Cam says as we approach the metal detector. Not many visitors are allowed through these gates except lawyers and villain groupies who fudge birth certificates to show they're "related" to the incarcerated. Sad. The only weapons allowed on-site are in the Hardcore Unit—their name not mine—where the criminals with superpowers are housed. We hand over our weapons to the guard, who sticks them in a lockbox before walking us through.

"Hell, I'd rather be here than where I was," I say, getting my keys and wallet back. We walk down the beige hallway with pictures of the guards on the wall. "Did you call Harry about this?"

"I left a message, but I think he's still at the Mike Spencer bombing site with Kowalski and Mirabelle."

"Well, better them than us."

The guard behind the bullet resistant glass at the reception area looks up from his magazine as we approach. "May I help you?"

"Detectives Cameron and Fallon here to interview prisoner Janus Manx," Cam says.

"One moment please," the guard says as he makes a call.

As we wait for confirmation, I turn around and lean against the wall with a sigh. I so just want to go home and crawl into bed, but no, instead I get to spend countless hours listening to a man tell me how he vivisected women. Fun all around. A guard wearing a Galilee Angels baseball cap with his head hung rounds the corner, followed by an Asian man dressed in a business suit. God, you could not pay me enough to work here.

As the guard passes, his head tilts up to gaze at me. I can only see half his face, but I can tell he's very good looking: about forty, six foot, and medium build, with wide lips and brown eyes, the visible one winking at me. My body tenses a little for some reason. I swear I've seen him before. Where—

Cam's angry booming voice interrupts my train of thought. "What do you mean he's in the hole?"

I turn around to see the guard hanging up the phone. "I'm sorry, but he's been in there all day."

"But that's impossible. His lawyer called us saying she spoke to him just hours ago."

"I don't know what to tell you. There is no way he made that call. I—"

"Holy shit! I need some help over here!" a man shouts around the corner.

Cam and I take off like rockets. About twenty yards away another guard kneels on the beige linoleum, beside him another man lies on the floor covered in blood and a pink frothy liquid that still bubbles. The smell of sizzling flesh with metallic acid and blood is overpowering. "Lockdown! We need a lockdown now!" the guard shouts into the radio on his shoulder.

Cam kneels down too, yanking off his jacket. "We need to stop the bleeding."

The prostrate man, if he can be called that because I doubt he's barely out of his teens, is as white as a ghost. His left hand is nothing but a pulpy stump, and he's not dressed. He's only in boxers and a gore-covered undershirt. Oh, fuck. I remember exactly where I'd seen that guard before. I look at Cam. "Alkaline! Fucking Alkaline is trying to escape!"

Instinct takes over. I take off running the way I came, passing the receptionist who shouts, "What the fuck is the matter with the security system?" into the phone. Not good.

As I'm going one way as fast as my feet can take me, the guard at the metal detector runs the other. We both stop. "What the fuck—"

"Did a guard with a baseball cap just leave?" I ask.

"Yeah, he—"

I don't wait for the rest. I sprint toward the entrance, retrieving my car keys from my pocket. Just as I step out, booming gunshots ring out from the watchtowers above, their guns pointed down the road on the other side of the fence. He's out.

As I approach my car, I notice a pair of legs on the ground about three spots away. The Asian man lays motionless next to his empty spot, his head at an odd angle and eyes open. I feel his broken neck for a pulse, but there isn't one. Nothing I can do here. I leap up and get to my car.

My spare gun is in the locked glove box, and I retrieve it before I peel out of my spot, tires squealing loud enough to overpower the waning gunshots and barrel out the open gate. I turn right, the only way off the island toward the bridge. As I super-speed as fast as Justice, I get on my own radio. "Attention, this is Det. Joanna Fallon, badge number 5757. We have a prison break at Xavier Prison. I repeat, James Ryder, AKA Alkaline, has escaped from Xavier. I am in pursuit, about to cross onto Xavier Bridge. Known one dead, one injured. Send back-up immediately!" Dispatch does her job, ordering all available units toward the bridge. I spot the only car on the road as I cross onto the bridge, a red SUV about a quarter mile away. My blood is pumping and I can feel every inch of my skin. I can see why some people become adrenaline junkies. I floor it.

I gain ground and he speeds up, so I do as well, but then out of nowhere he switches lanes and slams on the breaks so he's behind me. Motherfucker. Both feet punch the break, my heart and stomach almost leap out of my rib cage. Thank God I have on my seatbelt or I would have broken my ribs on the steering wheel, instead I lose all the air in my lungs. But I'm not totally lucky. I lose a second because, unlike him, I come to a complete stop, smoke from my tires visible in the back. I know what his next move is and I'm not ready for it. I accelerate as fast as I can but not fast enough. The SUV zooms alongside me, smashing me into the side, sparks flying as metal rubs against concrete. He pins me, but I keep my foot on the petal. He's still behind me and the bastard actually salutes me. I'll wipe that smug fucking attitude right out of him.

I aim the gun out the window, but he swerves to the other lane for a moment before smashing into my side again. My hand hits the car door and I lose the gun, my wrist vibrating in pain. I lose control of the car, spinning to the other lane, the back of my car hitting the concrete on that side. I've practiced this maneuver at the academy and my beautiful instincts are the only thing that keeps me alive.

Alkaline doesn't wait around to check on me. The SUV whizzes away toward the blinking lights of the drawbridge. I lose precious seconds before I realize my instincts forgot to remind me I set the parking brake to ease the crash. I turn the car around and continue my pursuit. That fucker is not getting off this bridge.

I'd put him five seconds ahead of me, and quickly spot him just as a huge foghorn bellows to signal the raising of the bridge. About fucking time. The wooden partitions lower as the bridge slowly rises. He's trapped.

But I've forgotten I'm chasing a crazy man. The SUV plows through the partition and up the incline. No way, no fucking way. I watch as the car accelerates up the metal to the top, and glides through the air like Blue Angel toward the other side.

There's no way my car can make that leap, so I come to a skidding stop right next to the splintered wood. I hold onto the steering wheel for dear life, my breath coming out in short bursts but only for a few moments. I barely realize I'm climbing out of my smoking, damaged car, walking past the stunned old man who must control the bridge, to the side. I have to know if he made it.

And there he is. He's leaning on the side too, a huge smile plastered on his handsome face. I watch, unable to do a damn thing as he blows me a dramatic kiss with both hands and waves before walking out of sight. Motherfucker.

"Was that really Alkaline?" the old man asks beside me.

"Yeah," I say though my ragged breaths.

"Then may God help us."

"Amen."

***

Pandemonium, pure and utter pandemonium.

I wait outside, sitting on the steps staring at the now clogged parking lot. Ambulances, fire trucks, police cruisers, and tech vans all vie for space in this mess. A blue tent is being set up where forensic techs in their white coveralls swarm, collecting evidence and taking notes. The coroner and her assistant stand by to take the Asian man's body to the morgue. I can't stop shivering and it's not from the cold. The adrenaline has worn off and now I'm spastic. Or it could just be the guilt.

A gray Crown Victoria is stopped at the gate, but then pulls through. I stand up and take a deep breath. I am not looking forward to this. Out of the car comes three men, the rest of my surrogate family. Detectives Seth Mirabelle and Mitch Kowalski, both in their early forties and each packing a few extra pounds in their wrinkled suits, are followed by our boss, Lieutenant Harry O'Hara. He's a few years younger than Cam, mid-forties, with medium height, medium build, and fine brown hair just starting to go gray at the temples that shines red in the light. His Roman nose is straight, his lips are thin, his chin is a little weak, and blue eyes are hidden behind rectangular silver framed glasses. He's handsome, though. Something about the eyes. Intense at times.

I stand as they get closer. "Evening, guys."

"If it isn't Speed Racer," Kowalski says.

"Shut up," I mutter.

"Are you alright? Are you injured at all?" Harry asks.

"Just my pride."

"You did all you could, I know you did," Harry says.

"Thank you, sir."

He meets my eyes with a nod. "So, get us up to speed. Who is the man in the lot?"

"Dr. John Qwan, psychiatrist here. Pretty straightforward. Ryder snapped his neck and stole his car. The real show is upstairs."

I lead them through the bustling lobby. They had to shut off the metal detectors because they were constantly screeching. We take the service stairs to the second floor and through the empty exit. The narrow hallway is packed to capacity with half a dozen techs taking blood and acid drops. Right as I step out of the stairwell, a forensic tech snaps a picture of a pool of blood by my right foot. A white numbered card sits just off to the side of the grotesque sight.

We join Cam near the second body, what was once a man in a brown guard's uniform, though anything else I can't tell about him. His head is nothing but red and white sludge on the beige linoleum. It's as if his head has dissolved, which I guess it has. The rest of him lays sprawled in front of the open cell door where more techs take pictures inside.

Cam stands and nods at the men. "Hello, sir."

"Get us up to speed quickly," Harry says.

Cam flips back the pages of his notebook, the detective's best friend. "At 7:18, James Ryder, AKA Alkaline's, cell door opened, cause unknown. Two guards were assigned to this section at the time, Steven Moore, this fellow on the ground, and Logan Dodd, who we found downstairs."

"Where is he now?" Harry asks.

"On the way to the hospital, sans hand. Poor kid. Only twenty. He was in shock when we found him and about a second later fell unconscious. He should make it, though."

"Did someone order protective custody for him at the hospital?" Mirabelle asks.

"Already done," I say.

"So," Cam says, "somehow Ryder got out of his cell, and best we can figure took Moore out right away when he went for his gun. Then he grabs Dodd and drags him to the stairwell. Like all locks between the blocks, you need both a keycard *and* fingerprint for the door to open."

"Explains why he took Dodd's hand," I say.

"Yeah. Took his uniform too. He, uh, made it all the way to the parking lot without incident," Cam says.

All eyes momentarily glance my way. I turn red from head to toe. Harry puts his hand on my shoulder, the smell of Old Spice wafting from him. It's an acquired taste. "Honest mistake."

"If you say so, sir."

"And if you had said something he probably would have killed you," Kowalski adds.

"Thanks." I turn to Harry. "Any news on the car he stole?"

"We passed it on the way here. They found it a half mile down the road on the shoulder. He could be on foot."

"We're not that lucky," I say. "I'll bet he either had a car waiting for him, or someone picked him up."

"Some unsuspecting good Samaritan?" Cam offers.

"Near a prison? Yeah, right. My money's on an accomplice picking him up, something he arranged. He knew he only had a matter of minutes, if he's lucky, before they realize he's gone and sound the alarm." Though Dodd and I screwed that up for him. "He's not going to leave it to chance that someone will drive by and pick him up. No way in hell. Remember, this guy planned the Arroyo bank heist. He was the head of a multi-million dollar underworld organization for over twenty years. He's a genius. Even Justice had problems capturing him. Two years we were all after this guy. Ryder left *nothing* to chance on this."

"I agree with Det. Fallon," an annoyingly familiar deep voice says. Oh, goody. Justice. If I were eight this would have been a thrill. I'd either faint or babble like an idiot. Now, I feel nothing but irritation, like a rash that pops up and bothers you for days. I've spent all of ten minutes of my life around him, and that was *more* than enough.

He's just about 6"2' and muscular, though how much is the dark blue leather-like suit and how much is him has been debated for ages. His suit is actually a lightweight Kevlar popular with all superheroes. Not that he needs it what with the super-healing ability, but I suppose it helps lessen bruising. Depending on the light, the suit is either black or dark blue with red piping and a white scale on his chest. Everything is covered, even his mouth, with wire over it so he can talk and breathe. Along his waist is his red belt with the usual: riot cuffs, stun gun, foam canister, and other gadgets I have no idea what he does with. Per the experts, they change depending on who he's chasing at the time. I don't give a crap enough to notice or care.

Not only is he able to survive a gunshot to the head with little more than a headache, he's fast. Clocked at a hundred fast. And strong. I saw this firsthand when he lifted a car above his head at Galilee Falls Day when I was ten. Pop took me. He liked Justice too.

"The best in America and he's all ours," Pop would say when we watched his latest heroics on the news. Pop would flip if he knew I got to work with him. That is if he was still alive.

"Gee, thanks," I say sarcastically.

"Justice. Good to see you," Harry says.

The two men shake hands, and I roll my eyes. Harry is a great detective, one of the best to ever walk the streets, but now he's a bureaucrat first. The more stripes on the uniform, the more butts they expect you to kiss. The day they want me behind a desk is the day I turn in my badge.

"I just heard," Justice says. "Tell me how I can help."

"We're still trying to figure out what happened here," Harry says.

Justice's masked face turns my way. "And you, Detective? I heard you pursued him and got into a scuffle. You seem intact. Did he harm you?"

"No," I say, glancing at Harry who remains impassive. "The car is another story."

"Chasing him on your own was ill-advised. He could have killed you, Detective," the superhero says harshly. "Please try to remember that next time."

I glare at him. "Yeah, the next time a psychopath tries to get away on my watch I'll just hold the door for him."

I can't see his face under the mask but I'd bet he's glaring back. "I will let you all get back to work. I'll assist in the search. Check his old haunts, interview a few key players. Keeping the public safe should be our top priority."

"Duh," I mutter.

"I couldn't agree more," Harry says, ignoring me. "We'll keep you in the loop."

"And if I find anything, I'll do the same. It's going to take all of us working together, but I have no doubt we'll find him."

"Bye," I say super sweet with a small wave before he zooms off like lightening. All the people who were watching go back to work now that the celebrity has left.

Harry shakes his head and flips open his ringing cell phone. "Yes, sir, Mr. Mayor," he says before walking to the stairwell.

"You can be a real brat sometimes," Cam says.

"I'll try to be more consistent in the future," I say with another smile. "Let's go check the psychopath's cell."

Cam's lips purse in disapproval before he steps into the cell with me right behind. With the two photographers, two forensic techs dusting and tweezing, former wrestler Mirabelle and just plain fat Kowalski this place is jammed to the point of claustrophobic. The cells at Xavier are double the size of a normal one as the inmates almost never get to leave them except for therapy, their seven hours a week walking around an enclosed gym in shackles, and their weekly shower, also in handcuffs.

All the standards are here: twin bed, metal toilet sans lid, desk, and now destroyed trash can. Alkaline spruced the place up with a few murder mystery books, a poster of the Galilee skyline and falls, and countless clippings about Justice that cover all the free space on the walls. There are even old ones dating back from the forties to present day.

"Holy crap. Someone has a crush," I say. One of the photographers smiles, and Cam gives me a look.

"There are blank spots," Mirabelle says, pointing to one or two places where the white wall is visible.

"I'll bet whatever was up on the walls is now in there," Kowalski says, gesturing to the demolished trashcan. The plastic is melted at the bottom and twisted where the splatters hit on the side.

"It melted straight through the floor to the lead," a tech says.

"Can you tell what was in there?" I ask.

"Doubt it, but we'll try anyway."

"I want all of this stuff processed and on my desk ASAP," Cam says. "Books, sheets, everything. And fingerprint all surfaces. If there is one latent that's not Ryder's, run it."

"You got it," the tech says.

"What about the security cameras? They must have captured this clusterfuck," I say.

"First thing we checked," the second tech says. "He uploaded a virus. It wiped out an entire week's worth of footage and blocked the possibility of a lockdown."

"Of course it did," I mutter.

"Let's pow wow," Cam says to us.

We follow him out and down the hall away from the blood and death. The rest of the cells are shut up, so not even the metal slots are open. I wonder what they think is going on. We're going to have to interview them, which is not something I'm looking forward to. Especially Chameleon. It's creepy when he morphs to look like me.

"First thoughts people," Cam says. He's the senior detective in the squad, and always leads the brainstorming session when Harry's busy. He'll be lead detective and I'll be his number two, just the way I like it. All the fun, none of the responsibility.

"He lured us here," I say. "He wanted us at the center of this for a reason."

"Any idea why? Either of you had any dealings with him before this?" Mirabelle asks.

"No," Cam says.

"I was the first responder on one of his murders a few years back," I say. "Luis Rivas, his documents guy. And we grew up in the same neighborhood, but I never met him. Ever."

"Speaking of the Ward, do we think it's just a coincidence that Alkaline's old Lieutenant Mike Spencer died in a bomb blast the same day his buddy busted out?" Kowalski asks.

"Hell no," I say. "He probably helped him plan this. Where did you guys get on that?"

"Not far. We have an eyewitness saying she saw a man in black flying away just seconds before the blast, but she was as high as a kite, so who the hell knows?" Mirabelle answers.

"Man in black flying away? Any theories on who he might be?" Cam asks.

"Not as yet, but I'm pretty sure this investigation will be melded with that one," Mirabelle says.

"So what else do we know?" Cam asks.

"He's obsessed with Justice," Kowalski says.

"Something a little less obvious," I say.

"He should be warned," Kowalski says.

"He knows, I'm sure," I say.

"It tells us he'll probably stay in the city," Cam says. "But just in case, we should notify buses, trains, airports to be on the lookout. Give them all his past aliases."

Harry reappears from inside the stairwell and starts walking down to us. "Here comes Harry," I say. We wait for him before continuing.

He pushes his glasses back up his nose. "That was the mayor and commissioner. They are officially ordering a task force. By midnight there should be about twenty officers on this, anyone who worked on any Ryder-related case just to start. Every officer in the city is at our disposal. Cam, you're taking point on this under me."

"Too bad Stackhouse ate his gun," Mirabelle says. "He helped find this guy last time."

"We have his notes and case files," Harry says. "We'll start pulling all files, trial transcripts, everything we have on this guy. Stuff from in here too."

"They're already on it," Cam says. "We'll get full cooperation."

"We should also pull in all known accomplices," Kowalski says.

"And interview *anyone* who had contact with him in here," I add. "I'm talking guards, inmates, if they washed his sheets we need to grill them. Hard. This was an inside job if ever I saw one."

"We should also reach out to all our CIs," Cam says.

"Agreed. Now, walk us through the night, Jo," Harry says.

"Okay. First, they tranq these guys within an inch of their lives, and if I remember correctly, during sentencing, they also ordered that he be given some cocktail Justice developed to reduce the pH level in his body. He had to be off both to do this. Either someone stopped giving them to him, or he was slipped more drugs to counteract them."

"We'll start with the doctors here," Mirabelle says.

"Second. How'd he get out of his cell? There are no acid marks on the door, so someone had to open it for him. Either intentionally or Ryder faked a medical emergency."

"The injured guard, Dodd, should shed some light on this when he wakes up," Cam says.

"And third, we're assuming he had outside help on this. Someone picked him up outside the prison, and the death of Mike Spencer is too coincidental. I'd bet money we'll find another set of tire tracks where he ditched the car. Someone picked him up, which means he had contact with the outside world."

"So?" Mirabelle asks. "Mail. E-mail."

"No, after he sent harassing letters to Grace Pickering and other witnesses, they cut off his mail privileges," Cam says. "He can get mail, but he can't send anything out. And since they have Virus here, who can import himself into a modem, they got rid of the internet."

"We'll get the visitor logs and copies of all letters he received," Harry says.

"It'll be a lot," I say. "Alkaline was popular with the villain groupies. At the trial they practically had to sweep all the underwear thrown at him. I think there's even thousands of fan fiction stories about him and websites."

"We'll still go through them, interview the more dedicated groupies," Cam says.

"What about tonight?" Mirabelle asks.

"I doubt he'll try anything tonight," I say. "If I had to guess, we have at least a day or two before he makes his presence known. He's a planner; he'll need time to set up whatever he's got up his sleeve."

"We're against the clock people," Harry says. "Because whatever he has in mind, it's going to be big. There isn't a single person safe in this city tonight."

"Then let's be big damn heroes," I say, grinning cheek to cheek.

***

Even Justice sleeps, or at least I imagine he does. Who the hell knows? I'm too tired to think about it. *This* hero has been on the clock over twenty-four hours, and fell asleep leaning against the wall of the prison. Harry shoved coffee down my throat and sent me packing. The prison is only about fifteen minutes from my apartment, and I barely make it. I park my borrowed brown work Sedan only a block from my building, something that never happens. I usually have to walk at least three.

My building is a five-story brownstone built in the early twenties by Justin's great-grandfather. He offered to let me stay rent free, but my stupid pride wouldn't let me accept. The apartment was just the last in a long line of things he kept trying to buy for me. Cars, clothes, trips, even ice skates once. I refused. Didn't want to prove his Aunt Lucy right that I was just there for the money. As if she has a job.

I'm on the fifth floor with one other person, Mrs. Jeffrey. Old woman, lots of cats. She's hard of hearing, so my late comings and goings don't bother her. She loves me. One time her water heater broke. I just called Justin and it was replaced within a few hours. I got a couple of muffin baskets out of that one. Had to refuse the cat, though.

The apartment's small but cozy with the original hardwood floors, stone fireplace, kitchen nook that is as pristine as when I moved in, a closet, one bedroom and bath. Simple, just the way I like it. I'm not much of a decorator, so the walls are pretty bare except for the odd family photo or poster Justin bought me as a gift. I have about five old noir movie posters like *The Lady from Shanghai* and *Double Indemnity*. They look pretty cool. My favorite has a place of honor above the fireplace. An authentic Japanese samurai sword from the sixteenth century. The handle is black with white writing in Japanese. "Duty before all else." Does my best friend know me or what?

I don't bother even turning on the lights. I kick my shoes off at the door, my jacket goes over the dark blue velour loveseat, the shirt and pants fall in a pile by my bed. I pull on my flannel pajamas before crawling in bed, setting my gun on the nightstand, and set the alarm for eight. I close my eyes.

I must have fallen asleep because the clock reads 4:23, an hour and a half after I last looked. The creaking floor boards should worry me. I'm still half asleep when I hear them, but fully awake when I catch a whiff of that familiar scent. Old Spice. I do love that smell.

"Harry?" I ask groggily.

He stands in the door, holding his shoes in his hand. "Sorry. Did I wake you?"

"It's okay."

He sits on the other side of the bed, and I flip over to face him. I watch as he shakes off his jacket and lays it on the chair in the corner. "I almost fell asleep at the wheel," he whispers as he sets his watch on the nightstand. "Didn't want to chance it. Your place was closer."

"I gave you the key to use anytime for any reason," I whisper back.

He strips down to his boxers and white undershirt, neatly folding everything before setting it on the chair. A person wouldn't know it by looking at him dressed in those stuffy suits, but he's got a great body. Toned chest, arms, and legs with only a hint of middle age spread around the stomach and waist. He hates it when I nibble him there, but they don't call them love handles for nothing.

I pull the covers back for him before he sets his gun and glasses next to the watch. "I'm exhausted," he says with a sigh as he lies next to me on his back. "And if I have to speak to one more city official, I'll throw myself in front of a car."

I settle in my favorite spot, my arm and leg flung over him and my head resting on his beating heart. He wraps his arm around my back, hand resting on my bare hip. "Can't have that. Who else would put up with me?" I whisper with a smile.

He smiles and kisses the top of my head. "Got that right."

I close my eyes, nestling in closer. We both lie there silent for a minute as he traces a circle on my hip. Even after five months, his touch still makes me tingle. "I'm scared, Jo," he finally says. "He wanted you there for a reason. He could have…"

I press his hand to my lips and kiss his fingertips. "Hey, I'm fine."

"What you did tonight was insane. Completely insane, reckless, and stupid."

"I know," I whisper. "I just…he *winked* at me. You're not disappointed in me, right? For letting him get away?"

"Of course not. You were a hero tonight. A stupid one, but a hero none-the-less."

With a smile I snuggle in closer to him. "Thank you." He continues tracing my hip but doesn't relax. "What?"

"He's had three years, who knows what the hell…"

"Hey," I whisper. I trace his thin lips with my thumb. "He made his first mistake tonight. He pissed me off. We'll catch him." I close my eyes, feeling at peace for the first time today. "There isn't a doubt in my mind."

CHAPTER THREE
HARRY

Like most mornings, I wake before the alarm. Harry snores lightly beside me, looking peaceful and content. A familiar tingle of lust charges through me and on any other day I'd wake him up with a little nookie, but not today. Evil genius with the ability to shoot acid out of his wrists on the loose. City in peril. No sex for Joanna today.

After a quick shower and blow-dry, I creep out of the bathroom and get dressed. The press will be swarming, so I put on my best suit. Tailored black pant suit with matching vest and sky blue dress shirt that makes my eyes pop. I'm buttoning the vest when I notice Harry watching me with a huge grin on his face.

I smile back. "Morning."

"Do you have any idea how beautiful you are?" he asks.

A yummy, gooey feeling like caramel fills me. "You don't have your glasses on," I say.

He slides them on and the smile widens. "I stand by what I said."

I never intended to sleep with my boss. I didn't take one look at him and say to myself, "I can't wait to see *him* naked." And I'm not doing it for the usual reasons. I'm ambitious, but not to the point of whoring myself. Hell, I don't know why I'm taking the risk except…he's the best.

Before I started working under him I'd heard of him, the Eliot Ness of the GFPD who led the investigation of the Borelli family that resulted in a hundred arrests and convictions. The few times we actually met I acted like a star-struck idiot, babbling away. He was always very cordial but nothing beyond that. When I heard there was an opening on his squad, the elite Priority Homicide, I tirelessly pursued it. Called in favors, had Justin put in a good word for me, all so I could work for one of my heroes.

For the first year there was nothing but mutual respect, at least on my part. I'd always had a little crush on him, but pushed it down when I started working with him. I never got a sexual vibe from him, but in hindsight I should have. When I'd invite him out alone for drinks after work, he'd decline. He never met my eyes. He never touched me, not even a pat on the back. The few times we'd accidently touch or brush against each other, he'd freeze and mutter an apology. I just thought it was because I was a woman and he didn't want a hint of impropriety.

Until the night of Justin's big news.

I sobbed the whole way to Neptune's and didn't leave for three hours. I'm pretty sure I had an entire bottle of Jack Daniel's with a vodka bottle chaser. Harry was working late, and Mick the bartender called him. When Harry came, I was in the middle of a heated argument with poor Mick, where things got a little…animated. My mom would be proud. Harry pulled me off the bar by the waist and dragged me back to the squad room, plying me with an entire pot of coffee until I rushed to the bathroom to puke my brains, intestines, and toenails out. After showering, brushing my teeth, and changing into my spare sweats, I felt almost human. He was waiting for me with more coffee and aspirin, not once asking me what had happened. I loved him for that.

Harry drove me home. I was sober enough to know how awkward the whole thing was. The ride was quiet except for the police band. I just watched as the buildings went by, so emotionally and physically wrecked it took strength for me to blink. He opened my car door and helped me out, following me to my door.

"Thanks, Lieutenant," I said in a small voice. There was just enough booze in me that hugging him seemed like a good idea. His body tensed as if he had turned into concrete. I didn't care, I just inhaled the hint of Old Spice and felt a little better. A moment later his arms enfolded me too, and the tension lifted. That's when I felt it. One good thing about being a woman, we can hide our sexual attraction. If we like a guy our boobs don't pop out involuntarily. Guys aren't that lucky.

I should have been offended. Pulled away. After all, he was my boss and all. But I was actually a little giddy. Be it the booze, the ever present crush, or crazed emotions, I felt good. He released me, the stone body returning. "I…" he muttered.

I wouldn't let him go. Before he could utter another word, I mashed my mouth against his, kissing him with all I had. No hesitation this time, he kissed me back. *Boy* did he kiss me back. All the sadness, all the rage evaporated, replaced with red hot lust. We ground into each other like teenagers. If we hadn't been standing on the street, I'm sure we would have gotten horizontal right there. But some catcalling idiot drove by, and we were brought back to reality. Harry all but jumped away from me, shocked and embarrassed at himself. He mumbled something and walked back to his car, not looking at me. I just watched silently as his car sped away.

I didn't sleep that night, processing everything. I *could not* have a thing for my boss. Besides the whole it's against regulations thing, and the threat of us both getting fired, there were several other issues. He's fifteen years older than me. He's divorced, though no kids thank God. His idea of fun is staying in and reading a book. He was fucking Harry O'Hara for God's sake! The legend! Was I that desperate for companionship that I'd risk my entire career with a stupid move like that? Or was it just a lame, girly attempt to make a man I admire and respect take some notice of me as a woman? My mind twisted itself up, down and sideways trying to make sense of it all. As the hours ticked by I convinced myself it was a fluke. I was semi-drunk, vulnerable, and self-destructive. I'd pretend nothing happened. That was the plan.

Until I got to the squad room and saw him. He was coming out of his office as I walked in. Our eyes locked and it took all my resolve not to run across the room, push him up against a desk, and kiss him for all my worth. His expression told me he felt exactly the same way. He turned back into his office and didn't come out until I left on a case. Still, after that look, I couldn't pay attention to work all day. That kiss, that look…I knew I should stay away. It'd be better for us both. I would deal with Justin and his perfect bride, *bride* Jesus Christ, without dragging my fantastic boss and livelihood down with me. I'd be alone, sure. But that's easier.

With those thoughts circling my head, I grabbed my keys and headed over to Harry's. He met me in the lobby, and I managed to wait until we were in the elevator before I did what I had wanted to do that morning. And more. I'm a bad girl.

That was five months ago. Five months of dinners in out of the way places, stolen kisses in his office, and hotel rooms at lunch. Harry could lose his job, and I'd be a laughing stock, but we can't stop. It's thrilling, all the sneaking around. I haven't even told Justin. And yet this has been my longest, most healthy relationship ever. I'll enjoy it while it lasts.

Like now. I walk over to him and sit on the bed, entwining my fingers in his. "You're already getting laid. You can lay off the charm."

"Never." He kisses my palm. "Why don't we both call in sick? Stay in bed all day?"

"Well, I would, but my boss is kind of a slave driver. He'd have my ass."

"Learn some new jokes, Fallon." He kisses my wrist where I have a massive bruise from last night.

"Well, the bad jokes are all part of my dastardly plan to get you to break up with me. I figure I say them enough, you'll get bored, realize you're far too good for me, dump me, and then I can have the bed all to myself again. Is it working?" He pulls me to him for a sweet kiss, his now ten o'clock shadow scratching my chin. "Eww. Morning breath." I sit back up. "You need a shave, O'Hara. Can't face the press resembling a hobo." I stand up and continue getting ready.

"You are such a ray of sunshine in the mornings, Jo."

"I've had about five hours of sleep in two days. You're lucky I don't grow snakes out of my head and turn you to stone."

"I think you'd look sexy with snakes in your hair."

"You have got sex on the brain! I don't think your girlfriend is satisfying you enough. You should dump her."

"I've grown accustomed to your face. And wise-ass remarks."

I stick my tongue out, garnering a chuckle. My expression softens. "I dry cleaned your spare suit. It's in the closet."

He tosses the covers off as I walk into the living room. While I make the coffee, he does his thing in the bathroom. I don't know when exactly we started that annoying ritual of leaving things at each other's apartments. It started with toothbrushes and toiletries, but somewhere around month three I noticed that in both our apartments we unconsciously made room for each other's clothes. Suits, pajamas, underwear all meshed together. It blew my mind, especially when I noticed the tampons in his medicine cabinet. Still makes me uncomfortable.

I turn on the radio as I down my black coffee. The prison break is on every station. Alkaline terrorized the city for two years, killing three dozen people, destroying buildings, and scarring superhero Ranger so badly he was forced to retire. Apparently, the city is "gripped in panic," people should "stay indoors," and "nobody is safe from this madman." I shut off the radio when the president of the Alkaline fan club comes on pledging her undying love. Sensationalist bullshit. If this city were gripped in panic every time the news says we are, this would be the biggest ghost town in the world. At least my name isn't mentioned.

The shower runs as I walk into the bathroom, setting the coffee cup on top of the toilet. "City's gripped in panic again," I tell Harry.

"It must be a Tuesday," he responds behind my powder blue shower curtain.

"I'm gonna get going. Your coffee's on the toilet. Lock up when you leave."

His wet, warm hand shoots out from inside the shower and grabs my wrist. "Jo?"

"What?"

He doesn't say anything and releases my wrist a moment later. "Nothing. I'll see you at work."

"Okay," I say skeptically. He does that sometimes, and it drives me nuts.

I clip on my phone, gun, shield, grab my jacket, and head out the door.

Time to catch a bad guy.

***

Priority Homicide, along with most of the investigative divisions, works out of Police Plaza. It's a six-storied, brown brick building as old as the city itself. Right next door is the courthouse, which is twice as tall as the Plaza. On its other side is City Hall, which is still under construction after Aura and Justice got into it a month ago. Every day since I've been greeted by catcalls and jackhammers when I walk into the building. My middle finger has been getting quite a work-out.

This morning a fresh hell awaits me. The press. All us civil servants park in the ten storied structure then trudge a quarter-mile to our respective buildings which share a courtyard with a fountain in the middle built to resemble The Falls. This is where the vultures lay in wait with their microphones, cameras, and tape recorders. Every reporter in the country must be here because uniformed officers man the barricades set up to create a path to the front doors of the three buildings. Their news vans are lined up three deep on the side of the road, the antenna coiled up like a field of stalks.

I smooth my frizzy hair and walk through the barricades. Dealing with the press is old hat for me. As the best friend and rumored paramour of the city's Golden Boy, I've been exposed to them since I was seventeen. Justin threw this big eighteenth birthday bash and he hooked up with starlet Amanda Garfoyle. The next day, I got about ten calls looking for quotes, and a few painted me as the jealous ex-girlfriend and stalked me at work. It hasn't gotten better since, especially after the engagement. I've gotten used to them, like someone who learns to live with chronic ringing in their ears.

They see me approach and all perk up, thrusting their instruments of torture at my face. An overwhelming cacophony of voices assaults my ears.

"How long until you catch him?"

"How did Alkaline escape?"

"Do you have any leads?"

"Which designer did Rebecca choose for the wedding dress?"

I do what we're told to do. Ignore them.

The inside of the plaza isn't any less of a zoo, just without cameras and annoying questions. The line to pass through the metal detectors for civilians is almost to the door, and the number of police employees is triple the norm. Uniforms, plainclothes, techs all take their turns showing their credentials to get to the elevators. The Galilee Falls seal of an eagle soaring over the falls is covered under dozens of feet.

The elevator doors open and we fill it to capacity. One or two people get off on the narcotics floor, only one on the fraud/computer crimes floor, but half pile out on the investigative support floor where the lab work is carried out. I'm sure they have their work cut out for them just as much as we do. The rest, me included, exit on the fifth floor: Violent Crimes.

Because we cover the entire fifteen miles that comprises Galilee, there are sixty detectives assigned to four different squads, each run by their own Lieutenant. Robbery is one, Special Victims is another, Homicide is the third, and Priority Homicide is the last. We distinguish regular homicide from priority by the number of victims, and off the record, which ones will get the most press attention. As a detective, we're all trained for each squad in case one needs extra bodies, but we pretty much stick to our specializations.

Priority Homicide, where I work, is packed so tight people have spilled into Special Victims in the next room. I can't even *see* my desk, let alone get to it. There is no order, only people milling around or looking bored. Wouldn't the reporters love this? There's an escaped maniac on the loose, and the people supposed to catch him are twiddling their thumbs and talking about the last Galilee Angel's game. Cam waves as I worm my way in, but disappears into the file room.

Kowalski, who had the privilege of staying up all night and dealing with this mess, steps out of Harry's office looking on the verge of collapse. I not so politely nudge my way through the dead weight. Kowalski's face almost lights up when he spots me.

"Jesus Christ, you are a sight for sore fucking eyes," he says as we step into the office.

Harry's office is cramped with only a desk, three chairs, a map of the city on the wall, and a gold desk lamp. The only window looks out onto the bullpen but the gray, vertical blinds are drawn for privacy. The desk is covered with files, pink message slips, and loose papers. When Harry gets in and sees this mess, he'll flip. Unlike me, he's a neat freak almost to the point of anal retention. Makes him great at paperwork but a lousy roommate. Not that we're even close to that point. Hell, we just exchanged keys two weeks ago.

"What the hell is all this?" I ask as Kowalski shuts the door. The inane chattering outside is cut in half.

"Messages from the press, city hall, supers offering their help," Kowalski answers as he falls into Harry's chair. "I haven't done jack-shit since last night but answer telephone calls and fill out requisition forms. At least now you're here."

I start gathering up all the pink slips, but raise an eyebrow. "Do I look like a secretary?"

"I need rack time Fallon or I'll pass out right on the floor," he pleads.

I sigh. "Fine. Go. I'm sure Harry will get here soon anyway."

He smiles. "Thanks. I have a uni handling the calls now, so it should be a little quieter. Get me if you need me." He rushes out before I can change my mind.

First things first, clean up this mess. As I am a trained multi-tasker, I gather up the notes, files, and forms while calling Justin. He picks up on the fifth ring.

"Pendergast," he says, out of breath.

"It's Jo. Bad time?"

"No. No, I was just...working out."

"Well, I'm alive. Exhausted, but alive." There is no way in hell I'm telling him I got into a car chase with a psychopath last night. I'd never hear the end of it.

"You're on the Alkaline case, aren't you?" he asks, not at all thrilled by the prospect.

"Yep. Cam and I are the leads."

Justin's end remains silent for a moment. "And there's no way I can talk you into taking an extended vacation starting today, is there?"

I roll my eyes. "You know, most best friends would be happy and supportive that I'm heading up the biggest manhunt this city has ever seen."

"The man shoots acid, Jo. He's a cold-blooded psychopath. Forgive me if the prospect of my best friend attempting to bring him into custody doesn't inspire enthusiasm."

"Whatever. Killjoy. You'll be eating those words when you're at my commendation ceremony."

"Joanna, I'm serious. I know I can come off as overprotective, and I know you hate that."

"Both true."

"But in this case…I'm scared for you. I'm begging you, *please*, ask to be taken off this one. *Please*."

The fear and desperation in his voice gives me pause. He's never sounded like this before, not even on the bridge. I hate to admit it, but my body temperature rises and a huge grin forms. He cares. He really cares. I quickly quash it. "I promise I'll be careful. And I'll be surrounded by half the force and God knows how many supers."

"You're not going to do it, are you?" he asks.

"This surprises you?"

"No. You've always been too stubborn to listen to reason," he says harshly.

I scoff. "Gee, thanks. I think the world of you too," I say. "Look, I gotta go. Don't be surprised if you don't hear from me for a couple of days, okay? I'll make sure someone calls you if my stubbornness gets me killed. You can say 'I told you so' at the funeral." I slam the phone down. Okay, that was uncalled for and I know it the second I do it, but he got my Irish up. After two decades of friendship, he should know better.

There's a knock on the door before it opens. Cam and the honorable Mayor Samuel Miracle step in. "I have no idea when he'll be in," Cam finishes saying. Both men notice me and smile. "Oh," Cam says. "There you are."

"Just getting things organized," I say. "Mayor Miracle."

"Det. Fallon," the mayor says.

Our illustrious mayor. For some reason, I've never liked him. Our last mayor, Harlan Flores, helped clean up the parks in the Ward, so Miracle had some big shoes to fill. The man isn't fit to collect Flores' trash. I don't know if it's his beady eyes, ferret face, or the fact he hit on me at a Pendergast gala with his wife not five feet away. The feeling is mutual after I told him that if he didn't stop touching me, I'd break the champagne glass and shove the shards into his fingers. Diplomatic I am not. I think he's been afraid of me ever since.

"I guess the Lieutenant isn't here," Cam says.

"Not yet."

"Any idea when he will be?" Miracle asks.

"How would I know? I'm not his keeper."

"I'm sure he's on his way, Mr. Mayor," Cam says. "We stayed at the prison very late."

"I appreciate all your hard work and dedication," Miracle says, "but as my campaign slogan said, 'As long as crime doesn't sleep, neither should your mayor.'"

"Oh, so you were up at two in the morning with us interviewing the prisoners and collecting evidence? Strange, I didn't see you there," I say.

Miracle glares at me, and Cam shoots me a look, but I just cock an eyebrow. "There is a crazed madman on the loose," Miracle says, "and—"

"And I'm sure even *he* needs to sleep before doing all his crazy madman stuff."

"I don't appreciate your attitude, Det. Fallon."

"Yeah? Well, Cam has the sign-up sheet for the club if you want to join."

"We have about fifty members," Cam says, voice dead-pan.

The mayor is not amused. "I heard you both were there last night. Bang-up job, guys."

"Well, we are city employees. Just following the example of our fearless leader," I say with a shit-eating grin.

He stalks out of the office, scowl affixed to his face. "Cops."

Cam chuckles and shakes his head. "You are a piece of work."

"That guy is such a douche bag."

"He's the mayor."

"I didn't vote for him," I mutter.

"Did someone wake up on the wrong side of the couch? Because if you're going to be this snotty all day, I'm partnering with Mirabelle."

"And have to hear about his gout all day? Are you that desperate to get away from me?"

"If you're in full on bitch mode? Hell, yeah. My blood pressure is high enough without your shit raising it."

I sigh. "Fine. I'll do my pretty pretty princess routine today just for you," I say, batting my eyelashes. "Can I get you some coffee, Det. Cameron? Your slippers?"

Cam sits in the chair across from me, folding his hands in his lap. "That lasted all of a second. Want to talk about it?"

"Not really."

"Come on, save me from gout. *Talk.*" God, I want to tell him. I trust him with my life, I really do, just not my love life in this instance. He's an amazing detective, so I'll bet he suspects, but to his credit hasn't said a word. Another reason for me to feel like a shitty friend.

"I just—"

Our conversation is cut short. Harry rushes in and Cam and I stand up as if caught being naughty. Usually it's me and Harry who act like this. I step aside to let Harry get behind his desk. "Morning," I mumble.

"Moring, sir," Cam says as he passes.

Harry tosses his coat on the rack behind him. "Morning, Detectives."

"The mayor is waiting for you," Cam says.

"I know. I spoke to him. Told him to give me five minutes so I can get my bearings. What is this mess?" he says, looking at his desk. He sighs and sits before milling through the paperwork. "Okay, talk fast."

"We've had over a hundred tips on the hotline," Cam says. "Jimenez in robbery and about seven unis are going through them. The lab is rushing all evidence from last night, and should have the majority of it done by the afternoon, including everything from the Spencer bombing."

"What about the injured guard?" Harry asks.

"Made it out of surgery, but is still unconscious. They'll call when he wakes up. Lost his hand."

"Poor guy," I say.

"So, basically, we're still stuck at square one," Harry says.

"Yeah, and the press is sniffing at our crotch like a dog," Cam says.

Harry picks up a few of the message slips. "Yeah, I can see that."

"Someone even called me at home this morning," Cam says.

"Hope you gave them a piece of your mind," I say.

"About seventy pieces, yes. I would have made you proud."

"So, I'm up to date on the bad news. Any good?" Harry asks.

"It looks like we have our own private army out there," I point out.

"Good. We're going to need them. Have the files from the prison arrived?"

"I don't know," Cam says. "Kowalski would."

"And where is he?"

"The nursery."

"Get him in here, *now*," Harry says.

Cam and I exchange a look. With a sigh, Cam stands. "I'll wake him." He walks out, shutting the door behind himself.

"You okay?" I ask.

Harry drops the messages on his desk. "Overwhelmed. It'll take me a day just to get through all this crap, let alone all the other crap that will no doubt be shoveled in as the day progresses."

"That's why you have minions," I remind him. "Let some of the bright, eager young things out there do your scut work. You just boss them around, do the fun stuff, and take all the credit. Why do you think supervillains have them?"

"You're very cute when you're diabolical," Harry says with a smile.

The door opens again before I can retort. Cam and Kowalski step in, Kowalski obviously not getting a wink of sleep. "Hey, Captain," Kowalski says with a yawn. They shut the door.

"Did the prison files arrive yet?" Harry asks, all business again.

"No, boss. They're holding them for us there."

"Fine," he says. "What about the list of Ryder's known accomplices?"

"The preliminary should be on your desk...somewhere."

Harry shuffles the papers around. "Where, Kowalski?" Harry snaps.

Kowalski rushes over and helps in the search. Harry's frustration grows with each passing second until it's found. "Here," Kowalski says, triumphant.

"Okay, go make twenty copies and divide the names into groups of three. Then go home. But I want you back here by two."

"Yes, sir."

"Get some sleep," Harry says as Kowalski leaves.

We all watch the lucky one go. "We're going to need more detectives," Cam says.

Harry finds another file and smirks. "I know. We'll get them." Harry stands up, as do I. "I'll try and get Pritchard and Wu from homicide to cover the Mike Spencer angle. Cam, I want you to head up the accomplice interviews. You and Mirabelle can take the real troublemakers. Fallon, you take point at the prison. I'll give you an officer to assist."

"I want Conover. He's had some psych training."

"You got it. Help me rally the troops first. Both of you."

He adjusts his tie and smoothes his hair. We follow him out into the bullpen, where the men and women continue their conversations, oblivious to us and the mission. Ever the narcissist, the mayor poses for a picture with a female officer. I wonder if he'll try to grab her ass too.

Harry, with us in tow, walks around the group to the huge whiteboard on the far wall. He stops, and Cam takes his position on his left and me on his right, flanking him like sentinels. We put on our best scowls.

"A-ttent-ion!" Cam bellows in his deepest, best drill sergeant voice. The chatter wanes and all eyes turn to us, even the mayor's.

"Good morning," Harry begins. "For those of you who don't know me, I'm Lt. Harold O'Hara, commanding officer of Priority Homicide, and for the foreseeable future I am the man who runs your lives." His voice sends tingles to my girl parts. "You sleep when I tell you, you piss when I tell you, and you see your families when I allow it. If I am not here, then Det.

Terrance Cameron to my left is in charge. He is the lead investigator on this case. Any information you get goes directly to him or his partner on my right, Det. Joanna Fallon." I nod at the group who size me up then look back to Harry. "Now, for the reason we are all here."

Harry opens the file in his hand and slaps the mug shot of Alkaline on the whiteboard. "James Malvern Ryder, AKA Alkaline. Age forty-two. Height, six foot even. Hair dark brown, eyes brown. Arrested three years ago for ten counts of kidnapping, twenty for assault, one count rape, and thirty-five for murder or manslaughter. Was a resident of Xavier prison until last night when he escaped by killing two people and maiming one. We believe he is still in the city, possibly preparing for his next wave of crimes. It doesn't get worse than this man people, and it is up to each and every one of us to find him before he strikes again.

"This is no time for egos, or misplaced heroics. If you are in this room right now, that means you have either had some tie to this man, or your superiors think you are fit for this task force. No doubt you know what this man is capable of, but in case you don't, we're dealing with a super who has two reserves of highly concentrated sulfuric acid in either arm that can melt you down to your spine. Add to that the ability to heal five times faster than normal, super-strength, and a keen intellect. He is smarter than every one of us in this room. What this mean is no going off half-cocked. You get a lead, you tell us. We have SWAT on stand-by at all times. No heroics. I *will not* lose any of you to this man, is that understood?"

The collective all mutter and nod.

"Then we understand each other. Now, those of you pulled from patrol duty this morning, we will be handing out lists of Ryder's known accomplices and associates. You will locate them, pick them up, and bring them here where detectives will interview them. Detectives, while you're waiting, I want you to go through the crime reports of Ryder's past offenses. Make note of anything, no matter how minute, you think is useful. If you don't fall into either category, then you're running down tips from the hotline. I will be pulling some of you for other jobs on the basis of need. Are we all on the same page people?"

Once again we all nod.

"We have to find this man. We *will* find this man. Get to work."

The group, now energized so much you can feel it, immediately springs into action. Cam proudly smiles and pats Harry's shoulder before walking off. I lean in and whisper, "I swear to Christ, if there weren't so many people here, I'd rip all your clothes off and ride you like the sexy, hot stallion you are until we both passed out."

His mouth drops open, but the idiot mayor saddles up to us before he can respond. "Impressive speech, O'Hara."

"It certainly was," I say cheerfully. "Maybe later, huh?"

"I certainly hope so," he says with a sly smile.

"Well, I'm off to prison now. Excuse me gentleman. Mayor." I turn on my toes and walk away.

I have the coolest boyfriend.

CHAPTER FOUR
INCARCERATION

I get my own office down the hall from the warden, a windowless cell not unlike the ones the prisoners inhabit. Just a table, desk, chair, and enough files to keep Speeder, fastest man alive, in this office for two years. Psych reports, physicals, fan letters, guard reports, even websites all about Alkaline. I start on the letters.

It makes me embarrassed to be a woman after reading just five of these things. My luck with men isn't the best. Once I've even gone a year without sex, but I've never been so delusional or desperate to write a convicted rapist and murderer pledging my undying love. What the hell are these chicks thinking? Most border on or just plain are pornographic. At least Ryder had *something* to do in his cell all day. I am so wearing gloves when I touch anything in there.

I just don't get it. There are letters from hundreds of women, and some men, to this butcher and rapist. Sure he's a handsome man, and there is the danger aspect, but he shoots acid out of his body. Acid. How the hell is that sexy?

These letters go in the pile of possible accomplices. Sadly, the pile is really fucking big. At least fifty women and men have pledged their devotion and love to Ryder. We'll have to interview all of them to get their alibis, not that I think the accomplice is any of them. A smart man, and Alkaline is that without doubt, would either destroy or keep the letters from his accomplice, but he might have made a mistake and forgotten, so these fans will be getting a knock on their doors today. This would be a hell of a lot easier if I could figure out how he communicated with them.

After two more pornographic tales of longing, I close the file. I'm not going to find anything here. I'll have a rookie sort through the rest. Time to move onto the light reading: psychological profile. Ryder had monthly meetings with Dr. John Qwan, prison psychiatrist who is now having his guts weighed by our medical examiner. It's mostly information I already know. Anti-social personality with extreme narcissistic tendencies. Feelings of persecution. Genius IQ. God complex. A basic psychopath.

Ryder was born to two loving parents in Galilee, where he lived five blocks from me. I probably passed him on the street a million times. We even went to the same high school, though at different times. Creepy. He had one sister who, along with the parents, died in a fire when Ryder was fourteen. The same year his power manifested. The fire marshal declared it accidental due to a gas leak. Yeah, right. Ryder was stuck in foster care, three different families, but ran away from each within days. Started his first gang then, building a small empire by age twenty. He was arrested twice, but released both times for lack or loss of evidence. He went pretty much unchecked until Justice resurfaced and made him a priority. Then Ryder got mad and became Alkaline.

Diablo's Ward wasn't enough for him, especially when he lost control of the piers. He went from mob boss to uber-villain, chasing Justice all over the city. He kidnapped and killed the police commissioner, robbed banks, and tried to release a stolen virus at the library. All of this just to get Justice's attention. It worked. Their war resulted in almost a billion dollars in property damage, multiple deaths, and worldwide interest. Now he's back out there, more pissed off than before.

There's nothing in this file to help me locate him, which is all I care about. Hell, the only real way we'll find him without relying on luck, is to tie Justice up on the bridge and wait for Ryder to slime his way toward him. This scenario brings a smile to my face.

I pull out the file the warden's secretary gave me with the list of people who had any contact with Ryder. The poor, overwhelmed thing had to go back and get me the complete list. She only had the names of people with direct contact. One theory I came up with was he left notes in his sheets, and one of the people in the laundry delivered them. Farfetched, but possible.

People from the library where he had books delivered, cleaning crew, guards, medical personnel, even the secretary of Dr. Qwan, the list is close to forty people. For a man in solitary confinement, there were a lot of people he had access to. The good news is Conover and I only have to interview a quarter of them. We took the interesting ones for ourselves.

Officer Dwayne Conover, one of my trainees from years back, with his rumpled brown suit, skinny frame, and gaunt face steps back into the room with two cups of coffee. "The warden's coming," he whispers as he rushes in.

Warden Gilbert Myers, a stocky man with shiny bald head, more than fills the door when he walks in. Right now he's the second most hated man in the city: the man who let Alkaline escape. I wonder what they'd say if they found out about my part last night. I'd feel for the guy, but since we got here, he's done nothing but make my life a living hell. The bastard yelled at me for not granting him access to the crime scene, for my constant demands of files, for him to call in personnel on their day off, even for wanting to interview him "like a common thug." It took a lot but I kept my mouth shut. I need him. I can respect the office even if I don't the man.

"Yes, Warden?" I ask with a faux sweet smile.

"Willie Lopez just got here," he says. Lopez is the supervisory guard in the Hardcore Block. "And the press conference is in half an hour."

Ugh, I had hoped Harry was kidding about that. I hate talking to the press. They always ask questions we're not allowed to answer, and mine is the third of the day. First the police commissioner and mayor had one an hour ago, and then right after that Alkaline's victim, socialite Grace Pickering, the woman who he kidnapped, raped, and who ultimately led Justice to him, had one. Finally, mine in half an hour. If it bleeds, it leads.

I know Grace. She was one of the first people Justin introduced me to. They dated for about a month years later. Sweet girl until Ryder became obsessed with her. After the trial she withdrew from the society scene, only coming out to a charity event here or there. I sure as hell hope we have people outside her penthouse in case Ryder wants to rekindle their old flame.

"Thank you," I say. "Come get me when it's time. Send Lopez in."

"Fine," the warden says with a sneer before walking away.

"What an asshole," I mutter.

"I'll bet he gets fired," Conover says.

"Oh, yeah."

Just as I locate Lopez's file, the man himself steps in. Latino, medium height and build inside a brown Correctional Officer's uniform, with black hair cut very short. He's a few years older than me, but not by much. Without a word, he sits across from us and folds his arms on the table.

"Officer Lopez, I'm Det. Joanna Fallon, this is Officer Dwayne Conover. Thank you for meeting with us today."

"You were the one who chased him last night, right?"

"I am."

"Thank you. I just left Stu Moore's wife and four kids. They had to sedate his mother. I'll help anyway I can."

"I appreciate that." I open his file, scanning it. "So, it says in your file you've been on Ryder's block for four years, the longest of any other officer."

"Yeah," Lopez says. "Most last about a year, if that. Those assholes freak out even the hardest hard ass. Me and Stu were the old timers."

"And only you, Stuart Moore, Logan Dodd, Ralph Marinello, Garret Leon, and Marcel Akwambe worked the block?"

"Sometimes, if someone called in sick we'd swing another guard in, but that hasn't happened in a couple months. For the most part, it's two shifts of two guys, twelve hours each. Since the prisoners are confined to their cells all day, we just watch them on the monitor and do a visual sweep every hour."

"Been any disturbances?" Conover asks.

"Not really," Lopez says. "Chameleon faked a seizure about a week ago, but we immediately subdued him."

"What about Ryder? Anything out of the ordinary with him in the last three months? Anything at all?" I ask.

"I've been wracking my brain since I found out, but nothing," Lopez says, frustrated with himself. "They keep him pretty doped up, so he'd either sleep or read. That's all he's pretty much done since he's gotten here."

"Were any of the other guards particularly attentive toward Ryder?" I ask.

"We're not allowed to talk to them beyond basic commands. The last guy who spoke to him was fired a year and a half ago. His name was Dylan Gunderson. I have no idea what happened to him."

"Who reported him?" Conover asks.

"I did."

"What did they talk about?" I ask.

"The weather, I think, but we have a zero tolerance policy," Lopez says. "He was just an idiot. And besides, he doesn't have access to the prison anymore."

"You seem to know the block better than anyone," I say. "Any theories as to how he got out of his cell? How he contacted the outside world to set this up?"

"The security cameras didn't show the escape?" Lopez asks.

"The ones on your block were hacked into," Conover says. "The past week's footage was destroyed. We have techs figuring out how it was done."

"So how did the cell door get open?" I ask.

"If he didn't burn through it, someone had to open it. Only way," Lopez says. "He could have faked a medical emergency, hung himself, any number of reasons for them to go in there." Lopez leans forward, arms still on the table. "You have to remember, we thought this guy was neutered. There was *nothing* to show otherwise. He was a model prisoner: quiet, obeyed orders, nothing physical. I wished they were all like that."

"Who gave him his drugs?" I ask.

"We did. One of the guards on duty. Every meal he took them, and we *watched* him take them. Checked under his tongue and cheek. The stuff for the acid came in liquid form. There was no way he could have pretended to take that."

I jot "switched liquid how??" on my pad. "Who had access to it?"

"Dr. Landry, our prison doctor mixed it, brought it to us, and we gave it to him once a day at dinner."

"So either one of the guards or the doctor's staff switched it," Conover offers.

Lopez's face falls. Now *him* I feel for. I couldn't imagine what I'd think if Cam or even Mirabelle was accused of helping a psycho escape. You're supposed to be able to trust these people with your life, you against them. I'll let this idea sink in before making him confront the hard truth. I clear my throat. "Do you have any theories on how Ryder could have communicated with someone outside the prison?"

Lopez comes out of his own head. "Um, what?"

"We believe that someone was waiting for Ryder outside the prison," Conover adds. "How would he be able to do that?"

"I don't know," Lopez says, still in a daze. "He received letters, but someone went through them before he got them. The only other items he was able to bring into his cell were books and newspapers, but they never leave the prison. We toss the cell once a month, but he never had anything out of place. I don't see how else, unless he had a go between."

I meet his dark brown eyes. "So, you know these guys. You work with them. Anything we should know about them? Or you?"

"They're good men," he says with little enthusiasm. "They do their job."

"Any make unusual purchases lately? Acting weird?" Conover asks.

"Not that I know of," Lopez says with no conviction. This is the first time he's lied.

I smile sympathetically. "I know you don't want to jam up your buddies, but you and I both know this was an inside job. Whoever organized it is responsible for the death and crippling of two of your friends. Logan Dodd lost his hand. Stu Moore lost his life. Who knows how many more Alkaline is going to hurt before we catch him. Please. Anything you know."

Lopez shakes his head and falls back in his chair. With a sigh he says, "Garrett's wife just had another baby, and they're hurting. Ralph likes to gamble, but I don't know how much he owes and to who. Marcel and Logan, as far as I know, are clean."

"What about Officer Moore?" Conover asks.

It's as if a switch is flicked inside our ally. One moment he's slumped in the chair, and the next he's all but reaching across the table at Conover, face contorted with rage. The young man instinctively leans back. "You leave Stu Moore the fuck out of this! You leave his wife alone, you leave his kids alone. Do you hear me?"

Conover's speechless, but I maintain my calm. It takes a lot to make me flinch. Conover will get the same tolerance after a few years. My gut is shouting at me, though. "Officer Lopez, please calm down. We didn't mean to offend you."

"Stu Moore was my best friend," Lopez snarls. "I've known him for ten years. I got him his job here. I'm godfather to his youngest. Don't you *dare* do anything to insult his memory. He died a hero, and I won't let anyone say otherwise."

"Yes," I say. "He did. I'm sorry if we offended you." I stand up, extending my hand to the still steaming man. "Thank you again for meeting with us. If you could send Officer Leon here when you get back to the block, I'd appreciate it." Lopez forcefully shakes my hand, glares at Conover, and stalks out. With a sigh I sit back down. "I thought he was about to punch you."

"Me too," a still shaken Conover says. "What was that about?"

"Could be grief, could be something else. My guess is a little of both. Not that he'd ever tell us. At least not today." I shut the Lopez file, and pull out the file on C.O. Garrett Leon. "So, what have we learned so far Officer Conover?"

Ever the eager student, Conover's face lights up at the chance to show his stuff. "Not much. Just background about the guards, right?"

I cluck my tongue. "You disappoint me, Officer Conover."

His face falls. "Why?"

"There's an old saying my Uncle Ray told me. It's KISS: keep it simple, shithead. We just narrowed the suspect pool down to six."

He considers this. "It had to be one of the guards. There's no one else."

"Correct. But why?"

He thinks for a moment. "Because…the more people who know, the more chance of one of them screwing up."

"We'll make a detective out of you yet," I say with a proud smile. "Three cardinal rules in the detective racket: easiest solution is usually right, follow the money, and the spouse always did it." I pull out my pad to write everything down. "We need to look at this in the most logical way, chronologically. He convinces one of the guards to start sending out his letters, either through charm or more likely through cold hard cash. We never found all of his bank accounts, so he's probably got millions stashed away God knows where. So Ryder bribes him to not only act as go-between, but to switch out his medicine. The same guard probably messed with the security system too."

"So we're not ruling out Moore or Dodd?"

"No, if anything they just became our prime targets. Maybe Ryder faked a seizure, or maybe he was simply let out and messed with the security system himself."

"But why kill Moore if he was helping him?"

"Loose end."

An obese man with a huge belly and balding red hair steps in dressed in a guard uniform. Officer Leon, I presume. He sits without a word, and I begin questioning with Conover occasionally interjecting. He has nothing new to add.

"You just had a baby, right?" I ask.

"Yeah. Our forth," Leon answers.

"Wow. Four. That must be hard on a guard's salary."

"That's why I'm in Hardcore. Better pay."

"Still," Conover adds.

"My wife's family helps when they can."

By now he should be acting defensive, or at least glaring at us, but he's not. He's too calm, which either means he knows he's caught or is too dumb to know what we're hinting at. From the rest of the interview, I glean it's the latter. Did Ryder take advantage of that? Would he trust his escape to this man? The famous gut says no.

"Did James Ryder pay you to help him escape?" Conover asks.

The guard's face twists into a look of disgust. "No, sir. That guy scares me. I didn't even like looking in his cell. He has *acid* for blood or something."

I believe him. We'll double check, but he's not our accomplice. "Did any of the other guards like him?"

"I don't think so," the giant answers.

The door swings open, and the Warden pokes his made up face in. Make-up on men is unnatural somehow. "I need you for the press conference," he says.

Great. "On my way."

The warden glances at the guard, lips pursed in annoyance for whatever reason, before walking out again. I wonder if the guy ever smiles. Probably only when he's ripping into people. I've encountered his type way too many times not to know the signs. If he did ever smile, he won't be doing it again for quite awhile.

"Officer Leon, thank you for your time. If we have any follow-up questions, we'll contact you," I say with a smile.

"How long until you think you'll find him? Will he come back here if you do?" he asks, noticeably scared.

"I have no idea."

"Oh. I hope he doesn't. Can I go now?"

"Sure," Conover says.

Leon leaves without another word, off to guard the rest of the freaks. I don't care how much it pays, if I had four kids there's no way in hell I'd even come within a mile of this place. Hope after all this Office Leon comes to the same conclusion.

"He didn't do it," Conover says.

I stand, and toss on my suit jacket. "Nope. But we'll treat him as a suspect until we have proof otherwise." I pull down my vest. "How do I look?"

He eyes me up and down. "Good. Any idea what they want you to say?"

"The usual. 'No comment' or 'We can't release that information.' While I'm gone, I want you to keep culling through the fan letters. I'm sure it's a dead end, but better safe than sorry. This shouldn't take that long."

Warden Myers waits at the end of the hall, arms folded. Not a man who likes to be kept waiting, even for a minute. Up close I can see the pancake make-up covering his entire face with a hint of blush on the cheeks. I probably should have done some touch–up, but it's too late now. Don't want to keep my adoring audience waiting.

"This your first press conference?" I ask as we walk toward the front of the prison along with his secretary and another guard.

"Yes," he replies gruffly.

"Do you have a prepared statement?"

"Of course," he snaps. "I'll do the talking. You're just there to back me up." He already has flop sweat and shaking hands. I'd be nervous too if I were him. Right now I'm walking beside a scapegoat about to be slaughtered on national television, and he knows it.

"It's your show," I say.

He ignores me the rest of the walk. Instead he rehearses his statement. Not that it matters what he's going to say. He's already been tried and convicted in the court of public opinion. The jackals are amassed in the parking lot, twelve deep with their vans and equipment scattered around. It's not just the locals either. No, our blunder will be broadcast worldwide through BNN and LBC, among others. Now I really wish I'd put on make-up.

The sacrificial altar, or podium with several microphones attached, waits for us just outside the glass doors. Two guards standing watch by the door nod at us for solidarity. We nod back. The warden takes a deep breath, and then his trembling hand opens the door. He's probably a good poker player. His face remains expressionless as he walks up to the microphones with me and the guard a few inches behind him.

"I have prepared a brief statement, and then I will take questions," he begins, voice neutral. "I'd like to begin by giving my heartfelt condolences to the families of the guards who were injured or killed in last night's attack. Officers Moore, Dodd, and Dr. John Qwan were trusted and respected members of our community. Moore had several commendations for valor, and Dr. Qwan served in his position for over ten years. What happened to them is a tragedy, and all our thoughts and prayers of our staff are with their loved ones.

"There is no excuse for what happened last night. We failed to do our jobs, even though every safeguard was in place and followed to the letter. What happened was a fluke, and we are already taking measures to make sure it does not happen ever again. The prison is cooperating fully with the investigation into this event. Thank you."

Immediately, a cacophony of voices starts. I can barely understand a word until the warden points to someone. The reporter shouts, "Have the other prisoners been moved from the obviously unsecure area?"

First blood drawn. "I cannot comment on the location of inmates due to security reasons. But let me stress, this was an isolated incident. There hasn't been an escape in three years, and there will be none from now on."

The reporters clamor until Myers chooses again. "How do you respond to Grace Pickering's demand for not only your job, but those of the mayor and commissioner?"

"As of this time, I have no plans to resign. This was an *isolated incident*, one that will not be repeated as long as I have my post."

"But *someone* is to blame," another reporter shouts. "Your so-called safeguards failed in this case. Who's to say they won't again?"

The top of Myers' head turns red, and he grips the podium so hard it creaks. He's lasted longer than I thought he would. It's sound bite time. "Look, we have the worst offenders in here. The scum of society. The freaks of nature. We do what we can to keep them in here, but we're bound by law and nature. They aren't. What the hell are we supposed to do when we have to mollycoddle them or be sued by you liberals if we don't?"

"And what do you propose, Warden?" someone shouts.

There's no way in hell I'm letting him answer that. I am, after all, his back-up. You don't stand by and let someone shoot themselves in the head. The foot maybe. I step up to the podium beside the Warden. "I'm Det. Joanna Fallon with the Galilee Falls Police Department. I'm sure you have questions regarding this investigation. *I'd* be happy to answer them."

A few faces fall, but my old pal Veronica Lilley with *The Galilee Standard* smirks. She's actually my first cousin, though we both like to keep that under wraps. I feed her information, and she does the same for me. Like me, she's the tiniest in the crowd, with the same color eyes and skin, but tawny straight hair. Her hand shoots up along with the others but I choose her, as she knew I would.

"Do you have any leads on how Alkaline managed to get out of his cell? Are the guards suspects?"

"We are investigating every possible avenue," I respond with the stock answer.

"And how do you respond to the allegation that Alkaline had an accomplice outside the prison? Any leads to who that is, if it's true?" V asks.

"It appears as if someone picked up Ryder outside the prison, yes. We are asking anyone with information regarding James Ryder to contact our tip line. Next question."

I field a few more routine questions about the investigation, our suspects, how he escaped, with the usual deflections and vague answers. We might as well be reading from a script. Of course it never remains that easy for long.

"The last time, Alkaline was caught by Justice. Is he involved in this investigation? Perhaps leading it?" the woman from BNN asks.

"GFPD is in charge of this investigation, with help from the Federal Marshal Service, and will remain so. As of right now, as far as I know, there are no plans to officially involve a masked vigilante in the manhunte."

"But last time Alkaline was free, it took years to apprehend him. Justice was the one who did it. What makes you think the GFPD will have more luck this time?" the same reporter asks.

Bait. These stupid reporters sure do know the right one to bring for a specific prey. My mouth takes over before my brain can stop it. "I want to assure the citizens of Galilee that there is not a single police officer in this city resting, and we will not rest until that murdering psychopath is back behind bars or dead. We will scour this city. Anyone he even *glanced* at will be put under a microscope. We will cut off all his allies, all his resources. He cannot run. He cannot hide. We *will* find him." I look straight into the cameras, my jaw set. I hope to God that bastard's watching. "Of that, you have my personal guarantee. If you have any more questions, please contact police headquarters or the Bureau of Prisons. Thank you."

I glance down at V, who holds up her fingers like a telephone, before I walk back into the prison with the others. The reporters shout their questions, but we ignore them. The voices end as the door shuts. The warden looks at me, wary and a little grateful.

"Good press conference everyone," I say with a smile before turning and walking away.

I am in so much fucking trouble.

***

My phone doesn't start buzzing for three whole minutes, enough time for me to return to Conover and send him to the cafeteria for lunch. I barely ate at Justin's last night and forgot breakfast, and my stomach throbs as a reminder of this. After a deep breath, I answer.

"Det. Joanna Fallon."

"Joanna, this is Grace Pickering."

If there was a feather, I'd be knocked out of my damn chair. Not who I was expecting at all. I never would have recognized her voice. When she was out on the social scene I noticed her voice was higher, more girly, like most of the women in that set. I swear sometimes I can't tell them all apart. Same hair, same clothes, same body, same nose, even same voice. You'd think Dr. Avatar fired up his cloning machine again. Grace's voice is huskier now, and a little surer of itself. I guess a month trapped by a psychopath makes you grow up.

"Wow. This is…unexpected."

"I got your number from a colleague. I hope you don't mind."

"Of course not. How are you?"

"As well as can be expected. The police officers parked in front of my penthouse are reassuring. As are the half dozen press vans."

"They'll be on you twenty-four seven until we find him. He won't get near you," I say with utter certainty.

"Thank you. And how is Justin? I haven't seen or spoken to him in over a year. I have seen the pictures in the paper though. He's happy?"

"Blissfully."

"Love does that to a person. I received an invitation to both the wedding and the engagement party. I haven't decided whether or not to attend yet." She pauses. "But, of course, I did not call to catch up."

"I figured."

"I phoned because I was wondering if you would stop by this evening," Grace says.

"I don't know. I'm really busy."

"I promise to make it as quick as possible. I would *greatly* appreciate it."

Hell. I hope she just wants to grill me about all we're doing to find her rapist, not looking for someone to hold her hand when she cries. I'd rather have a root canal than be witness to an outpouring of emotion. Though how can I say no? "Okay. I'll swing by when I can."

"Thank you." She hangs up. Okay, it seems as if she's lost her manners in three years. I flip the phone shut. Now I'll have to watch her press conference.

Just as I'm about to clip my phone back on my belt, it rings again. "How do you people expect to me get any work done if I'm constantly on the phone?" I mutter to myself before answering. "This is Det. Joanna Fallon."

"Jo, it's Harry," my bed buddy says.

As I always do when I hear his voice, I smile. "Hey. Please tell me this is going to be a fun call."

"Sorry."

"Then I take it you saw my stirring performance. How much trouble am I in?"

"Minimal. Although I doubt Justice will be sending you a Christmas card this year."

"It kind of all just slipped out."

"Actually, I just got off the phone with the commish. He was impressed."

"Really?"

"Yeah. So impressed, he wants you to handle the press from now on."

"Ugh. I thought you said I wasn't in trouble. Why are they punishing me then?" I whine.

"The general consensus is your conviction and passion makes us look good. They want you to keep doing that. You're someone people can get behind and believe. Plus, you look really good on TV. Hot even."

"Why, Captain O'Hara, are you sexually harassing me?" I ask, voice sultry.

"I doubt I'll be able to tonight," he sighs.

"Darn. Guess one of my other boyfriends will have to service me then. Rudolpho maybe."

"Hardy har. So, how are things going at the prison? Have you found anything of use? Please tell me you have. Even if it's a lie."

"Nothing concrete, but I'm convinced it was one of the guards. More than convinced." I read off my notes, finishing just as Conover returns with my hamburger and soda. "That's all we have so far. The other guards are on their way in, so we'll see what happens with them. What about you guys? Having better luck than us?"

"Not in the least. Just getting the usual stonewalling from these bastards. All claim they haven't seen or heard from Ryder since he went in."

"Harry, I really think our focus should be here at the prison. On the guards. We need to pick their lives apart."

"That's why I have my best woman on it."

"As fabulous as Conover and I are, we are not miracle workers. We need to grill them. Talk to their neighbors, wives, even their grocers. I can't do that here."

"Jo, I swear I'll take that under advisement. Just keep up the good work, okay? Bye." He hangs up.

"They getting anywhere?" Conover asks.

"No, we are the rock stars of the GFPD at the moment." I reach across for my burger. "Let's eat, and then call in our next suspect." I bite into my wafer-thin, probably horsemeat burger. I spit it out and sigh. "I am officially tired of prison."

***

After interviewing the final guard, C.O. Marinello, I take a much needed break. We've been here for ten hours and the pot of coffee I've had has made me pace around the interview room like a caged panther. I excuse myself to the bathroom and splash some cold water on my face with a sigh. Some days I hate this job. Ten hours and precious little to show for it. Just an unsubstantiated theory and a sore butt. We're done here.

As I walk down the hall I pass the guard's break room, the TV is playing a re-cap of the day's events. Chuck O'Connell from Channel Four, his steel gray hair, so obviously a toupee, blowing in the breeze, stands outside an apartment building I recognize. He's surrounded by his fellow bloodsuckers, all waiting for the delivery of fresh meat.

I really don't know why Grace called this thing. After she escaped, they were relentless. They tried to sneak into her penthouse, swarmed her like mosquitoes in Florida when she went shopping, even printed lies from ex-boyfriends. I don't blame her for becoming a hermit. First the trauma of the kidnapping, then the media scrutiny and trial. I would have moved to Antarctica.

"This is Chuck O'Connell, reporting live from outside the apartment of philanthropist Grace Pickering, whom you might remember as the woman who helped Justice locate and capture the notorious supervillain Alkaline, who last night escaped from Xavier Maximum Security prison. In just moments this brave woman is scheduled to make a statement regarding last night's events."

The doorman opens the door, and all the reporters snap to attention, shouting questions one over another so not a single word is decipherable. Flash bulbs pop in tandem with the voices. Grace walks out with her pointed chin held high. She's thinner than I remember, almost skeletal in her black trousers and pink cardigan. Her long golden hair is pulled back into a tight ponytail. She's pale almost to the point of sickness with hollowed out cheeks. Her wide cornflower blue eyes appear sunken in. Concentration camp survivors looked healthier, though not as stylish.

She approaches the reporters, and if she's nervous it doesn't show. She raises a hand to stop the onslaught and within seconds the pack settles down. "I would like to make a statement," she says in a polished voice. "To the families of those who lost their lives last night, I want to give you my heartfelt condolences. You are in my thoughts and prayers from this day forward. I know what it is to lose a loved one. The only comfort I can give you is that with time, the pain fades. But I am sorry to say it does not vanish."

Her fiancée Chad Caldwell was murdered by Alkaline when he kidnapped Grace. I knew Chad a little, just in passing at parties. Nice, but a tad boring. I went with Justin to his funeral. They were in the same frat in college. He actually introduced the couple.

"I would also like to speak to the people responsible for allowing this to happen." Grace looks directly at the cameras, eyes and jaw set with fury. "To Warden Myers, Commissioner Craven, and Mayor Miracle I have three words for you: shame on you. You promised us multiple times that this very event could not happen. That every possible safeguard was in place. You promised that the reign of supervillains terrorizing our city was coming to an end. And yet, the incidents have gone up. It is your job to keep your citizens safe. You have failed in every conceivable way. So, shame on you. I am calling for your resignations at once, and I can only hope that other conscientious citizens do the same. This must stop, and if you cannot do it, then we will find someone who can.

"And finally, to James Ryder, the monster who calls himself Alkaline. Please. Whatever you are planning, whatever you think you must do, please don't. Give yourself up. If there is even a spark of humanity left inside of you, let this end. If not for my sake, then for yours. Thank you."

She turns around and the reporters shout more questions, but she ignores them, retreating into her building. Short, effective, and to the point. Wouldn't expect anything less from her. I shut off the tape.

Well, that put my conference to shame. Maybe they should have her give the updates, not me. For someone who shuns the press, she sure does know how to work them. The Mayor and Commissioner must be shitting bricks because if

Grace Pickering wants them gone, they better have their U-hauls at the curb.

The woman on that tape sure as shit wasn't the Grace I knew. The Grace I have known since I was twelve giggled and went to the salon religiously. She never raised her voice or acted as if the world wasn't as sweet as a bowl of marshmallows. Ryder killed that part of her, and she can never get it back. He may not have killed her body, but he sure as hell killed her soul.

CHAPTER FIVE
GRACE

After dropping Conover off at the station to start typing up what will end up being a novel-sized report of today's investigation, I swing by the upper-scale downtown neighborhood of Parkscale where Grace Pickering lives. A few news vans remain outside the gothic apartment building, lying in wait. I seriously doubt Grace or Ryder will appear outside, but if they did it would be a great story. Better safe than sorry, I guess.

Our patrol car stands guard right at the front entrance with another down the block. The doorman is on guard, his eyes moving from side to side as if he's reading. Scanning for potential threats. Grace's last line of defense against the acid spewing psycho killer.

The press spots me as I get out of my car. They're on me with their microphones and tape recorders as I walk toward the door.

"Are you here to interview Grace?"

"How do you respond to her request?"

"Are you any closer to finding Alkaline?"

The doorman opens the door for me, then blocks the annoying horde after I pass. "Please leave," he says before shutting the door.

I don't wait for him to call up. I walk down the mirrored hallway to the elevator. Impatiently, I press the button a few times, of course not getting the desired result. I still have to glance at the guard's bank statements, run through some of the three hundred or so tips we received, write a statement for the press conference tomorrow, and maybe eat something and get an hour of sleep, and the stupid elevator is taking forever.

The doors finally open and take me up to the penthouse. I step into the foyer where a boulder of a man dressed in all black blocks the apartment door. The gun on his hip is the next thing I notice, and then don't take my eyes off it as I approach.

"Det. Joanna Fallon," I say, flashing my shield. "Miss Pickering is expecting me."

He presses a finger the size of a tree branch into his ear piece. "A detective here." He waits for a response. "Very good. Please enter." The boulder opens the door for me.

Grace's apartment, unlike her, hasn't changed that much through the years. Antiques meshed with state-of-the-art technology. An armoire from the eighteenth century with fine crystal figurines has a plasma TV on it as well. Next to that, another black clad guard packing heat watches as I step in. We appraise each other as two alphas do when they come into close proximity. I don't like this one. He makes the hairs on the back of my neck stick up. "Got a permit for that?" I ask with a smirk. The man scowls, and I know I've won the dominance match. I usually do.

"Be out in a moment," Grace calls from the back rooms.

I plop down on the ten thousand dollar sofa and prepare. I get out my pad, pen, and sympathetic face. The guard watches my every movement with a glare. I know he's just doing his job, but I hate people looking at me as if I'm a perp. That's *my* job.

Grace steps out in the same clothes she wore in the press conference. The camera does add ten pounds because if she looked like a gulag survivor on screen, she looks like one who didn't make it out in person. Those size-zero clothes literally hang on her, and her cheekbones could cut diamonds. I'm no expert on anorexia, as my scale will tell you, but Grace could be the poster child. Guess after what happened she needed to find control some way.

"I was beginning to think I was stood up," Grace says with a gracious smile.

"It's been a hell of a day. I got here as soon as I could."

Grace starts pouring herself a drink. "Would you like something to drink?"

"I'm on duty," I say.

She replaces the tumbler and sits across from me. "Something to eat?"

"I'm good, thanks."

She nods then turns to the guard. "Arnold, why don't you wait in the kitchen? I don't think I'll be needing you for awhile." Arnold lumbers out of the room without a word. Grace smiles. "I think privacy is in order, don't you?"

"Pretty serious looking guys."

Grace sips her drink. "Arnold was a linebacker for the Independence Eagles."

"I'll bet."

Grace sips again, and settles into her chair, folding her legs underneath her. "You look well, Joanna. What's it been? Two years?"

"The zoo fundraiser."

"Right. I remember you spent the night talking to Clinton. He always did have a bit of a crush on you."

Clinton Bell, my stalker at most society functions. Good guy, but very dull. "Clinton is very nice, but not my type," I say with a chuckle.

"Well, we all know who is," Grace says without malice. I still feel sucker punched. "Not that he knows it," she adds.

"I have no idea what you're talking about," I say like a guilty perp in interrogation. I suppose it is the worst kept secret in Galilee. The only people who aren't privy to the knowledge are Justin and Rebecca. Too close to it, I guess.

"I apologize," Grace says, shaking her head. "I fear my years of isolation have made me feral. I forget how to act in polite society. Let me try this again." She smiles. "How *is* Justin these days? Well, I hope."

"He's wonderful."

"Love does that to a person, I suppose. I received the wedding invitation two months ago. It was very sweet of him to invite me. To the engagement party as well." She sips her drink. "And what is the bride-to-be like? I understand she's a doctor."

"Pediatric surgeon. And she's...perfect. Sweet, smart, incredibly beautiful. She has a daughter, as well."

"Does she?" Grace asks, surprised. "Huh. Then Justin has found exactly what he's always wanted."

"What's that?"

"A family. An instant family to welcome him in. To never be alone again."

"I never thought of it like that." I scoff. "I guess you're right."

"You only knew him after his father died," she says to make me feel better. "They were very close. His mother passed when he was so young. All they had was each other all alone in that big house. I remember Mr. Pendergast would take him out of school to go fishing on a whim. I always envied that. My father barely acknowledged my presence. The only thing a girl was good for was marrying well. At least he died before he could see that dream fail."

"That's a little fatalistic," I say. "I'm sure there's a dozen men who—"

She waves her hand. "That part of my life is over," she says. "I've actually come to enjoy solitude. I don't have to spend hours getting ready just to go outdoors. I don't spend thousands a month on trivial things like my nails. No more small talk or gossip. It's actually very liberating."

"Never pegged you for the hermit life," I say with a smile.

"I'm not. My priorities just changed. I volunteer three times a week at the battered woman's shelter, among other places. After my…experience, everything about my life seemed so shallow. It was such a wake-up call."

"Well, I'm glad something good came out of it."

"As am I," she says. "But we aren't here to reminisce, and I'm sure you're eager to get back to work." She takes a sip of her drink. "I'll bet you were surprised to hear from me, especially after my little rant."

"Yes. I heard you refused to be re-interviewed when we called this morning."

"Understandably I was in shock. I thought that ordeal was behind me, and then I wake up in the middle of the night to find it's not. Then shock turned to fear, which turned to anger. That's when the other detectives approached me, and I called that silly press conference." She shakes her head at the memory. "I sounded like a lunatic."

"No, you didn't," I say. "You did a better job than I did."

"That's why I called, you know," she says. "I've been watching the news coverage all day. All those talking heads. The mayor. Commissioner. That idiot warden. All swearing to capture James, bring him to justice and all. You were the only one I believed."

"Thank you. I meant it."

She nods in reverence. Twenty years I've been around these people, the rich, privileged, and snotty as hell, but this is the first time any one of them has shown me the slightest hint of respect.

Grace downs the rest of her scotch. "Okay, I think I'm ready to answer all your questions now. Ask away."

"In the three years since his incarceration has he contacted you?"

"Not personally since the trial. The day of his conviction I did receive a letter."

"What did it say?"

"Nothing really. He professed his undying love. Said he didn't blame me for testifying. I turned it over to the police."

"Nothing since?"

"Not really. I do receive a bouquet of pink roses on my birthday from him. I hired a private investigator to track the payment, but he had no luck. I pulled the file of his findings. It's over by the door."

"Thank you." I jot that down. "That's it? The only contact?"

"Nothing else, thank goodness. I can only hope that he's forgotten about me. Moved onto his next obsession."

"How did you two meet?"

"Chad, of all people. Caldwell Inc. was working with one of James' legitimate businesses on some project. Chad invited him over for drinks, and I just happened to be there." She scoffs. "He told me later it was love at first sight."

"How did he act with you at first?"

"Cordial. A little flirty, but nothing overt. Then he started showing up everywhere. At my gym. Outside my charity meetings. Even at the opera. We'd chat, nothing more. I didn't really think anything of it until a month later."

"What happened?"

"I was 'mugged,'" she says, doing the quotation marks with her fingers. "James just happened to be strolling by to rescue me. He, of course, set the entire thing up, not that I would find that out until it was too late. I invited him up to this apartment to wait for the police. I'll admit I was shaken, and I let him kiss me, but I *never* slept with him, despite what his attorney insinuated.

"After I came to my senses, I pushed him away and he grew...angry. He told me he loved me, and I ordered him to leave. He actually apologized, and left. The next day I received a necklace. And the next day, matching earrings. I called James and told him to stop. That I was in love with Chad, and nothing would change that.

"The next night at the AIDS gala Alkaline showed up, as I'm sure Justin told you. It was...frightening. I'd never seen a supervillain in person before, at least not that I knew of. I feel like such an idiot now. I should have known. Seen the signs or something."

"We didn't know who he was then," I offer.

"Still. Only a total ignoramus couldn't have put two and two together." She quickly grins. "Anyway, Alkaline zeroed in on me and Chad, attempted to kill poor Chad and to take me hostage, but thank God Justice showed up when he did."

"But Alkaline got away," I say.

"Even so, I was saved. At least that time."

"What happened the night of the kidnapping?"

She hugs herself a little. "Do I really have to go through this again? Isn't it all in a file somewhere?"

"Yes, but you might remember something new now. A forgotten detail that surfaces that could help. I wouldn't ask otherwise."

"I suppose." She looks down at the floor and continues. "After the gala, Chad and I went to the Bahamas for a week to recover from the whole ordeal. We were back maybe two hours when three men broke in. They just kicked the door down and ran into Chad's townhouse. We were in the living room, and they shot Chad on sight right through the head. The blood..." She closes her eyes. "It was all over me. I couldn't move, I couldn't even scream. That's when another man pointed what looked like another gun at me. But it was a Taser. Next thing I knew, I woke up in a windowless room."

Those men were found the next day with two holes in their heads. A five million dollar ransom was demanded, but the kidnapper wasn't forthcoming with his identity. James Ryder's name popped up a few times, but he had disappeared as well. On paper, he seemed like a legitimate businessman with a crush. It was Justice who suggested that the gala and kidnapping were connected. Within three days, it was confirmed. James Ryder was Alkaline, the supervillain who ran Diablo's Ward. With this revelation, the biggest manhunt in the city's history was underway. The psycho made his first mistake in all his years. Love makes even the most methodical sloppy.

"James showed up hours later with my still packed suitcase. I begged him to let me go, but he refused. I spent the first few days curled up in a ball in bed almost catatonic. James would just open the door and check on me like a nurse does a patient. He'd say, 'Everything will be alright, Grace. I promise,' and he'd leave. Hunger finally got the best of me, and I left the bed to eat. Mind you, I only had the finest. All my favorites from the top restaurants. The room had a TV, books, all I could want. He knew all my tastes.

"I think it was the fifth day that I was allowed out of my room. We were underground somewhere, so there were no windows and most doors were locked. There were guards on duty at all times, but I could walk around. I had access to the living room, dining room, office, and kitchen, though the forks and knives were locked up."

"He took you home," I say.

"Yes. And he treated me like a guest. As best as I can figure, with hindsight mind you, he brought me there so I would fall in love with him. For us to get to know each other better. He believed that if I was alone with him, and we spent enough time together, I'd forget about Chad and love him instead. At the time I just knew to play along with whatever he wanted. We'd play chess or watch movies, and we'd always have dinner together."

"Did he talk to you about his crimes? His accomplices?"

"Some. He spoke about his childhood in the Ward, coming into his power. I gave the names he mentioned and crimes when I was rescued. I haven't been able to recall any others since."

"What about places?"

"None," she says sadly, "and since last night I've been trying. I want him caught as much as you do. Probably more."

"That's okay," I say with a sympathetic smile. This is a waste of time. I'm not doing anything but torturing her now. I start to stand up, but she grows tense.

"You're leaving?" she asks.

"I can get the rest of this from the case files. You don't have to—"

"I want to," she says. "I *need* to. I need you to hear it. So you can understand who you're dealing with. So when he's in your sights, you don't hesitate."

A chill fills the room spurred on by her voice. I sit again. "Okay."

Grace's gaze moves to the outside of her window. "I did my best to be a good prisoner. I was attentive when he'd drone on for hours about Justice and his crimes. I'd help him make dinner. And yes, I even let him kiss me on a few occasions. He actually believed I loved him after a week or two. But at night when I was locked back in my room, I'd cry myself to sleep. Every night."

"What happened the day you escaped?"

"He'd just had the fight with Justice at the library."

Ryder was at the library in a disguise, but a patron still recognized him and called the police. Justice got there first. It took a year before they could re-open it. Many said it was a miracle that the entire place didn't collapse. If you look closely, you can see the patches they had to put in where the acid ate away the wall.

"He was so enraged, like nothing I had ever seen before. I can only equate it to demonic possession. He threw things, destroyed a chair, and...even killed one of the guards who tried to calm him down." Tears glisten in her eyes. "His body...there was nothing left of his chest but blood and pulp. I ran screaming into my room, barricading the door with anything I could. I was so terrified, I huddled in the corner.

"Then perhaps five minutes later, as if nothing had happened, James knocked on my door. He apologized for the outburst, for scaring me, but I refused to open the door. After half an hour he pushed his way in, calm as could be. I couldn't stop crying. He tried to smooth my hair, but I cringed. He asked if I still loved him, and...I lost it. I told him I hated him, thought he was worse than the devil. He told me he loved me. I spit in his face. That's when he…you know."

"Yes."

"After it was over, he curled up into a ball beside me, whispering for forgiveness. I just got off the bed and walked out. He simply let me leave. I've spent many a sleepless night wondering why he did that. He had to know what I'd do."

"Maybe he didn't care," I offer. "He knew that he'd lost you." An image pops into my mind of Rebecca walking down the aisle toward Justin. My stomach momentarily knots up. Hell, I think I just sympathized with the devil.

"Perhaps," Grace says.

Grace was spotted wandering down the street by a vendor, who immediately called the police. Within an hour Justice had Alkaline in custody. The villain didn't even put up a fight.

"Do you think he'll contact you?" I ask.

"I don't know. It's been years, I doubt I'm anything but a memory to him by now. At least I hope so."

"He's not stupid," I say. "He'll know we're watching you closely. If you want it, we can have officers posted right outside your door."

"I have Warren and Arnold," she says, referring to her guards. "I'm more than confident in their abilities."

"Well then," I say, standing up again, "if you need anything else, just call me. If you think of anything else, or just need to talk…"

Grace stands as well, ushering me toward the door. "I will." We reach the door, she hands me the file. I open the door. "You know…"

I stop and turn around. "What?"

"I never used to like you."

"Huh?"

"I thought you were just some pathetic hanger-on maneuvering for a way out of the gutter. We all did."

"I kind of figured that," I say.

"But we were wrong, weren't we? You're genuinely in love with him. And he has no idea, does he?"

Sucker punch right into the gut. "He's my best friend," I say, the old stand-by.

She smiles sympathetically. "Can't help who we fall in love with, can we? It has no rhyme, it has no reason. And it's usually so fucking unfair." She quietly scoffs. We stand in silence for a moment before her faux smiles returns. "Well, then. Will you please give Justin my best wishes? I doubt I'll be attending the engagement party or the wedding. I hope he'll understand."

"Of course he will."

"And good luck." She starts closing the door. "You will need it."

The door shuts in my face.

Chapter Six
Tips

Alkaline's been a busy boy today. He's visited the zoo, every grocery store in the city, and apparently can now be found in the fifth plane of existence, whatever the hell that is. We received over two hundred fifty tips, and they all have to be logged. The ones that don't involve inter-dimensional travel have to be investigated. Scut work, not my favorite thing. I've gotten through about twenty, most dismissed with a simple phone call.

The squad room is quiet now. All non-essential personnel were sent home to catch a few winks. I got mine last night, so I'm stuck here. Cam and Kowalski are in our now empty interview rooms reviewing the preliminary reports on the guards. Harry's in his office with the door closed and the blinds drawn. Probably asleep at his desk.

"This is stupid," Mirabelle says across the room from his desk. "I've been yelled at four times in a row for calling so late. It's past midnight. Even Alkaline's asleep right now."

"That's why we're better than him. He rests, we don't."

"Maybe I'm in the wrong racket."

"I really can't picture you in a spandex costume, Mirabelle."

A young uniformed officer walks in holding a piece of paper. "Um, ma'am?"

"Yes?" I ask.

"There's a woman on the tip line who's asking to speak to a detective. She's pretty insistent."

Ugh. "Fine. Transfer her."

The officer walks back into the other room.

"You want me to take it?" Mirabelle asks.

The light on my phone blinks to let me know I have a call. "I got it." I pick up the phone. "Det. Joanna Fallon."

"Are you like in charge of the Alkaline case?" a young woman asks nervously.

"Yes," I lie. "You say you have information? Can I get your name and telephone number, please?"

"Can't this be, like, anonymous or something? I don't want them to know it was me. They'll, like, kill me."

The certainty in her voice with those last words grabs my attention. I signal to Mirabelle, mouthing "trace the call." He hops to. "That's fine. What can you tell me?"

"It's my boyfriend. Robbie. I think he's in trouble. Like major trouble. And I'm like totally freaking out."

"What's his connection to Alkaline?"

"If I tell you, you have to promise you won't arrest him, okay?"

"That's not up to me, that's up to the DA. But if his cooperation leads to Alkaline's capture, the DA will take that into consideration." The girl is quiet as she considers this. I'm going to lose her, so I add, "Miss, if your boyfriend is involved with Alkaline, then he is in grave danger. This is a man who could very easily kill Robbie just so he won't talk. You as well."

She waits a moment before saying, "I think Robbie is making a driver's license and passport for Alkaline. I saw him printing one with Alkaline's picture on it. He doesn't know I saw it."

Yes! Yes! A legitimate break. Finally. I'm so happy, I could cry. I smile at Mirabelle, who has been listening to my every word. "What's Robbie's last name?"

"Munoz. I'm not saying anything else. I gotta go." She hangs up before I can ask another question. I sigh. "Crap."

Mirabelle listens into his phone for a moment, and then hangs up. "Call came from a payphone on McFarlane. The Ward."

"Is the name 'Robbie Munoz' familiar to you?" I ask Mirabelle. "Counterfeiter?"

"Munoz? Yeah. We had him in today. He was Luis Rivas' old apprentice. You know, the documents guy Alkaline offed? Weren't you the first responder on that one?"

"Yeah." I get up to retrieve the file on the interview today. Mirabelle helps me with the other box. I think we set a new record for number of interviews in one day with not a damn thing to show for it. Munoz is about a third of the way through. I open the file. Munoz swore up and down he had nothing to do with Alkaline and wouldn't, even if asked.

"Why would a guy work with the man who melted his boss?" Mirabelle asks.

"A shitload of money?" I copy down the address, and put the file back. We're going to the Ward. "You coming with me?"

"Think this is legit?"

"Worth a look." I grab my coat, clip my gun back on, and rush out with Mirabelle behind me. I briefly consider filling Harry in, but don't want to wake him if this doesn't pan out. He's grumpy without enough sleep.

The streets are near empty as I drive us to my old stomping ground, Diablo's Ward. It boasts a hooker and junkie on every street corner. Really a wonderful place to raise kids. I made pocket money turning in dirty needles I found in parks to clinics. Fifty cents a pop. Treasured childhood memories.

Every election year some politician swears on his or her own mother that their first priority is cleaning up the Ward. The rotting, splintering, condemned buildings where junkies inject their fixes will come down, replaced with schools and parks. There must be a lot of dead mothers out there judging from the state of this place. The only people out tonight are dealers, the homeless pushing their carts, and the pros drumming up business.

Munoz's place is in the heart of the Ward, a small apartment complex of maybe four stories of white cinderblocks. We park alongside the building, surveying the area. Far as I can tell, there are no lookouts to cause trouble.

"What do you think?" I ask Mirabelle.

"Let's rock and roll."

Just as we're about to get out, three gunshots ring out above us. Instantly, we each reach for our guns and crouch down, but the shock lasts for a millisecond before we leap out of the car, guns at the ready. With his free hand, Mirabelle pulls off his walkie from his belt.

"Dispatch, shots fired in the vicinity of 4763 McFarlane Street. Plainclothes officers in need of assistance."

I see nothing. No people, no weapons, nothing. I hate flying blind. For all I know there's a fleet of crack-heads with Uzis charging around the corner. As I'm assessing, there's a large thump on the hood of the car. Metal hitting metal. We swing our guns at the source. A Glock lies on the hood of our car in the middle of a crater. But before we can even register this fact, a man's screams from the roof grab my attention.

My legs start pumping of their own accord before I'm aware that I'm running toward the building, then through the unlocked front door. I glide upstairs, checking every corner for danger. Mirabelle is behind me, managing to keep up all five flights.

The access door to the roof lies on its side against the wall, along with a piece of plywood in three pieces. The barricade obviously didn't work. A piece of lead wouldn't either. The man hollers again, but I can't make out the words. Adrenaline pumps through my system as I make my way up the final flight of steps, and goddamn I do love that feeling. Anything could be out there. These could be my final moments on the planet for all I know. What a fucking rush.

Mirabelle is a few inches behind me and I look at him. He nods. I run out the door onto the gravel roof with my gun pointed. "Police! Freeze!" I shout before I realize who I'm drawing on. Fuck.

Justice stands by the edge of the roof, holding a crying man over the side one handed by the belt. The man, who I recognize from his mug shot as Munoz, is near hysterical and praying in Spanish.

"Good evening, detectives," Justice says as if greeting us at a party.

"Put him down," I say.

"I haven't finished questioning him," Justice says with his gravelly voice.

"Put him the fuck down!"

Justice complies. The moment Munoz's feet hit the roof, he falls onto his knees and kisses the gravel, murmuring in Spanish. Justice holds his hands up in surrender. "If you wouldn't mind pointing those guns somewhere else, please. I've already been shot three times today. We are on the same side, you know."

"Debatable," I say, but put my gun back in the holster, as does Mirabelle. "Det. Mirabelle, can you please escort Mr. Munoz to the squad car?"

Mirabelle pulls out his cuffs, putting them on Munoz, who doesn't even seem to mind. Mirabelle yanks the almost relieved felon up and escorts him off the roof. Justice nods respectfully at Mirabelle, who I'm fairly sure blushes and nods back. "Sir."

"What the hell are you doing here?" I ask when they're gone.

"Following up on a lead, the same as you detective."

"And how did you hear about Mr. Munoz?"

"I have my sources." Meaning he's tapped into our phone lines or computers. Sneaky bastard. He starts walking toward me. "He was contacted two days ago by an unknown person via e-mail asking him to make a passport, birth certificate, and driver's license. He received a wire transfer the same day, but didn't know who he was making it for until today when the same person e-mailed a photo of Alkaline to put on the documents. I was just about to find out about the delivery details when you arrived. He'll probably lawyer up now."

"Geez, sorry for doing my job, asshole," I say as snidely as humanly possible.

"The man shot me the moment he saw me."

"We'll make sure to charge him for it."

"It could have been you, detective. You're not even wearing your vest. I noticed you weren't wearing it last night either. He could have killed you if I hadn't gotten here first."

My Irish flares up. "Excuse me?" I almost yell. "Are you criticizing me after I find you dangling a perp off a fucking rooftop? His lawyer's going to have a field day. Anything he told you is inadmissible."

"Good thing I don't work for the police. Though, I'm told starting tomorrow I'm your Federal Marshall liaison. We should be seeing more of each other in the future."

"Oh, goody."

The sound of sirens, our late back-up, draws his attention. "Time for me to depart. And wear your vest, Joanna. Please." He vanishes, leaving nothing but a gust of wind as he super-speeds past me down the stairs.

The. Fucking. Nerve. I'm literally vibrating with anger, though it could be the adrenaline wearing off. Wear my vest. Not a bad idea, but if he tells me I have to eat all my vegetables I just might shoot him myself. Prick.

***

One sleepless night later, to my credit, I have fifty pieces of evidence logged, thirteen interview requests from the press, an eight-page incident report, two angry phone calls from the motor pool for the dented car, and one lawyered-up suspect. Not to mention a stern talking to by Harry for not keeping him in the loop or waiting for back-up. All this sudden interest in my safety is getting old and stifling. I feel like a pissed-off China doll.

At least the whole debacle wasn't for nothing. The computer guys are working on tracing the e-mail and wire transfers. We know one of Ryder's aliases. A scumbag is off the street. But according to city hall, the best news is that we actually have a lead. We don't look incompetent for a change. The press conference I just gave went as smooth as Don Juan. Too bad I looked like a gargoyle.

And now to cash in my superstar award. I get to go home and sleep. Maybe even eat something, take a shower, and change my clothes. I'm on call if anything comes up, but even God isn't that cruel not to allow me eight full hours of sweet oblivion.

Harry isn't in his office as I walk out, but Lt. Pete DiQueeno of Special Victims is. He waves as I pass, and I do the same. I guess we've all been relieved for a few hours. My off-duty car is exactly where I left it over twenty-four hours ago, though there are five fliers under the wipers. I reach my bed ten minutes later. I kick off my shoes, put on my pajamas, climb in, and pass out thirty seconds later.

A loud ringing by my ear jerks me out of Jo's Happy Place. I look at the clock. A little past noon. Almost three hours. I'm too tired to think of something witty to say.

"Det. Joanna Fallon," I say when I answer the phone.

"Jo, it's Cam," my partner says.

"What?"

"The guard, Dodd, is finally awake. Thought you'd want to be there when I talk to him."

This perks me up like a verbal cup of coffee. "Yeah. Hell, yeah."

"I'll swing by your place in twenty. Bye."

Twenty minutes to turn human again. I toss on my gray suit, purple shirt, brush my teeth and hair, scarf down a Pop Tart, and clip on my badge and gun just as Cam buzzes his arrival. Out the door I go.

Cam sits in the idling car and barely waits until I get in before pulling away. Like me, he resembles the walking dead with bloodshot eyes and sallow skin. At least he didn't go on the national news looking like that.

"When did Dodd regain consciousness?" I ask.

"About an hour ago, poor bastard. He's still pretty fucked up. We only get a few minutes with him."

"Then we better make them count."

One of the many things I love about Cam is that silence doesn't feel awkward with him. Neither one of us is a big talker, so we barely say three words on the ride to the hospital. Not that either of us has the energy for anything so superfluous as small talk.

Our Lady of Perpetual Sorrow Hospital, Galilee's crowning glory, sits right at the edge of the Andalucía River which separates the city proper from the state park and The Garden. I turn my head to the left and I see The Falls in the distance. The thirty-story white building is always busy with doctors, patients, and visitors filing in and out. Two ambulances pull up to the ER as we park. As we walk to the elevator behind an orderly pushing an old woman, I spot Veronica sitting in the waiting room, jotting down notes. She doesn't see me. Crap, I really owe her a call.

Logan Dodd is on the fifth floor, the critical care burn unit. His private room is under guard by two uniforms. A middle-aged Indian man in blue scrubs and white lab coat approaches us. "I'm Dr. Amil Sharma, Logan Dodd's physician," he says. "Before you go in, you'll need to put on protective gear to prevent infection."

Both the doctor and the two of us don our paper gowns, latex gloves, and face masks. We look ridiculous, but we don't want our witness dying on us before trial just because I breathed my cooties on him. Cam looks at me and his eyes crinkle with a smile.

"How's he doing?" I ask.

"As well as can be expected," the doctor says. "We had to amputate his hand at the wrist, and he'll need more skin grafts where the acid splattered his thigh. He's in for a long recovery process, in all respects."

"At least he's alive," Cam says.

"He's on heavy pain medication," Sharma says. "Morphine. Please avoid agitating him, if possible."

"We'll be gentle," I say.

Lying in his hospital bed, Logan Dodd looks less like a 6"3' prison guard and more like a pale child. IVs and other tubes in nasty places hang from his body. The sheet covers the carnage inflicted on him. He's awake, but his eyes are barely open. Doped out of his mind.

"Officer Dodd, I'm Det. Cameron and this is Det. Fallon," Cam says. "We were the ones who found you at the prison. We wanted to ask you a few questions about your attack."

Dodd tries to prop himself up using his good hand, but doesn't have the strength. The other hand comes out from under the sheet. It's wrapped in white gauze with a net over it. There are a few yellow spots where the ointments have leaked through. At least I think they're ointments. "Um, okay," Dodd says, still groggy.

Cam sits in the chair by his bedside, and I pull out my notepad. "We'll try and make this as fast as possible, okay? What can you tell us about the night you were attacked?" I ask.

"Everything was normal. Everything was fine," he says through the drug haze. "We'd just checked on the inmates."

"You and Stu Moore?" Cam asks.

"Yeah. I was in the office reading a magazine, when I heard Stu shout something, I don't know what. I checked the monitor. Alkaline was out. He stood across from Moore, something coming from his wrist. Then Stu's head, um..." The boy can't finish. As part of Alkaline's sentence, the holes where Ryder's acid reserves spring out, through the extra hollow bones in his wrists, were surgically closed. It must have hurt like hell when the bone pushed through.

"Where was Stu when this happened?" I ask.

"By Alkaline's cell. Where he died."

"How did Alkaline get out?" I ask in hopes of sparing the poor kid.

"I don't know. I wasn't watching the monitors. I should have been when Stu was walking the block, but…" Dodd tears up. "I don't know."

"What happened next?" Cam asks.

"I ran out there. But…he got me. I couldn't think. He had Stu's gun on me. I was so freaked, I forgot to pull mine. He told me to take off my uniform and give him my card key. I did."

"And then?"

"He said 'Thank you.' He took the card, smiled, and then…it came out of his wrist again. That bone, and then the acid. It hurt so bad." He's crying now, almost sobbing. "My hand. It just fell off. I've never felt anything like that in my life. That's the last thing I remember."

"I think that's enough for now," the doctor says.

"Just a few more questions," Cam says, "please. Is that okay, Logan?"

"I guess," Dodd says, trying to calm himself down. He takes a few deep breaths. "I want this over with."

"Were any of the guards particularly attentive to Alkaline?" Cam asks.

"I don't know," he says, "I noticed he had an extra brownie for desert once."

"Any idea who gave it to him?"

"Maybe Stu, I don't know. It was like a month ago."

"Did he ever speak to you? Alkaline?" I ask.

"We weren't allowed to talk to him. He never even tried with me."

"Did you ever see Officer Moore talk to him?" Cam asks.

Dodd is quiet for a second. "I don't think so. I don't know! I don't know how he got out! When are you going to find him? He—he's gonna come back and finish me off! Why haven't you caught him yet?" The kid has gone wild, trying to kick his covers off.

Dr. Sharma steps over to him, acting as a buffer between us and Dodd. "Okay," the doctor says, "that is more than enough."

"He's gonna kill me!" Dodd shouts, near hysterics.

"You have protection," I say.

"Leave. Now," Sharma says.

The big, bad police walk out just as Sharma injects a drug into Dodd's IV. I rip off the stifling protection in frustration. "You woke me up for *that*?" I ask with a sigh.

"Could have gone better," Cam says.

"They're not going to let us back in there," I say, "not until he's discharged. Not that it matters. He didn't see shit."

"Or he's lying and he's the one who let Ryder out," Cam says.

"We're not going to find out anytime soon. They won't let us press him, and we're running out of time. If that psycho isn't about to do something heinous, then I'm a supermodel."

We start walking down the hall toward the elevators. I punch the button hard enough to break it. "You need to chill," Cam says. "You'll get an ulcer."

"You sound like Justin," I say. The elevator doors open and we step in. "I'm being held together by coffee and adrenaline. If I chill, I'll fall to the ground and start babbling like an idiot."

"Still."

We get off a few seconds later. Just as we pass reception, a woman calls my name. Rebecca, dressed in purple scrubs and white lab coat, runs over to us with that perpetual sweet smile on her face. Just what I need.

"I heard you were here," she says as she reaches us.

"Lucky me," I say with a fake smile.

"It really is lucky! I just got done assisting on a five-hour surgery when one of the nurses told me she saw you." Five hours of surgery and her make-up and hair are still flawless, where as I resemble a three-day piece of road kill. She holds out her hand to Cam. "Hi. You must be Joanna's partner, Cam. It is so nice to finally meet you."

"Cam, this is Rebecca Thornton, Justin's fiancée," I say.

They shake hands. "I've heard a lot about you," Cam says. And he has. I try to keep my thoughts about my private life to myself, but I sometimes spend sixty hours a week with the man. Things slip. Okay, *a lot* of things slip.

"Me too," Rebecca says. "So, you two are here to interview that poor guard?"

"Yeah," I say, "but he's in no shape to talk."

"I heard it was ghastly."

"It wasn't pretty."

"So, are you heading back to the station now? Because I sort of had an ulterior motive for coming down here," she says sweetly, her nose crinkling and shoulders rising.

"You did?" I ask.

"Everyone I normally have lunch with is busy, and I hate going to the cafeteria alone. People always come up to me with questions. I can't finish my meal."

"Um—"

"You have time," Cam interrupts. The traitor. "You're technically not on the clock."

"But you drove me here," I say with a fake sweet smile

"Take the Metro. You need to eat, don't you?"

Rebecca's smile stretches from cheek to cheek. "Oh, please? Please?"

Lack of sleep and yes, nourishment have made the lying part of my brain go on the fritz. I'm sure when she's babbling on about the honeymoon or china patterns, a trillion will come to mind. But not right now. Now, I'm screwed.

"I can't think of a reason why not," I say.

If at all possible her smile grows. "Wonderful! I'm starving." She wraps her arm around mine and pulls me away. Cam has a huge grin on his face. So much for my brother in blue.

CHAPTER SEVEN
GIRLFRIENDS

This is the only hospital in the country that has gourmet chefs on the payroll and a ballroom. Since Rebecca's paying I load up with scallops, pork chops, and chocolate mousse. She just orders the watercress soup and Caesar salad. "Must fit into my wedding dress," she chirps with a broad smile. Rebecca looks so beautiful it almost hurts my eyes. Plus she saves people, whereas I arrest them. Whenever I'm around her I leave little drops of self-esteem in my wake. I really have to stop that or I'll have none left.

All the other doctors grin and wave as she passes and a few patients' families do as well. I'll lay even odds she was popular in high school too. Voted "Most Likely to Succeed" and prom queen. The only people I was popular with were the truant officers. I trail behind her like her shorter, less attractive shadow. We find an empty table next to a window, and I can see The Falls in the distance across the river. I love looking at it. The waterfall, a quarter mile wide, cascades off black rock. That white water over black onyx always draws a crowd.

"I am starving," she says as she takes a baby bite of her salad.

"Me too," I mutter with a good helping of pork chop in my mouth.

"But I have to lose five pounds before the wedding. I just *had* to choose satin. It leaves nothing to the imagination. Have I shown you a picture of the dress yet?"

Only half a dozen freaking times. "Yeah. It's beautiful." And it is. Sleek ivory satin, sleeveless, with crystals and tiny pearls swirling around. Only ten grand for something she'll wear once. Okay, I have to stop thinking like this. She's wonderful. Justin is the happiest he's ever been. I have an awesome boyfriend. I'm a lucky girl. If I just keep telling myself these things, maybe I'll start believing them.

"I can't wait to show it to you on," she says with another bite of lettuce. "Will you still have time on Saturday to meet us at the dress shop? They really need to fit your dress. I finally decided on sky blue to match your eyes. You are going to look gorgeous! I'm dying for you to see it. I have the whole day planned. The shop, then lunch, then I was thinking we could go for pedicures. Mom's never had one before."

Oh, lord save me from female bonding. "We'll play it by ear," I say. "If something comes up or there's a break in the case…I'll do my best."

"You have to be there. At least for the fitting. Half an hour, tops."

"I can't control these things."

"But if you're not there, then they won't have time to alter the dress."

Why do I get the feeling that after this I'm going to get a nasty call from Justin? "Look, I'll do everything in my power to be there. I promise. Same with the party tomorrow night."

"I know, I'm sorry," she says with sincerity. "I swear I'm turning into the supervillain Bridezilla. It's just that my last wedding was at city hall, and I always regretted that."

Her previous husband Micah, the father of Daisy, was an abusive bastard who she divorced when she was seven months pregnant. Brave of her. He is currently doing a stint in prison for assaulting his boss and shares a cell with Big Bubba. The woman learned her lesson and has definitely upgraded.

"Maybe we should just fly to St. Tropez and elope," Rebecca continues. "Get married on the beach with just family there, but I guess it's too late. The invitations are out and the food is ordered." She sighs. "I'm just so exhausted. It's like I have three full-time jobs, what with here, the wedding, and Daisy. I wish I knew Dr. Avatar. Maybe he could clone me. Never a supervillain around when you need one, huh?"

"I seem to be having that problem as well."

"Oh! I'm sorry! That was a silly thing to say. How is that going? Have you been working around the clock? I'll bet you have. Justin says you're the most tenacious person he's ever met."

"It's going well. We have a few leads. We'll find him."

"Well, Justin is just frantic with worry about you. I had to convince him not to phone the mayor and bar you from the case."

"He was going to do that?"

"He had the phone *in his hand*. But I told him you were a grown, more than capable woman who the people of the city needed out there if we expected to find this monster," she says with utter conviction.

"Thank you," I say, and to my surprise I actually mean it.

"He is just so protective of you." She takes another bite. Almost all my food is gone, but half her salad and all of the soup remains. "To be perfectly candid, it bothered me a little in the beginning. I thought maybe he was in love with you, or vice versa." My heart skips a beat. "But then, as I watched the two of you, I sort of fell in love with him because of your love for each other. How open, how honest and warm he was with you. It showed me what a good man he is, and how much I wanted someone to feel those things for me too. That connection. That love." Her smile doubles, if possible. "And having you in my life is just an added bonus. I would like nothing more than for us to be best friends." She shakes her head. "You're so strong and fearless. I feel like a meek little nothing compared to you. I wish I could be that way. And I can't believe I'm admitting this to you, but I'm still sort of threatened by you. I mean, I know Justin loves me with all his heart, and I know you both have too much integrity to ever cheat, but I am. You two have this bond like nothing I've ever seen. I'm a little jealous. I just hope one day you and I could have a relationship like that. I want it more than almost anything."

Okay…I feel like total and utter shit. They could do a full-scale model of the Eiffel Tower with the amount of shit I feel like right now. For months I've been praying that a hole would swallow her up. Or aliens would abduct her. I've been standoffish, and just a bitch behind her back. And all this time she's been admiring me, and wanting nothing more than to be my best friend. They're reserving my spot in hell right now.

It's hard to process that she's been comparing herself to me and not stacking up, as I've been doing with her. "I don't know what to say."

"You don't have to say anything. I'm sorry I put you on the spot like that." She covers her face. "I'm so embarrassed."

"Don't be. It's…I'm sorry if I did anything to cause you to feel like that," I say, genuinely meaning it.

"You didn't. It's me. It's all me and my stupid insecurities." She lowers her head, shaking it. "Anyway, the uncomfortable soul bearing portion of our meal is over with." She smiles again. "Time for the fun stuff. Are you bringing anyone to the engagement party tomorrow? Or the wedding?"

Subtle. "I'm afraid I'll be flying solo tomorrow night *if* I can go."

"Oh," she says sadly. "Well, maybe you'll meet someone tomorrow night. A lot of people from the hospital are coming. There's actually this really brilliant neurologist I worked with in Independence who I'm just *dying* to introduce you to. He's one of my oldest, dearest friends, and the sweetest man alive. I think you'll really hit it off."

I take a bite of my brownie. "Please stop trying to set me up. Between you, Justin, and Cam's wife, I think I've had dinner with the whole male population of Galilee by now."

"We just want you to be happy."

"I am happy," I say quickly. "I'm happy for you. And Justin. The rest, well, it'll come when it comes. No rush."

"Maybe with Dr. Ambrose," she says with a knowing smile.

"Maybe."

It's times like these I wish I could tell the world about Harry. Shout it from the rafters that there's a descent, hardworking man who thinks I'm worthwhile. But that would be too much like right. Too grown up. Too real.

The rest of lunch is filled with the dreaded girl talk about the wedding, Daisy, and of course Justin. The way she talks about him, and looks when she's talking about him, grates me. It's akin to hero worship. Her eyes double in size, she gets a silly grin on her face, and giggles more than any grown woman should. V's told me I look exactly the same way when I talk about him. Strange to see the same look on your rival's face. No, not rival. No doubts now. She loves him just as much as I do. No. Stop. Not doing this. Not anymore. She's not a rival, there wasn't even a contest. You lost years ago. Think of other things.

I keep a smile on my face and half listen, my mind wandering a tad. If Dodd's recollections are correct, then Moore was the only one who could open the cell. It is possible that one of the other guards left it unlocked and Ryder waited until night, but I doubt it. Why take a chance that someone on duty would notice? No, Stu Moore just became suspect number one. Ryder killed him so he couldn't talk, poor bastard. But what if—

"Don't you think?" Rebecca says, pulling me back.

"I'm sorry?"

"Our hair. I think I'll have an up-do with daisies, and all the bridesmaids will too. Are you okay with that?"

"Fine. I'll do whatever you want."

Her face scrunches up. "I'm boring you, aren't I?" she asks.

"No, sorry. I've just got work on my mind. I actually should get back to it." I take a final bite of my brownie before rising.

"Okay," she says, also standing. Before I can stop her, she pulls me into a hug. I hesitate for a moment, my arms suspended at my sides not wanting to put forth the effort, but I force them to embrace her back. "Be safe."

I pat her back. "I will."

She releases me, a smile of course there. "Thank you for having lunch with me. I really appreciate it."

"Of course. Bye." And I rush out of there before she can say another word.

Veronica remains at her post, waiting for something to report. She perks up when she notices me coming at her like a cruise missile. "Hey," she says.

I grab her arm and pull my surprised cousin out of the chair. "I promise to answer all your questions if you leave with me. Right now."

"What? Why—"

Rebecca walks to the reception desk to ask something, but spots us. She smiles and waves. We respond in kind, though the sentiment is different on this end. "Oh," V says through her smile.

I lock my arm in V's and pull her away toward the exit. I need a drink.

***

V's Irish genes are recessive, at least in regards to the desire to consume alcohol. The girl, and I use the term loosely as she's a year older than me, barely touches the stuff. She's always been the good one of the family. College graduate, owns her apartment, and until recently was in a long term relationship with a criminal defense attorney. He and I had fun conversations at Thanksgiving.

The story goes that my Pop was dating my hell-beast mother when she introduced him to proud new Papa, Uncle Ray, Aunt Emily, and three-month-old Veronica. Pop held the little baby and that was it. That night he knocked up Mom just so he could have his own little angel. Don't know if I should thank her or smack her. Depends on the day.

Where alcohol is my drug of choice, V's is coffee. She has about six cups a day, and since it's more socially acceptable to indulge her addiction in the middle of the day, we stroll down the riverwalk to a coffee shop a few blocks away. We sit inside as far from everyone as possible in the corner.

"You know, I've seen her all of three times," V says as she sips her drink, "and *every* time she's had a smile on her face."

"I've seen her a billion times and can say the same thing," I say.

"Nobody is that happy all the time without pharmaceutical intervention. You sure she's not on happy pills? Cause if she is, I want a prescription."

"No. She's just like a fairytale princess with birds fluttering around her head, chirping a melody or something." I sip my black coffee. "And why not? She escaped the evil ex-husband, has a precious daughter, she saves babies all day, and now she's got the handsome prince madly in love with her. Hell, I'd smile all the time too."

"And in this fairy tale, who do you cast yourself as?"

"I alternate between the wicked crone thrusting a poison apple in her face or the troll under the bridge. Depends on my hair that day."

V chuckles and shakes her head. "I don't know how you do it. I'd want to rip her hair out." My dear cousin is the only person I've actually admitted my feelings about Justin to. Everyone else just *knows*.

"If I did that, it'd just grow back more lustrous than before."

"Most likely, but at least you'd feel better for a few seconds."

"She's so nice, V," I say. "You know what she said to me today? That she wishes she was like me. That I'm fearless and strong, and that she's threatened. By me! Can you believe that shit? I felt like such an asshole. I wanted to run screaming from the table or slap her to stop the words."

"That bitch," V says, sarcastically. "Liking you. The nerve."

"Funny, cuz."

V sips her coffee. "I don't know. You've always had such a blind spot when it comes to Justin. Always. You justify his every action. You can't see his faults, and he can do no wrong. It's not healthy. Maybe it's time you started distancing yourself from him. He is not worth the pain. Put away fucking childish things and move on. He's gone. You will never have what you want. She's the one he's marrying. She's the one who will have his children. She's the one who gets to share his bed. His life! *She's* the most important person to him now. You're the one he'll go out for drinks with after work to bitch about trivialities like her snoring and playful nagging. It's not you and him against the world anymore, it's her and him. He's not alone anymore; he doesn't need you like he did. He has a family now, a real one. And the sooner you realize that, you moron, the sooner you'll get a life of your own. Like you deserve. You deserve to be happy, Jo. It's *okay* to be happy."

The words sting like acid, but I know they're true. "It's not that easy. I've been in love with him for almost twenty years. A fucking lifetime! We've seen each other through the worst of the worst. He saved my life, V. I can't just turn it off and say good-bye. I can't."

"Then start preparing yourself for the inevitable and try to make the best of it. Maybe actually truly try to embrace Rebecca and Daisy. Look at all her good traits, which I'm sure are legion. Think of it as gaining a friend, and not losing one."

"You sound like an advice column," I say with a sneer.

"I got this stuff from 'Ask Mary.' If it was me, the second I realized he would never love me back, I would have run the other way. But you know this. I think you just like torturing yourself. You're only happy when you're miserable. You get that from Aunt Maeve." She sips her coffee. "Speaking of, so I no longer have to listen to this crap for the trillionth time, cousin dear, Dad's planning on going out to the cemetery on her birthday next week. He wants to know if you want to go too."

"He can give her my regards." Ten years ago my mom fulfilled my prophecy of her death, passing out drunk with a lit cigarette and burning her apartment down. I hadn't spoken to her in four years, and only found out when someone at the department contacted me as a courtesy. Didn't shed one tear for that abusive alcoholic. I used to go to the cemetery with Uncle Ray, the only one of her siblings who still gave a damn about her, but the whole thing felt phony. "I'll pass."

"He also wants to know why you haven't called him back."

"I'm busy. I've only slept about eight hours in four days, okay? I'll try to make Sunday supper this week."

"And Bobby wants to know how to get a permit to carry a handgun. And Eamon wants to know if his application to Pendergast Productions went through. And R.J. needs another speeding ticket fixed." V's the eldest and only girl, poor thing. "And I shouldn't have to play messenger girl. You need to call them back, if you can pull yourself out of your own misery for a minute. We're your real family, remember?"

"I know, and I will. I promise."

"Good." She takes a generous sip of her coffee and pulls out her notepad. "So. Is the GFPD any closer to catching Alkaline?"

"On the record, we're pursuing multiple leads and are confident we'll apprehend him within days. Last night's arrest and confiscation of counterfeit IDs have opened up many new avenues of investigation." We both roll our eyes, but she writes this quote down. "Off the record, it took us a decade to get any dirt on him and catch him, and that's only because we lucked out with Grace Pickering. We have no idea where he is, what he's up to, or how he even escaped. It's going to take him fucking up or blind luck to snag him this time, and my money's on neither. He's smarter than us, and we all know it. We're royally screwed."

"God, I wish I could print that," V says. "So, nothing? You guys have found jack?" I fill her in on the documents guy, Munoz, but leave out the meeting with Justice. Mention his name to any reporter, and the article becomes a loving tribute to the man."Well, that's something," she says, jotting it all down. "Do you think it means he's still in town?"

"I cannot speculate at this time," I say in a monotone. "Off the record, he is so still here. He's been planning something, probably since he went in. What, I have no clue."

"Come on, Jo. Give me something new here. Has he tried to contact Pickering? Who helped him escape? Something!"

I do owe her. "Okay, but this didn't come from me. Just write it came from someone close to the investigation. You can run with it or not."

"What is it?"

"When we entered Alkaline's cell, it was covered with pictures and articles about Justice. Like every inch of his cell. He's obsessed with the man. And that's all I'm saying."

"I'll need confirmation on that," she says.

"Call the lab. I think the count was one hundred twenty-one different clippings. But you didn't hear it from me." I finish my coffee. "I should get back to work."

"Okay," V says.

I stand up. "You don't, by any slim chance, want to be my date to the engagement party tomorrow night, do you? Free food, booze, rich men?"

"You don't have a date?"

"Of course not. I'm a loser." She doesn't know about Harry. I've wanted to tell her a dozen times, but I know she wouldn't approve. Yeah, that's the reason and I'm sticking to it.

"I think I'm going to pass. Like you should."

"I'm the best man," I say with an uncomfortable smile. "I have a speech to make and all. About their love, God help me. They'll be crushed if I don't. I think I should start drinking *right now*."

"Maybe good old Alkaline will pop up and give you an excuse, you never know."

"I'm not that lucky."

"It'll be fine." She stands up too and air kisses my cheeks. "Remember: you're getting a friend, not losing one."

"'Ask Mary' needs to find a new trade," I say.

"'Ask Mary' is a fifty year old man named Duke. He used to write obituaries."

"It shows." I hug my cousin. "Bye."

As I get outside and start toward the subway, I do something I try never to do: think. It always leads to problems, followed by depression, followed by drinking, ending with a hangover. So thinking actually hurts me. But that ever stopped me from doing anything. V inherited the common sense in the family. Per usual, she's right. I need to adapt, grow. Come to terms with the state of things.

Rebecca is not going away. He loves her, and she him. There is nothing I can do about that. He doesn't love me, not in the way I want him to. He never will. That wouldn't be different even if he had never met Rebecca. It's been twenty goddamn years, why can't this fact just sink in?

So, I have a choice to make. I can be happy, truly happy for my friend that he found such a warm, giving woman to love, and who loves him back. I can share in their joy and embrace her as a new friend. Though this time, I'll actually mean it. Slay that green-eyed monster that stands in my way. Or I do what V has suggested for years. I walk away. I don't answer his phone calls, I don't go where he will be, and if I see him I walk the other way. I cut him out of my life. But that would be akin to cutting out my own heart. I couldn't live. I just couldn't. I need him. Me, who everyone thinks needs nothing and no one. Guess I've made my choice. I'll carry on as I always have, with my head held high and smile on my face, even though inside I'm sobbing. Good thing I've had a lifetime of practice.

I stop walking and turn to stare at The Falls. This is it, the moment. The fork in the road. Justin Pendergast has been my life for twenty years. My love has been the one constant in my fucking rollercoaster of a life. Besides the job, it's sustained me. Gave me hope to carry on. The belief that one beautiful day that man would turn to me and with such brilliance in his eyes tell me he loves me just as much as I do him. But it was just a dream. Accept it. Move on. It's not fair. It's not fair to me, to Rebecca, Justin, even…Harry. I bite my lower lip to stop the tears. This is it, Joanna. Time to wake the fuck up. You can do it.

Okay, then.

CHAPTER EIGHT
ENOUGH

Sleep is impossible now, so I'm back at the station skimming C.O. Moore, Lopez, and Leon's HR files, financials, telephone records, just about anything we have on them. There are no red flags. They all went through extensive background checks that came back clean. None have been arrested or have more than five grand in their bank accounts. The forensic accountants are digging deeper. I close the last file, and I'm at a loss at what to do next. Someone else interviewed the spouses and friends yesterday, and there was nothing out of the ordinary. Even the Mike Spencer explosion front has stalled. This entire case is nothing but a brick wall behind a lead one.

I have nothing to do now. Strike that, I can run down more tips, which have trickled down to three an hour after Gearhead took control of all machines at the docks a few hours ago and is getting all the press. Last I heard he and Geronimo were beating each other to a pulp. Glad I'm not on that one. Half our underlings are down there now, and I'm enjoying the quiet.

Cam just finished reviewing his half of the guard's information, and I'm not speaking to him. Throw me under a bus like that? No, I will not pass you the Lopez file. Get off your betraying butt and get it yourself. I've already forgiven him, but can't appear to be weak. And I'm lazy. He's down in the lab reading them the riot act. We still don't have the clippings back or the reports on the burnt trash can. I'm not looking forward to reading through all the Justice clippings, but maybe I can find a pattern.

I push my chair away from the desk. I need a task. I hate having nothing to do. Thinking follows it and I've had enough of that today. I can snatch the other three files off Cam's desk, but my brain has stopped functioning. Maybe I'll dash off to the library down the block to see if they have a self-help book. Or twelve. "Get Over Your Man" or "Acceptance, it's Not Just a Scrabble Word." I hate reading, though.

Harry isn't in his office or SVU. I stop one of the uniforms on the tip line who directs me toward the nursery, as we call the back room where officers on duty catch a few winks. I spend more nights in there than at my apartment. It's nothing more than a ten-by-twelve windowless room with two bunk beds. The sheets are scratchy, the room is barely ventilated, but if you're tired enough, it's heaven.

There is only one human shaped lump on the bottom bunk in the back. The reason we call it the nursery is because even the most grizzled, hardened officer sleeps like a baby in here. Harry is no exception. He lies on his side facing me, light snores escaping. I'd tease him about it, but apparently I snore louder. I lock the door and tip toe over to him, sitting on the bed opposite his.

I just watch him for a minute, taking him in. He's not as handsome as Justin, no man really is, but he turns me on like no other has before. He's funny, charming, and strong. I respect him. I trust him. So what the hell is the matter with me? I have this wonderful guy who I respect, adore, and for some reason sees something worthwhile in me. That should be enough. I'm beyond lucky to have him, and I keep him at arm's length.

I really haven't been fair to him. The one time he ever attempted to discuss our relationship I played coy and distracted him with sex. I justified it, of course. Why get serious? Why ruin the fun? It couldn't *possibly* go anywhere. It was just some fun on both our parts. He's been slumming it for a mid-life thrill. That's what I've been telling myself anyway. Probably to protect us both. He deserves better than a woman whose heart is full of another. No room. No room for him. Maybe it's time to make some.

I pull up his blanket to make him more comfortable and the snores stop. His eyes open, and he blinks to focus. I remain above him smiling and he smiles back. "What time is it?" he asks.

"About four."

"Anything going on?"

"Quiet as a crypt," I whisper with another smile. "Scoot over."

He raises an eyebrow, but moves toward the wall. I climb into the twin bed with my back to him, resting my head on the pillow and wrapping his arm around my chest. With a sigh, I close my eyes. He nestles in closer to me.

"What if someone walks in?" Harry asks.

"I locked the door." I kiss his hand. "Don't worry."

He relaxes a little, laying his head back down. This is one of the reasons he's such a great boyfriend. Most men would be taking advantage of this situation, trying to make a move for public sex, but Harry just holds me and traces a circle on my sternum with his thumb. "Did you get any sleep?" he whispers.

"Hour or two."

"I could kiss Gearhead. I got approval to send everyone home at five."

"Yourself included, I hope."

"Why do you think I asked? Forget the rest of you, I'm bone tired. I remember I used to do thirty-six hours with nothing but coffee and willpower. I hate getting old."

"You're not that old, Harry."

"My body begs to differ."

"Your body didn't seem to think it was that old last Friday. Remember? All *three* times?"

He chuckles. "I must still be recovering then. You do take it out of me. Literally."

I playfully slap his hand. "Filthy talk, old man. And at our place of business no less."

"You are the one who climbed into bed with *me*, Det. Fallon."

"I hate it when you're all logical and right." I tilt my head back and he pecks me. I kiss him deeper and roll over, facing him now. I break the kiss and nestle into my Harry nook. He wraps his arms around me. "Thank you."

"For what?"

Being you. "Nothing."

"Have a bad day?"

"No more than usual. Just needed a hug."

He kisses the top of my head. "Happy to oblige, ma'am."

We lay like this, the only sound from his heartbeat and breathing. I want to talk to him about today, hell about everything. He knows about my Pop, about Mom, but how can I talk to him about Justin? He knows we're close, but like most things we've never discussed how close. I'm sure he's guessed my feelings, but he's never called me out on them. Another reason I need to hold onto him. He just…accepts me. As is. Screwed up, ornery, cranky, and yet here he is. Petting my hair and risking his reputation for me. I'm nuts. I can have it all. Respect, acceptance, even love, if I just let go of the impossible.

Just let go.

"I want you to come with me to Justin's party tomorrow," I say.

He does a double take. Guess I surprised him. "You're going?"

"If I can. Do you…want to come?"

He's speechless. He opens and closes his mouth a few times, then chuckles. "Really?"

"Definitely. It has to happen sometime. It has been five months. It's only a matter of time before someone finds out, we both know that. This way we'd have control over it."

"I—I just don't know if it's a good idea," he stammers.

"You can say no if you don't want to go. It's fine." Of course it isn't. I flip over again so he can't see my face.

He sighs. "There's just a lot to consider."

"I know," I say, keeping my voice neutral. "I said it's fine. Just a thought. I'll just go alone like I was planning to, no biggie."

He's quiet for a few seconds, then says, "I want to go. I really do. I want to walk in there with the prettiest girl on my arm, and dance with her, and show her off. You know I do. I'm just, I'm worried. We've both worked so hard to get where we are."

"Harry, we've been damn lucky so far. If we keep seeing each other, it will come out, we both know that, and we know what they're going to say. I'm sleeping my way to the top, you're going through a mid-life crisis and taking advantage of me. I don't care. People have been saying nasty things about me all my life. You get used to it. You survive it. They're not going to fire either of us. We're both too high profile and too good at our jobs."

"They could transfer one of us."

"If they try, I'll have Justin blackmail and threaten everyone in city hall and the department. It's one of the few pleasures of being the best friend of the crown prince of Galilee. If they do transfer me to vice or homicide, then so be it. I can come back when you're promoted and they bring in someone else." I pause. "You're worth it, Harry."

He's quiet again. "This is important to you, isn't it?"

I flip back over to face him. "I just think it's time to shit or get off the pot, you know?"

"That's possibly the most romantic thing you've ever said to me."

"Well, I am something of a poet, Harry. It's one of my many talents." My smile drops. "Seriously, though. I don't want to pressure you into this. I just…want you by my side. I want to let everyone know I'm dating the nicest, handsomest, most wonderful man in Galilee. The aftermath, well, we'll handle it. Together."

He's quiet for a moment, weighing his options. But only for a moment. He smiles. "Okay, then. Guess I'm your plus one."

My smile resurfaces. "Really?"

"I've wanted to meet the famous Rebecca. And I do look great in a tux."

I kiss him once, twice, three times. On the forth he kisses me back deep enough to push away any doubts on either of our parts. I roll on top of him, still kissing. He's just about got my top off when the door handle jiggles and we both freeze. There's a knock on the door. "Det. Fallon?"

I leap up, tucking in my shirt as I walk to the door. Harry pulls his covers back up and tosses the blanket on the opposite bed back as if I had just gotten out of it. This is not the first time we've gone through this charade. I unlock the door, rubbing my eyes. A uniform stands outside. "What is it?" I ask groggily.

"A package just arrived for you," the woman says.

"Thank you."

I slip out the door, blocking her view of Harry and walk back to my desk. A huge dress box wrapped in dark blue paper and a big red bow is in my chair. Cam sits at his desk across from mine with a huge grin on his face. "You have an admirer," he says.

"What the hell is this?"

"Don't know, but ask me who it's from."

"Who?"

"Justice. He just delivered it himself."

"Justice? Justice bought me a present?" I ask, shocked.

"Maybe he has a crush on you. Or you've been knocking boots in his hideout without telling me."

"Yeah, we're having a secret affair, and we're madly in love with each other."

"Are you?"

"Please. I'd sooner fuck Gearhead." I rip open the wrapping paper. Word must have gotten around about my not so secret admirer. A crowd, Harry included, forms around my desk. I was right, it is a dress box. If he bought me a dress, I will track him down and shoot him. I don't do girl clothes unless absolutely necessary. But it isn't a dress, it's a jacket. A black leather-like, fitted trench coat with silver buttons with "J" on them. The impossible has happened. I am going to say something nice about Justice. He has excellent taste in coats.

"Nice," Cam says.

I pull the jacket out. It's lighter than leather with a different texture too. I put it on, and sure enough it's a perfect fit. Looks awesome too. Stylish, yet bad-ass. "I don't think it's leather," I tell the murmuring audience.

"There's a card," Cam points out.

Inside the box is a white card. "'Dear Det. Fallon,'" I start reading aloud. "'Like you, I have found the traditional Kevlar vest an eyesore. Perhaps now that you own a more fashionable version, you will be more inclined to wear one. Enjoy. Justice.'" I scoff. The fucking nerve!

Cam touches the coat. "I think it's made of the same material as his uniform."

"You mean his costume?" I ask snidely.

"It looks really good on you," the officer who summoned me says.

I take it off, tossing it on my desk. "What the hell am I supposed to do with it? I can't exactly return it. I don't know where to return it to."

"You could wear it," Cam says.

"Oh, yeah? What if it's not really bulletproof?"

"I doubt Justice would lie to you," Harry says.

"But why send me this? He barely knows me, and I'm not exactly his biggest fan."

"He's just doing what he does," Cam says. "Protecting the citizens of Galilee. Even your ungrateful ass."

It is a nice coat. It's exactly what I would pick out for myself. And it was given in the spirit of camaraderie. Maybe being part of the new me should include accepting Justice. He's never been anything but nice to me, even when I'm bitchier than normal. He does do a lot for the city. We are colleagues after all. Okay, I just *really* want to keep the coat.

"It would be rude not to take it," I offer. "He went to a lot of trouble and all."

"Did you just say something nice about a superhero?" Cam asks.

"No! I simply stated a fact."

"Okay, people," Harry says, "excitement's over. It's just a jacket. Get back to work."

The crowd disperses, mumbling to each other about my gift. The gossip mill has already started weaving its tale. By tonight Justice and I will be involved in a torrid affair or I'll be his secret sidekick. Good thing I'm the new and improved Joanna or I'd be inclined to kick his superhero butt from here to the ocean even though he gave me a bitchin' coat.

"What's that old saying?" Cam asks. "First comes coat, then comes marriage?"

I point my finger at him. "I *will* kick your ass."

"Play nice you two," Harry says. "Did the lab finish with the newspapers?"

"Yeah. Just Ryder's fingerprints and those of five of the six guards. The ones he burnt are gone forever. The lab couldn't pull anything useful."

"Another dead end," I say.

"The autopsies are done too. Nothing we didn't already know."

"Forensic accountants?" Harry asks me.

"Should be done by tomorrow morning."

"We are too good at our jobs," Cam says. "Anything we can do, we've done. What now, boss? Want us to run down more tips?"

"No. We've got people already on it." Harry sighs. "Alright. There's no point in you two being here with nothing to do. I want you to finish up your reports for the day and go home. Sleep, see your family, whatever. Just keep your cells on in case you're needed. I want you both here at eight in the morning tomorrow."

"Yes, boss," Cam says with a huge grin.

Harry walks back to his office. Cam looks at me, and I shrug. "I'm not going to complain." I put on my jacket and toss the box on the floor.

"You want to come over for dinner?" Cam asks.

"You think I'm going to forgive you for what happened at the hospital with the promise of pork chops, Judas?"

"Worth a shot. So, when are you going to forgive me?"

I sit back down. "Cam, I'm Irish. We hold grudges even after we're dead."

"So what are you going to do with your free night?"

"Well, because of you, I have to go buy a new dress for the party tomorrow night."

"Can't you just wear an old one?"

"These people give you shit if you show up with your old face, never mind a dress. I'll just stop by the consignment shop near my place."

"Something funeral black, maybe?" he asks with a raised eyebrow.

My phone rings. "No, I'm saving that for the wedding," I say with a sneer. I pick it up. "Det. Joanna Fallon."

"Jo?" Justin asks.

"Hey," I say.

"I haven't heard from you since yesterday. Just wanted to touch base and see how things are. Still hard at work?"

"Always. I did, however, have time to have lunch with your better half today which I am sure you've heard all about by now."

"Yeah, she told me. I'm glad. She said you'll be at the party tomorrow."

"That is the plan."

"I had Shannon send you a few dresses and shoes from our new line. I know how much you hate shopping."

I smile to myself and lean back in the chair. He knows me so well it's scary. "What is it about men sending me clothes today? One more person does it, and I'm gonna start taking offense."

"Who else sent you clothes?" Justin asks.

"The great Justice sent me a Kevlar coat."

"Really? That was nice of him. Why did he do that?"

"Who knows, who cares?"

"Is it nice?"

"Very. Hey, maybe he's gay!"

Cam narrows his eyes and shakes his head at me. "No way," he mouths.

"Yeah it's…possible," Justin says. "I have no idea."

"Anyway, quit your worrying. Unless something big comes up, I promise I'll be there tomorrow. With a surprise even."

"A surprise? Should I be worried?"

"No. You'll like this one. At least, I'm pretty sure you will."

"Can't wait."

"I'll see you tomorrow, okay?" I pause. "Say hi to the family. Send them my love. Bye." I hang up the phone.

"What's the surprise?" Cam asks.

"None of your business. Quit eavesdropping and finish your work. I want to get out of here before Harry changes his mind."

It takes an hour and a half to leaf through the clippings and compose a one-page report about absolutely nothing. There's no rhyme or reason to the articles that I can tell. He just cut out everything he could on the man for his own reasons. Know thy enemy, I guess.

Cam leaves before me, as do Mirabelle and Kowalski, who saunter in and out after chasing a false lead. A few of the uniforms have to remain behind for clean up, but I slip out. I grab dinner on the way home and find five dresses on my couch to choose from. Justin must have given Shannon his key.

Considering the woman has no problems with my occasional demands for errand running, I let this invasion of privacy slide. I settle on the cerulean one with black netting underneath that flares in a bell skirt down to my knees. Brings out my eyes and skin, my two best features. As I'm putting the other four back into their garment bags, my phone chirps letting me know I have a text. When I read it, a huge smile stretches across my face.

I pull up to his apartment building half an hour later. His doorman, Bruce, opens the door for me. "Spiffy coat," he says. I smile and nod. Harry lives on the second floor at the end of the hall. I fluff my hair, check my breath, and knock on the door.

He's still in his work clothes, but his shirt is untucked and sleeves rolled up to his elbows. He has a phone to his ear, but smiles and waves me in. "No, I'm happy with our progress. We know—"

The sight of me almost makes him drop the phone.

The now open coat falls to the floor, leaving me in nothing but my birthday suit and black knee high boots. His mouth drops open. "Um, Randy, can I call you back? Something just came up." He hangs up the phone, and we more than make up for lost time.

I just can't get enough of that man.

CHAPTER NINE
INTERVIEWS

I wake up to the smell of coffee and bacon, in my opinion the second best way to wake up. The first is a variation of what Harry and I were up to all last night. There's always tomorrow morning. I stir in his four poster bed with a smile.

He's fully dressed at the stove pushing the sizzling cholesterol around. I open the paper on the table. V's story is on the front page, though it's below the fold and doesn't get the headline or space Gearhead does. Besides the information I gave her, she contacted the prison, a few of Alkaline's old goons all of whom both she and I went to high school with, and a forensic psychologist. Good reading, but it doesn't tell me anything I don't already know. Harry sets down the plate of bacon and eggs in front of me, and sits down across from me with the same on his. "Thank you," I say.

"You're welcome."

We both dig into our meals and read our respective papers. "So, quiet night?"

"Yeah. You know, I'm beginning to think he did leave the city. He would have put his plan into effect by now."

I sip my coffee. "You do realize you just jinxed us, right?" I smile and nudge him with my big toe. "He's probably setting charges at city hall as I speak. That's on you."

"Cute."

"You know, there are other cases out there we can work. Murder doesn't stop just because James Ryder busted out of prison."

"I know. That's why I'm going to call the commissioner and see if I can get Kowalski and Mirabelle released from the task force."

"Why them?" I whine.

"Because you're the face of the investigation. If he does wreck havoc, and the press finds out we reneged on our promise, it'll be a political bloodbath." He drinks his coffee. "Speaking of faces, you'd better put yours on. You have another press conference this morning. The press office faxed the statement you'll give a few minutes ago."

"They still want me to do that? Nobody cares anymore. If I speak, and there's nobody around to listen, did I ever speak at all?" I lean back, all proud of myself for deep thinking. "Think about it."

He smirks. "You're quite philosophical this morning."

"I will try anything not to have to put on make-up. You know that."

"Well, I don't think you need it. You're gorgeous just the way you are."

"Aww," I say. "I'm glad you think that, but I've been on the Galilee worst dressed list far too many times to believe that. Sorry."

He blinks a few times, shakes his head, and then sighs. "You *really* have no idea how beautiful you are, do you?" Harry asks, both sad and shocked.

"Shut up," I say, blushing. "I am not. I'm short. I need to lose ten pounds. I have cellulite. My hair's frizzy and wild. I'm the color of paper. My nose is crooked. I can get away with many adjectives, but not beautiful."

He leans across. "You just named every aspect about you that drives me wild." He kisses the bump on my nose. "You're beautiful. And trust me, I am not the only one who thinks so. You should hear some of the comments the men make about you."

"Do you defend my honor?"

"Well I will, starting tonight."

"You still want to go through with it?" I ask.

"Do you?"

I bridge the gap between us and kiss him. "More than anything."

And we prove our sentiments on the table.

Later, he leaves while I gussy myself up for the cameras. When I get into the office, Cam and Kowalski sit behind their desks reading files and Harry's door is closed when I saunter in. The press statement is on the top of my desk, and after a quick glance I push it aside. This is a happy zone and insipid writing is not allowed.

"Jesus Christ, are you actually smiling?" Cam asks.

I guess I am. I stop. "I got a good night's sleep."

"Naw, that's an 'I got laid' smile," Cam says. "Who's the lucky guy?"

"His name is Mr. Rabbit and I met him at my local sex shop, okay?"

Cam grimaces. "Girl, I know you're my partner and all, but sometimes you over share."

"You asked."

"I will never do it again." He leans back in his chair. "You ready to face the cameras again?"

"Never," I say. "But I will. Anything come up last night?"

"The dead guard's wife is on her way in. The accountants found something interesting an hour ago."

"He had a secret bank account?"

"In Switzerland of all places. The transfers originated from an account in the Caymans, so we can't get the name of the person who holds that account."

"Naturally," I say. "I told you."

"Fat lot of good it does us. The man's dead. He can't tell us jack."

"True, but I was still right. Makes *me* feel better."

A middle-aged woman with short hair, glasses, and suburban chic clothes is escorted in by Mirabelle. She's nervous, glancing around the room like a skittish mouse. I guess I'd be the same if I was dragged out of bed and more or less strong-armed by the police to come in. She's gonna need a friend. Kowalski gets up and joins his partner.

"Who's handling the interview?" I ask.

"Kowalski and Mirabelle," Cam says. "They got here before we did."

Damn that irresistible Harry. Almost makes the orgasm not worth it. Almost. I stand up. "I need coffee," I say, standing up.

"They're not going to let you in there," Cam calls as I walk away.

"Yes, they will," I shout back.

"You have a press conference!"

I ignore him. The press can wait while I do my job. Mirabelle and Kowalski are in the control room with Chip, our computer tech, while Mrs. Moore is on the monitor from Interview One. She bites her nails, on the verge of tears. Mirabelle examines the file with his partner looking over his shoulder.

The control room has four computer monitors, each hooked up to the video feed from the interview room. Like this one, all the interview rooms are the size of a prison cell and beige without windows. There's nothing in them but two to four chairs, and a tabletop with a steel hook toward the edge in case we need to restrain someone. They're depressing and cold for a reason. If you want out, just tell us what we want to know. I've gotten used to the rooms, but I don't like spending any more time in them than I have to. Great motivator for the people on both sides of the table.

"Morning, gentlemen."

"Fallon," Kowalski says. "Is that the famous jacket?"

I've gone all black today with the silver buttons providing the only color. I run my hand over it. "Yep. But don't worry, I'm sure yours is on its way."

"What do you want, Fallon?" Mirabelle asks.

"We've worked together for years now. Thought I'd be transparent by now."

"You are. We're doing this interview," Kowalski says.

"It'd be better if I did," I say.

"Because you're a woman?" Mirabelle asks.

"I am the face of this investigation. I chased after the villain who killed her man. I am personally trying to find her husband's murderer." I pause. "*That* and we both have boobs. It helps."

"No," Kowalski says.

"She'll open up to me. Mirabelle, you just dragged her from her breakfast and fatherless children. We can do good cop/bad cop best. You scare her, I tend to the widow. You both know I'm right."

Kowalski sighs. "She is. Fine."

"Okay, Mirabelle go in there and just start pounding on her. I'll come in a minute later and save her. Sound good?"

"Sounds fine," Mirabelle says before leaving.

A few seconds later, he reappears on the screen with the widow. She does not seem happy to see him. She rubs her right temple as if she has a headache. As Mirabelle sits, I reach into the desk and retrieve two aspirin, putting them in my pocket.

"Thank you for coming in, Mrs. Moore," Mirabelle says.

"Didn't have much of a choice," she says, still rubbing.

"This is Det. Lawrence Mirabelle with Kelly Moore. It is Friday, May eighteenth, at approximately nine AM." He opens the file. "You were married to C.O. Stuart Moore, is that right?"

"Yes."

"Did you have a happy marriage?"

"As much as anyone else does, I guess."

"Guess it's easy when your husband keeps secrets from you."

"I'm sorry?" she asks.

"Your husband. Did he keep a lot of secrets from you?"

"I don't know what you're asking me."

Mirabelle scoffs. "Okay, I got an easier one for you lady. A yes or no. Was your husband a good man? Law abiding?"

"Of course!" she says, looking bewildered. "What is this about?"

"I'm just trying to understand what kind of man your husband was. You know, was he an asshole? The second coming? Someone who cheats on his wife and taxes?"

"Why are you asking me these things?" she asks, now as hostile as he is. "Why am I here?"

"Oh. He getting a hero's burial? They going to give that traitor a twenty-one gun salute?"

I take that as my cue. I walk out of the control room with a bottle of water, take a moment to get into character, and then "barge in." Mirabelle is sneering and Mrs. Moore is on the verge of tears. "Det. Mirabelle, why don't you go get a cup of coffee?"

"What? How dare—"

"*Now*, please," I say, my voice hard. As he walks past me, he glares hard. I just shake my head and shut the door behind him. I smile sympathetically at Moore, handing her the water and aspirin. "You looked like you could use this. It's just aspirin."

She looks at the offering, no doubt wondering what the catch is, but takes it anyway. "Thank you."

I smile again and sit where Mirabelle was, and he is now where I was. She swallows the pills and sips the water. "I'm sorry, about him. We're just all under a lot of pressure to find Alkaline. We've barely slept in days. He shouldn't have taken it out on you."

"It's fine," she whispers.

"No, it's not," I insist. "It's not. You're the victim in this just as much as Logan Dodd, Grace Pickering, or anyone that monster has touched. Your husband was just trying to keep us safe from him. It cost him his life. And that's seriously fucking unfair."

The widow looks down from my gaze. I think it's the first time a person has vocalized something she's thought a hundred times. "I guess."

"How are your children doing?"

"They're fighting. A lot. With me, their grandparents, each other," she says, exhausted even from the memories.

"It's tough losing a parent at such a young age. I was only twelve when my Pop died. I hated everything and everyone that reminded me of him. It was too much having to deal with the unjustness of it all, let alone the realization that he'll never hug me again, talk about my day, stupid stuff like that."

"How did you get over it?"

I shake my head. "I didn't. Not really. It's always there. But time and people who loved me helped. They didn't give up on me. That's about as good as it gets."

"I don't know what to say to them. Everything just becomes a battle," Kelly says.

"They're angry, and rightly so. They're mad at Alkaline, they're mad at you, they're even mad at your husband. It's not fair, but it is what it is."

Kelly contemplates this, saddened even more. My heart goes out to this woman, it really does. Her husband has been murdered, her kids are a wreck, the press is hounding her, and now she's stuck in a police station. Just one of those things could send a person over the edge. And it's not her fault. *She's* not the one who took a bribe from a convicted murderer. She's not the one who killed him either, but she's the one who has to clean up the mess. I more than know how that is. "I think I'm just still in shock. I've been going through the motions. With everything. My mom's helping out."

"That's good." I smile sympathetically. I pause. "So, you're probably wondering why you're here."

"Yeah. I thought maybe you caught him or something, but…"

"Sorry. Not yet, but you may be able to help us on that end."

"How?"

I glance down at the file, scanning it while she watches. "Who handles the finances in your family?"

"I pay the bills. Why?"

"Do you know anything about an account in Switzerland? Have you ever set one up for your son Michael?"

"A what?" she asks.

I pass her the file. There's account information in her son's name, social security number, and several deposits totaling $250,000, the last one the day before the escape. She reads it, confused as hell. "I take it you knew nothing about this," I say.

The widow looks up, eyes bugging out of her head. "$250,000? What? How?" Her voice is so desperate I can't help but believe her. "I—I've never seen this before in my life."

"Could your husband have?"

She gazes back down at the file and it dawns on her. The realization seems to begin at her eyes which grow again, then moving to her mouth which shrinks, then down her back which straightens. From the look she gives me, I believe the mouse is about to roar. "Absolutely not. I know what you're implying, and how dare you? My husband was the best man I ever knew," she says, her voice breaking. "He was proud of his job. Proud he was helping to keep us all safe. You said it yourself, it cost him his life. There is no way in *hell* he would help that psychopath. Not even for a million dollars." She shoves the file back at me.

"Then how do you explain the account? And the fact that the other C.O., Logan Dodd, said your husband was the only one in the room when Ryder was let out?"

"He's lying!"

"Mrs. Moore, you have to see this from our point of view. A limited number of people had access to James Ryder. Of those, only two were there the night he escaped, and only one of those has a secret account with hundreds of thousands of dollars." I lean back in my chair. "Now, I know you loved your husband and what I'm suggesting is unthinkable, but you have to face facts. This," I say, pointing to the file, "is the only lead we have right now. So *anything* suspicious, anything you might know or suspect, no matter how small, might be the key to finding him. Did he act out of the ordinary at all? Buy extravagant gifts?"

"No, because he didn't do anything."

"There's nothing? Not a single moment when you thought, 'There's something wrong,' or just a feeling?"

"No, and I am done with this." She bolts up.

Ah, love. You always make my job such a pain in the ass. "Mrs. Moore, you should know we have a search warrant for your home."

"What? You can't—"

I stand up too, closing the file. "I'm sorry. I'll have a patrol car take you home." I leave as she calls me nasty names and return to the control room. Mirabelle and Kowalski smirk and cluck their tongues. "Shut up."

"You two going to have a sleepover and braid each other's hair?" Kowalski asks.

"Like you could have done any better," I say. "She doesn't know a damn thing."

"You don't think she's lying?" Mirabelle asks.

"No way."

"I agree," Kowalski says.

"Then let's hope we have more luck with the warrant," I say.

"We're going there right now. *You* have a date with the press," Kowalski says.

"Sure you wouldn't rather do it? Lotte would love to see your handsome face on the screen."

"No, thanks," Kowalski says. "Besides, I don't think that woman will want you anywhere near her house." He glances at his partner. "You either. I'll take Cam."

"We're sure he's our guy?" I ask.

"Seems like it," Mirabelle says.

"Then I might actually have something to feed to the jackals."

On my way out I peek into Harry's office, but he's not there. I need to know whether or not to release this information. We should probably wait for final confirmation. There's always tomorrow. I'll play it by ear. After a quick hair and make-up fix in the ladies room, I grab the prepared statement and walk out.

About two thirds of the usual lot are not there. V is front and center, but I only recognize a few others. Guess the big guns are onto better things. I read off the bland account of our progress, and few even bother to take notes. Going through the motions, I open it to questions.

"Can you comment on—" V begins.

Out of nowhere Mrs. Moore, with Cam and Kowalski close behind, saddle up to me. Her rage is palpable enough for the reporters to perk up. I'm too shocked in that moment I can't think of a thing to say. Kelly Moore doesn't have this problem.

"My name is Kelly Moore. My husband was Corrections Officer Stuart Moore, who was brutally murdered four days ago by the man who calls himself Alkaline." She looks down at her sneakers. "My husband worked at Xavier for over five years. He was a good man. He was active in AA, sponsoring three people. He coached our youngest son's Little League. He provided for me, for our children, and kept this city safe by watching over criminals like Alkaline. He's dead because of it." She gazes at me, hate brimming through the tears. "And the Galilee police department, instead of searching this city for my husband's killer like they have promised numerous times, is instead wasting their time and the taxpayer's money slandering my husband's good name." Her gaze returns to the salivating journalists. "My husband died protecting all of you. He's a hero. He did nothing wrong."

She walks away, the reporters shouting questions which she ignores. Cam and Kowalski both give me a pitying look before they follow her. A few reporters chase after her, but the rest stay, unleashing their questions on me.

"Is Stuart Moore a suspect?"

"How long has he been a suspect?"

"What evidence have you found to link him to the escape?"

"Are any of the other C.O.'s involved?"

A cacophony of the same question phrased differently assaults me. V's mouth moves, but I can't hear her over the others. I hesitate, the wheels in my head turning. I have no idea what to say, what they would want me to say. Probably nothing, but I'm trapped.

"One at a time," I shout. I point to the WHEN reporter, an intern judging by her age. "You."

"Is Stuart Moore a suspect?"

"At this time, he is a person of interest. Veronica?"

"Why is he a person of interest?"

"Through the course of our investigation, we discovered a large sum of money in one of Mr. Moore's accounts. How it came to be in there has yet to be determined."

"Do you think he was murdered to silence him?" another reporter asks.

"We will have to ask James Ryder that when we arrest him."

"And you're still confident you will find him?"

"I stand by my promise to this city. We are doing everything in our power to find him."

"What about reports that Alkaline had a shrine to Justice? Can you substantiate those claims?"

I glance at V who takes notes. "I would not use the word 'shrine,' but yes he did have multiple news clippings on Justice. What that means, once again, we will ask Ryder when we apprehend him. And we will."

"It's been four days. Only one arrest has been made. Are you sure he is still even in the city?"

"No, but no matter where he is, we will find him. If it takes years, if he's on the moon, we will find him and drag his butt back here to face justice for the heinous crimes he has committed, including the death of Stuart Moore," I say passionately. "Whether he was complicit in the escape or not, he is still a victim. He and his family deserve justice. We will get it for them, of that I have no doubt. James Ryder will not win. He *cannot* win. You have my personal guarantee that he will not."

"Have you found any evidence as to what he might have planned?" V asks. "Potential victims, if any? If he is in the city, could it have something to do with Justice and his obsession?"

"We have uncovered no evidence that Ryder's plans extended beyond his escape. But once again, if he does, we will stop him. We did once, we will do it again. That's all for today. Thank you."

I spin around as the reporters shout more questions that I won't answer. Harry waits outside his office, arms folded, none too thrilled with me. He doesn't have to say a word. I walk straight into his office, sitting myself in the naughty chair. He shuts the door.

"What the hell was that?" he asks.

"I couldn't stop her. I was just as surprised as you were."

He sits at his desk. "You should have shut it down the moment you saw her."

"How? Tackle the widow of a murder victim?"

"We're going to be back in the spotlight now, you know that right? They'll be hounding Moore, rooting around in his background."

"I know! But Harry, what the hell could I have done? Tell me! Because, under the circumstances, I think I did a pretty damn good job turning things around."

He shakes his head. "The mayor's pissed."

"So what else is new?" I mutter.

"You're off press duty."

"Oh, thank God."

"You're also in tip duty today, and you're not allowed to even look at a reporter, let alone talk to one. That includes your cousin."

"Tip duty?" I whine. "We haven't had one in hours. I'll have nothing to do all day."

"Exactly." His phone rings. "Dismissed."

I leave the office feeling like a chastised child as he starts talking to the Chief of Detectives, probably feeling the same way. Me and my big mouth, getting us all in trouble. I should be used to it by now, but I do hate disappointing people and dragging them down with me. Justin's lost more than a few acquaintances because of me. I sit at my desk with a sigh. I've been grounded by my boyfriend.

As I begin typing my millionth report this week, a familiar swish of air pulls me away from the monotony. Normally, Justice works at night, as he most likely has a day job to keep up appearances, so having him here in full regalia is a surprise. As I am trying to be more accepting—and he gave me an awesome coat—I will call this a pleasant surprise, though the office stops working and starts gawking.

His masked face scans the bullpen, stopping when he sees me. I muster a smile as he approaches. *I will be nice. I will be nice.* "Good morning, Det. Fallon."

"Justice."

"I see you received my gift. Does it fit well?"

"Yes. Thank you. Is it really bulletproof?"

"Bullet resistant, yes. It's made of the same material as my uniform. Wear it in good health, though do please wear it."

This rankles me, but I keep my smile on. "I will. So what can we help you with today?"

"I saw your press conference regarding Stuart Moore. Are you confident regarding your findings?"

"Yes. It was a Swiss bank account in his son's name."

Justice opens a packet on his belt and pulls out a small zip drive. "Here is all the data I've complied on Stuart Moore. Telephone records, known associates, his entire life. I have reviewed it, but found nothing useful. Perhaps you will have more luck."

I take the drive with a nod. "Thank you. I'll have a look."

"Have you made any other progress?"

"No. Have you?"

"No," he says, emotionless, "and I am getting worried. I know this man. He will never be content living life without causing others misery."

"So you don't think he's on a beach drinking tequila and laughing at us?"

"Laughing at us, definitely. Left the city? Not a chance in hell."

I do a double take. I've never heard him swear, not even in the heat of battle. "Do you think he's sticking around for you?"

"It's entirely possible. I've been trying to be more visible, giving him ample chance to confront me, but he has not taken the bait. He'll strike when I least expect it, I'm sure. I'm almost looking forward to it."

"Yeah, you haven't had a real nemesis since you put him away. How boring it must be being you, what with all the epic battles with all the other supers."

"Point taken, Det. Fallon. All I meant was I will enjoy the moment when I finally apprehend that monster once again."

"I may beat you to it, you know. I'd enjoy slapping the cuffs on him just as much as you would."

He steps toward my desk, almost looming a foot away with his hand on his hip. I know this pose, I used to practice it in the mirror with my Justice shirt on. It's his, "I'm ready to kick your ass in five seconds" stance. He is intimidating, no question, but damned if I'll let him know it's working on me. I fold my arms across my chest and tilt back in my chair. "Det. Fallon I have never doubted your ability or dedication with regards to this job."

"O-kay," I say, not sure where this is going.

"You are one of the finest officers on this force."

"Thank you." Okay, now I really have no idea what is going on. Is he going to ask me out or something? That'd be rich.

"James Ryder is a monster. An actual monster, one who has no remorse, compassion, or possibly even a soul. He is more dangerous than you can fathom."

"I know his history. I've seen firsthand what he's capable of. I've smelled it, okay?"

"And he will do that to you without a second thought. Possibly worse."

"Why are you telling me this?"

"Because I know you don't like me." My cheeks heat up, but he keeps talking. "Because he wanted *you* and your partner there the night he escaped. Because I know you're stubborn and hate asking for help, especially from supers. In this case, you'll have to. If he is cornered, he will not hesitate. He will harm as many innocent people as he feels is necessary to get what he wants. And better it be me than you. If you or anyone on your force locates him, or think you have, you need to contact me personally."

"Why? So you can get all the glory?"

"So I don't have to have another innocent person's death on my conscience."

"Maybe you're not giving me enough credit."

"There is no one more I'd trust with the welfare of this city than you," he says, sounding as if he means it. "But this isn't your battle to fight. If you or any of your fellow officers try, you will lose. Then where will we all be?"

I have absolutely no idea what to say right now. He's genuinely concerned and downright scared for me. Me, who passed around a petition to stop supers from being granted law enforcement status, and never said a pleasant word about him in ten years of interactions. I'd be weirded out if I wasn't so touched. I can't help it. My old hero is actually living up to my expectations. And he likes me. He really likes me. Thinks I'm great. More than that, he respects me. Damn.

"Well, um, thank you," I say unevenly.

"I mean every word. I know that when the time comes, you will do the right thing. You always do. Good hunting, Joanna."

He speeds out in a blur, the papers on my desk flying around in a swirl. I grab a few, but the rest fall on the ground. Underneath the second one is a dark blue card with a white "J" on it. On the other side is a local telephone number. His phone number. First a coat and now his private number. If I didn't know better I'd swear he was into me, but I didn't get that vibe at all. I have no idea what's going on.

But I don't hate it.

CHAPTER TEN
SHINDIG

There was nothing of use in the zip drive or at the Moore house. I get to leave the station twice, one time when Ryder was spotted at a *bodega* and the other time he was seen at the library. Neither pans out, but it feels great getting away from my desk and all the chitter chatter. Teenage girls got nothing on cops when it comes to gossip. Justice hadn't even left the building when the tongues started wagging. Pretty sure we're engaged or we were making out on my desk by now. Everyone who walked by gave me a sideways glance, Harry included. I cornered him in the locker room and planted one on him for reassurance. Tomorrow they'll really have something to talk about.

It's about five and the party begins at seven, so I have to get the hell out of here. I need to shower, shave, eat, straighten my hair, apply make-up, and try to get a cab on a Friday night. Ugh, girly things. Kill me now. I shut off my computer and put on my coat. Tomorrow I get the whole day off and that comes straight from the top. We've spent too much money on this investigation already with too few results. Harry's off too, so we'll just spend the day in bed or go to the movies. Get some needed rest. Or not, wink wink.

My boyfriend's on the phone again when I poke my head in. He waves me in, and I shut the door. "No sir, we'll take it on a case by case basis." He listens and tosses files in his satchel. "I've already taken care of that." He pauses. "I'll do that. You too. Bye." He hangs up then looks at me with tired eyes. "You ready to go?"

"Yeah. So, do you want to get ready at my place? How do you want to do this?"

"I have a few errands to run before," he says.

"Well, your place is on the way to the hotel. I'll swing by and pick you up around seven."

"That sounds perfect. I'll be ready."

"Okay." I blow him a kiss before leaving.

Cam holds the elevator for me. "You looking forward to your shindig tonight?" he asks.

"As a matter of fact, I am."

"You going stag, or is Justice picking you up with a corsage?"

The elevator doors open and we step off. "I have someone much better lined up, thank you very much."

"Who?"

"It's a surprise. See you Sunday!"

The streets are clogged so it takes forever to get home and almost as long to find a parking spot three blocks away. I shower first, and then eat a tuna sandwich over the sink in my towel before starting on my mop of hair. Blow-drying forty-five minutes, straightening thirty. Then I realize I don't have any pantyhose and have to run out to get some. Of course there is a line almost to the door. I get back at seven and call Harry, telling his machine I'll be a half hour late. It ends up being closer to forty-five when the cab pulls up to his building.

Bruce, the doorman, whistles as I approach. "Looking sharp."

I do look quite spiffy. The dress fits perfectly, my hair is sleek and shiny, and make-up flawless. I clean up real good. "Thank you."

"But if you're here to see Mr. O'Hara he left half an hour ago."

I stop walking. "What? Did he say where he was going?"

"No. Sorry."

Huh. I check my cell phone, but there are no new messages. Maybe he's going to meet me there, but he can't get in without an invitation which I have. "Thanks, Bruce," I say as I return to the cab. I call Harry on the way to the hotel, but he doesn't pick up. "Hey, it's me. I just went by your apartment. Where the hell are you? I'm on my way to the party. I hope you're not there already. Just call me, okay?"

The line of cars to the Galilee Grand Intercontinental is ridiculous. Limos for over half a mile. I wait in the cab, literally watching my money tick away for fifteen minutes. I'd get out and walk, but I'm in three inch heels. I'll be lucky to make it through the night without twisting my ankle. It's happened more than once before.

The Galilee Grand is the premier hotel in the city and looks it. Twenty stories with three pools, one with a wave machine, two night clubs, the It spa, and the biggest ballroom within a thousand miles complete with two story waterfall. As my meager transport pulls up to its grandness, I'm bombarded with flashing lights that would bother the blind. The security guard, who wears sunglasses even though it's night, opens the door and helps me out.

I'm not even fully upright when the questions start. I totter down the red carpet with a smile plastered on. Some of the others on the carpet pose and speak to the press, showing off their designer gowns and designer breasts. Every socialite, athlete, politician, and captain of industry is here. I pass Lorcan Betts, running back for the Galilee Angels and his hoochie of the week. We hooked up once four years ago after Justin's birthday party. He was more interested in my panties than the sex. The reporters shout their questions, but I ignore them and don't pose. Never have, never will.

The lobby is quieter. Tourists and upper echelon meander around, separated by the red carpet and velvet rope. Security guards line the rope, keeping the gawking have-nots from the haves. A teenage girl even takes my picture. I scan the room for Harry, but no joy. His phone switches straight to voice mail again. "Harry, where the hell are you? I'm at the hotel already. I have to go in, but I have the invitation. You can't get in without it. Please call me when you get here."

If he thinks he's getting any tonight after all this trouble, he's nuts. Now I have to go in there alone. Except on rare occasions I always come alone, unless Justin escorts me. It should be old hat by now, but tonight I'm almost afraid to walk in there. The looks. The questions. The playing nice. I just don't want to do it alone.

"Joanna!" Brittney "Bitsy" Armstrong calls to me as she drags her husband Thayer from the entrance. Both are thin and tan, but so is everyone in this set. She wears a pink floral gown, her signature. Bitsy air kisses me. "You look fabulous."

"You, too. Love the necklace."

She touches the pink diamond the size of a gumball. "Thank you. Thayer got it for our ten year anniversary. He has such good taste."

Thayer isn't paying attention. His fingers dance over his Blackberry. They come up with a new way to be rude every year.

"Isn't this wonderful? Justin finally tying the knot? You can hear the sound of a thousand hearts breaking. Though I absolutely adore Rebecca. And that little girl! So cute. We had them over for dinner last month and our Preston just fell madly in love with little Daisy."

"It must be genetic," I say with a smile. Might as well get this thing plastered on right now. It won't be coming off until I get home tonight and put it back into my medicine chest.

"Are you going in yet or are you waiting for someone?" Bitsy asks.

"Um…no. I think I may have been stood up."

"Oh, you poor thing. Well, whoever he is, he's an idiot." She locks her elbow in her husband's, who doesn't even notice and starts walking. He's probably e-mailing Giselle Larkin. Everyone knows they're having an affair, maybe even Bitsy. The criminals I chase have more morals than most of these people.

Time to face the music. I follow a few feet behind the Armstrong's toward the ballroom. A security guard checks the invitations of the guests before allowing them to pass. I pull out mine and he nods. Welcome to the lion's den.

There have to be two hundred people here, all dressed to the nines and swilling champagne as if it was the elixir of life. An orchestra plays big band music near the waterfall while guests shake and shimmy on the dance floor. Silver and black balloons are scattered around along with lit-up crystals that match the chandelier in the middle of the ceiling. Simple, tasteful, and elegant, just like the happy couple. Almost the moment I step in, I grab a passing champagne glass and down it.

After a deep breath, I join the horde. Twenty years of practice has made me damn good at small talk. The key is to ask questions about everyone's favorite topic: themselves. People can talk about themselves for hours. I have two more glasses of champagne while listening to Emma Gilroy blabber on about her new Italian villa. I smile and nod like a moron. This just encourages more talking, but at least it's her doing it, not me. Italian villas are a safer topic than acid spewing supers or abandoning boyfriends, which is all I have on my mind right now. I'm just about to grab my third glass of booze when Marnie, Rebecca's mother, starts toward me, looking very elegant in a long sleeved green velvet gown and hair in a bun.

"Joanna, there you are," she says, almost relieved. "We've been looking for you."

"Excuse me, Emma," I say before following Marnie.

"Thanks for the save," I say when we're far enough away.

"Seemed like you needed it. We thought you weren't going to make it."

"Took longer than I thought to get ready."

"Well, it was worth it. You look smashing."

"Thank you. So do you." We stop at the buffet and I snag a few crab puffs. "So, where is the happy couple?"

"I lost track of them ages ago. Lucy was introducing me to people, but she's vanished as well. And let me tell you these people are not my crowd. Who are Dolce & Gabanna, and why does everyone insist I visit them?"

I chuckle. "Yeah, they are an acquired taste. Better get used to them, though. You'll be seeing them at Christmas, New Year's, and all summer long. They show up like a rash and are far more annoying."

"Please don't tell me that. I want this to be a happy night, not one that will give me nightmares."

We both chuckle this time and shake our heads. It's official. I like this woman. But the fun police find us. Justin's Aunt Lucy, in a matronly black dress with gold jacket, swans over. Her lips purse in disapproval, as they always do when she's around me. I could graduate valedictorian at charm school and she'd still think I was nothing more than a guttersnipe. But in the spirit of the new me, I choose to remember the good things about her. Like when Mom split my lip Lucy iced it, let me spend the weekend at the mansion, and then went and spoke to Mom. I have no idea what she said, but that was the last time Mom ever laid a hand on me. Or the fact that both she and Justin showed up at my graduation ceremony from the police academy. Or the time when I was fifteen and broke my arm at school. Mom was passed out, Uncle Ray was out of town, so Lucy not only stayed with me at the hospital, but paid the bill too. She's not so bad. I think deep down we like each other. Way deep down. Not that either of us would ever admit it to the other.

"I see you've found her," Lucy says to Marnie.

"Fashionably late, you know me," I say.

"Justin and Rebecca were asking for you," Lucy says in that tone reserved only for me, annoyance mixed with…well, really just annoyance.

"Where are they?" Marnie asks.

We scan the crowd, but I spot them first talking to the mayor and his wife. As always, he's drool worthy in his tux, golden hair brilliant against tan skin. She compliments him, wavy orange hair cascading down over her blue-gray draped goddess dress. His arm is around her waist. For once, and I credit the power of positive thinking for this, I feel no jealousy or longing. I see it. They fit together perfectly.

"They're talking to the mayor," I say.

"Oh. Him," Lucy says with distaste. "Begging for money, no doubt. Insipid man."

"I guess it's my job as best man to save them," I say with a swig of champagne. "Ladies."

Justin's face lights up when he spots me crossing the room. Always nice to be appreciated. Mayor Miracle continues talking. "…and that's why we failed. I mean, with no support from the constituents, how can anything get done?"

"Sorry to interrupt, Mr. Mayor," I say.

"Joanna!" Rebecca almost shouts. She breaks away from Justin to give me a huge hug. "You're here!" She releases me. "You look so beautiful! Doesn't she look great, Justin?"

"Most definitely." He hugs me too. "Thanks for coming."

I pull away. "And miss the party of the year? Never."

"I'm happy the city could give you the night off, Detective," the mayor says.

"Me too, sir." I try to be on my best behavior around Justin. My shenanigans shouldn't impact his business relationships. "Thank you. Justin, one of the caterers was looking for you. Something about the champagne?" We always use this excuse when getting the other person out of an uncomfortable situation.

"Oh. I'm sorry, Mr. Mayor, we have to deal with this. Excuse us." He ushers Rebecca away, and I trail behind. As we walk back toward Lucy and Marnie, they smile and nod at the other guests.

"Thank you," Rebecca says. "He would not stop talking!"

"My pleasure."

"So, where's this surprise you promised?" Justin asks.

"Um…it didn't pan out." Justin and Rebecca exchange a look. "No biggie, guys."

Marnie and Lucy meet us halfway. "I told the photographer we're all here now," Lucy says. "He's setting up by the waterfall."

"You guys waited for me?" I ask.

"Of course," Rebecca says.

"They're waiting," Lucy says impatiently.

"Oh, wonderful," Marnie says as if reading my mind. We smirk at each other as Lucy leads us toward the waterfall. The photographer and his assistant set up a tripod in front of the lit-up, blue waterfall that twinkles like sapphires. Sparkle Cohen, the grand dame of society reporting for the past fifty years, is taking notes while chatting with the photographer. Her withered frame is encased in an ornate yellow dress with huge collar. She reminds me of a cobra with that collar and skin pulled tight across her face. As we walk Justin whispers something into Rebecca's ear, and she pecks him on the lips. Sparkle jots that down.

"Are you enjoying yourself, Sparkle?" Justin asks before kissing her cheek.

"You know I always love your soirees," she says. "They're always so elegant and tasteful. Much like your choice in fiancée. Hello, Dr. Thornton."

Rebecca embraces the woman. "Sparkle."

"I want to get the future bride and groom first," the photographer says.

As Justin and Rebecca arrange themselves for the photo, Sparkle turns her attention to me. "So, Joanna, I've been meaning to ask, how are you and the future Mrs. Pendergast getting along? She's exquisitely beautiful." Sparkle loves needling me, hoping I'll flub up and give her something juicy to write. Hasn't worked yet, but I do admire her tenacity.

"Oh, yes. Both inside and out. The woman's a living angel. To be quite frank, he doesn't deserve her."

"And I heard you two didn't get along," Sparkle says.

"Well, you heard wrong. How can I not like her? She makes my best friend happy. She's like my sister."

"Right," Sparkle says with a fake smile.

Justin waves the rest of us over. "Excuse me, Sparkle. Duty calls."

The photographer sets up again as Rebecca and Marnie fix each other up for the next shot. Lucy hangs back, talking to Sparkle. "Long time no see, stranger," Justin says. "I was beginning to think you were mad at me."

"I've been living at the station. I haven't had time to be mad."

"Well, I appreciate you taking time away from saving the city. I know you hate these things. Though you look great."

"Thanks."

We stand side by side with the trumpets and piano playing "In the Mood," but the silence between us is unbearable. He glances at me, but I just watch as Rebecca and Marnie pose for the camera. "Now, just the Pendergast family," the photographer says.

Justin signals to Lucy, who excuses herself from Sparkle, and rushes right over. "Our turn," Justin says. He takes Lucy's hand and then grabs mine. I look up at him, surprised. "If you're not family, I don't know who is."

And the Grinch's heart grew three sizes this day. I follow them to the waterfall, trying and failing to hide my pride. As always, when he puts his arm around my back I get a little tingly. Baby steps, Jo. Baby steps. The photographer snaps the three of us, then have Rebecca and Marnie join us. He releases me and greets her with a loving smile. We position ourselves: me, Rebecca, Justin, Lucy, and Marnie. His arm instinctively wraps around her waist, and she takes my hand.

One big happy family.

After the photos Shannon, Justin's assistant extraordinaire for the last nine years, whisks the couple away to chat with the Ambassador of France while Marnie goes to call the baby-sitter. Lucy and I exchange an uncomfortable glance then go our separate ways, she to Sparkle and I to the bar. Jack Daniels keeps me company. After watching Justin stare into Rebecca's eyes as if she was the only woman in the universe and kiss her, and after I suppress the hint of anguish it stirs, I check my cell. There are no calls or texts. All the joy from the last few minutes shatters. It hits me. I've officially been stood up.

He must have weighed our relationship against the job, and the job won. *That* I can understand. I can. We are the job. It's our calling. I was having a tough time with this too. I never took him for a coward, though. Not that this is all his fault. I got my hopes up. I know better. There's only one man I can really trust. I just stand at the bar for a few minutes, watching the crowd and trying to hide my embarrassment and pain. The perpetual wallflower who no one dares to come near. I'm just not worth it.

A cute man with glasses, dark curly hair, and killer cheekbones takes pity on me, nervously asking me to dance. The booze is working its magic, and I'm in dire need of a distraction, so I agree. Neither of us talks, I think he's afraid to, but when he opens his mouth for the first time Justin taps him on the shoulder.

"Mind if I cut in, Jem?"

My partner steps aside to allow Justin to take me in his arms. Lucy insisted on dance lessons for her nephew, and I just happened to be around to act as partner. I know all his moves and cues so well, I could dance with him even if I had no legs. He smiles down at me, and I quickly smile back. "So, are you? Mad at me?" he asks. "Because I was just trying to protect you. I know you hate it, but it's sort of my job."

"I do appreciate it. I do."

"Well, if you're not mad at me, who do I need to beat up?"

I chuckle. "No one. I'm just…tired." Angry, afraid, and heartbroken.

"I know the feeling. I have this project at work that's going nowhere. I'm frustrated as hell because if I don't crack it, a lot of people could suffer."

"Lot of that going around," I say.

"And I have to fly to New Urbana tonight for a meeting because I've been neglecting everything else. I've barely seen Becks or Daisy all week. What my future mother-in-law must think of me."

"Better get your priorities straight there, rich boy, before you say 'I do.' I doubt your lovely fiancée will put up with your workaholic ways for very long before she wises up and dumps you for a man who will actually be home for dinner and make those ballet recitals."

He doesn't say anything for a moment, his face falling a little. We dance in silence for a few seconds before he asks, "Do you think I'll make a good father?"

I'm a little taken aback. We've never discussed this topic before. I always put him in the same category as me, the forever childless. Freedom and fun before all else. Crap, he's going to be a father. How am I just realizing this now? He's going to have massive responsibilities. The welfare of others will be entirely in his hands. "Of course you will. You'll be a great Dad," I say without reservation. "You were born to be a Dad. That little girl adores you."

"I'm so scared about screwing this up, Jo," he says in a tone I didn't think he knew of, let alone felt. Terror.

"Justin, I don't think you could mess this up even if you wanted to. She's over the moon for you, they both are. You've never failed at anything, let alone the most important thing to ever happen to you. Just be a partner, a friend, a confidante, and most importantly, show up. That's all any of us can do."

"You always know what to say to me."

"My mouth can on occasion be used for good. You just bring it out of me, I guess."

"You don't give yourself enough credit. You never have. You're my strength, Jo. Everything I am, I owe to you."

"Hey, if memory serves, *you* saved *me*. You more or less took me in, stood by me when I had no one else. You believed in me. You…kept me sane. You're my hero, in every possible way."

He stops dancing to hug me. I stiffen at first, but then go with it, even savoring it. "I love you, Jo."

Twenty years I've been waiting to hear that. No one but my Pop has ever said it to me. It's not the way I want it, but I'll take it. "I love you too, rich boy."

The song ends and the dancers applaud. He pulls away first, beaming down at me. "We're going to take a short break," the bandleader says before stepping away from the stand. There's a clinking of glass and all eyes turn to the source. Lucy holds up her glass and hits it as she walks toward the bandstand. Rebecca and Marnie are close behind, whispering to each other. Must be nice to have such a good relationship with your mother. The ladies step next to us, Rebecca sliding her arm through Justin's.

"May I have your attention, please?" Lucy asks. The conversation stops as we all listen. "I ask you all to raise your glasses to the future bride and groom." Everyone who has one raises them. "May you always have wealth, health, and above all, happiness. To the beautiful couple."

"To the beautiful couple," we all say. They nod in appreciation.

Lucy looks at me for a few seconds, why I have no idea. Her eyes narrow in annoyance. Oh! That's my cue. I climb up onstage as Lucy steps off. I was trying to think of something to say on the ride over, but nothing came to mind. Some best man I am. The crowd waits as I smooth my skirt and clear my throat. Mouth, don't fail me now.

"It is customary for the best man to get onstage and roast the future bride and groom, and you would think that after twenty years of friendship, I would have some doozies. Tales of debauchery and venereal disease, or running from the Mexicali police." I hang my head, shaking it. "Alas, this is not *my* wedding." Everyone, including me, laughs. "My best friend has not made it easy on me with all his virtuous behavior," I say with fake disgust, "so I'll just have to talk about that, won't I?" I look straight at my friend, right into his eyes. "You trust him the moment you meet him, and he never abuses that trust. He is one of the few people who earn it every day. He always looks for the best in people, always tries to help them even when they don't want him to. He's loyal, strong, kind, giving, and above all, loving." I turn my gaze to Rebecca. "Now, I haven't known Rebecca as long, but in the short time I've had the pleasure, I can say with utmost certainty everything I just said goes double for the bride-to-be. She's a good woman. Better than most. You two are going to have a wonderful life together because you are both compassionate, loving people, and I thank you from the depths of my heart for letting me be a part of your family." I raise my glass again. "To the happy couple."

Rebecca, eyes brimming with tears, runs up on stage and embraces me as the audience applauds. I hug her back. "Thank you," she whispers.

And damned if I didn't mean every word.

***

I think it's time to go home. I've lost track of how many glasses of champagne I've had, but I always know that I've had enough to drink when I start getting touchy feely with strangers. Most of my one night stands were a result of this trait. Since I'm in an unofficially monogamous relationship, the fact that I'm seriously considering kissing cheekbones, now known as Dr. Jonathan "Jem" Ambrose, the neurologist Rebecca wanted to set me up with, is very bad. I'm no cheat, even when my boyfriend is a total jackass. I need to get out of here before I do something I regret.

It's rude, but I get up and slink away before he returns with my glass of water. Everything, the music, the lights, the air, has a soft edge to it. It's difficult to walk, but I manage to make it to the dance floor where Justin and Rebecca slow dance like they're at the prom, rocking side to side, completely enveloped in each other. A person could set off a bomb here and they wouldn't notice.

I also tend to get emotional when I'm plastered. Watching them so in love, so together, just makes me want to puddle into tears, which I can feel coming. They'd do anything for each other, and my boyfriend doesn't even want to be seen with me. We could be dancing right there with them, but I'm not even worth a phone call from him. Why is it that some people are so lucky and others have to fight and struggle for scraps? It's so fucking unfair.

The song ends and all couples disengage. "Hey, guys, I'm gonna get out of here."

"Okay," Rebecca says, disappointed. "Guess I'll see you tomorrow, huh?"

"Tomorrow?" I ask.

"The dress fittings!"

"With your Mom and Daisy. Right. I remember now. Noon?"

"Yeah. I'll take us all out to lunch after."

"Great." I turn to Justin. "Have a safe flight. See you in a few days?"

He kisses my cheek. "Take care of my girls when I'm gone, okay?"

"I'll guard them with my life. Night, guys."

I walk away. Time to go back to my empty apartment and eat an entire carton of ice cream, and then…wait. Was that…

A very familiar looking man brushes past me as I leave the ballroom. He has the same dark brown hair, though in a different cut, build, age as…I turn back around to get a second look, but he's faded into the crowd of tuxes. No, it couldn't be him. He had glasses, a goatee, and graying temples. Besides that, how could he have gotten past the press and security? Or gotten in without an invitation? And there's the fact this is about the seventh time I've "seen" him in the past few days. One guy I actually tackled. Overcompensating, obviously. No, that guy was too old. I definitely need to sober up and have a day away from all things Alkaline.

There are a few cabs waiting, and I all but fall into the closest one. As soon as the cabbie pulls away, the tears make their way to my eyes. No. No. Unacceptable, Joanna. We do not cry over a man ever again. We do not cry, period. That son of a bitch is in no way, shape, or form worth it. Not even one tear. After years of practice, I'm a master at pushing down my emotions. The tears retreat, but they're calling in the cavalry. Anger. "I've changed my mind. Take me to 14635 Gaiman Street."

Bruce is at the front desk when I come storming into the building. "He in?" I ask as I pass. I don't wait for an answer. I get in the elevator and keep pressing the button until it closes. As the elevator lifts, so does my rage. I'm almost vibrating with it when the doors open. I knock and knock continuously until he opens the door, dressed in pajamas.

"You asshole!" I push past him into the apartment. "You unbelievable piece of shit!"

He shuts the door. "Jo—"

"No! You don't get to talk, I get to talk. I'm the one who had to go to her best friend's party alone. I'm the one who had to deflect and lie about why she didn't show up with someone when she said she would."

He seems confused. "Jo, I—"

"Shut up! I'm not done!" I step toward him, fury cutting through the hooch, so I'm fast. "You made a promise to me, and I take promises seriously. I don't ask for a lot, Harry. I don't pressure you, I don't smother you, and I haven't asked you for any kind of commitment. I listen to you, I help you out at work, I never turn you down for sex, and I have lied to everyone I know and love to protect *you*. This was the first time I ever asked you for anything. *Anything!* And you said you would. You said you would be there. I needed you tonight, and you weren't there! You didn't show up! You lied to me!"

"I didn't—"

"I'm not even worth a damn phone call to you. I'm nothing but a fuck to you. A roll in the hay to make you feel virile. You've been using me, haven't you? You've been pretending to care for me, but you don't. Not really. And if you were just honest about it, that'd be different. I'm used to it. I just thought you were better than that, but obviously I'm an idiot. Because I forgot. No one ever gives a damn about me. I don't get a happy ending. What's the matter with me? Why can't anyone…" I ball my hands into fists, digging my fingernails in so deep I almost draw blood to stop those fucking tears from falling. My chin trembles. "I thought you were one of the good ones, Harry. I thought you wanted…me. And here I thought *you* were too good for *me*."

Harry takes a step toward me. "Jo…"

I back away, holding out my arms to stop him. "Don't touch me. Don't come near me. Just…go to hell. Go to hell." I turn around and storm out before he can see the tears I can't stop this time. Bastard doesn't deserve them.

He doesn't follow me. I don't expect him to.

Fuck.

CHAPTER ELEVEN
HORROR

Light is bad. Light hurts Joanna. It burns my eyes, and makes the percussion band in my brain double their rhythm. I'd stay in bed until Armageddon if it wasn't for the immediate need to vomit up all my internal organs. I rest my head on the cool porcelain after my second round. I shouldn't have mixed drinks like that. I know better. Punishing myself, I guess. I'm very good at doing that.

Last night I got home and just dived into bed. Fell asleep in my dress, which did it no favors. Neither do the specks of spit, vomit, and sweat on it now. Shannon is going to kill me. Sadly, I'm not one of those drunks who black out. I can never get a break. The whole awful night came back the moment I woke, adding to the general "I want to die" feeling. I push the memory of Harry's confused face, then that final look of betrayal as I walked out far from my consciousness. It just makes me sad and angry, as if *I* did something wrong to him.

Yeah, the repression of the memory lasts all of a minute. As I replay the scene over and over again as the near boiling water of my shower works its magic, I realize I'm not that innocent in this. I was horrible. I was needlessly cruel, like bringing an Uzi to a pillow fight. But he hurt me. Deeply. I'm madder at myself than him. I let myself get involved, and I know better. I saw a future for us that he obviously didn't. I can understand that, God knows the roles have been reversed before, but it's the fact that he lied about it. I don't suffer liars well.

After half an hour in the shower, I feel almost human. I grab the newspaper and plop down on the couch with my black coffee. New record. I made the front and society pages. The front just has an article about Stu Moore. Looks like V landed an interview with Kelly Moore. There's just a mention of me and my "impassioned speech," about how Moore deserves justice, and how we'll catch Alkaline no matter what. There's a picture of me and Kelly at the press conference. I really need a haircut.

The society page is much kinder to my vanity. Taking up half the page is a photograph of all of us looking like a royal family, arrogant and classy. Underneath are candid shots of various guests and one of Marnie and Rebecca laughing at something I'm saying. Sparkle's article is a loving piece about how magical the night was, and how perfect the couple is together. I'm quoted here too. "She's like my sister…he doesn't deserve her."

I should call and cancel the fitting. I am in no way ready for human contact, but the only other option is to spend all day alone in here brooding, which will probably lead to more drinking. I finish the paper and get my lazy butt up.

Blue jeans, black shirt, and boots are my weekend attire and my new jacket matches perfectly. I grab a piece of dry toast and change purses. When I grab my wallet from the counter, I notice the light blinking on my answering machine. Please God, let it be from Rebecca cancelling.

"*Jo, it's Harry,*" my ex says over the machine. "*I know you're still there because you just left a message on my machine. God, I hope you get this. I know it's short notice, but I can't make it tonight. I'm actually running out the door right now. The Commissioner just called. I have to meet with him, the DA, and some Marshal. They're talking about taking the case from us. I am so sorry. I'll call you when I get a chance, okay? Have fun.*"

Immediately, I grab my cell phone and turn it back on. I shut it off because I kept checking it every three minutes. One message. "*Hey, it's Harry,*" he says, concerned. "*I guess you didn't get my message. I can't make it. I'm getting my ass handed to me by the Commissioner.*" He sighs. "*God, what a night. Look, I'll make it up to you, I promise. I'll take out a full page ad in the paper about us, okay? Hope you're having a better time than I am. Bye.*"

Oh, fuck. Oh…God. Oh, fuck! Fuck, fuck, fuck! I plop down in the couch, staring at the phone in disbelief and horror. No. This is not happening. He…I…I have to get the fuck out of here. I'm going to be late.

Millicent's Bridal Boutique is the "It" place in town for the bride-to-be to purchase her gown. They have access to all the best designers newest lines and in-house tailoring, not to mention an attached flower shop for one-stop shopping. Inside the airy store, gown technician Libby greets me with a mimosa. I decline.

The rest of my party hasn't arrived, so I sit in a Chintz chair off to the side and wait.

Happy young women with their friends and mothers filter in, giggling and chatting about the beaus and dresses. I was never that young. When I was their age, I was taking down meth labs and planning my mother's funeral. They glance at me slumped in my chair with sunglasses on, dressed mainly in black and their smiles falter a bit. I should be quarantined. I suck the joy out of everyone I come in contact with. I'm toxic.

And I'm an idiot. A huge fucking idiot. He wanted to be there. He tried to explain. But no, my self-loathing and negativity clouded my judgment. I know Harry. He'd never intentionally hurt or play games with me like that. He's loyal and good. And well rid of me. So well rid of me. I was right. He *is* too good for me. He deserves better. So much better. I ruin everything. God, what is the matter with me? I fuck everything up. Everything. I don't deserve him. Never did.

"Miss Fallon?" Libby asks.

I look up. "Yeah?"

"While you're waiting, would you like to try on your dress?"

"Um, sure." I follow her into the dressing room where a sleek blue dress with yellow ribbon around the waist hangs on the mirror. I begged for a tux, but it fell on deaf ears. At least there isn't a big bow on the butt.

It fits and looks beautiful, hugging my curves in the right places. I am going to need a wrap to cover my arms. Not my best feature. The tailor comes in and marks the spots that need taking in or letting out, then leaves to let me get dressed.

As I'm putting on my boots, there's a knock on the door. Libby pokes her head in. "Excuse me? Millicent wants to know when Dr. Thornton and her family will be in. Her next appointment is here."

"They still haven't arrived?"

"No. We've tried calling, but there's no answer."

"They were out late last night. Let me try." I pull out my cell and call. The machine picks up on both her house and cell phones. "Hey, it's Jo. I'm at the boutique. Where are you guys?" I sigh. "Look, I'm going to pop by, okay? See you soon." I hang up. It's not like Rebecca not to call or hell, be late period. I pull out one of my cards and stand up. "If they show up or call, can you please let me know?"

Libby takes the card. "Of course."

As I walk to my car, I try the house again. No answer. I'm going to feel like a total idiot if they're on their way and I have to go back. Maybe they forgot or got the time and place wrong. I drive faster than usual out of town and into the Garden. Rebecca lives in a quaint community where all the streets branch off from a huge park where parents chat while their offspring play. I circle around once, but don't see Daisy or her adults.

The two-story, single family home is quiet as I pull in behind Rebecca's Prius. The curtains are drawn too. The horrible feeling that grew with each unanswered call I have doubles. I try the house phone again and can hear it ring inside, but nothing else. No TV, no laughs, it's as quiet as a...

I unlock the glove compartment that holds one of my back-up pistols, a snub nose .38 I keep for just such occasions. I button up my bulletproof coat which hides the gun, and carefully make my way up the path toward the front door, checking all the windows for movement. My knock garners no response, so I try the handle. It's open.

"Rebec—" is all I can get out before a familiar smell stops me dead. Burnt flesh and metallic acid. God. Fuck. I stumble back to get away from the smell and pull out my cell phone. I take a few deep breaths as my shaky hand dials dispatch. "This is Det. Joanna Fallon, badge number 5757. I have a possible 187 at 5672 Kirby Street. We're gonna need a bus, and please call Lt. Harold O'Hara and Det. Terrance Cameron." I hang up, stick the phone back in my pocket, and take out the .38. I draw in breath, doing what I always do before viewing a body. Shutting off. I flip the switch. This is no time for emotion. Then, breaking about twenty policies, I enter the quiet house.

I feel nothing beyond the adrenaline. The living room is clear, just dolls and crayons scattered around. No one in the kitchen or backyard either. My heart pounds in time with my pants. The smell is making my eyes water. In the backyard I take deep lungful of fresh air. Where the hell is my back-up? I don't want to be the one who…I glance at Daisy's pink playhouse and straighten up. This is my job. I can do this.

Gun pointed, I return inside and make my way upstairs, checking every corner again, all my nerve endings and muscles tightening. I'm halfway up when I see a body lying face down in the upstairs hallway. A pool of blood and pink fluid is underneath what's left of the face. I can tell by what's left of the hair this is Marnie. I know there's no point but I check her cold neck anyway. No pulse. I cough and gag from the smell and practically leap away. Breathing through my mouth, I take huge gulps of air. "Oh, fuck, oh fuck," I whisper. Gotta keep going, Jo.

Careful where I step because of the acid and blood drops on the carpet, I check the spare bedroom. Marnie's gown from last night hangs on the armoire and the only things out of place are the covers tossed off the bed. She must have heard a noise and gotten up to check. The other two bedrooms are down the hall. Master on the right, Daisy's on the left. I go right, passing an indentation on the wall with blood in it.

I've lost track of how many murder victims I've seen. They run the gamut from peaceful to slaughterhouse, but this…this is just… Rebecca's tied naked to the headboard with purple rope, arms and legs spread eagled for everyone to see. Her head is turned to the side, but I can see there's a gag in her mouth. Her chest is nothing but an empty hole of jagged ribs and red gore. I back out of the room as if it was on fire, straight into Daisy's. I don't want to turn around, but I do.

The four-year-old lies on her bed with a pillow over her head, her tiny arm hanging over the side. Though my hand is violently shaking, I touch her wrist. No. That's it. That's all I can take. As quick as I can, I run out of that house, taking steps three at a time. My back-up arrives, sirens shrieking just as I step outside and puke my brains out right on Rebecca's perfect rose bushes while my legs give out on me.

Dear God in heaven. What have I done?

***

At my command the uniforms that respond first do not enter the house. I don't want anyone to contaminate the scene, so the men set up a perimeter. The moment they pull up, the neighbors peek out of their homes to check out the commotion. When the coroner van appears, there are a few gasps. Right behind the ambulance is the CSI van, followed by the first of the press. Let the circus begin.

I haven't been back inside the house. I can't. The ME and techs know their jobs and don't need me breathing down their necks. There are other things I can be doing, interviewing neighbors for one, but instead I'm sitting in the backyard staring at that pink plastic house, trying not to feel anything. I walked back here through the gate like a zombie and just sit down in the same chair I was in a month ago for a bar-b-que. Rebecca at the grill, Justin teaching Daisy how to somersault, and me sipping beer and as always feeling out of place.

My hands haven't stopped quivering. Even balling them into fists doesn't help. Everyone's left me alone out here, even Cam. I heard his voice barking orders a few minutes ago. It's only a matter of time before he comes looking for me. I have to give my statement. I'm not an investigator on this one. I'm a witness. I'm part of the case now, and I think I'm the only one who realizes how big a part right now.

"Jo?" Harry asks behind me. I don't turn around. I can't look at him. I don't think I could move if I wanted to. He comes around, pulling one of the chairs with him, sitting down across from me. "Jo, look at me. Please." He touches my hand, and I turn away from the pink house to my ex. He should hate me, I would, but there's no malice in those blue eyes. He looks as sad as I feel. "Oh, Jo."

"It was…" I can't finish. I want to fall into his arms and cry, but after last night I've lost that privilege. So I don't. I don't even look at him. I gaze down at the stone. "Have you been in there?"

"Not yet. I wanted to check on you first."

"Sir?"

We both turn around. One of the ME's assistants, who has blood on her gloves, stands at the door. "Yes?" Harry asks.

"The ME's asking for you."

"Give me a minute."

The woman walks back inside the house of horror. She's going to poke and prod as if they were slabs of meat. Then they'll be autopsied, cut apart and…God. "You better get in there. I'm okay, boss."

"Do you need anything? Do you want me to call someone?"

"Uh, Justin's out of town. I tried his cell, but it's turned off. I left him a message. I don't know when he's supposed to be home. I don't think Rebecca has anyone else. I don't know. I should call Lucy, I guess. She might know."

"I meant call someone for *you*. Your uncle? Veronica?"

"She's probably out front with the rest of them. No, I'm fine. Go to work."

He isn't at all convinced, but he knows better than to press me. "Okay. I'm just inside if you need me." He gets up and walks to the door.

"Harry?"

He spins around. "Yes?" I open my mouth to apologize, beg for forgiveness, but the words don't come out. I shake my head. He smiles sympathetically. "We'll talk later, okay?"

"Yeah," I whisper. "Okay."

He walks inside, leaving me as I should be. Alone. I just want to give my statement and leave. I would, but I can't move. I have no place to go. I need to do *something*, anything. Justin. I have to think of Justin, he's all that matters now. I pull out my phone and try his number again, then his assistant Shannon's, but neither answer. Lucy does.

"Lucy Helms."

"Lucy, it's Joanna."

"Oh," she says, more than a little surprised. I've never called her before. I only have her number for reasons such as this. "Is everything alright?"

"Um, no. Not at all." I pause, biting my lip. "I need to reach Justin right away, and he's not answering. Do you have another number for him?"

"No. He's probably on the plane."

"He's already on his way home? Do you know when he lands?"

"They're just stopping here to refuel. He has to go to London next. Joanna, what is going on? Do you need help?" she asks, genuinely concerned for me.

"No," I say, my voice quaking. "Um, it's…um…, Rebecca's dead. Daisy and Marnie too."

There's nothing but dead silence on the other end for a few seconds. "How?"

"They were murdered. It looks like it was Alkaline."

Now there's nothing but the sound of ragged breathing. "Are—are you sure?"

"I—I found them. It—it was him. No doubt."

"Oh, Joanna," she says, "I'm so sorry."

I didn't know she was capable of pity. I'd be touched if I wasn't trying so hard to remain numb. "Look, I don't know how long I'll be stuck here, but I think we should both be there to tell him. I'll get away somehow."

"Right. Of course. Just call me when you're on your way." She pauses for a moment. "Thank you for telling me, Joanna."

"I'll see you soon." I hang up the phone and let out a shaky breath. She thanked me. *Thanked* me. Why would she do that? Why—

A camera peeks over the back fence followed by its owner, a skuzzy man I recognize as one of the paparazzi. Then another pops up next to him. "Detective Fallon! Detective Fallon! Is it true this is the work of Alkaline? Whose house is this?"

I can't deal with them right now. Where there are two, there will be more. I'm a hot draw. I stand up and back into the house away from the shouting people.

The smell has almost dissipated with all the doors open. Forensic techs dust for prints on the front door and living room while others take pictures. For once I feel out of place at a crime scene, when I usually feel out of place everywhere else. I stand off to the side near the wall filled with pictures. I never look at the pictures of people at the scene, but now I can't take my eyes off these. Rebecca and Daisy at the playground. Daisy in her christening gown. Rebecca as a beautiful teenager in front of a yellow VW beetle. Rebecca, an Indian woman, and Jem Ambrose from last night all smiling and hugging. Justin and Rebecca on the beach holding hands. Maybe I should go back outside.

Cam comes down the stairs before I can flee, still holding a handkerchief to his mouth. He lowers it when he sees me. More pity. I can't abide it. Never could. "I'm fine," I say before he can open his mouth.

"Of course you are," he says as he approaches.

"Look, can you take my statement? I have to meet Justin's plane."

"Does he know? What about next of kin?"

"I don't know. Her father's dead, but I guess her ex-husband should be notified. He's in prison in Donnersville. I think his name's Micah, but I don't know the last name. Oh, her brother's in the Army. He's overseas, I don't know where. His name's Sam."

"We'll find them," Cam assures me.

"Okay." I glance at the photos, suddenly feeling sick again. "Can we do this in the kitchen, please?"

"Sure. Of course."

Techs work in there too. Nothing seems out of place, not even the Disney princess placemats on the table. I sit in front of Snow White with Cam beside me. He takes out his pad. "I was supposed to meet them at Millicent's Bridal Boutique at noon. Approximately forty-five minutes after I arrived, a salesgirl told me that the Thorntons hadn't shown up and could not be reached by telephone. I called the house and Rebecca's cell, but there was no response on either, I decided to check on them here. When I arrived approximately twenty minutes later, the car was in the driveway, and the front door was unlocked. When I opened the door, I could smell the acid and blood and called for back-up. There was no one on the first floor, and no signs of struggle. When I went upstairs, I found all three Thorntons dead. The only things I touched were the front and back door handles, the neck of the corpse in the hallway who I can positively identify as Marnie Thornton, and the wrist of the child Daisy Thornton. I did not allow anyone to enter the house until CSI arrived. Um, I know I'm forgetting something. I covered…"

Cam pats my hand. "You got it all, Jo."

"Did the ME determine time of death?"

"Looks to be about 6:30 this morning."

"What do you think happened?"

"As best we can tell, he either found a spare key or picked the lock. The older woman must have heard him or was up already, and he shot acid into her face and neck area to keep her quiet. If this alerted the other two, we don't know yet. We assume yes, because Dr. Thornton has a broken nose."

Harry steps in without a word and hangs back by the fridge. He folds his arms and gazes at me. I can't look back. "Um, there was a splotch of blood down the hallway," I say.

"There's a contusion on the back of the child's head. We think he threw her against the wall and knocked her out there. After he was done with the mother, he carried the child to her bed and smothered her."

"He didn't…" I can't even fathom it.

"No, she was fully clothed and there are no other marks on her besides the head wound."

Thank God for small mercies. "Rebecca was the target."

"Yes. He subdued her, restrained her, and killed her."

"Were there signs of sexual assault?"

He hesitates, but says, "Yes. I'm sorry."

"That's not his M.O., Grace Pickering notwithstanding."

"None of this is his M.O. There's no way we could have predicted this." He clears his throat. "Do you have any idea why he targeted the Thorntons? Did any of them mention someone following them? Anything out of the ordinary?"

"No." I avert my eyes down to the tile floor. "But, um, at the party last night, I think I saw Alkaline."

"What?" Cam asks.

"At the time, I didn't think it was him. I only saw him for a second." I look at Harry. "And I had *a lot* to drink last night." I look away again. "He had a beard and glasses on, but after this it had to be him."

"How sure are you?" Harry asks.

"Now? Ninety percent. It just happened so fast. He walked right by me, didn't even acknowledge my presence. I turned to get a second look, but I couldn't see him."

"You didn't think to call this in?" Cam asks.

"Like I said, I was drunk and upset, and it wasn't the first time I thought I saw him. Not to mention the fact that there was security everywhere and the only way past them was by invitation, which was checked at the door."

"Okay, I'll call the hotel and get the security footage from last night," Cam says. "Is there anything else you remember about him?"

"He was wearing a tux. His hair was shorter, parted to the left. He had rimless glasses and a goatee. Nothing else was different."

"Do you remember seeing him anywhere else?" Harry asks.

"Nothing substantiated. I don't think anyone's been tailing me, and Rebecca never mentioned anyone tailing her either."

We're all quiet for a few seconds, I'm sure all thinking the same thing. The most important question of our jobs. Why? Was it because of her high profile? Maximum shock value? Or was it more personal? *She's like my sister...*

A tech rushes in, eyes wide. He looks at me, almost afraid, before turning to Harry. "Sir, we found something." He glances at me again. "You should all see this."

We follow him out into the living room where three techs huddle around the now closed front door taking pictures and dusting for prints. They stop and part as we walk up, worry all over their faces. There's a photo tacked onto the back of the door. It's from today's newspaper, the same one I was reading a lifetime ago. The first family of Galilee all smiling. Except for me. My face is burned off by a single drop of acid.

All eyes turn to me to gage my reaction, but I feel nothing. Not anger like Cam or terror like Harry. I'm just numb. Maybe I'm in shock. I'm not cold, which happens to people in shock. I'm more upset by the people watching me. I don't like it. I walk back to the kitchen.

"Everyone back to work," Cam barks behind me.

As I sit at the table, Harry and Cam walk in. "Can you please leave us?" Harry asks the techs. They bow their heads and do as he says. "You too, Cam."

"Sir?"

"I need to talk to Det. Fallon alone."

The always protective Cam straightens his back. "Sir?"

"You are needed upstairs, Detective. *Go.*"

Cam begrudgingly obeys, throwing me a sympatric look as he does. I'd still rather be in here getting my butt handed to me than up there with them. "I can't believe I missed that," I say. "It's from today's paper. It must be Rebecca's. Maybe one of the neighbors saw him—"

"You're going to have twenty-four hour police protection until we find this fucker," Harry says forcefully. I'm surprised by his vehemence. He's scared, probably more so than I am.

"No way."

"This is not up for debate, Joanna. If I thought you'd stay there I'd put you in a safe house. You can't stay at your apartment. It's not secure."

"I'll probably be staying at Justin's. It's got a gate and a state-of-the-art security system. I don't need babysitters following me around. I'm police. I can take care of myself."

"The man who has killed about forty people and raped at least two has just threatened your life. I am not taking any chances, okay? If you don't agree to the guards and fully comply, I'll toss your ass into a cell at the station and watch you myself."

This is where I would make a kinky comment if the last twenty-four hours had never happened. I can't even think of one, let alone fight him on this. "Fine. I'll do whatever you say."

"And as of right now, you're off the case."

"I figured."

He sighs and hangs his head. We don't speak for a few seconds, and for the first time I'm uncomfortable in his presence. Part of me wants him to leave me alone, but the bigger part wants to fall into his arms and cling to him until it's all over. I can't even look at him, let alone touch him. I don't deserve to, and I think he finally realizes it. "Do you need anything? I can call Dr. Newman."

"I don't need a shrink. I'm fine."

"Of course you are. You're always fine." He pauses, trying to pull up the correct words. "This isn't your fault, Jo."

I can't be in this house a moment longer. I stand and walk over to him, though I don't meet his gaze. "Of course it is. It's all my fault. All of it. Always. It's all on me. You of all people should realize that. Bye, Harry."

With my head hung I walk out of the kitchen, past the glancing techs, the shouting reporters with their cameras, to my car. Their swarming doesn't stop me from pulling out and driving as fast as I can out of there, as most guilty do when they leave the scene of their crime. I'm no different.

CHAPTER TWELVE
BROKEN

A police cruiser follows me to Justin's but waits outside the gate as I enter. I'm sure Harry's ordered them to stay within ten feet of me at all times, but I shut the gate before they can get in. I need them to keep their distance for today. Justin and Lucy have more important things to worry about than me.

Dobbs, the butler/chauffer, opens the door for me. His grief is written all over his wrinkled face. He's been the Pendergast butler for forty-four years, running this house like a tight ship, thirty of those years with the help of his wife Leigh, who was the maid before she passed away. He's always been kind to me, having the cook make my favorite meals and dropping or picking me up when I'd come over. He's even the one who taught Justin and me how to drive and sail. Justin practices that last one a lot more than I do, but I'm a great first mate when I'm there.

Dobbs shuts the door and we stand in the large entranceway, the crystal chandelier glittering like fairy dust above our heads. At least that's how Daisy described it. Bowing his head, Dobbs says, "Terrible day."

"The worst."

"You found them?"

"Yes."

He squeezes my arm. "I am so sorry."

"Me, too. I know how fond you are—*were* of them."

"Yes. I was looking forward to the sound of children once more. Now, I fear these walls will never hear them again." I have no idea what to say to that, so I hang my head and say nothing. He swallows down his emotions and is his professional self again. "Miss Lucy is in the parlor."

"Thank you, Dobbs."

I start toward the parlor until Dobbs says, "Miss Joanna?"

I turn around. "Yeah?"

"When it comes time to meet Master Justin, would it be possible for me to drive you two? I just want to…be there for him."

"Of course. It'll mean a lot to him, you being there."

"Thank you, Miss Joanna."

I nod before going to find Lucy. On the way, I pass the paintings on the walls. "The Hall of Pendergast," I call it. It's a family tradition dating back nine generations to commission a family portrait and hang it here. They're always the same with the husband on the left, children on the right, and mother sitting in a chair between them. The first dates back to the seventeen hundreds when the city was founded. Jeremiah Pendergast was one of the first to settle here, quickly building his milling and then shipping empire while his wife Ellen started the Daughters of the Falls, a charity organization still around today that every socialite is in or trying to be in. The last portrait is of Justin when he was nine with his father and mother. She had to be painted in using a photo as she died of breast cancer when Justin was six. He got her lips and chin, but the rest belongs to the Pendergast's. All are blonde, blue-eyed Gods and Goddesses right down the line.

One night, when I was about twenty, I accompanied Justin to his cousin Jeanne's wedding in St. Croix. While we were walking along the beach, he asked me if I ever thought I'd get married. Of course I wanted to blurt out, "Yes, to you," but instead said, "I don't know." Good thing I did, because he said with utter confidence, "I never will. *Never*. And I won't bring children into this world either. I wouldn't do that to any of them." Then she came and it all changed. She melted his heart, brought it to life. She gave him hope. Now, I doubt this wall will ever get a new edition.

Lucy sits behind the desk at the bay window overlooking the ocean, the telephone pressed against her ear. There's a glass on the desk of what I think is Bourbon, her drink of choice, which she plays with nervously. "No, I don't think they'll release the names until the family has been notified. If anyone else calls, just tell them no comment. I've already called Gene and he's drafting a statement. He'll release it when he deems it necessary." She listens. "Shannon, Joanna, and I can handle the funeral preparations." She listens again. "Thank you. Good-bye." She hangs up the phone, taking a moment before acknowledging me. "You arrived quickly."

I sit on the couch, crossing my ankles like she's told me to do for years. "Ladies do not sit like cowboys, Joanna." Now I only sit like a cowboy in her presence just to tick her off. No desire to do that today. "I just had to give a statement."

"Oh." She sips her drink with a slightly shaky hand. Mine stopped shaking on the drive over through sheer force of will. "A few members of the press, it seems, have already contacted Pendergast Industries in search of Justin."

"One of the neighbors probably told them who lived at the crime scene. I'd give it another half hour or so before the entire mess is leaked out. You should probably call a security firm and get them to guard the gate. This place is going to be a madhouse."

"For how long, do you think?"

"Week, maybe two. Definitely at the funeral."

"Yes." She takes another sip. "I don't know where they would want to be buried. I doubt Marnie would want to spend eternity in Galilee. She didn't like it here at all. Too dirty and loud. Though Rebecca and Daisy…should we separate them all? Maybe we should just have the funeral in Lake City." She sips her drink. "And would they want to be buried or cremated? I just don't know."

"Maybe they had wills. Might be in there?"

"Perhaps." She takes a final sip and stands up, going to the bar to fill up. "When will they release the bodies? They'll have to autopsy them, I suppose."

"Yeah," I say quietly.

She nods a little, no doubt to shake out the image of them lying on the autopsy table missing organs. "I'm forgetting my manners. Would you like something to drink?"

"No, thank you." I'm never touching that shit again if I can help it.

"The last time I had a drink in the afternoon was twenty years ago," she says, pouring. "I had just been informed that I had inherited control of a seven billion dollar legacy and a thirteen-year-old boy I had only met five times before. If there was ever a time, right?" She sips. "As you may have figured out, I don't like most people. I have no real use for them. I remember now why that is." She walks back over to the window to watch the waves crash below. "Even after twenty years, I miss my old life. I was the head of the board at the Independence Museum of Art, you know. I made or broke exhibits. I went on archaeological digs all over the world. I even negotiated with the Louvre for a Monet. I had my cats, the occasional girlfriend, my committees, and I flew around the world on a whim. I never wanted to get married or, God forbid, have children. Freedom trumped all. It's hard to get close to someone as fiercely independent as us. You know how that is."

I nod. I'd say something, but my input doesn't matter. I just have to listen.

"Then J.T. dies, and I'm responsible for a grieving child. Two total strangers stuck in a mausoleum. I had no idea what to say or do, and neither did he for that matter. He barely spoke the first few weeks beyond the polite pleasantries. I did the best I could. We soldiered on."

"He loves you," I say. "And he knows you were the one who was there for him when he really needed it. Even though you didn't want to do it, you came. You raised him. Who knows where he'd be without you?"

She turns from the window with a small smile. "You're good at this. It must make you an effective law enforcement officer. It's a rare gift, knowing the exact right thing to say or do in a given situation."

I scoff. "That is *so* not the case."

"Don't sell yourself short, Joanna. I know it may seem that I never liked you. At first, I didn't. He had enough on his plate without a suicidal teenager following him around like a lost puppy." A sip. "Then, as time went on, I saw how good you were for him. You gave him what I couldn't. A purpose. Affection. Someone who made him laugh. I never did thank you for that."

"You didn't need to."

"I've treated you badly. I'm a snob, and I know it. You're uncouth, vulgar, and stubborn to a fault." She scoffs. "And I see a lot of myself in you, if you can believe that. You have so much potential, and I hate to see it squandered. Though considering your upbringing, I'm amazed you're as well adjusted as you are. A lesser person would be some type of addict, criminal, or emotional cripple. You should be proud of yourself."

One out of three isn't bad. "I am," I lie.

"I do have a point to this ramble," she says, stepping toward me. She sits in the chair next to me, back straight. "I know how you felt about Rebecca, because I know how you feel about Justin. You're in love with him." I open my mouth to protest, but she holds up her hand to stop me. "Don't bother denying it. I could tell the moment you stepped into our limo that first night. You were all but drooling." She sips her drink. "Do you know the reason he's never reciprocated your feelings?"

"I'm uncouth, vulgar, and stubborn?"

"Oddly, he likes those traits in you," she says with a smile. "No. You lost him before you ever had him, my dear. The moment you stepped onto the edge of that bridge, any chance of romantic love was over. If you two had just met, say at a function or on the street, he would have fallen madly in love with you, without a doubt."

"Then why not then?"

"Because you're a symbol to him, Joanna. You are the first person he ever saved, and that saved him. You're an extension of himself, and everything he stands for. You represent his whole world. All his pain and sacrifice for the greater good. He'd never let such a base thing as sex sully that. You have to go out in the world, live a good life apart from him, contribute, otherwise what is all this sacrifice for? And that's what makes you the most important person in his life."

"What sacrifice? He talked me off a bridge. Nothing else."

She chugs her drink. "Then he met Rebecca," she says, ignoring me. "She meant something different. A blending of both worlds. She needed him at first exactly as you did, but could provide him with normalcy free of the darkness, or so he thought. Sometimes there's not enough light in this godforsaken world to keep the darkness at bay."

"I suppose," I say for lack of something better. I'm confused as to half of what she's said.

She closes her eyes for a moment, probably to focus her thoughts. "My point is you saved him once. You gave him a sense of purpose, and now you need to give him a reason to continue. This is going to destroy him. Mind, soul, and maybe body. I know that's a lot to put on you, but I wouldn't ask if I didn't think you were up to the task. I'm asking you to put your own feelings, especially the misplaced guilt you are no doubt feeling, aside. I'm asking you to be strong for him, no matter what." She purses her lips. "I know you must have resented Rebecca for usurping your place at his side. I would have. But wishing a person dead does not make it so. Any guilt rests solely on the monster who killed her. This is not your fault, Joanna. Please believe me."

For a moment, mind you just a moment, if feels as if a weight has been lifted off my shoulders. I can actually believe those words. Then that image of the photo on the door crashes me back to earth. Not that I'll let her see any of this. "I will do whatever I can to get you both through this. I know you were fond of her. You lost her too. All of them."

Lucy looks away. "That little girl. She was…precious. Did she suffer?"

"No. She was unconscious when it happened."

Lucy collects herself, and then turns back to me with an awkward smile. "That's good," she says quietly. She takes a final swig of her drink and sighs. "I believe I will go upstairs and have a lie down." She stands and as manners dictate, so do I. "I'm sure you can handle any telephone calls that come."

"Of course."

She sets down the glass. "Wake me in two hours. I've already contacted the airfield. They won't grant clearance until we arrive."

"Okay."

We face each other, neither wanting to speak. Then she does something I never thought she'd do. She leans in, wrapping her thin arms around me in a stiff hug. I'm too shocked for a moment to move, but quickly remedy that, hugging her back. It's over in a second. She pulls away first, a little embarrassed by this show of emotion. "Thank you."

"Go rest."

On unsteady legs, she totters out with her head up to maintain dignity. I've never seen her drink more than a single glass of champagne. I run my hand through my hair with a ragged sigh. If she's reacting like this, Justin's going to be inconsolable.

My hands begin shaking again and I have the strongest urge to sit. Really, I want to run out of this house, hop into my car, and drive as far away as possible. Check into some random hotel, drink myself into oblivion, and sleep for a month. And I could. I really could. They'd be better off without me. Everyone would. I—

The telephone rings, making me almost jump out of my seat. My nerves are shot. I could really use a drink. Or Valium. Or both. But no, I'm not touching the crap.

Okay, I failed one job, I'm not going to do it twice. I'll just do the best I can. Just show up. I can do it. I can.

So I do.

***

The ride to the airport is a quiet one. Dobbs sits in the front of the vintage Rolls Royce separated by a clear sliding partition. Lucy and I sit side by side in the back, looking out our respective tinted windows. Even with the car in relative darkness, Lucy and I wear sunglasses to help with our hangovers.

The adrenaline that was keeping mine at bay wore off soon after Lucy left me to field a thousand phone calls from concerned friends and business associates. I told the truth, which turned out to be a mistake. Bitsy even began to sob, blubbering for close to five minutes. I let the machine pick up after that, only answering those which needed immediate response. The aspirin helped with the headache and a sandwich settled my stomach, but I'm still exhausted. My body feels as if I've just run across the country.

I rest my head against the cool window, watching my city go by. The airport is on the mouth of the river where it meets the ocean, though Justin has his own hangar across the street from the real airport. To my left is the urban jungle, to my right the dark water of the Andalucía River with huge boats parked at the docks. Longshoremen in yellow hard hats unload crates with cranes and mill around chanting to their colleagues and drinking coffee. In the distance, a line of trucks wait to leave the port terminal. Overhead planes begin the descent, engines roaring. If I didn't already have a headache, the noise alone would give me one. Lucy presses her temples to help assuage hers. What a pair we are. Justin would be better off with a hyena to comfort him.

Dobbs pulls into the private airport with my police escort following behind. The guard at the gate lets us pass. Justin does a lot of traveling and gives a mean Christmas bonus, so they all know the car. The rich people airport, as I think of it, is nothing more than five hangars, two air strips, a small terminal where they bring your plane to the door, and tiny access roads. Normally we'd wait at the terminal, but since the plane's only here to refuel we drive toward the hangar itself. It's fairly deserted except for the fuel trucks, tiny prop planes, and bigger private jets scattered around with mechanics tinkering on them. The hangar that Justin shares with the Pickering and Lockwood's is the last on the tarmac. We're just in time as Justin's jet lands when we pull in.

"Should I tell him or do you want to?" I ask Lucy.

She takes off her sunglasses, revealing red eyes. "Want is in no way is associated with this endeavor." She places the glasses into their case. "We'll play it by ear." Dobbs opens Lucy's door, but I don't wait for him.

This isn't the first death notification I've done. They come with the job. Ask any officer what their least favorite part of the job is, and they'll say death notification. You become the most important person in the worst day of their life. Some people burst into hysterical tears. Some throw things. Some just stare blankly as if you're speaking a foreign language. You never can tell.

I remember my first. It was around three in the morning when I heard the knock on our apartment door. At first I thought it was Mom in the kitchen looking for another bottle, but the second knock woke me fully. I got up thinking Pop had forgotten his keys, but when I saw the two officers in the hall my stomach dropped. I'd seen enough detective shows to know something bad had happened. The patrolmen were both young, early twenties if that, and visibly uncomfortable. Sands and Webb were their names. I made it a point to remember them in case they were lying. I'd sue their butts if they were. I was grasping at straws, working very damn hard at denial at that moment. When I joined the force I sought them out. Sands had quit, but Webb was a fraud detective. He remembered me after a little prompting. Like I said, it's hard to forget your first notification.

Sands, the taller of the two, asked if my mother was home. Too stunned to talk back, I ran into her bedroom. Mom was asleep, or should I say passed out on the top of the bed. I shook her for a few seconds to no avail. She'd fallen off the wagon a week before for no conceivable reason, and would never climb back on again. This was an especially bad night for her. Pop threatened to leave her, taking me with him, if she didn't start attending meetings again. I was overjoyed. We'd finally be free of her drama and bullshit. Before I went to bed I got the newspaper and began circling possible apartments we could move into.

After slapping her face, she jerked awake. I told her the police wanted her. Still half asleep and drunk, she stumbled to the front door. The officers exchanged a glance, one I'd seen on neighbors and family members' faces when she was like this. They asked if she was Maeve Fallon, wife of Sean Fallon. When she asked why, they ignored her, asking if there was anyone else at home. I found out later this is standard in case one person flips out, there's another there to calm or comfort her. Otherwise the officers could be there for hours, especially with a fainter. Mom said no. Having no choice, they told us what happened. Pop was shot three blocks from the apartment in an apparent robbery.

"I'm sorry, but he didn't make it."

Mom clutched her stomach as if stabbed, gasping and doubling over. The officers helped her to the couch as she burst into tears and wasn't able to stand on her own anymore. Until that moment I thought she hated him. They fought constantly, especially after she'd been drinking. I can count on one hand the times I saw them be loving to each other or even hug. I think the only reason they married was because of me. But in her way she loved him. After his death she never seriously dated, instead choosing one night stands with other alcoholics. She was so distraught she couldn't even handle the funeral arrangements.

Mom was a crumbler. I just went into shock. Those words came out of Sands' mouth and it was like a two-ton iron door shut inside me. Everything just closed. My emotions, my ability to think, my belief in anything decent and fair. It only opens on rare occasions, usually to let one of the demons out that can't be contained anymore to wreak havoc on my life. Like last night.

I think I was catatonic for a minute, floating outside myself for that time as my brain assimilated the information and prepared me for my new life. Then Sands touched my shoulder and I snapped out of it. He asked if I was okay, an insanely stupid question. I looked into his eyes and told him I needed to call my uncle for my mother. Mom sobbed even louder, resting her head on Webb's shoulder. He later told me that I looked at her with such utter contempt he got a chill. I went into her bedroom to make the call as her cries were too loud to hear over. This would be my life until I emancipated myself when I was sixteen. Mom falling apart and me having to handle everything from paying the bills to doing the repairs.

It was twenty years ago, and I remember every detail, down to the pajamas I was wearing. Justice t-shirt with purple shorts. My first next-of-kin notification. Now, I have to take center stage on the worst day of my best friend's life. The day when all of his hopes and dreams are shattered with a few words. Will he fall apart? Take a swing at me? Never look at me the same way again? I'm about the find out.

As the jet taxis into the hangar, three mechanics hop to, grabbing tools and the fuel hose. I walk around the car to join Lucy and Dobbs. Her arms are folded across her small chest, already defensive. Dobbs has his hands crossed in the back and chin up, even now the proper servant. I don't know what to do with my arms, so they stay at my side, the shakes that started again when we pulled in controlled by balling my hands into fists.

Justin peers through one of the small windows, smiling but confused. Shannon, Justin's assistant's, head bowed, lifts her cell phone to her ear. She better not tell him before we do. The plane stops and one of the mechanics opens the door. After saying something to Shannon, Justin stands to deplane. I sigh before starting toward the plane with Lucy behind me. *I can do this.*

As Justin comes into view at the door, Shannon's face falls. She looks at us, stunned, her mouth gaping open. I keep walking but glance at her, lightly shaking my head to signal her to keep her trap shut. Her tiny mouth closes.

"This is a nice surprise. What are you doing here?" he asks with a chuckle as he steps down.

I have no idea what to say. He's smiling. *Smiling.* I keep my face neutral as I keep walking. His grin grows as I approach, but so does the confusion. He tries to read me, but I'm not giving anything away. Lucy isn't either. "Seriously guys, what are you doing here?" We keep walking. His smile wanes. "Jo? Aunt Lucy? What's going on, you guys?" He tries to meet my eyes. When I don't let him, the smile disappears. A dumbstruck Shannon appears in the plane door, trying to stop her oncoming tears. "Jo, you're starting to scare me." I'm only a few feet away, and I can't not meet his gaze.

We know each other too well. Confusion changes to fear when our eyes lock. "Jo, where's Rebecca?" This is one of the few times I'm glad for my walls. The look on that handsome face, the abject terror and sadness, would kill me otherwise. He grabs my upper arms, shaking me. "Joanna!"

I do my job. "I'm sorry to inform you that Rebecca Thornton, Daisy Thornton, and Marnie Holt were found dead this afternoon in their residence. I'm so sorry."

My face is pressed against the glass as my best friend's heart breaks. Fear turns to anger which becomes unfathomable sadness. He clutches onto me with quivering arms so tight I want to wince. I don't. I accept the pain. "Daisy?" he asks, voice cracking.

I shake my head.

He releases me, wide eyes tearing. Disbelief fills his face. "No. No," he says, shaking his head. He looks at Lucy, who averts her gaze down. Shaking his head even harder he turns to Shannon. She covers her mouth with both hands to stop the sobs. Justin gasps, running his hands through his hair as he looks back at me. Tears fall down his cheeks. "What happened? Jo, *what happened?*" he roars.

"They were murdered," I say after a pause.

"Who?" I don't answer. He grabs me again, eyes wild. I've never seen him like this before. There's something inhuman about his expression. Feral. For an instant, I'm scared of him. "*Who?*"

"Alkaline. It was Alkaline."

His mouth slacks open as he gasps and doubles over, just as my mom did. He twists away from me, away from all of us, staggering back to the side of the plane. He keeps gasping, unable to draw in enough air. "No," he says in between the chokes. "No!" he bellows. He hits the side of the plane so hard it shimmies, leaving a huge dent.

It's my turn to gasp. I've never seen anything like that outside of a superhero fight. "Justin!" I rush over to him.

He rests his head on the plane, fist still imbedded. As I take his hand to check for broken bones, he gazes up at me through tear-filled eyes. I've seen that look. My mom had it all her life. It's in my eyes every moment of the day. I can barely look at myself in the mirror because of it. It's something I wouldn't wish on my worst enemy.

Broken. He's broken.

"Oh, Jo," he cries as he crumbles into my arms.

I do the only thing I can. I hold him as tight as I can as he falls apart.

CHAPTER THIRTEEN
AFTERMATH

The press began to show up an hour before we left, but by the time we pull through the gate every reporter on the continent is on Justin's doorstep. The usually calm Dobbs grips the steering wheel, breathing heavily as he plows through the shouting horde, horn honking continuously. Flashbulbs pop and cameras are thrust against the windows, though they can't see anything. Gotta love tinted windows. That doesn't stop them. If anything they take it as a challenge, swarming us. They screech their questions, but I can't make out a single word. Everywhere we look, there they are. Dobbs can barely go one mile an hour, but we make it through the gate.

"Cretins," Lucy says. "Have they no shame?"

"None," I say.

"I'm on the phone to the police right now," Shannon says, pinning a stray strand of brown hair back in her tight bun. "They'll clear them out."

"It's a public street. The police can't do anything," I say.

"Bastards," Lucy says.

Justin stares out the window, lost in his own world. He doesn't even register their presence.

The reporters stop at the gate, but their questions continue. "Oh, good," Shannon says. I turn around and see my armed escorts get out of their car for crowd control. "Why were they following us?" Shannon asks.

Justin looks away from the window to me for the answer. "Standard procedure in high profile cases," I say. "For just this reason. Nothing to worry about."

As Dobbs retrieves the suitcases from the back, the rest of us retreat inside away from the loud voices. We follow Justin into the foyer where he just stops. Nobody says a word or even moves. We stay like this for almost a minute, even when Dobbs joins us. He looks at Lucy, who turns to me. Justin hasn't let go of my hand since the airfield. I squeeze it. "Justin?" He says something, but so faintly I can't hear him from a few inches away. "What?"

"I don't know what to do," he says only a little louder. "I have no idea what I'm doing. I don't know what to do next. Do I…start the funeral arrangements? Do I go into the living room and just sit down? I don't know what I'm supposed to do."

"Hey," I say, positioning myself in front of him. He won't look at me. "We'll handle everything, okay?" I look at Dobbs. "After you bring the suitcases upstairs, can you make us some sandwiches and coffee?"

"Yes, miss," Dobbs says as he starts toward the staircase.

"Shannon, why don't you handle everything at Pendergast? Meetings that need cancelling, worried staff, whatever crops up. Unless there's an emergency, I don't want anything work-related to get past you. I've already been in contact with Gene Tully in public relations and he's drafted a statement and is coordinating with the press. On the desk in the parlor there's a pad with notes about everything he and I spoke about and others who have called. It'll help you catch up. Dobbs can drive you back to the office when you're done."

"Okay," she says as she walks away, already fiddling with her phone.

"And I think I'll begin returning phone calls," Lucy says. "I'll be up in my room if I'm needed."

Tentatively, Lucy approaches her nephew. She squeezes his shoulder and with his free hand he pats hers. "Thank you, Aunt Lucy," Justin says before leaning in and kissing her cheek.

She nods and walks up the stairs to her sanctuary. Just the two of us now. "Why don't we go into the living room? Or would you rather go upstairs and lie down? I can call Doc Swenson. Get you some Valium?"

"No. Thank you."

"Okay." I start toward the living room for lack of something better to do. Justin doesn't release my hand, so he comes with me. In his shock I could lead him into the ocean and he'd follow.

I choose the living room because it's the calmest room in the house. The mansion was built over a hundred years ago when the first burnt down. The rest of the house is a cold museum with antique furniture, ancient statues and paintings. When I first stepped in, I was struck by how dark and stuffy it was. Definitely a house, not a home. For the first year I was petrified to even look at the art, let alone touch anything. This room and the library are the only two I'm comfortable in. And since we've spent the majority of our friendship in the living room, that is where we end up.

Justin's dad, J.T. renovated it just before Justin was born. He knocked out an entire wall and replaced it with glass so there's a panoramic view of the sapphire blue ocean below. There's a deck and patio where we sunbathe or barbeque when weather allows. Inside there's a full bar with stools, popcorn maker, cotton candy machine, small fridge, and dart board off to the side. The L-shaped fluffy black couch takes up most of the room with glass coffee table separating it from the sixty-inch plasma TV. Every videogame system invented is attached to the TV. Hundreds of wasted, yet fun as hell, hours have been spent on those things. We're both very competitive, almost to a fault, and once spent eighteen hours straight trying to kill each other. I won. Taking up half a wall is a bookcase filled with DVDs, mostly comedy and action. Justin's a cineophile. Last count was a thousand. The digital juke-box is next to a giant stone fireplace big enough to burn a human with the oldest map of Galilee hanging above it. I've always thought it's out of place in here, but elegant.

I sit him on the couch, pulling my hand away. "Can I get you anything? A drink?"

He looks up at me. "You need to tell me everything that happened. *Everything.* Start with this morning."

I sit next to him, grabbing one of the throw pillows to hug. "Justin, I don't think—"

His eyes grow wide. "I don't care what you think. I need to know. *Tell me.*"

With a sigh, I walk him through the day's events, omitting the more gruesome or disturbing aspects, stopping before I get to the threat. He listens, only flinching a few times. "That's it. That's all I know."

"That's everything?" I nod. His eyes narrow. "You're lying."

"I've told you everything important."

"I want every detail."

"No, you don't. And I sure as hell am not going to tell you, okay? So don't ask again."

He seems to accept this for the time being. "The door was unlocked when you got there?"

"Yeah. I think he picked the lock."

"And what time did he, um, enter?"

"Sometime between six and six thirty this morning."

"I was already in New Urbana," he says to himself.

"Don't start that," I say.

"What?"

"When Pop died I came up with a dozen things I could, would, or should have done to stop it from happening. I turned it around in my head so much, I made it my fault. Stupid things like if I had packed him an apple, he wouldn't have stopped at that mini-mart. Or if I hadn't needed all of that Justice crap he would have gotten a safer job. And then I ended up on a bridge." I reach across and touch his hand. "Listen to me. There is nothing you could have done. They didn't die because you went on a business trip. They didn't die because you forgot to tell them you loved them before you left. They died because a psychopath killed them. Nothing more. Making it your fault and torturing yourself will do nothing to change that fact. It'll just make you crazy. I'm speaking from experience."

"But—"

"Listen to the words coming out of my mouth like you have never listened to anything before. This…is not—your—fault." It's mine.

He pulls his hand away. "I think I need to be alone now."

"That's the last thing you need."

"Joanna, you need to leave me alone." He looks up at me, eyes like ice. "Right now."

If anyone else had spoken or looked at me like that, I'd pull my gun just to be safe. "Fine." I stand and walk to the door. "I'll be in the kitchen if you need me."

I'd take it personally, but I know how he feels. I didn't want anyone within a hundred feet of me when Pop died. All those people looking at me, coddling me, it drove me nuts. I screamed at Aunt Emily when she tried to hug me. I locked myself in my room for a whole day after that. Isolation didn't make things better, but it didn't make things worse. At least I didn't have to keep up a strong front.

I make it down the hallway when Dobbs comes up to me. "Miss Joanna, the police are at the front gate."

"Already? Crap." I sigh. He's in no shape to answer invasive questions. "Okay, let them in and show them to the parlor. I'll be there in a minute." Dobbs begins walking to the front door, and I go back the way I came. So much for alone time. When I get back to the living room, Justin's gone. He's not out on the patio either. I even check the stairs down to the beach, but he's nowhere to be found. How the hell did he get past me? I rush back inside into the parlor where Harry and Cam wait. I smile graciously as I enter. "Hello."

"Would you gentlemen like something to drink? We have fresh coffee," Dobbs says.

"We're fine, thank you," Harry says.

Dobbs nods, and then turns to leave. I stop him and whisper, "I can't find Justin. Can you locate him? Have him come in here?"

"Yes, Miss Joanna," he whispers back before walking out.

"Sure you don't want anything to drink? Eat?" I ask.

"No," Cam says. "How are you doing?"

I sit on the loveseat, and they sit across me on the couch. It's kind of strange not being on the same side as them. Usually I'm the one on the couch next to my partner ready to grill a witness. But not today. Right now my one and only loyalty is to Justin, and I'll do whatever I can to protect him. "I'm exhausted. It's been a long, God awful twenty-four hours." I glance at Harry whose mouth twitches.

"How's he doing?" Cam asks.

"He's in shock. The press outside doesn't help matters."

"I already called it in," Harry says. "There'll be another patrol car around to corral them."

"Thanks." We all sit in uncomfortable silence. That's never happened before. Usually, we're a well-oiled machine finishing each other's thoughts. I'm the host, so it's my job to make everyone comfortable. "So, have you been making progress?"

"Neighborhood canvas came up with nothing," Cam says. "Neighbors saw no one, heard nothing."

"Have they determined a definitive time of death?"

"Between six and seven this morning," Harry says.

"CSI find anything of use?"

"His fingerprints were all over. DNA will be back tomorrow," Cam says. "When we catch him we'll have more than enough to charge him."

"What about the security footage from the hotel last night? Has anyone started reviewing it? Interviewing the security detail?"

"We're still processing the crime scene. The hotel's sending it over," Harry says.

"I've been playing those seconds over and over in my head. It was him. I have no doubt now."

"Doubt about what?" Justin asks behind me.

The three of us stand as he walks in. Cam and Harry put on their professional, sympathetic expressions that I see every day. "Hello, Mr. Pendergast," Harry says, holding out his hand. "I don't know if you remember me, I'm—"

"Lt. Harold O'Hara," Justin says, shaking his hand. "We met at the policeman's charity ball two years ago." Justin shakes Cam's hand. "Det. Cameron."

"Mr. Pendergast."

We sit on our opposite couches. Us versus them. Harry clears his throat. "Um, Joanna, I think it would be best if we questioned Mr. Pendergast alone."

"I'd like her to stay," Justin says before I can protest. "If you don't mind."

Harry's mouth twitches, but quickly becomes a small smile. "Fine," Harry says. "Mr. Pendergast, let me just first say how sorry we are for your loss. We'll try and make this as quick as possible."

"I appreciate that."

He pauses. "When did you last see Dr. Thornton?" Harry asks.

"Around midnight last night. The limo dropped her and her mother off, and then drove me back here. My plane took off an hour and a half later."

"Did you notice anyone following you last night?" Cam asks.

"No, but I wasn't looking. Have you spoken to Kim Liu? She's, I'm sorry, *was* Daisy's nanny. She was watching Daisy last night."

"We have. She didn't notice anything out of the ordinary in the past week," Cam says.

"Did Dr. Thornton or her mother mention any strange people or cars hanging around? Any hang-up phone calls?" Harry asks.

"No. Nothing." Justin turns to me. "What about you?"

"No. Sorry," I say.

"Did Dr. Thornton and her daughter spend the majority of their nights at their home?" Cam asks.

"Yes, but I would normally stop by after work and spend the night. It was easier for Daisy that way."

"How many nights a week, on average, would you spend there?" Harry asks.

"Three to five, and usually once a week they would stay here. It depended on Rebecca's work schedule."

"So typically you would be with them," Harry says. "Who knew you would be out of town?"

"My immediate staff, and I told a few friends last night. But anyone could call and get my schedule if they wanted to make an appointment to see me."

"This was a planned trip?" Cam asks.

"No. The arrangements were made yesterday, mid-morning. I was supposed to be gone until tomorrow evening."

"Would it be possible to get a list of all the people who knew about this trip? The people you told at the party last night too?" Cam asks.

"Of course."

"Now, about last night," Harry says, "did you see anything odd? A person or persons hanging around you for most of the night?"

"No. Why?"

Cam glances at me, but I keep my poker face. "We have reason to believe that Alkaline was at your party last night."

"What?"

"An eyewitness believes she saw Alkaline there last night," Cam says.

"What?" Justin asks, flabbergasted. "Why the hell didn't she report it?"

"She wasn't sure it was him at the time," Cam says.

Harry decides to save me. "I'm sorry, we have to ask. Can you verify your whereabouts this morning between six and seven?"

My eyes narrow. "Is that really necessary?"

"It's okay, Jo." He nods at the men. "My assistant Shannon and I were in New Urbana. My pilot and colleagues were with me at the time. Shannon can give you their contact information."

"Did Dr. Thornton have any enemies? I understand her ex-husband is in prison," Cam says.

"He didn't know where they were living, and he certainly had no contact with Alkaline."

"What about you?" Harry asks. "Is there any reason why James Ryder would want to hurt you?"

For the first time Justin looks away, the strong façade momentarily crumbling. I'm surprised it took this long. I jump in. "His only connection to that monster is through Grace Pickering and me. That's it. Right, Justin?"

"Yes." He recovers, meeting Harry's eyes again. "I've never met or had dealings with the man. I have no idea why he'd target Rebecca or me."

"Just to err on the side of caution, I'm going to have a patrol car parked out front and another to escort you and your," Harry glances at me, adjusting his glasses nervously, "um, loved ones when you leave. I'd also recommend hiring private security. Just a precaution."

"Is there reason for concern?" Justin asks.

Harry and Cam glance at me, but I narrow my eyes to warn them off. Harry clears his throat. "As I said, just a precaution."

"Lieutenant, why do I get the feeling that there is a lot you are not telling me?"

"Mr. Pendergast—"

"Lt. O'Hara, I am friends with both the mayor and commissioner. Do not make me go over your head."

I touch his hand. "Justin…"

Harry sighs, and I yank my hand away. "Mr. Pendergast," Harry says, but I shoot him a pleading look, "I, um…"

"At the crime scene," Cam interjects, "there was a threat. Alkaline left a burnt picture of Jo tacked onto the front door."

Justin's gaze whips to me. "What? Why the hell didn't you tell me?"

I glare at the defiant Cam before turning to Justin. "I didn't want you to worry about me. We don't know it's a threat. It could just be a ploy to get us all worked up, make mistakes." Or it's a message. To me.

"Bullshit, Jo!" Justin says. "You lied to me! That's why the cruiser was following us."

"We're worried about everyone's safety, Mr. Pendergast," Harry says. "That's why I suggest you hire additional security for yourself, your aunt, and…Joanna."

"That's it? Security? Two police cruisers? Why isn't she in protective custody? Don't you people take care of your own?"

"We offered, she declined, Mr. Pendergast," Harry says with a hard edge.

"You're her commanding officer. Order her to!"

"Nobody makes Jo do anything she doesn't want to. You should know that better than any of us, Mr. Pendergast," Harry says.

Justin glares at Harry, who glares back. "She also doesn't have a death wish," Justin says. He remembers that I'm in the room, and the glare gets focused on me. "I'm sending you and Lucy to the house in Paris until he's captured."

"I'm not—"

"I think that's an excellent idea," Harry says.

"Excuse me!" I shout. "Stop deciding my life for me without my input. Justin, you and Lucy should go to Paris, no question. I'm not running. I am not giving him that satisfaction."

"It wasn't my face burnt off a picture, Jo," Justin counters.

"And I've had combat training. I spend three hours a week at the shooting range. I am a police officer. You aren't."

"You're going to use yourself as bait, aren't you?"

"If I have to."

Justin leaps up. "You're so fucking stubborn sometimes, you know that?" He storms out, probably before he can smack me. I always have that effect on people.

"Justin!" I say as I follow him out.

He's pacing the hall, running both hands through his blonde hair. He comes out of his own head when I step in. "You're a fucking idiot, you know that?"

"I've been told."

"Jo, in twenty years I've never asked you for anything. Not a damn thing. But I am asking this. I'm *begging* this. Please go. I just lost the love of my life. I couldn't survive losing you."

"I'll go if you go."

"I...I can't. I have a business. I have to plan my fiancée's funeral. I can't go."

I knew he wouldn't agree. Neither of us has ever backed down from anything. "Then neither can I. I am not running away. And I am sure as hell not leaving everyone I care about unprotected in this city. If something happened, I would never forgive myself. *Ever*. I won't risk that."

Justin sighs angrily, and turns away from me. "There is nothing I can say or do to change your mind, is there?"

"No. Sorry."

He doesn't talk for a few seconds, but judging from his tense shoulders he is not happy. They slump and he hangs his head. "I'm so tired, Jo. I don't...I don't have any fight left in me. Do whatever you want," he says walking away.

"Where are you going?" I call.

"I haven't slept in over thirty-six hours. I'm calling Pelham Security to get round-the-clock guards for us and your family, and then I'm taking a sleeping pill and passing out for as long as I can so I can start planning a triple funeral. Okay?"

I rankle at this one. "Fine," I say, not meaning it. "I'll be here if you need me."

"I know." He slowly walks down the hall like a man on his way to the execution chamber. I shake my head, rolling my eyes. He's never spoken to me like that. I know it's the grief and anger, but it still hurts. I don't do hurt well.

Cam and Harry remain seated but stand when I come in. "You just couldn't keep your fucking mouth shut, could you?" I ask, not hiding my fury.

"He has a right to know, Jo," Cam says.

"Is he coming back?" Harry asks all business. "We have more questions."

"Well, they'll just have to wait, won't they?"

Harry looks into my eyes, challenging me, but I'm never one to back down. It only lasts a few seconds before he looks away. "Fine. Then I guess we have everything we need here. When Mr. Pendergast is up to it, have him call us."

They move toward the door, Cam squeezing my shoulder as he passes. Harry refuses to look at me. Knife to the heart. When they step out, I hug myself and pace around the room like a mad woman. God, I've ruined everything. Everything. I've hurt everyone I care about. Too much. This is too much. I can't...I see something pink in the corner behind the grand piano. I kneel down and reach for it. It's a fluffy pink bunny with a white nose. Daisy loved this thing. She carried it around in the crook of her small arm and chattered away to it like it was an old friend. She must have left it the last time she was here. She would have been devastated without him. Scared without her security blanket. I'm suddenly sick to my stomach and throw Fluffy Bunny back where I found it. I have to get out of here. I can't stay in this house.

I catch up to the men outside just as they're about to pull out. Cam rolls down his window as the press goes nuts. "Wait. I'm coming with you," I say as I jump into the backseat.

"I don't think that's a good idea," Harry says.

"You guys keep harping on my safety. Where's safer than a police station?" Harry opens his mouth to protest, but I talk before he can. "Look, I'm sorry for what I said back there. I know you were just looking out for me, but I can't stay here. I'll go nuts. I know I'm not on the case, but I can help in other ways. I'll man the tip line. I'll fetch you coffee, whatever. I just need to keep busy. Be productive. Please."

"She does need to fill out her report as first responder," Cam says.

"Don't you want to stay with your friend?" Harry asks, emotionless.

"Yeah, but he doesn't want me around right now. Harry, *please?*"

He turns back around and sighs. I wait in anticipation for a second before he says, "Fine."

"Thank you."

If I can't stand my first home, then there's always my second.

**

The squad room is usually quiet on weekends. There's the odd spousal murder, but regular homicide usually handles those, not Priority Homicide. Today, we're not so lucky. Phones ring off the hook. Officers race in and out with eyewitnesses and staff from the party last night. I even recognize a few employees of Pendergast, taken away from their restful weekends to be grilled because they knew Justin would be out of town. A harried Shannon has been in and out twice. The poor woman isn't paid enough to juggle the police and the entire Pendergast Industries. There is a big Christmas bonus in her future.

Me, I spent the first half an hour on my incident report, an hour calming down Uncle Ray, Aunt Emily, and Veronica after burly men with guns showed up at their doors and wouldn't go away, and then another hour reviewing security footage from the party last night. I've started with the entrance to the ballroom where the invitations were checked. Shannon, on her last trip here, brought me a guest list, so if I recognize a person on the tape, I check their name off. Those who got invitations but didn't show might have given theirs to Ryder. Straw grasping I know, but at this point it's all I have.

Mirabelle walks in with a cup of coffee for me. People keep bringing me things. Kowalski brought me two donuts. Cam's wife Tawny came with a hug and cookies. Everyone's being so nice it's starting to freak me out. "How's it going?" Mirabelle asks. "Any luck?"

"No. How about you guys?"

"Bubkus, and Harry's getting reamed a new one by the mayor and commish."

"That's constructive." I turn back to the screen. "My shadows still out there?"

I was here about an hour when two hulking men in dark suits and guns arrived. Justin sent bodyguards to the station. They flanked me at my desk. They followed me into the bathroom, checking the stalls before they'd let me alone. Now, they're at the door like gargoyles. "They made me show my badge before I could come in. They're hardcore."

"Yeah, I feel safer already." On the screen Tasha Stone and her girlfriend Melina stroll into the party.

"Do you really think he's going to…you know…"

"Melt me like cheese? Hell if I know." Liz Theron and Byron Blake. When did they start dating?

"Are you scared?"

"I'm not an idiot, Mirabelle. I'm scared shitless."

He pats my shoulder. "I'm sorry about your friend. If you need anything…"

I squeeze his hand and he smiles down at me. "Thanks. Appreciate it."

"We'll catch him." He's the ninth person to say that to me. He walks out, leaving me to my task. My cell phone buzzes with yet another call that I ignore. There's only one person I want to talk to, and he's asleep according to Lucy. When it stops, I check the number. I don't recognize it. I do have twenty messages. The only one I plan to return is Grace's. She—

Wait. On the screen, a dark haired man the right height and weight walks up to the guards behind Rose and Leo Giffin. As the couple bicker per usual, the man looks up at the camera. My heart clenches in my chest. It's him. The footage is grainy, but I know it's him. Especially after the huge grin forms on his face and he waves at the camera. The same wave he gave me the night on the bridge. The Giffins walk in and Ryder lowers his head again, handing an invitation to the guard before stepping into the ballroom. "Motherfucker."

I back-up the DVD and watch it again. After making note of the timestamp, I switch over to the hotel lobby footage five minutes prior to his arrival. Sure enough the same man strides into the lobby from the elevators, under the rope, and toward the ballroom right behind the Giffins. Almost vibrating with excitement, I eject the DVD and rush out of the media room.

My guards, Geoff and Bryan, follow me into the bullpen, scanning the area for potential threats. I give it two more hours before they drive me batshit crazy. Harry's door is closed and the blinds are drawn, so I knock. That isn't to say I wait for an invitation.

Harry is behind his desk looking exhausted while Mayor Miracle, Commissioner Craven, and U.S. Marshal Frank Napier wear angry faces. The Marshals have jurisdiction over escaped convicts, but since Justice works for them, they waited until last night to try and kick us off the case. The murders changed things, so we're now part of a unified Federal task force since the department knows the area and the players. The men's expressions switch into neutral when I step in. "Sorry to disturb you," I say.

"Det. Fallon," Commissioner Craven says as he stands. He's a thin man with thick gray hair, bushy eyebrows, and a scar down his left cheek from his legendary fight with Supernatural twenty years ago. "I'm sorry for your loss."

"As am I," Miracle says. "Terrible tragedy."

"How are you doing?" Craven asks.

If one more person asks me this, I'm going to scream. "Fine. Shook up, but fine."

"And Justin?" Miracle asks.

"Devastated."

"Well, will you please tell him that the whole of the force and Marshal Service is doing everything in their power to find Alkaline," the mayor says. That line must have come straight out of the press release.

"I may have found something to help you do that, sirs." I hand the DVD to Napier. "Ryder was at the engagement party last night. He arrived at 8:12 with an invitation in hand."

"Alkaline was at the party last night?" Miracle asks, stunned.

"He probably walked right past us both ten times last night," I say.

The mayor gulps. "I didn't see him."

"It gets better. He was staying at the hotel. There's footage of him getting off the hotel elevators." The men perk up. A lead. "Though he seemed to know we'd review the footage, so I doubt he's still there."

"We can cross check the names of guests who checked out last night or today to Ryder's known aliases," Napier says.

"We already gave that list to every hotel in the city," Harry says. "He must be using another name."

"He smiled at the camera. He wanted us to know he was there," I say. "We would have found out eventually."

"Five other guests have come forward," Harry says, "to say they saw him, but didn't believe it was him either."

A tiny weight lifts off my shoulders. I'm not the only one who screwed up. "I didn't see him," the mayor says again.

"Why risk it?" Napier asks.

"Ultimate taunt," I say. "'I was right under your noses. I drank the same champagne as the detective on my case and the mayor, and I got away.'"

"Let's just hope his narcissism is his downfall," Craven says. "Our people are already at the hotel interviewing staff from last night. I'll have them get the list and pull the security tapes since Alkaline escaped. See if he met with anyone."

Napier holds up the DVD. "I'll get this over to our lab for enhancement."

"I haven't finished going through it. I don't know what time he left."

"We'll take care of it," Napier says. He stands up and walks out with the stunned mayor behind him. Probably cycling through the excuses to use when the news breaks.

Craven smiles down at me. "Good work, Detective."

"I was just doing what Lt. O'Hara told me to."

"Then good work to you both. Let me know if you need anything else."

"Thank you, sir," I say.

Craven nods at Harry. "O'Hara."

"Commissioner." Craven walks out, closing the door behind himself. Harry sits back with a sigh. "Thank you."

"For what?"

"Coming when you did. I think I was about five seconds from being demoted to parking enforcement. I have the distinct feeling I'm being prepared as the department scapegoat for this mess."

"Sorry."

"There's a psychopath killing children out there. The city's in an uproar and terrified, but all they're worried about is looking bad at a press conference." Harry sighs. "Politics."

"If things get too bad you can tie me to the sacrificial altar. I am the one who let him walk right past me twice."

"Well, you aren't the only one. Half the city was there last night, including our vigilant mayor. No, your involvement is being kept on the Q.T. Strict orders from Craven."

"Why?"

He looks away. "Didn't ask." Liar. "They also don't want you anywhere near the case anymore. They're right. We can't give Ryder's future lawyer any ammunition for impropriety. Craven had to use every inch of his clout to keep us involved at all. So, as of right now, you're on paid vacation. I shouldn't have let you come in the first place."

"For how long?"

"Until Craven says so. I tried to get you temporarily transferred to another squad, but he wouldn't go for it. You're too high-profile right now, and your guards don't help matters."

"So, I'm being punished for my friend getting killed?"

"Jo, you have a target on your back. What the hell do you expect us to do?" I have no idea. If I was in his position, I'd do the same thing. "I'm sorry. Look, we'll re-evaluate in a week, okay?"

"Fine," I say quietly.

He rises from the chair. "I have to go back to the scene. I'll drive you to the mansion, okay? Police escort so your friend doesn't kill me." We both know that's not the real reason, but I hold my tongue. Even after all the horrible things I said, he's still worried about me. It makes me want to cry. "Mirabelle," he says as we walk out, "I'm dropping Jo off and heading to the scene. You're in charge until Cam returns."

Geoff rides in the backseat of Harry's sedan with Bryan following close behind in their black BMW. Nobody talks except when Harry asks if I'd like to swing by my apartment to pick up a few things. I hadn't even thought of that. I just have the clothes on my back. Some reporters lie in wait, and for the first time I'm glad for the guards. They push them aside like gnats. This gratitude lasts all of a minute. With guns drawn, Bryan checks my apartment for bogies before Geoff lets me go in. Lets me. *Into my own fucking apartment.* The coil inside me tightens almost to the breaking point.

"Can you guys wait outside while I get ready?" I ask.

"We're not supposed to—"

"I don't want you in here!" I shout.

Harry touches my back. "Guys, wait out here. We'll only be a few minutes."

Him they listen to. They even let him shut the door without protest as I walk into my bedroom. Had I known I would have company I would have cleaned up at least the bra and panties on the floor. For some reason my hands shake as I pick up the strewn clothes from last night. That feels like a decade ago. Harry waits in the doorway, just watching me. "Those guys are driving me batshit already."

"They're just doing their jobs, and they seem good at it."

"I feel like a fucking convict. I can't even go to the bathroom without clearing it with them." I toss the clothes I wore last night back down on the floor in frustration. "Fuck these! I'm burning them." I go into the closet and grab a suitcase.

"Jo," Harry says, stepping in.

I start tossing random clothes in the suitcase. "Oh, I forgot to tell you. I got your message. Finally. Guess right now you're damn glad you didn't go."

"That doesn't matter now."

"Of course it matters!" I say, my voice breaking a little. "I said horrible, *horrible* things to you. Even if you did decide not to go to a stupid party with me, you didn't deserve that. And I should have known better. I should have known you'd never do that to me."

"Jo…" he says, getting closer.

I keep packing. "I should have trusted you. I…" I chuckle. "I let my own fuckedupness cloud my judgment, and I ruined everything. *Everything.*" Tears start streaming down my face and I can't stop them. I go to the dresser and practically rip the drawer out. "Always have, always will. With you, with Justin, with…" The image of them lying there flashes into my mind. Senseless. This is all so senseless. One fell swoop and all the hopes and dreams for so many were destroyed. Because of me. I gasp and burst into tears so hard I double over. "Oh, God!"

Harry doesn't let me fall. He takes me into his arms, holding me tight. I clutch onto him for dear life, sobbing into his shoulder as he strokes my hair. "Shush, baby," he whispers. "It's okay. It'll all be okay."

"He…they…"

"I know," he says soothingly as he strokes. "It's not your fault. I *swear* it's not your fault."

"I'm sorry," I say to anyone or anything that might be listening. "I'm *so* sorry."

He kisses my hair. "Baby."

He is so warm. Familiar. Old Spice. I love that smell. It's comforting. *He's* comforting. Always has been. I lift my head, my lips meeting his in an almost chaste kiss. That spark ignites a firestorm. The tears subside as we literally rip each other's clothes off. He pins me to the bed, kissing me into depths I didn't know I had. I'm not ready for him but he doesn't give a damn. He pushes inside me so hard he reaches the end of me, punishing me for my sins against him. I cry out in pain but meet him with each thrust. All that pain, all that anger morphs into all consuming passion. For a few mind-blowing minutes everything but the need vanishes. Agony and ecstasy in perfect balance. It feels so good. So *right.* Even if I've lost him, at least I have this.

We lay on my bed unable to move for a minute afterward. Tiny pinpricks of blood rise on his back from where I mauled him. I'm not unscathed either. I'm already sore inside, stretched and torn, but find the pain welcoming. "Did I hurt you?" he asks breathlessly.

"Nothing I can't handle." I gulp. "Did I hurt *you*?"

He looks into my eyes, concern falling into sadness. "Yes," he says after a pause.

We let that word hang between us like a millstone. He might as well have plunged an icicle into my heart. I didn't think it possible, but I hate myself even more. I've lost him. He sits up then slides off the bed, collecting his clothes from the floor. More tears threaten stream out, but I push them back. If I start again, I'll never stop. Never.

* * *

The mansion is quiet when I return. Harry doesn't walk me to the door and mutters, "Call me if you need anything," as I get out. We couldn't even look at each other since the bedroom. First time things have been awkward between us. I hate it more than anything, and that's saying something. Geoff the guard carries my suitcase inside, but Bryan joins the third guard in walking the grounds. Harry drives away, off to try and save the woman who broke his heart.

Dobbs greets us, looking as exhausted as me. Despite this he smiles as he says, "Welcome home, Miss Joanna."

"Hi, Dobbs."

He takes the suitcase from Geoff. "I'll take this upstairs to the blue bedroom."

"Thanks. Is Justin up?"

"No, and Miss Lucy has retired as well. She was not feeling well."

"Why don't you go to bed too? I have a feeling we'll be very busy tomorrow."

"Thank you. I will." Dobbs glances at Geoff. "We've left out food for you and your men."

"Thank you," Geoff says in his baritone voice.

Dobbs nods, then starts up the stairs, leaving me with my jailer. I'm in a fancy prison, but a prison none the less. "Look, I'm completely safe now," I say to Geoff. "This place is a fortress. I'm going to the living room, and I'm going alone, okay? Don't follow me." I'm shocked when he actually listens. Like the rest of the house, it's as quiet as a crypt in the living room. My first impulse is to race over to the bar and down a whiskey bottle. I actually have to stop myself walking midstride toward it. God, I want a drink. It takes all my strength not to make those last few steps.

Instead, I plop down on the couch with a sigh. I turn on the TV, finding the news. The story's gone national. Top story on BNN and every other news outlet. Some woman interviews Bitsy, who tearfully recounts last night's party and Justin's tragic love story. There are a few more testimonials from Rebecca's co-workers and friends from Independence. As people talk pictures from last night and today are intersliced, including the rolling out of the bodies. Tasteful.

I flip to MSCBC where the mayor, commissioner, and Marshal Napier stand in front of the city hall answering questions. Napier does most of the talking, saying the same crap the other two promised a week ago. Terrible tragedy. Doing all we can. We'll catch him. Being on the other side of things, the victim's side, is odd. Listening to them talk with self-serving platitudes and empty promises makes me want to spit in their faces. They don't really give a damn. They just don't want to look bad in front of their constituents. I change the channel.

We even made Jury-TV. They're replaying Ryder's trial. One of his henchmen, now in the witness protection program, recounts the plot to hijack a boat with a deadly virus on it. Ryder sits next to his thousand-dollar-an-hour attorney staring impassively at the man on the stand. A flash of the moment he passed me last night pops into my head. Both of them. My opportunities to get him, and I blew them. Doubt I'll get another unless he crawls out of his hole to take a shot at me or someone I love. I need to—

Through the glass doors I see a man appear out on the patio. My heart stops as I leap up and grab for where my sidearm usually is. The terror subsides a moment later when my brain connects to my instincts. Justice stands on the porch looking directly at me. "Superb."

As I open the patio door, Bryan and a third guard come running from both sides of the house, guns up and pointed at the superhero. "Freeze!" the other guard shouts. Geoff barrels into the living room with his gun out too. I suddenly feel underdressed for this meeting.

"I'd put those down, guys," I say as I step out. "I'm pretty sure he can take you."

The men lower their weapons. "Sorry, sir," Bryan says. "We didn't know it was you."

"It's fine, gentlemen," Justice says, lowering his hands. "Good response time, but I'd post someone back here at the staircase down to the beach. If I made it undetected, so could Alkaline."

"Yes, sir," Geoff says.

All the men holster their guns and return to their posts, leaving us alone. "I'm sorry for startling you," Justice says.

"It's okay. I'm a bit jumpy tonight."

He nods. "That's to be expected after your ordeal. I just came by to check on you and Mr. Pendergast and to offer my condolences."

"Thanks. He's, uh, asleep right now, but I'll tell him you stopped by," I say as I step toward the house.

"I was also hoping to ask you a few questions," he says, stopping me. I turn back around. "If you don't mind."

"I'm sure you've read my statement." He has some supercomputer that's linked to every law enforcement database and all the CCTVs in the city. "It's all in there."

"I just have a few follow-up questions."

I shrug. "I'm a captive audience. Not supposed to leave unless I'm in a tank with the National Guard around me. Fire away."

"I understand you're frustrated, but the precautions are for your safety. You should not try to find a way around them."

"If he wants me, he's gonna get me. The more people around me, the more collateral damage. Maybe I should just let him get me. Be bait."

"No," he says forcefully. "We will find a way of capturing him without putting you in harm's way. That will *never* be an option. If I hear you have attempted that foolhardy plan, I will kidnap you myself and *really* lock you away. Do you understand me, Det. Fallon? I will not stand for it."

I have no idea what to say. He actually sounds concerned and scared. For me. My heart warms a little. Not that I'll let him know that. "Fine, I won't. Ask your questions."

After we sit, I walk him through the party last night, through finding the bodies and all that we've uncovered today. He knew most of it, and even clued me in to some new facts. Like Ryder checked into the hotel the night of the escape under the name "Joe Fallon." He had a credit card and driver's license in that name. The bastard might as well have just spit in my face.

It was booked a week before he checked in, and checked out at 5:37 this morning.

"Fat lot of good that does us," I say.

"I already have my system working through the security footage for the past week. It can pinpoint him and see if he met with any accomplices."

"If you need me to run down anyone, my schedule is cleared indefinitely."

"I'm sorry this has caused your life such an upheaval."

"Yeah, well it frees me up to be your Girl Friday. I mean, if you don't already have one. Do you have one?"

"I work alone, and it will stay that way." He stands up. "Thank you for all your help."

I leap up. "Wait. You're not leaving already, are you? I can help you. I *need* to help you, okay? I can't just sit in this cold museum waiting, doing nothing. I'll go nuts."

"Your friend needs you far more than I do. What you need to do is stay here and help him through this. Be his strength. Leave the rest to me."

"He's angry at me and doesn't want me to help."

"He'll get over it. No one can stay mad at you for too long."

"You talk about me like you know me," I say with a scoff.

"If I'm not mistaken, I've known you for ten years," he says without sarcasm. "And he does need you, by his side. Just be there when he's ready. He may push you away, scream at you, but never take it to heart and never give up on him. Not that I think you ever would."

I stare at him, really wishing I could see his face. I can never get a read on him. "I don't get you. For years I've been a total bitch to you. Now you're complimenting me, even sending me presents. Why? You're not...you know..." His head cocks to the side. Ugh. He's going to make me say it. "I'm not going to sleep with you. *Ever.*"

"What? No," he says, sounding offended. "I don't think of you in that light, Det. Fallon. At all." I do a double take at his vehemence. "I mean, you are aesthetically pleasing, I realize that, but—"

"Just forget I said anything," I say, now mortified on top of everything else.

"Don't be embarrassed," he says, "it's a perfectly natural thought. I have momentarily entertained the notion, but your attitude toward me quickly dispelled it. No, I just…admire you. You're tenacious, brave, and brilliant. This city, but especially your friend in there, needs you. And you need him too. You lost a friend today as well."

A sarcastic laugh escapes before I can stop it. "I guess."

"What does that mean?"

I shake my head. "It means I was a two-faced bitch who only pretended to be her friend when in reality I wanted to push her off a cliff a lot of the time."

"Really? Why?"

"Nothing she did. It wasn't her fault. She was nice. Kind, funny, smart, just perfect. I would have liked her if I let myself. There was just one thing I could never get past about her."

"What?"

I look up at the superhero and smile sadly. "That he loved her, not me."

Justice's shoulders slump. "Who? Your…friend, Mr. Pendergast?"

"Worst kept secret in Galilee. I'm surprised you never heard."

"No, I didn't." He pauses, clearing his throat. "How long have you harbored these feelings?"

I scoff. "Forever." I sit back down, suddenly tired. "From the moment he opened his mouth twenty years ago, my heart belonged to him." I shrug. "But he didn't want it. Probably never will." I bite my lower lip. "Then she came. She was everything I wasn't: sweet, charming, gorgeous. And he wanted *her*. So I hated her. Him a little, too. But they got their comeuppance, huh? Ha fucking ha," I say sarcastically as my voice breaks. "Sure showed them."

Justice sits across from me. "Wishing a person dead does not make it happen, Joanna. You know that."

"I brought a monster with a grudge into their lives. I let him walk past me. Twice." I run my hands through my hair. "I was so pissed at him I let my anger cloud my judgment. I bruised his ego. Dared him to come out. I knew what he was, what he was capable of, but I did it anyway to prove what a badass I am. You have the right idea, hiding behind that mask. You know, going after me I understand. I poked a rabid dog with a stick, he should bite me. But going after an officer's friends and family is something you just don't do. You don't. He did."

"There was no way you could have known," he says after a long pause.

"They wouldn't even be on his radar if it wasn't for me. Everything, everyone I touch, I damage. My dad, my mom, Har—" I stop myself. I take a moment to collect myself. "Justin saved my life, you know. Now I'm the cause of the rape and murder of the love of his life and future daughter. He'll wish he had let me jump. He'd be right to."

"Never think that. *Never*," Justice says vehemently. He leans across the table, reaching for my face. He lifts my chin up to where his hidden eyes are. "Listen to the words coming out of my mouth like you have never listened to anything before. This is not your fault. This is in no way, shape, or form your fault. He did not target them because you called her your friend, your sister. He didn't target them because you didn't like her for whatever reason." He pauses before saying, "He didn't do this because you're a horrible person who deserves misery. He did this…" he says, voice quaking, "He did this…"

He can't finish the sentence. He falls back into his seat, and looks away as if I can see underneath the mask. I'll bet this is the closest he's let another person glean what's behind it in a long time. I guess sometimes we all forget that under the costume and powers there's a human being in there. He pays his bills, he washes his clothes, and maybe he cries in the shower so no one can hear him just like me. We're not so different, him and I.

"This isn't your fault either," I say. "You're only one man. You can't be everywhere. You can't know everything. You caught him once. You're the one who got him off the streets for three years when no one else could. We need you now. We need you strong. Fierce. We need our hero."

As those words pop out, I realize I mean them. I've resented him for an event that wasn't his fault for decades. He's not God. He wasn't there that night to punish me. He's as fallible as the rest of us. A pang of regret hits me. All these years working together with my old idol and I've squandered it. I could have learned from him. We could have helped each other more. All for nothing.

For a moment he looks at me. *Really* looks at me. I'm uncomfortable, but don't let it show. "And here I thought you hated me," he says.

"I don't hate you. You've pissed me off sometimes. Made me feel inept. Obsolete. And…you let me down once, but that wasn't your fault." I take a deep breath and say it because it's true. "I just, I—I feel better knowing you're on my side."

"I feel the same way about you, Detective." He pauses again. "I'm so sorry you were dragged into this. I'm sorry it's affected you so. I will do everything in my power to keep you safe. To find him. I give you my word, and I never give it lightly. I will not let him harm you," he says with utter conviction. "I *swear* it."

Listening to those words with his severity, it hits me. There's really a madman who wants me dead. He's going to try to rape and burn me alive with acid. I'm a police officer, I know every day on the job I take my life into my hands. It could happen at any time. Leaving to interview a person, walking through a door even. I can rationalize it away. Most police barely draw their weapons in a career, let alone get involved in a shoot-out. But this…it's inevitable. I know the man after me. He'll battle his way through an entire legion of superheroes and police to get what he wants. Me. He can't be stopped. He can't be reasoned with. He is pure evil and he is coming for me. At some point in the near future, probably when I'm least prepared for it, I will be fighting for my life. The odds of coming out of it are against me. I'm living on borrowed time. I'm going to die.

I glance at Justice. "He's really coming for me, isn't he?"

The terror must have leaked through to my face because Justice doesn't respond right away. "Not if I get him first." Clearing his throat, he stands up. "Stay in the house as much as you can. Be surrounded by people at all times. Don't go anywhere without the guards, no matter how much you dislike having them around. Keep your eyes open for anything suspicious."

"I will."

"Good. I'll be watching. Be safe."

"But what if I need—" I feel the whoosh of air beside me before I can finish. He's gone.

The curtains inside waft in the breeze, but I shut and lock the door. It does nothing to stop the chills. I rest my head against the cool fabric and glass underneath, clutching onto the thin drapes as I push away the panic and desolation.

"Jo?" Justin asks behind me.

I give myself a second, just a second to rein my emotions in. They whip back into their prison, and I turn around to my friend with a small smile. "Hi."

He's in a white undershirt and pajama bottoms, hair messy from sleep. "Are you okay? I heard voices."

"It was no one," I say, walking toward him. "What about you? Are you alright?"

He shakes his head slowly. "No. Not at all. I could use a hug."

"I think I can handle that."

He opens his arms to me and I do the same, pulling each other close. I lay my head on his pounding heart and he rests his on the top of my head. For the briefest moments, wrapped in his arms, I feel peace. I hope he does too. Because I'm sure we may never feel that way again.

CHAPTER FOURTEEN
FAULT

The ride to the church takes so long I begin to worry we'll be late. Surely Reverend Matthews won't begin the service without the guests of honor. We can't help that crews are taking forever to clean up after Hexen's latest bid for attention. I heard on the radio they've caught two of the unicorns he summoned on Infantino Avenue.

Three days. It's been three days almost to the hour since I found them. It's flown by, I've been so busy. Lucy handled the funeral plans, Shannon the work-a-day problems and I helped with both, along with fielding the press and a million phone calls from old friends. When I wasn't glued to the phone, and he wasn't asleep, I watched old movies with Justin and played pool. He's been sleeping a lot. Close to sixteen hours a day. Mom did the same thing after Pop. I'll start to worry in a week.

I have found tiny pockets of time for myself, mainly used to aid in the investigation whether anyone liked it or not. It's hard to do when you can't leave the house, but I've managed. The photographer sent me the pictures from the engagement party, and in the hundred shots, I found about six with Alkaline in them. He wasn't speaking to anyone, but in each he was close to me, Justin, or Rebecca. Stalking us. I phoned the others at the party who claimed to have seen him, but like me they only noticed him in passing.

Cam's been feeding me information. He and Mirabelle stopped by for a follow-up interview with Justin and me. As far as I can tell, they've garnered no new information. Three days and nothing. He checked out of the hotel and vanished. No more dead bodies, no more leads, just dead quiet. He's biding his time, waiting like a snake to pop out of a hole and strike. Where better than his victim's funeral?

St. Agatha's Church is the oldest standing building in Galilee. Even the heroes and villains leave it alone. People of all denominations flock here for the sheer beauty of it. Anyone who is anyone in Galilee celebrates their milestones here. Weddings, christenings, and funerals for the elite. It's a beautiful, gray stone building with cathedral ceilings, statues of St. Agatha and the Virgin Mary, and six stained-glass windows each a story high. The ones in the back and front of the church are glittering rose windows with a red cross in the front. The other four are of Archangels Michael, Gabriel, Rafael, and Uriel, all in epic battle. They added those a hundred years ago when Madman, one of the first villains, tried to blow up the church. Lightening, the protector of the city at the time, managed to stop him, but the church was in tatters. It's been neutral ground since. Hope Alkaline remembers that.

Police presence is palpable with patrolmen walking up and down the sidewalk two blocks in either direction. As we move closer, the press outnumbers the mourners and police. They've been pushed over to the other side of the street, held back by barricades. The police have also cordoned off the blocks surrounding the church. Bryan, the guard, pulls up to the barricade and shows the invitation to the patrolwoman. She orders all the windows rolled down and she peeks in. It takes her a second to realize who we are, and she's suitably mortified. "Sorry, ma'am. Sir."

"Just keep up the good work," I say.

We roll up to the front of the church. Justin looks at it and sighs. He was supposed to be walking in here to get married a month from now, not to attend his fiancée and her daughter's funeral. None of us moves. I take Justin's hand, squeezing it. He looks at me, indecision all over his face. "We can stay here as long as you need to," I say.

He takes a deep breath, and then slowly lets it out. "Let's get this over with."

The moment I step out of the car following Geoff and Lucy, it is as if a rock concert erupts. Screaming reporters overrun the usual city sounds. We've become national celebrities. Front page of newspapers across the country. My life has been picked apart and analyzed by every talking head with a microphone. I'm either a strong victim or as a few have hinted at, a possible murderer in league with Alkaline. The popular theory is that he butchered them at my behest so I could have Justin all to myself. Plausible, but only the tabloids were running with that one, and they stopped after Justin's battalion of lawyers went after them. Besides that blip, I'm now considered a tragic hero and Justin is just tragic. And here we are in our designer funeral attire looking very melancholy and beautiful surrounded by police in case a mass murderer tries to melt us. I'm shocked they're staying behind the barricades and not rushing us like groupies.

As quick as we can, the four of us—me, Lucy, Justin, and Dobbs—rush into the church. It can seat three hundred and will today. Lucy just took the wedding guest list and sent out funeral invitations from it. Though instead of pastels the guests are in black and instead of pink and white daisies there are solemn lilies and a cornucopia of wreaths from mourners at the front of the church. In the center of the field of flowers there is a recent picture of the Thorntons taken at the beach. Marnie gazing down as Rebecca and Daisy build a sandcastle. I'll bet Justin took the picture. There are no coffins as they were cremated. The remains were delivered this morning and we're keeping them at the mansion until Sam, Rebecca's brother, can fly back from the Middle East to bring them to Lake City. They'll be interred near her father. Makes the most sense, I guess, keeping them all together. Justin didn't object.

People offer their condolences to Justin as we pass, some I know, but the others must be from Independence, Lake City, or the hospital. Scattered around are police in dark suits trying to blend in with the crowd. Mirabelle nods at me, and I do the same back. I wonder if Harry's here. The mayor and commissioner push their way toward us, no doubt to suck up or beg for forgiveness. Either way while Justin is distracted, I worm my way around the group and down the aisle to the less populated front with my shadow a step behind me.

I barely have time to take a breath before Bitsy rushes over to me, her eyes red and swollen. Without a word, she hugs me tight. My bodyguard doesn't stop her, the louse. "Oh, God, I don't know how I'm going to make it through this," she says.

I pull away as politely as possible. "Yeah."

Bitsy dramatically turns to the photo. "They were so beautiful. This is just such a tragedy. I still can't bring myself to tell Preston. He'll be heartbroken. He loved Daisy too." She looks back at me. "We try and shield him from unpleasantness such as this."

"Probably a good idea," I say.

"And how are you? We haven't spoken since...the day."

"I'm fine. I'm coping."

"And Justin? How is he?"

"Holding up well, considering. You should go over. He'd love to see you."

"You think? Okay, then." She squeezes my arm. "If you need anything, please call."

Yeah, right. "Thank you."

She walks away, and I plunk myself in the front pew, already exhausted. A few guests walk up to the altar to examine the flowers or put checks in the donation box just underneath the photo. My kind-hearted friend has spent most of his waking hours organizing the "Dr. Rebecca Thornton Pediatric Recovery Wing" where parents and children will have a mini-apartment to stay in if the child needs long-term care. That way they can all be together and maintain a sense of normalcy. Good thing he's on the hospital board as it cuts through a lot of red tape. There's going to be a gala fundraiser in two weeks if all goes as planned. The cute doctor that Rebecca tried to set me up with, Jem something, puts his check in. He glances at me, smiling awkwardly and blushing, before rushing away. Probably counting his lucky stars we never got past flirting.

"Mind if I sit for a minute?" a woman asks.

I turn and smile at Grace. "Only if you dare. I am a marked woman."

"Welcome to the club." Her sunglasses envelop half her face, a tiny bid for anonymity. They match her black suit with large diamond brooch. "I snuck in through the back. The press hasn't stopped phoning me since Saturday."

"I'm surprised you came. It'll mean a lot to Justin."

"That's the only reason I'm here. I almost told my driver to turn around three times." We sit in silence for a moment as she gazes to the photo. "They were beautiful. All of them. I wish I had met them."

"You would have gotten along."

"It's such a waste, and to die like that." She pauses again. "He didn't…um…with the child, did he?"

"No. He smothered her with a pillow. The other two, he burnt alive."

"How much evil can one man be capable of?" she asks to herself.

"I stopped asking myself that question years ago. Just when you think you know the answer, someone goes and does a thing like this. It makes me want to go and live in a cave."

"I'm surprised you aren't in one right now," Grace says. "I heard he threatened your life. I'd be halfway around the world if I were you."

"Doing what's in my best interest has never been my strong suit." I pause. "You have just as much reason to be afraid today as I do."

She looks down at the floor. "Not really. It would seem James has a new obsession to occupy him now. I don't envy you."

For some reason the word "obsession" grips my attention. "Why do you assume he's obsessed with me?"

Before she can answer, Justin and Lucy approach. Grace and I stand. "Hello, Grace," Justin says, hugging her tiny body. "Thank you so much for coming."

"How could I not? You were so wonderful to me after everything. This is the least I can do. I'm just sorry I never got to meet them. I've heard nothing but lovely sentiments."

"How are you doing?" Justin asks.

"Isn't that my line?" We all smile. "I'm fine, Justin. I am so sorry, though. I know what you're going through. It's complete and utter hell. If you need to talk…"

"Thank you, Grace."

She kisses his cheek, nods at Lucy, and walks off to find a seat. The reverend starts preparing for the sermon at the pulpit so the guests begin sitting, as do we. The bodyguards sit behind us and when I glance back, I spot Harry a few pews behind with Cam next to him. My stomach clenches. I haven't seen or spoken to Harry since Saturday. I've wanted to, and have actually picked up the phone, but just couldn't dial. No idea what to say, I guess. Both he and Cam smile sympathetically and nod. I do the same.

"We are here today," Reverend Matthews begins, "to mourn the passing of three young souls who were ripped from our lives too soon. Marnie, Rebecca, and Daisy Thornton were new to our city, but judging from the sheer number of you here, I can say that they have made their impact, and that we are all better for having had them here."

Reverend Matthews continues on, showcasing their accomplishments mixed with bible verses. Behind me, people sniffle or weep. This is only the third funeral I've ever attended. Mom's was merely a formality. Quick and painless. But Pop's...it was small, only about ten people showed. Uncle Ray and Pop's boss Dominic gave eulogies, but they could barely be heard over Mom's sobs. She hadn't stopped crying since the police came to our door. Four days of her crying and I was in shock. I'm the one who planned it. She couldn't even decide which suit to bury him in. I didn't cry once, not until I was alone in my room that night. Everyone had gone home, Mom was passed out in her bedroom, and I felt completely and utterly alone in every sense of the word. The unfairness of it all was crippling me. A girl shouldn't know the world is a shithole with no chance of it ever improving at age twelve. My heroes were gone, leaving me with nothing but misery on the horizon.

I sat on my bed just looking up at all my Justice crap. Posters, action figures, even a mask like his. Fury and desolation just washed over me. I felt betrayed. I worshiped the man, and the one time I needed him, he didn't show up. I thought he actually *cared* about us. No. Another lie. I couldn't take it anymore. I ripped off, smashed, and then burnt anything with his face on it before running out of that apartment. I hopped on my bike and rode until I couldn't anymore, finally stopping on Pendergast Bridge, willing myself to jump. You can only be strong for so long before you break. I broke.

Like now. I'm sitting here, head up high, stoic, representing their family when I really feel like screaming at the top of my lungs, but I can't even cry. I'm the strong one, forged by fire and ice. Dobbs blots his tears with a tissue, Lucy remains stony, but when I glance at Justin my façade crumbles. He's desperately trying to keep himself together, though his eyes are rimmed with tears and his chin quivers. It literally feels as if someone plunges a knife into my heart. I can't look at him for the rest of the service.

As the eulogizers speak about the deed's multitude of achievements, I scan the pews. More than a few mourners whisper to their friends, eyes on me the whole time. My hands start shaking, and I ball them into fists as I set them in my lap. It takes every ounce of self-restraint not to run out of this church. The guilt is suffocating. I can do this. I *will* do this for him.

Rev. Matthews concludes the service with a prayer about forgiveness, and the moment I can I leap up, excuse myself, and rush toward the door behind the altar. I know there's an empty office. I shut the door, and take several deep breaths. I pace back and forth, wringing my hands to stop the shaking, trying and failing to expel the pent-up energy that's about to explode out of me otherwise. Geoff steps in, but I tell him I need a minute. He listens, but I'm sure stays close. I keep pacing on those wobbly heels, now my whole body shaking while I try to catch my breath. I was doing so well. No tearful breakdowns or drinking binges, and now I'm a second away from a full-blown panic attack.

They all know. All of them in there know. How I feel about him, how I felt about her and God knows what they're all thinking. Who knows how long it will be until he figures it out too? I can't keep this up. The pretending. I almost wish Alkaline would just come in and kill me already. He—

There's a knock on the door. "Jo?" Harry asks on the other side. He steps in, and I stop my crazy person routine. "I saw you run in here. Are you okay?"

"You know, I am *so* sick of people asking me that. 'Am I okay?' No. No, I am not okay. Not in any way am I okay. I am…exhausted. And pissed off. And scared out of my mind. All I want to do is take a few pills and fall into oblivion for a few months, and when I wake up I'll find out this was all a dream. That my friend hasn't shattered into a million pieces, that you don't hate my guts, and that I'm not responsible for either."

"Jo—"

I start pacing again. "Everyone is just being so fucking nice. It's driving me insane." I can feel my blood pressure rising. "They just want to keep hugging me, and saying kind things to me. I can't stand it. I can't. Especially when I know it's all fake. All those people in that room know who I am. What I've done. Then why won't they just fucking say it? Once, just *once* I'd like someone to look me in the eye and say, 'Joanna, this is your fault. You let him slip through your fingers twice. You challenged a cold-blooded murderer, and he just rose to that challenge. We know you didn't mean it, but there it is. Their blood is on your hands.' Just one person, instead of platitudes and—and—and fucking comfort I don't deserve!"

Harry doesn't respond right away. He just keeps looking at the floor as I keep walking. "Okay," he finally says as he takes a step toward me. "Speaking as head of the investigation, the strongest motive for the murders we have found is revenge." I stop pacing. "We have surmised this due to the savagery inflicted on Dr. Thornton, the fact he used your name to check into the hotel where he stalked her, that he most likely summoned you to the prison that night, and the picture left at the scene. No other known connection to the victims has been found, so that leads us to conclude that you are at the center of this. We have examined the lives of the victims and Justin Pendergast, and none have had dealings with James Ryder or any of his known accomplices, and believe me we have looked."

"See? I told you—"

"I'm not done talking, Joanna," he says with another step my way, "so kindly *shut up* and let me finish." He's never spoken to me like that. I'm stunned into silence. "As I was saying, as best we can figure, this was retribution." Suddenly, he takes my arm and pulls my ear toward his mouth. "But that still doesn't make this your fault, Jo," he says quietly. "He didn't do this because you cared for her, which I know you did despite everything you said or did. He didn't do this because you asked for it in anger a few times. And he didn't do this as some divine punishment you feel you deserve. He did this because he's insane, and cruel, and evil. *You* are none of those things. So stop torturing yourself. Stop feeling sorry for yourself. It's wasted energy."

He releases my arm. "And I don't hate you," he continues. "Am I pissed off you didn't trust me? Hell, yes. Am I hurt? Damn straight. But I could never hate you. You try my patience, and you make me nuts sometimes, but you also make me laugh and make me feel good about myself. I like being around you. You're beautiful, and strong, and fiercely loyal. I just don't know why you can't see that. That's why you're in love with a man who can't love you back. You think that's all you deserve—misery and heartache. You've built this damn wall around your heart, and I don't know if I have the strength to bust it down. I don't." He shrugs. "You gotta help me here."

Before I can respond, there's another knock on the door. Without permission, Justin steps in. Harry steps away and composes himself, but I have to take a deep breath and turn my back on the men. "I'm sorry," Justin says, "am I interrupting something?"

"No," I say, struggling to calm down.

Justin steps next to me, trying to read my face. "Are you okay?" I turn away, and his gaze whips back to Harry. "What's going on?"

"Jo, you want to tell him?" Harry asks with an undercurrent of anger.

I open my mouth, but have no clue what to say. Each of them stares at me, waiting for an answer. I don't know where to look. "I, um…we were just talking."

"Were you harassing her?" Justin asks Harry. "I know what people are saying, but she—"

"Justin, we were just talking! Calm down!" I say. "Can we just get the hell out of here, please?" I pull Justin away before he makes things worse. Harry watches with a small scowl as we pass. I can't leave like this. I turn back. "Thank you."

"For what, Jo?" Harry asks, no longer hiding his anger.

"Trying."

I walk away.

***

Only about twenty people are invited back to the mansion for the reception. The mourners stand around with their plates of food and stories. Since I've never been good at gatherings, big or small, even in the best of circumstances, I help Dobbs with the serving and clean-up. Keeping busy has gotten me this far. When I have time to think I'll end up going crazy in a church.

About an hour into the reception, I notice Justin has vanished. The last time I saw him he was talking to one of the eulogizers, but she says he excused himself. I check the whole house, but he's nowhere. Even the guards have lost track of him. There's only one other place he could be.

He sits alone on the beach facing the ocean, barely moving. I tell Geoff to hang back by the stairs and walk over to him. He doesn't turn around, doesn't look at me even when I sit next to him. There are two bottles of Jack Daniels in the sand, one almost empty. In all our time, I've barely seen him finish a glass, let alone a whole bottle.

"Hey," I say.

"Hey." He picks up the bottle and finishes it off, tossing the empty glass into the surf.

"Where's Bryan?"

"I'm the boss. I told him if he followed me down here, I'd fire him. He believed me. You gonna give me shit for it?"

"Considering I got a lecture for making Geoff wait inside instead of outside when I was on the patio," I pause and pretend to think hard about it, "um, yes. Yes, I am." I punch his arm. "What are you thinking?"

"Ow. Don't hit the bereaved. I just…had to get away from everyone and their good intentions."

"Just you and Jack Daniels, huh?"

"*You're* going to lecture me on drinking? How many times have I held your hair while you puked?"

"Countless. And I'm not going to lecture you."

He opens the second bottle. "Good." He takes a swig and holds it out to me. "Want some?"

"No, thanks."

"The woman who drank my entire frat under the table is abstaining?"

"Yep. It makes me…horrible. But as an authority on the subject, I will tell you that if you take one more sip, I will probably have to take you to the hospital for alcohol poisoning where the entire staff will fawn over you and smother you with love. Is that what you really want, lots and lots of love from hot nurses?"

He holds out his arms and touches his nose with each pointer finger. "I can recite the alphabet backwards too, Detective." He picks up the bottle again and drinks. "I'm barely buzzed. Me and my freak metabolism. Can't even drink myself into unconsciousness. I sure as hell am going to try though."

We just sit and watch the ocean crash for a minute while he chugs the whiskey. I can practically feel the anguish coming off his body. It seeps into me like an itch I can never scratch. "Do you remember that summer before you went to college? We tried to learn to surf?"

He smiles after another swig. "Aunt Lucy hired that, I don't know what the hell he was, a stoner, hippie Martian or something. What did he want us to call him?"

"Buddha Moon, but we just called him B.M."

"Right," Justin chuckles, "and before we could go into the ocean we had to thank mother Gaia and father Poseidon for creating the waves we were about to disturb."

"Well, you did something to piss off Poseidon because he kicked your ass. I don't think you ever were upright on that board."

"I guess I'm not a water person."

"Understatement of the damn year." I tick his shoulder with mine.

"What? Like you did much better. At least I didn't laugh my ass off every time you fell like my best friend did."

"I had just never seen you fail at anything. I was so overjoyed to find you were actually human."

"That's up for debate," he mutters as he swigs. We're silent for a few seconds, all the mirth gone again. I wait for him to speak. "I was going to teach Daisy to swim this summer. It was to be my first official act as her step-father. I even read a book on the correct approach."

My heart clenches. "She would have loved that. She adored you."

He shakes his head. "At first, I was so scared around her. What did I know about four-year-old girls? That lasted all of a second. It was like I looked at her and I knew. With both of them, I guess."

"Knew what?"

"That they were for me. That I was supposed to love them. To care for them. To be there for them. That I'd lay down my life for them. Same thing happened when I saw you." He pauses and chokes back a sob. "And I failed. I failed. Oh, fuck!" He leaps up, and then almost falls back down. "I have to get out of here," he says as he stumbles away.

"Justin, where are you going?" I ask as I follow.

The alcohol is working now as he can barely walk. "I—I don't know. Not here. I can't breathe here."

"Okay, but I'm coming with you."

"No! I need to be alone. Why do you even want to? You should stay away from me. I'm useless. It's never enough. All I do and it's never enough." He's talking to himself now. My best friend is drunk for the first time in his life. "Why do it? What's the point?"

I grab him by the arms. It's worked on me. "Justin, stop it!"

His face crumbles until he's near tears. "I can't go back up there."

I put his arm around my shoulder to help him walk. "You don't have to."

We go up the stairs and sneak him around the side of the house to the garage. Getting upstairs for my purse and car keys is harder. Five people stop me to ask after Justin. The one person I tell the truth to is Lucy, who promises to cover for us. Justin is nursing the bottle by the Cobra convertible when I get back. Geoff steps in behind me.

"No! Not him!" Justin shouts. "He can't come!"

"Sir—"

"Just follow behind us," I whisper.

I get into the driver's seat and Justin plops into the passenger's. "I can keep you safe," he mutters. "I saved you once, I can do it again."

"I know you can." As can the snub-nose .38 in my purse, but I'm not telling them that.

"He wouldn't dare come after me," Justin mumbles. "I want him to, so he won't. Coward."

I start the car, the Cobra's engine roaring then purring like a lion. We peel out and I drive down the coast. Justin gazes out at the ocean in silence, holding the bottle to his chest when he isn't drinking it. I know him well enough to not engage in conversation right now. When he wants to talk, he will. Until then, I enjoy the wind blowing through my hair and the forward momentum. It's freeing. There's no destination. Just the ocean, setting sun, and us. I don't think about anything but the road in front of us. Not Harry. Not Rebecca. Not even Justin. My body settles, and for the first time in days I'm not on edge. Last time I felt this way was that last night at Harry's, just laying in his bed in my nook and listening to him breathe. I push the image away.

I don't stop for an hour and wouldn't except we need gas. I get us some coffee too. Justin is slumped against the door snoozing when I return. He passed out about ten minutes into the drive, much to my relief. I wave at the black BMW that's been tailing us. Hope they're enjoying the ride too. When I shut the door, Justin stirs and mumbles, "Rebecca." I have the strongest urge to run my hand through his blonde hair and kiss his forehead like Pop used to with me. I restrain myself and start the car.

Halfway back Justin wakes, opting for more booze instead of cold coffee. "Where are we?"

"Almost home."

"No. It's a fucking crypt."

"Justin, we've been driving for almost two hours. Where—"

"The Falls. I dreamt she was at The Falls."

It's almost full dark by the time we reach the park. I pull into the parking lot deep in the forest. I'm not big on nature, so I've only been here a few times on school field trips and with the occasional boyfriend. There's no one around, because the park is closed now, but that's not stopping me now. I park the car right at the edge of the tree line and Justin jumps out, sort of falling against the door. He is so drunk. My attention swings to the car coming into view. The BMW rolls up, blinding me with its headlights. When I turn back, Justin's gone. Crap.

"Justin!" I shout. As the guards climb out of their car, I ask, "Did you see which way he went?"

"No, ma'am," Bryan answers.

"Shit. Do you have a flashlight?" Geoff reaches into the glove compartment and tosses one to me. "Okay, stay here."

"Ma'am, I don't think—" Geoff says.

"Just stay here. That's an order." I grab my purse and run down the path, which I really hope he took. I'm in a dress, high heeled boots, and my Kevlar coat, so not proper hiking attire. The path is fairly easy to follow, but the trees scratching in the wind and haunting hoot of an owl ratchets up the fear factor. I kind of wish I had my guards with me to protect me from raccoons or whatever, but they'll just aggravate the situation. I call out for Justin twice. No answer.

As the roar of The Falls gets closer, I begin to find clothes along the path. One shoe, then another. A sock hangs on a branch with its mate a few paces away. Coat, tie, and shirt in succession as I continue on. The pants appear right at the edge of the woods where the trees open onto a small clearing that overlooks the waterfall. It's sixty yards away with a large lagoon blocked off by railings and "No Swimming" signs. Hanging from one of them is Justin's underwear. Oh, boy.

I approach the railing and in the distance see a white silhouette gliding back and forth in the black lagoon toward the side of the fall. There's a reason it's cordoned off. Rocks and trees tend to fall from the cliffs above. "Justin!" I shout. "Get out of there!" He either can't hear or just won't listen. I scream again with the same result. "Justin, I am not coming in there after you! You have thirty seconds before I call in the goons and have them drag your naked butt out of there! Then I'll tell everyone about it! Get out!"

That captures his attention. He turns around and begins swimming toward me. "Come swimming with me, Jo," he pleads. He stops half-way to the shore. "It feels nice."

"Hell, no. Come on, it's not safe in there."

"I am invincible!" he shouts.

"You are drunk! Please get out of there before you drown!"

"You know, that might actually kill me."

"Duh!" I snatch his briefs off the sign, hanging them by my index finger. "Ten seconds before I call Geoff and Bryan. Nine, eight, seven…"

He swims as fast as he can back, reaching the shore at two. As he climbs out I turn my back and hold out his underwear behind me. Twenty years and I've never seen him naked and vice versa. In a towel, yes. Him shirtless, lots. *Never* naked. He takes the underpants, putting them on, I hope. "And you're supposed to be the fun one," he says.

I wait three seconds then turn around. The sight before me takes my breath away. I'd forgotten how perfect he is. Not an ounce of fat on his lean body. Sculpted pecs, six pack, toned arms and legs. He slicks back his wet hair, showing me that body. I know I'm staring, so I look down and hand him his pants and shirt. "Here."

He attempts to put on the pants, but can't stay steady. I lean down just inches from that bulge, helping him with both legs and pulling the pants up. I can feel him watching me and become self-conscious. I don't dare look up. As I button the pants, my fingers accidently—I swear—brush up against his cold stomach. I can see the goose pimples rise and fall with every one of his deep breaths. Too much. This is too much. This is too intimate. This is wrong. I try to step away, but he takes my hands in his. "Jo."

I don't know what to think. What to do. I'm spent. I can't take another blow. This is a cage with no way out. There is no win here, and I know it. Any declaration of love would be a reaction to a loss he can't cope with. Maybe a few months ago, in another life, this would be good enough. All I know is that it's not good enough right now. For either of us. I just…

My best friend lifts my chin up and lowers his mouth onto mine. It's tentative and soft, lasting only a moment. He opens his eyes to gage my reaction, but a million emotions and thoughts are racing around my mind. Shock. Happiness. Confusion. And a whole lot of lust. His mouth finds mine again, this time with no hesitation or care. I kiss back with the same urgency. Our tongues dance and tease as he pulls me into his wet, hard body. I cling to his bare back, digging my fingers in. I'm intoxicated by him. His taste. His smell. It's exactly how I'd imagined it. Better.

He lowers us onto the ground, him pinning me as if I'll escape. Tiny rocks poke into me, but I try to ignore them. We kiss and caress, grasping at each other as if we'll be torn apart. He squeezes my breasts, and I run my hand through his hair. His hand moves under my skirt and up my thigh. I part my legs for him and almost die from pleasure as his fingers thrust inside me. And it's that beautiful agony that brings me crashing back to earth. What the hell am I doing?

I've wanted this more than anything almost since I met him, so why do I have a rock in the pit of my stomach right now? This is wrong. I know it's wrong. He's drunk. He just lost the love of his life. He's beyond vulnerable. I want him to want *me*, not a distraction. I'm not this person. This will change everything. He'll wake up tomorrow, hating himself and probably me. *Harry…*

No. I will not do this.

Without hesitation, I push his hand away and break the kiss. "No. Stop." I pull away, sitting up and pulling my jacket tight for protection.

"What's the matter?" my friend asks.

"We can't do this. You're drunk. You're mourning. It's wrong."

He touches my shoulder. "I want to, Jo."

"Why?"

"Because…I want to make you happy. Because you're in love with me."

Those words slap me in the face. I leap up, suddenly disgusted with both of us. "So you're finally drunk and sad enough to give me a pity fuck?"

He stands up. "What? No, of course not! You just looked so beautiful, and I wanted to…I don't know." His shoulders slump and he looks away, completely lost. "I love you, Jo."

"But not in that way," I finish for him. "And you never can, can you? Never."

As the words escape my mouth, I know it's true. More important, I can accept it. He can never give me what I want. He'll never look at me with lust or deep abiding love like he did her. He'll never ache for me. I'll just always be that girl on the bridge he needs to fix. All those years. Over half of my life waiting for something that can never be. Letting no other man in just in case he decided to love me back. I'm pathetic.

He steps toward me. "Jo."

I leap away. "Don't. I can't…" I turn around before he can see me cry. I run away as fast as I can, sobs escaping as I do.

Geoff and Bryan rush over to me when I come into view. "Ma'am?" Geoff asks.

"Um," I sniffle, "he's at the end of the path." I keep walking toward the Cobra, fumbling for the keys. "Can you, um, go get him? I'm afraid he might hurt himself." I struggle to unlock the door. "Just, um, take him back to the house when he's ready."

"Ma'am," Bryan says as I slam the door shut. "What about—"

I start the car, the engine drowning out his voice. I speed away before either can stop me. I almost hit three other cars as I dodge and weave through traffic. My mind has stopped functioning, but instinctively I know where to go. It's the only place I want to go. Hell, where I *need* to go.

Harry opens the door in his pajamas, bewildered by the sight of me. I'm sure I'm covered in dirt and leaves, so God knows what he's thinking. "Jo?"

"You were right," I say for possibly the first time ever.

"Jo, what—"

"Everything you said about me is right. I'm fucked up. I am *so* fucked up I don't know why anyone would want me. Mom didn't. Justin sure as hell doesn't. So why would anyone, let alone someone as wonderful as you? Because you are. You're the most wonderful man I've ever met. And if I believe or…" I say, my voice cracking, "*hope* that someone as remarkable as you wants me, and it doesn't happen, I'm not sure I could live with that. There is a huge part of me that doesn't believe I deserve even the hope. I'm scared to hell of even the possibility because if everything does turn up roses, I'm not sure I'd know what to do with myself. All I know is pain and—and struggle. It drives me, makes me strong. It'll always be a part of me."

"Why are you telling me this?" he asks calmly.

"Because…you deserve to know this. Because I miss you. Because I really need a hug, and you're the only person I want to hug me. Because, in spite of everything, I think this thing can go somewhere, be real, and I really want it to. Because you're worth *hoping* for. I trust you. And I want *you.* I need *you.* No one else. I'm tired of living in a dream, especially when you've shown me reality can be a hell of a lot better. I only hope it's not too late."

We stand at an impasse, moments growing heavier with the uncertainty as he decides our fate. Luckily, only about three pass before he says, "Come in."

My whole body loses four hundred pounds with those words. I step in and he shuts the door. The moment it closes I fall into his arms. He hugs me as tight as I do him, and for the first time in days I feel...right. My hot tears soak his shoulder as I weep. He picks me up and carries me into his bedroom, gently setting me on the bed before tucking himself in beside me. He doesn't say a word. He envelops me until I run out of tears. Welcome to reality, Jo.

Chapter Fifteen
Revelations

I wake at six, and we really make up. Twice. Afterward, Harry showers as I whip up breakfast, using all of my culinary skills to impress him. Meaning, I try not to burn the toast. All is well until I open the front door to get the paper. I about jump out of my skin when I see the midnight blue clad figure standing in the hall with his arms crossed. "Jesus Christ," I say, clutching onto my frantic heart.

"This is the residence of Lt. Harold O'Hara," the superhero says with disapproval. "Your supervisor."

I step into the hallway, closing the door so Harry can't hear. "Yeah?"

"You're wearing his pajamas."

"So?"

"I just…I'm surprised. I had no idea you two were intimate."

"It's none of your business."

"How long have you two been…together?" he asks with distaste for the idea.

"Again, none of your damn business." I cock my hips and put my right hand on the joint. "Who are you, my father?"

"I meant no offense. I—I hope you're both happy together."

"We are. Thank you." I stare into the impenetrable mask. Neither of us utters another word for an uncomfortable moment. "So, what are you doing here? Harry's in the shower if you—"

"I knew you were unguarded. I came to keep you safe."

I do a double take. "And how'd you know that? Hell, how'd you know where I was? Did you follow me last night?" The thought of him watching as I rolled around in the dirt with Justin turns my stomach.

"There's a tracking device in your coat."

"You LoJacked me?" I shout.

"Of course. I have to keep track of you somehow," he assures me. "And now you know, please do not destroy or leave the coat behind. If you do, I will have no choice but to shadow you. I promise only to use the device when needed. I have a feeling you may be grateful for it one day."

"Not today," I say with a scoff. "Just go away, okay? I'm safe, but completely creeped out right now. Shoo before one of the neighbors sees you." I snatch up the paper and retreat into the apartment in total shock.

Harry comes out of the bedroom buttoning up his shirt. "Who were you talking to?"

"Um…" I say, trying to find the right words, "Justice. He, um, bugged me and tracked me here to make sure I was properly protected."

"Really?" he asks, sounding not at all concerned. "Would he like breakfast?"

I swack Harry with the paper with an amused smile. "This is serious! He put a tracking device in my coat! He stalked me here! He stood out in our hallway while we were…you know! I'm not feeding the man!"

"He's just a good detective. Right now, you're his only lead. We have you under surveillance too, remember? Though they called and said they lost you last night. As for him knowing we're together…" He kisses my nose. "I don't mind if you don't. Is the coffee ready?" My boyfriend walks toward the kitchen as I just shake my head. I glance at the door before following him. No superhero is going to ruin my day.

After breakfast, which is edible for the first time ever, Harry collects his things for work while I lounge on the couch with the paper. I've made the front page again. A photograph of Justin and me walking into the church takes up half the page, but when I look at it, I get a knot in my stomach. I skim the article, just a re-cap of the funeral. Harry comes back out with his coat and tie on, looking quite dapper. I wolf-whistle. "Looking very smart there, L.T."

"The governor's driving up. Have to look my best. What about you? Any plans for the day? You're welcome to stay as long as you want to."

"Thank you," I say, beaming. "I don't know. Rearrange your ties? Clean your bathroom? Have a tea party with Justice?"

Harry leans down and kisses me. "A full day." We both smile. "I'm just a phone call away if you need me."

"I know." We smile at each other. Harry pecks me again before picking up his briefcase and walking to the door. As he opens it, I turn around. "Harry, I lo…" I say, but the words won't come out. My face scrunches up with frustration. Shit. The truth is I want to love him, even think I can, but don't know if I'm there yet. Crap.

Once again, Harry saves me from myself. "One step at a time," Harry says with a smile, which I return. He walks out.

After finishing the paper, showering, and dressing, I flop back down on the couch, watching TV for all of five minutes before I'm bored and anxious. There's something I need to do, but so don't want to. After five minutes of psyching myself up, I pick up the telephone. Dobbs picks up on the second ring. "Pendergast residence."

"Dobbs, it's Jo."

"Oh, Miss Joanna, we were so worried!"

"I'm fine. I'm staying with a friend. I'm safe."

"Would you like to speak to Master Justin? He's at the office, I can transfer you."

My stomach tightens. "No. Just tell him I called, and I'm fine, okay? Bye."

That went better than expected. Now what? I get off the couch and saunter around the apartment awhile, then watch more TV until there's a buzz on the intercom. "Yes?"

"There are two men here to see you," the doorman says. "They claim to be your bodyguards."

"Big? Dark suits? One has a crew cut, the other a scar on his right hand?"

"Yes. Should I send them up?"

"Yes." Ugh. I don't know which is worse, Justice or them. How the hell did they find me? Harry, or maybe Justice, must have ratted me out. Oh, hell. They're going to tell Justin. He'll know I've been lying for months. In spite of last night I don't want him to be angry or think any less of me. Nothing I can do now.

A minute later, through the peephole, I see Geoff and Bryan step into the hallway. They exchange a few words with

Justice before he speeds away, off to play hero while I go mad in here. TV ain't cutting it. Books either. I wander from room to room, settling on the office. I can't help myself, I have to snoop. The files on the desk and boxes call to me. He's left them out for a reason. It's almost as if he wanted me to look. So I do.

Most of the files are on old, unsolved cases he must peruse from time to time, looking at them with fresh eyes. I have a few of those files myself. Maybe we can help each other. You know what they say, the couple that investigates together... I turn on the computer, enter the password he gave me when I needed to get on before, and find the Alkaline case.

The tip line's six hundred fifty leads were all discounted. None of the physical evidence at the scene or his hotel pointed to his current location. "Joe Fallon" has not popped up on any database or other hotels within fifty miles. He must have moved onto another alias. As I'm reading through a list of all the evidence collected at the hotel, a thought strikes me. He checked in under my name the night he escaped. He had an ID and credit card in that name, which meant he had them made before the escape. Before I was even on the case. I've asked myself this question a million times, coming up with no answer: Why me? I was nothing to this man. Never met him, never had any dealings with him. I don't have a clue how I got on his radar before the press conference. The working theory was that I put away one of his friends, but that didn't pan out. It just doesn't make any sense.

The next file in the computer is a report on the second interview with Logan Dodd, which took place yesterday. Still in the hospital, poor guy. He went into great detail this time, even down to the magazine he was reading when Moore was making rounds. Nothing new there, but when I'm scanning the rest of his file, I come across a name that gives me pause.

Logan Dodd's father was Desmond Logan. I knew him, or of him, through the neighborhood. He brought cars into Uncle Ray's shop sometimes. I remember him because he got a seventeen-year-old pregnant, Sophia Dodd, and then before he could marry her, he was gunned down outside her high school as she watched. The scuttlebutt was she traded one mobster from a rival gang in for Desmond, and the ex didn't take kindly to that.

Double homicide time as both men killed each other in the shoot-out. When it happened, I overheard Uncle Ray talk about how Desmond was a driver for Ryder's then fledgling gang. Desmond was never arrested in connection to Ryder, so he wouldn't pop up as a known accomplice. Dodd never knew his father, so maybe it's just a coincidence. I hate coincidences.

I should call Harry or Cam, but they'll just tell me to stay put and go themselves. If I go, it'll just be a friendly chat among two victims of Alkaline. And I was one of the people to save him that night. Those excuses work for me. I fix myself up a bit, check to make sure my .38 is still in my purse, and spend a few seconds debating whether or not to put on the coat. The bulletproof factor trumps the tracking factor, so I do. Joanna Fallon, back in action.

Geoff and Bryan follow me without any questions, only sideways glances. Lord knows what they think or God forbid know about what happened last night. I won't mention it if they don't. They follow behind the Cobra all the way to the hospital. When we reach Our Lady, nurses and doctors approach me to offer condolences, but I just smile and walk on. I'm on a mission. There's no time for pleasantries.

When I reach the burn ward, I spot Dr. Sharma. He seems surprised to see me and my boulders. "Det. Fallon?"

"Hi. I just came to check on Logan. How's he doing?"

"I assume well," he says with a hint of frustration. "He checked himself out AMA this morning."

"Why the hell did he do that?"

"Claimed he didn't feel safe here. I couldn't persuade him otherwise."

"He say where he was going?"

"Home, I suppose. Your colleagues went with him."

Crap. Luckily, I wrote down his mother's address in the Ward just in case I needed to interview her. We drive there and park on the street. I really don't want to leave my friend's hundred thousand dollar car with only a crackhead on the corner to watch it, but I don't have a choice. Want both guards here for this. Good thing he has six others to drive if it gets stolen. The men and I walk past the police cruiser parked outside the apartment building. I don't recognize them but I still wave. They wave back. I push several buttons until an unsuspecting resident allows us entry.

For the Ward this building is upper class with fresh paint, uncracked windows, and no druggies passed out in the hallways. The Dodds live on the sixth floor. I have the men hang back so as not to scare anyone. Nice and friendly, that's what this'll be. A woman in her late thirties with graying brown hair and thick body opens the door, the intense smell of cigarettes wafting from inside. She eyes me up and down, not liking what she sees.

I smile. "Hi, Miss Dodd. Is Logan home?"

"Aren't you that cop?" she asks with distaste.

"Yes, I'm one of the detectives on your son's case. I found him the night he was injured, and I just wanted to check on him. I heard he was released from the hospital. May I come in?" I don't wait for an answer. The apartment is nice with recliner, new wallpaper, and big entertainment center. Nothing flashy, though a little on the odd side for an unemployed woman. "You know, I didn't realize it until today, but we know some people in common." I pick up a picture of young Logan playing video games in this apartment. "Ray Lilley's my uncle."

"Who?"

I put the picture back. "He has a garage on the corner of Miller and Frank."

"I don't know it."

I saunter back to the door with the Galilee Angel's pendant on it and stop. "Oh. Well, Logan's father did. Desmond."

"That was a lot of years ago."

"I know. I was just a kid when he died, but I remember it. Very dramatic."

"Not the words I'd use to describe it," she says with a cruel smile.

"It was, even for the Ward. The pregnant girlfriend watching her up-and-coming mobster boyfriend gunned down right in front of her by her ex. It was all anyone could talk about for a week. All the details are seared into my brain. *All* of them."

Her mouth twitches. "What do you want?"

I smile as brightly as I can. "I told you. I'm looking for your son."

She folds her arms. "He's not here. He's told the police everything he knows. He needs to rest."

I raise an eyebrow. "Well, if he needs to rest, why isn't he here? Gallivanting all over town can't be good for him," I say with a chuckle. "Neither can going out without protection. Huh."

"Get out of my apartment, Detective," Dodd says. "You have no right to be here. Get out!"

I cock my head to the side. "Why so serious?" I reach behind, opening the bedroom door as I spin around. A scared Logan, bad arm in a sling, stands on the other side of his bed filling a duffel bag. "Going somewhere?"

The kid reaches down onto the bed with his one hand, and my instincts take over. As he raises his arm, I barely get a glimpse of the gun before leaping behind the wall for cover. Two gunshots ring out, hitting the doorframe where I just stood, missing me by an inch. I reach into my purse for my weapon and there's another shot, this one hitting the recliner in the living room. The front door pounds open at the same time. Geoff and Bryan, guns out, bust in. Sophia Dodd screams and backs into a corner. Not so tough now. Geoff covers Sophia, but Bryan runs over to me. There are no more shots. I peek around the corner carefully, but no shots ring out. I check again and take in the empty room and open window.

"Geoff, go out the front! He's running!" I shout as I enter the room with Bryan.

Logan is halfway down the fire escape when I leap onto it. The rickety metal shakes as we storm down it. Logan fires, the bullet hitting and sparking a few inches from my hand. It doesn't stop us. Nothing will. Bryan returns fire, missing too. Logan hits the ground first, sprinting down the narrow alleyway as he fires wildly before rounding the corner onto the street.

When we reach the street I spot him crossing Ditko Ave and disappearing behind the shops. The police cruiser does a U-turn, lights flashing. Geoff runs out of the building and the patrolmen jump the curb to stop him. He can take care of himself. I stay on Logan's tail. No way in hell I'm losing him.

We haul ass after him for three blocks, gaining ground, until he goes inside a bodega. People inside the store stare as we run through. I can tell his path by the fallen food in the aisles. He went out the back, the door slamming shut as we enter. Logan's about halfway down the alley when we run out. At the same time an SUV skids to a stop on the street, cutting off his means of escape. I'd be thrilled if I didn't recognize the car as one parked down the street from Logan's apartment. The gun pointed out the window doesn't help my general "Oh, shit" feeling.

Dodd sees it too. He stops dead, holding up his gun at the car. It takes me all of a split second to figure things out. Bryan pulls me back into the store. Logan and the men in the car fire at the same time as he runs for cover behind a dumpster. Dodd hits the side of the car, but the assassin misses. The passenger leaps out of the car as he opens fire. At the same time the driver fires as well. Two against one. When the passenger starts running toward Logan, who is huddled behind the dumpster, too afraid to move or fire, I can't wait a moment longer. I know it's a stupid move the moment I make it. I run out, shooting at the men to cover my ass. Logan could easily hit me, but he just watches as I race toward him. Prison or death, he's picking the right one. Bryan is right on my tail, returning fire too. There are so many gunshots I lose track.

I'm just about to reach Dodd when an invisible truck hits my chest, knocking the wind out of me. I spin around and fall behind the dumpster. I don't know if it's the shock or adrenaline but I feel no pain, just pressure below my right breast. There's a flattened gold slug in my coat. It burns my fingers when I pull it out. I have the wherewithal to point my gun at Logan, whose own hangs limp in his hand. He's in shock too.

Bryan runs toward the car and I hear tires squeal as the car drives away. There are no more shots. A moment later, my bodyguard returns, gun pointed at Logan. "Drop it," he commands. Like a zombie, Logan does. "You okay?" Bryan asks me.

"I'll live," I say, still having a hard time breathing. "The men?"

"One's dead, but the other got away. I couldn't get the license plate."

Sirens come closer. My brothers in blue. I look at Logan, who stares into space with his knees pulled into his chest like a small child. I almost feel sorry for him. "Logan Dodd, you are so under arrest."

***

All it took for me to get back on the case was a gunfight and bullet to the chest. Small price to pay. I'll have a bitch of a bruise, and be in pain when I turn, but the bullet broke nothing. I got shot and only have a bruised rib. Thank you, Justice. They wanted me to go to the hospital, just in case, but there was no way in hell I was missing a minute of the drama I set in motion.

Cam arrived first as I was being examined by paramedics. I gave him the Cliffs Notes version of the events and after a minute of screaming at me, he went off to take charge. Geoff wouldn't leave my side, even when I had my shirt off. I did convince him not to call Justin. I don't need that right now. I also instructed all the first responders not to mention names, so the press doesn't get wind of the Alkaline connection. Right now this is nothing more than another shooting in the Ward.

Poor Bryan was taken away in handcuffs to be questioned. I gave Mirabelle and Kowalski my statement, so Bryan should be released by tonight. If this isn't justifiable homicide, I don't know what is. The poor guys drew the short straw and have to investigate this mess. I don't envy them, or me for that matter. Internal Affairs is going to kick my ass.

Kowalski is still going over my statement as I sit in a patrol cruiser with ice on my ribs when Harry lifts up the crime scene tape and sprints over to us. A tech tries to stop him to ask a question, but he waves her away. It takes effort, but I get out and stand. Without a word Harry takes me into his arms. It hurts, but I don't let on. I squeeze him back. "Are you okay?" he asks.

"I'm fine," I say, pulling away.

Kowalski clears his throat, all of a sudden extremely uncomfortable. Gee, I wonder why. He can't even look at us. We can be expecting more of this from now on. As I said, so worth it. "Um, sir, we, uh, still don't have an ID on the dead guy. We have an APB out on the make and model of the car his accomplice was driving." He looks at me. "And I, uh, need your gun for comparison."

I bend down to pick up my purse but wince in pain. "I'll get it," Harry says. He retrieves the gun from my purse, handing it to Kowalski.

"Right. Thanks. I'll just, uh, leave you two…yeah." He scurries away.

"Guess the cat's out of the bag, huh?" I ask as I watch Kowalski tell Mirabelle.

Harry grabs my arm, drawing my attention back to him. "Are you out of your fucking mind?" he hisses. "What the hell were you thinking?"

"I just had a hunch. If I was wrong, I didn't want to waste your time. I didn't think it would turn into Gunfight at the O.K. Corral. And I had back-up."

"Your back-up killed a man. You were shot!"

"I'm fine, it's just a bad bruise. I was wearing my supercoat."

"You were shot, Joanna!" he screams, his face tight. "Do you have any idea what I thought when I—"

He can't even finish, the idea of it too much for him. He steps away from me, running his hand through his hair. He thought I was dead. Shit, I've done it again. I hurt him. I wait a few seconds before approaching. I hug him from behind, resting my cheek on his shoulder blade. "I'm sorry. I'm so sorry. I just, I don't think sometimes. I'm sorry."

After a few seconds, his body relaxes and he pats my hand. "Don't do that to me again. I mean it."

I squeeze him again. "Promise."

I let go when I see Cam walking toward us. If he's shocked by our PDA he doesn't let on. "Sir, Logan Dodd and his mother are waiting at the station. I'm headed over there now."

"He lawyer up?" Harry asks.

"Not yet. I told them to wait until we're there before talking to him."

"Then let's go," Harry says, walking away with Cam.

I chase after them. Neither says a word when Geoff and I climb into the backseat, though Cam glances at me with a hint of annoyance. They both know it'd be pointless to say or do anything. I'd run all the way to the station for this. We don't talk on the way, or at least to each other. Harry fills the commissioner in on recent events and for once he seems pleased. A rare occurrence.

When I walk back into the squad room it feels like any other day. I've missed this place. My desk remains as I left it, a mess. I miss my messy desk. There isn't time to greet everyone as I stay on the heels of men with a purpose. I do wave to a few. Chip, our A.V. guy, sits behind the two monitors, one with a petrified Logan just staring into space and the other with Sophia, arms folded and out for blood. Gee, I wonder who will break first?

"We locate anything pertinent at the apartment yet?" Harry asks.

"Just started the search, but we did look earlier this week and turned up nothing," Cam says.

"Why didn't we know about his connection to Ryder before?" Harry asks.

"His father was never officially linked to Ryder's syndicate," I say. "It was just a rumor. The official motive for Desmond Logan's death was due to his relationship with Sophia, not his job. I didn't know Sophia Dodd was Logan's mother until I read it in your notes. Put two and two together."

"So, what's your theory?" Cam asks.

"Ryder kept in touch with his old friend's girl and kid, maybe passing them money or work from time to time. Or maybe Dodd's worked for Alkaline his whole life, I don't know."

"We interviewed his friends and extended family. They didn't mention any criminal activity in his past. There was no juvie file and the prison did a background investigation," Cam says.

"Then I'd go with St. Alkaline asking for a favor," I say.

"We can ask the mother," Cam says.

"Have we charged her with anything yet?" Harry asks.

"No. We have nothing on her," Cam says.

"Then there's no way she'll talk. My money's on Logan."

"Okay," Harry says, putting in his earwig. Cam does too. "I'm thinking high intimidation factor."

"I agree," Cam says. "I'm going to enjoy this one."

"Just try and stay objective," Harry says. "Let's go."

I sit next to Chip for the show. Wish I had some popcorn. This is going to be good.

On the monitor Logan wipes a tear away with his stump. If he hadn't tried to kill me, I'd feel bad for the kid. He's facing a life behind bars if the psycho who spews blood doesn't get him first. Not an enviable position.

Cam and Harry step in, both sporting scowls that would frighten the blind. Cam slams the door shut as hard as he can, jolting Logan out of his pity party. A calm Harry sits, but Cam picks up the chair and smashes it back down, freaking the man again. He'll be peeing his pants in a few minutes. Glaring, Cam leans back in his chair and folds his arms.

"This is Lt. Harold O'Hara and Det. Terrance Cameron with Logan Dodd. It is Wednesday, May twenty-third, at 2:56 pm," Harry says. "Mr. Dodd, you are under arrest for the attempted murder of a police officer and accessory to first degree murder. Have you been read and understand your rights?"

"Yes," he says quietly.

"Do you wish to have an attorney present for questioning?"

"N—No," he almost whispers.

"Speak the fuck up!" Cam says.

"I said I don't want a lawyer," he says, glancing at Cam. "You—you're going to protect me, right? Me and my mom?"

"That depends on what you can tell us," Harry says. "You cooperate and the DA should take that fact under advisement. No promises, though. You helped a serial killer escape, who then raped and killed an entire family. Then you shot at a police officer who is near and dear to my heart. If it was up to me, I'd string you up on Pendergast Bridge myself and let him have you."

So much for being objective. Cam nods in agreement. "You'll be lucky if we give you a spoon to paddle up shit creek."

"So start talking. When were you first in contact with James Ryder?" Harry asks.

"I only met him once or twice when I was a kid. About every three months, there'd be a grand in cash in our mailbox. Mom said it was from James, for my father being such a good soldier and her lying to the police when he was killed. She just said the other man used to be her boyfriend to keep James' name out of it. I saw him around the Ward before he became, you know, Alkaline. We only spoke to him twice, once when I was eight and Mom dragged me over to thank him. The second was when I was eleven and he happened to be in the same store. He bought me a magazine."

"When did he reach out again?" Cam asks.

"*He* didn't," Logan says. "I was having a hard time finding a job. I guess it got around the neighborhood because about a year ago this guy, Mike Spencer, approached me on the street. He said he might have a job for me."

"Mike Spencer, one of Alkaline's old lieutenants?" Cam asks.

"Yeah." And the mystery of Mike Spencer's death is solved. Ryder had him killed to shut him up. "I'd tried to join the organization a couple times, but Mom made sure they wouldn't accept me. I was so excited when they asked, I forgot to ask what the job was. About a week later, Mike called me in. Said his connection inside the prison was quitting and they needed someone else to look after James."

"Did he give the name of the man you were replacing?" Harry asks.

"No, but it had to be Denny Darcy because all the guys said how sad they were when he quit."

"What happened next?" Harry asks.

"I filled out the application, and it was pushed right through. I think they had someone inside to help with that, but I don't know who."

"What did they have you do?" Cam asks.

"Stupid stuff. Pass notes back and forth. When I could, just talk to him. And once a week give him some pills. That's it."

"Who gave you the pills? Mike?" Harry asks.

"No. After I got hired, I never saw him again."

"The notes you passed, who were they to?" Cam asks.

"Jane Smith at a P.O. Box in town. He'd give them to me sealed and I'd just stamp and mail them. Then Jane would mail hers to my apartment, sometimes with the pills. I never opened the letters. I was under strict orders not to."

"How much were they paying you?" Cam asks.

"Two grand a month in cash on top of my salary. James told me not to put it in my bank account or make big purchases."

"How considerate of him," Cam says.

"Do you remember the P.O. Box number?" Harry asks.

"Um, it had a one and a seven."

"Did you keep any of the envelopes your payments came in?" Harry asks.

"Maybe. All my cash is hidden in the Bible in my duffel bag."

I flip open my cell phone and dial Mirabelle. He picks up. "Det. Mirabelle."

"It's Jo. You're at the Dodd apartment, right?"

"Just walked in."

"In the duffel bag on his bed is a bible with a stash of cash. Check the room for letters or envelopes with a woman's handwriting. Oh, and have someone pick up former C.O. Denny Darcy for questioning. He was working for Alkaline."

"On it."

I shut the phone and return my attention to Dodd. He's chewing on his lower lip as if it was made of chocolate. "...they were all from Jane Smith, but I never met her."

"Who first approached you about the escape?" Harry asks.

"James. I usually worked nights with Leon up until last month when Moore switched so Leon could be home with his new baby. Leon would fall asleep, and I'd talk to James. About two months ago he brought it up, just in passing, how he was thinking of getting out. The next time we talked, he said he'd decided it was time. Asked if I'd help."

"You agreed?" Cam asks.

"Not at first. I said hell no, *hell no,* but then he started crying. Crying! He said he was going crazy. He said that a lot. That if he had to stay another minute inside, he'd string himself up. Said Jane was thinking of moving away, leaving him. I—I just couldn't say no. You don't know what he's like. It's like you get sucked in. He mesmerizes you with his voice, his look, I don't know. The things he says. The way he listened to me. I thought he was my friend. I thought..." He vigorously shakes his head, and his face scrunches up as if he's about to cry.

"What happened next?" Harry asks.

"Um, Moore switched with Leon and I couldn't talk to him anymore. I could still pass letters and the pills, but none of the others really slept on duty."

"So how did you know what to do?" Cam asks.

"Well, I didn't hear anymore about it at first, not until a week before. There was a letter for me from James. He gave me the date and time it was happening and detailed instructions of what I was supposed to do."

"Which was what exactly?" Harry asks.

"When I was walking the block, I'd shout that James was trying to hang himself. Moore would come running as I unlocked the door. I'd pretend to revive him and when Moore came in, James would knock him out, take his uniform, pass, and gun. While he changed, I'd wipe the security system. Then he'd pretend to take me hostage and release me in the parking lot." Logan looks away from the men down at the table. "He promised he'd send for me when the dust settled. I believed him."

"So what really happened?" Cam asks.

Logan starts playing with his stump, as if stroking his non-existent hand. "The night came and I was scared as hell. Shaking. I even threw up. Moore wanted to send me home, but I refused. I think he got suspicious." Logan shakes his head. "Then the time came and I did everything he told me to. Shouted, opened the door, pretended, but…instead of coming in to help me, Moore pulled his gun and told me to move away. I don't know what happened. James just sat up, cool as ice, and shot that acid right in Moore's face with that tube thing that came out of his wrist.

"Moore started screaming like nothing I've ever heard. He was in so much pain. I just, I was too scared to even move. No one was supposed to get hurt. I don't know how long I just sat in that cell, watching Moore die. Seconds maybe? James had left and come back twice, the second time grabbing me off the floor. He slapped me and dragged me to the control room. Asked where the disc with the computer virus was."

"How did you get that?" Harry asks.

"Jane sent it. There were instructions on how to install it. It was in my CD player in my bag. As he got it out he told me to strip, that Moore's uniform was no good anymore. I said, 'Won't that be suspicious, me walking around with no clothes?' He ignored me and got the disc. That's when I realized he hadn't taken the pistol off me the whole time. It was pointed at me since the cell. He told me to strip again, so I did. Then he dragged me to the door, telling me that I was now an accessory to a murder and if I didn't keep my mouth shut, he'd make sure me and Mom would never make it to trial. Then that acid thing came out again, and all I felt was pain. I don't remember stumbling down the stairs to get help."

"Why didn't he do us a favor and kill you that night?" Cam asks.

"I don't know. Mom came by the hospital yesterday. Said she found an envelope with twenty grand and a fake passport with my picture in it. The note read, 'Thanks for giving me a hand. You have two days before I come for the rest.' I was about to leave when that detective came."

"Why did you shoot at her?" Harry asks.

"I wasn't trying to hurt her. I just wanted to get away."

"The men who shot at you, have you seen them before?" Cam asks.

"No, but he must have sent them. I—I get protection now, right?"

"What else can you tell us about Jane Smith?" Harry asks, ignoring him.

"Nothing. I never spoke to her or even met her."

"You said you and he had conversations," Harry says. "What did he say about her?"

"He barely talked about her. I'd bring her up, just ask questions, but all he'd say was they'd do anything for each other, and he loved her for it." Logan scoffs. "Said he felt the same about me. All we really talked about was me. Girls I liked, my future. He said he'd talk to Mike again, get me in the organization when I got bored working at the prison."

"So you have no clue who she is?" Harry asks.

"None! I'd tell you if I did! I'll tell you anything if you just keep me and my mom safe!"

"Did he tell you his plans about when he got out? Did you know he was going to rape and murder an entire family?" Cam snarls.

"No! God, no! He was supposed to meet up with Jane and go to Rio."

"Do you have any idea why he targeted them? What else he might have planned?" Cam asks.

"No."

"And here I thought you were his best friend," Cam says.

"What else did you two talk about?" Harry asks. "Did he mention any other names? Locations? Is he going to butcher another family? Blow up another building?" Harry pounds on the table. "Tell me!"

He can't hold it in any longer. I'm surprised he's lasted this long. Logan bursts into hysterical tears, wiping them away with the stub while he winces in pain. "I'm sorry. I'm so sorry. I didn't know. He…and I…that little girl." They let him cry for a minute until he's capable of coherent words.

"Do you know why he killed the Thorntons?" Harry asks gently.

My body tenses. I don't want to hear the answer.

"One—One time, a week before the escape, when I was checking his cell, I found some newspaper articles on them. And pictures. Real pictures someone took. There were names, addresses, times, all typed up. And not just on them. He had the same stuff on that detective and this rich old lady, the one who was at the funeral with the lady detective."

"Why—Why?" Harry asks, visibly upset.

"I don't know, I didn't get a chance to ask him. But it must have to do with Justice."

"Justice?" Cam asks.

"I mean, you saw his cell. James was obsessed with him. When he did talk it was about their battles and how Justice ruined his life right when everything was going great. He hated him. Said he needed to be taught a lesson in humanity or something. The only time I was ever afraid of James was when he talked about Justice. His lip would quiver he was so angry. Then he'd snap out of it and be nice again."

"What does this have to do with Rebecca Thornton?" Cam asks.

Logan sniffles, looking back and forth at the men with confusion. "You don't know? You've worked with him for like a decade. It took me all of a minute to figure it out after I heard about the deaths. Why else would James kill them? He hated Justice. Wanted to punish him. And he knew the best way to do that."

I stop breathing.

"What—what are you implying?" Harry asks as Cam glances at the camera as if he can see me.

The room begins to spin along with my thoughts. Please don't say it.

Don't.

Logan scoffs. "Justin Pendergast is Justice. Duh."

And the bottom drops out of my world.

CHAPTER SIXTEEN
CONFRONTATION

I'm vaguely aware of the commotion around me. Cam asking furious questions to Logan. Harry shouting at Chip to turn off the feed. The always steady Chip struggling to get to the button on the computer, accidently brushing a stack of DVRs that go clattering all around. Harry and Cam walking in, almost arguing about what to do next. Cover it all up or haul him in for questioning. But I'm too damn busy going through twenty years of memories to be helpful.

How could I have been such a fucking idiot? So blind? I didn't have a clue. Not an inkling. I've often wondered who the man behind the mask was. I thought maybe it was ex-Olympian runner Salvatore Rossetti. I'd met him a few times in person, and he was always cordial. He was even the right height and build. The age was wrong, he's in his late forties, but I figured he just replaced the previous Justice when that Justice retired. I wasn't wrong on that front, I guess. J.T., Justin's father, must have been Justice before, and his father before him. Guess old J.T. didn't die of a heart attack. It must have been in that battle with Ache. I watched in horror with my Pop as that giant snapped Justice's neck and tossed him off that boat. They never found the body. About ten years later he resurfaced. Same costume, same powers, claiming he was traveling the world. We all knew the truth, but went along with the lie. Is that what I've been doing? Living in denial?

There were signs, there had to have been signs. All those times we were hanging out and he got a call. "Business emergency," he'd say. There were a lot of those. Or the times I'd be walking around the mansion and one second he wasn't there, and then he was. Just appeared, chalking it up to his "stealth ninja training," he'd say with a laugh. Or the way he'd grow uncomfortable when I'd badmouth supers. The annoying way Justice would single me out for conversation or protection. Or the countless times it seemed like he wanted to tell me something but chickened out. Or a hundred other fucking clues I chose to ignore or was too stupid to notice.

He lied to me. Lied to me for our entire friendship, about a fundamental part of his life. Himself. He didn't trust me. He's never trusted me. Everything I thought we had, everything I thought we meant to each other was just bullshit. All in my head. Why didn't he tell me? Why wasn't I smart enough to see what was right in front of my face?

"Joanna?" Harry asks, and I think for not the first time. He shakes me by the shoulders. "Jo!"

I snap out of my haze to see my confused and angry boss staring at me, looking for answers that I just don't have. Without a word I stand, push my way past the men, and sprint out of the squad room, not even waiting for the elevator. I have the wherewithal to grab my purse, but when I get outside I realize I don't have a fucking car. I all but body slam some bureaucrat for his cab. I have twenty minutes of driving while I try to wrap my head around twenty years of lies.

The anger and humiliation grow with each passing mile. I'm shaking again, especially when we drive over Pendergast Bridge. He appeared by my side like magic, and I thought nothing of it. *You were the first person he saved...* Lucy said that. I thought she was drunk. She knew. Dobbs too. And Rebecca? Did he tell her? Did she know what she died for? Of course she did. He probably told her on the second date. Twenty fucking years.

The press pounces when I get out of the cab. I ignore them, punching in the code and running through the gate before I deck one of them. Dobbs is at the front door, but I rush past him without a word. He calls after me, but I ignore him. Liar.

My destination is the living room. Justin has disappeared from in here more than any other room. I would walk in looking for him, check the empty room, and then a few seconds later he'd stroll out claiming he was on the patio or at the beach. I'm such a fucking idiot.

Back in my hero worshiping days I read every article I could on Justice. My collection of clippings rivaled Alkaline's. One was about his command center. He wouldn't give the location, but said it had a lab for evidence analysis, gym, and super-computer with access to every law enforcement database, CCTV in the city, and communication system hooked up to it so if he's in the field he can access the information right away. He's better equipped than the entire department. If it's here, I'll find it.

I start at the bar first, checking under every surface for a button or switch. Not on the bar, not in the cabinets, not under any painting. I've just started tossing the movies on the floor when Dobbs and Lucy rush in. "Joanna, what in the hell are you doing?" Lucy asks.

I keep going. "Looking."

There's a buzz from the front gate. Lucy gestures for Dobbs to go and he does. She steps toward me. "What are you looking for?"

I whip my head to the side, giving her the look of death. "You *know*."

Her face slowly falls. I've seen that look a hundred times on a perp, right when they know I've caught them. Guilt and fear, usually so satisfying, now just sickens me. We stare at each other, and to her credit she doesn't leave my punishing gaze. Her shoulders slump and she nods. I just watch as she walks toward the fireplace and reaches into it. A second later, the entire stone structure moves to the side. I find myself gasping and holding my hands over my mouth. Tears appear in my eyes, and I almost double over as if I was just sucker punched. "I'm so sorry, Joanna."

I guess I didn't believe it until this very moment. No way he'd do this to me. Not him. Not ever. He was the only person I could trust. I'd do anything for him. I thought it was a two-way street. I spin around from Lucy, not wanting her to see me like this or look at the fucking hole in the wall. I will not cry. I *will not*. I take a few deep breaths, pushing down sad and making room for fury. When I'm composed enough, I turn around and stalk into that hole.

It's cold in here. Dark. The only light comes from the bulbs every few feet as I walk down a metal ramp. I must be underground in the cliff. The ramp twists around a corner where the light is brighter. Then I'm in it, Justice's Command Center with the man himself sitting with his back to me in front of a computer monitor. It's one of three on the bank with two rows of TVs in the wall above them, all with real-time streaming footage from around town. It's smaller in here than I imagined, maybe the size of the library upstairs. I thought it'd be as big as the mansion for some reason. There isn't much in here either. A big black couch, a rack with a gaggle of costumes, a whiteboard covered with papers, crime scene photos, and reports. A red light flickers above. There are two doors on the far wall, one maybe to the lab and who knows about the other. In between them is another ramp exit, with a third next to the whiteboard. Not very homey.

"I know. Dobbs called down," Justin says but doesn't turn around. "I'm busy."

I start shaking again, fingernails drawing blood in my palms. I hug myself. None of this helps. He's sitting there nonchalantly in his hidden fortress hard at work on his secret life while I'm falling apart not ten feet from him. I can't talk. I can't move. I'm stuck here in this fucking depressing room with the man who shattered my everything.

After five seconds of silence, his head tilts to the side. His back straightens and his neck elongates. He feels my hatred as if I'm screaming it at him. Slowly, he swivels around, face filled with shock and fear. The moment our eyes meet, it turns into sadness. Sadness for me or for him, I don't know. Yesterday I'd say the former, but sure as hell not today. He leaps out of the chair and for some reason I take a step back.

"I'm not...I..." he says, holding up his hand to reassure me.

He's hurt. *I've* hurt *him*? That's it for me. I snap.

I bridge the gap between us at a rate even he wouldn't be able to achieve. My hand connects hard on his gorgeous face. "You son of a bitch! You son of a bitch!" It's like hitting a slab of granite, but that doesn't stop me from doing it again. And again. "You motherfucker!" Small smudges of my blood smear his face. I keep hitting and hitting him wildly with my fists now on his shoulders, chest, and face. "You piece of shit! I hate you! I fucking hate you!" I shriek at the top of my lungs. He grabs my flailing arms and I try to pull away. "Don't touch me! Don't you fucking touch me!"

He tries to pull me into a hug. "I'm sorry. I'm so sorry," he pleads.

"Let me go! Let me go, you bastard!"

His arms wrap me into a bear hug, so I'm pressed against his chest. "I'm sorry. Please. *Please*." He hugs me even tighter.

For a moment I relent, clinging onto his shirt and breathing in his familiar scent I used to get lost in. This is my best friend. My essential person. But he's not. He never was. "No!" I break away, sickened by his touch. "Stay away from me!"

"Just let me ex—"

"No!" I shout, holding out a finger to stop him from coming closer as I back away. "No. We have nothing to say to each other. Ever again. You stay the hell away from me. You don't talk to me, you don't look for me, you don't even *think* about me. You are dead to me. If you ever come near me again, I'll turn you over to Alkaline myself, I swear to fucking God!"

"Jo, please just—"

"If you ever gave a damn about me, just stay away. Just…go to hell."

I turn around and run out, past Lucy, Cam, and Harry who stand at the entrance all shocked by our scene. Footsteps follow me. When I climb out of that hole, I let out the breath I didn't know I was holding and take another. I'm gasping as if I've just run miles. Harry emerges from the darkness. "Jo—"

"Don't. Don't," I say breathlessly. "Just don't do…anything." I take a few more ragged breaths. "I can't do this. I can't." I'm close to hyperventilating. My chest hurts and I see spots. This must be a panic attack. I'm going to pass out in a minute, and I don't even mind.

Harry rushes over to my side, hugging me. "Calm down," he whispers as he pets my hair. "I'm here. It's okay, I'm here. Just breathe."

I force the air in and out and after a few seconds it's back to normal. "Please get me out of here."

"Of course."

I lean on him as he walks me out of that house.

***

Harry drives me home in my car, which I was last in when I drove it over from Rebecca's house a lifetime ago. A week hasn't even passed and since then I've lost and regained a boyfriend, planned a funeral, made out with my dream man, been shot, and found out that my best friend lied about who he is. I need a vacation.

I'm lying in my own bed on my side, knees pulled into my chest. It helps with the pain. The adrenaline has worn off and now my ribs ache like hell. There's a bruise the size of a fist every color of the damn rainbow. The Oxycodone left over from my root canal manages the worst of it and blurs the edges of my life. Maybe I'll switch from booze to pills. Fewer calories at least.

Harry walks back in with a cup of tea as he flips his phone shut. In between long calls to the station, he's been coming in and out to check on me, bringing food and kisses as if I had the flu. It's sweet, nobody's ever done this for me, but it's driving me nuts. He sets the tea down and sits on the bed, gazing down at me. We smile at each other. "Who was on the phone this time?"

"Mirabelle. They've just finished at Dodd's apartment. They found a writing sample of Jane Smith. Latent's working on it now. And your guard friend Bryan's been released."

"Kowalski get anything useful from Denny Darcy?"

"Not really. He was hired by Mike Spencer, just passed notes and pills. Never met Jane, has no idea where Ryder is."

"Of course he doesn't," I sigh. "Did Mirabelle mention anything about, you know?"

"We have Dodd in isolation, so so far the only people who know are you, me, Cam, and Chip. I'm going to have to tell the Commish, though. If he doesn't know already, that is."

"Probably not. I mean if he didn't tell me, his so-called best friend, he sure as hell didn't tell Craven." I scoff. "Or he did. For all I know he's told everyone in Galilee but me." Harry takes my hand and I wrap my fingers in his. "Have you spoken to Cam yet?"

"When you were in the bathroom. He's back at the station with all the evidence Justic—I mean, Justin provided. They might have a lead on the car the shooters were driving. The whole shoot out was caught on CCTV. Got a license plate, but lost the car when it went into an underground garage. We'll see what we find there."

"At least some good came out of this mess." I pull my hand away with a sigh. "You should go. They need you down there. The case is breaking now."

"I don't want to leave you alone."

"There's a cruiser out front, and I'm sure my guards will track me down soon enough."

"I'm not talking about that, and you know it."

I look away from his well-meaning face. "I'll be okay. I just need time to process, I think."

"Jo, I—"

"I can't talk about it right now, okay? I just can't. Seriously, go. You can't really do anything for me here. Not really. You need to fix this. There's still a psycho out there gunning for me, and I don't have the energy to go after him right now. You'll have to do the job for both of us. Go. I'll be fine."

I'm touched by his reluctance to leave my side, but we both know he's needed more there than here. This is my second cup of tea, and I didn't even touch the first. "Are you sure?"

"Absolutely, yes. Go."

Reluctantly, he stands up. "I'd feel better if you'd let me take you back to my place."

"I want to sleep in my own bed, watch my own TV, and stare out my own window. I'll be fine."

"I'll post another patrol car out front until the guards arrive."

"I feel safer already."

He leans down and kisses me. "I'll be back as soon as I can." We kiss again before he walks to the door, and a few seconds later I hear the front door close and lock.

Alone at last, thank the Lord. I sigh but then wince in pain. Stupid gunshot wound. I've never been shot before. Despite what the shows portray, very few of us ever get involved in shoot-outs. Most only draw their side arms about ten times with the intent to shoot, but never pull the trigger. Of course they also never have an acid-throwing psychopath after them because their best friend is a superhero. Or ex-best friend, I guess. Maybe Alkaline will leave me alone if I shoot the bastard myself. The enemy of my enemy and all that.

No, it's time to flee. I have come to the decision that I need to get the fuck out of this town ASAP. I should have listened to everyone and left the moment I saw that picture on the door. I wouldn't have been shot, humiliated, and broken hearted. I'd still have my best friend, bastard fucking liar that he is.

I'm thinking Fiji. Get a bungalow, burn in the sun, maybe rent a sailboat and go scuba diving. When Harry can join me, he can rub suntan lotion on my back. I'll send the bill to the bastard fucking liar who made me go to ground. It'll be the last time he hears from me.

I manage to get up and shuffle into the kitchenette to forage for food. There's a few apples, bread, moldy tuna, and peanut butter. I go for apples and peanut butter and stumble to the couch. Nothing on TV about the shoot out or me. I settle on a vampire movie to assuage my blood lust. I keep alternating between intense anger and bottomless despair with a sprinkling of humiliation thrown in.

As the busty woman gives herself to the dead man, and I find the most expensive hotel in Fiji, there's a knock on my front door. I damn near drop my laptop in surprise. No one buzzed to come up, but I doubt Alkaline would knock. Can't be too careful though. Not only do I get my spare gun, but I even throw on the coat. If I had realized I was still wearing it on the ride home, I would have thrown it out the window. I'll toss it in the trash at the airport instead.

I look out the peephole and roll my eyes. Crap. I wish it was Alkaline. I put the gun on the counter and unlock the door. "How the hell did you get in here?"

Lucy stands in the hall, as usual lips pursed with disapproval. Bryan and Geoff loom behind her, looking scary as always. "We own the building," Lucy says. "May I come in?" She doesn't wait for a response.

I shut the door. "Guess it's time for me to move then."

She glances around the living room, not liking the décor. "Are they all like this?"

"Well, the owners are kind of assholes, so yeah." I put my hands on my hips. "What the hell do you want?"

"I've come as a goodwill ambassador to explain."

"You can shove your goodwill and your explanation. All I want from you and your freak of a nephew is for you to forget you ever met me."

"We're your family."

My mouth slacks open, and I begin to chuckle. "*Family?* Oh my God, you did not just say that. Not even you are that cruel."

"We had our reasons, Joanna."

"Sure you did. Everyone always has their reasons. The reason my mom drank was she had a disease. The reason some punk shot my dad was that he needed money. The reason Ryder liquefied three innocent people was he was pissed off that he lost." I shrug. "So yeah, I'm sure you all had your reasons. But my parents are both dead. Rebecca, Daisy, and Marnie too. My so-called family, people who supposedly loved and trusted me, have been lying to me from day one. So fuck your reasons!"

"You have every right to be angry. I know you see this as a betrayal."

"Got another word for it?"

"But we lied to protect you."

"So you were being cruel to be kind." I fold my arms across my chest. "Yeah, I've heard that one before too."

"Do you know what you were like when we first met? A hate-spewing, prejudiced, angry girl who found a scapegoat in Justin's dead father for her own. Not much has changed through the years. Do you have any idea how hurtful that was for him to hear? To endure from his best friend?"

She's right on that front. My back straightens. "Ever think my opinion might have changed had I known?"

"He wanted to tell you. A thousand times. He did. I'm the one who convinced him early on not to. That you wouldn't understand. Then the years went by and it became harder and harder to tell you for this exact reason. And if you really think about it objectively, you didn't really need to know. It had no bearing on your life or friendship up until now."

"Did he tell *her?*"

"It's not a competition, Joanna."

"He did. He trusted her and not me. And then…I've been torturing myself, thinking this whole mess was my fault. He knew that and let me go on thinking it."

"He lost a part of his family. He didn't want to risk losing the rest of it."

"Too fucking late."

"You're being unfair." She raises an eyebrow. "You didn't tell him about an important part of your life, of who you are. How is that any different from what he did?"

My eyes narrow. "I didn't tell him about a five month relationship, don't you compare the two."

"I wasn't talking about your dalliance with your supervisor. Since the night you met, you kept an essential part of yourself concealed." My stomach seizes up. It must show on my face because Lucy takes a step toward me. "You didn't trust him with your true feelings. You did all you could to conceal your love from him. To protect the both of you from the havoc it would bring. How on earth is that any different than what he did?"

I'm shamed into silence, the wheels in my mind spinning in vain to come up with an argument. "I—"

The sound of gunshots hitting brick outside the window startles us both. I count three, followed by glass shattering in my bedroom. As I rush toward the noise, the front door opens, Bryan and Geoff rushing into secure the confused Lucy. A black figure flies across the living room window as more gunshots ring out, one hitting the window and lodging in the poster behind me. I'm not even through the bedroom door when I see it on the floor surrounded by broken glass. A gray brick of C-4 with wire and a timer. Shit.

"Bomb!"

The men shove Lucy out the door with me running close behind. The moment I pull the fire alarm in the hall, the explosion rocks the building. The noise and heat from the blast knock me down, with Geoff falling on top of me. I don't know which hurts more, the explosion or the two hundred fifty pound man in top of me. Either way I can't breathe. Bits of ceiling and wall, some flaming, rain around us. My ears ring so loud I have an immediate headache.

Geoff rolls off me, and I flip over. Black smoke, tinted orange, billows out of my front door burning my nose and throat so badly I'm hacking my lungs out. The walls around and across are stained black with huge cracks branching out into the ceiling like a spider web. My apartment's a crater.

Geoff grabs me by the collar and pulls me off the floor. He shoves me down the hall right behind the shaking Lucy and serious Bryan. My neighbors fill the stairwell, some crying hysterically, and the rest in a blind panic. Thank God the majority are still at work. My next-door neighbor Mrs. Jeffrey and her seven cats rush down with the rest of us.

When we get onto the street, it's havoc. People from inside and out all stagger around, coughing, and some are even bleeding. The two police officers sent to guard me help corral the stunned people away from the smoldering rubble. Cars on the street honk, though I can barely hear them. The drivers get out of their cars, looking up. I do the same and wince. There's a huge hole with flames and smoke wafting from it. What's left of my apartment lies in hot heaps on the sidewalk. Like the rest of them, I'm too shocked to know what to do next. I've just become homeless. Someone just tried to kill me. Again. What—

A man in a leather jacket, one of the few not sporting a deer-in-the-headlights expression, saddles up to Bryan. I don't know what he does, but Bryan jerks and falls down. The people around him seem confused except for leather man. He takes another step and the same thing happens to Lucy. She swoons into the man's arms. It's all over in a second. As I'm turning to alert Geoff, two cold metal prongs touch my neck, followed by a painful jolt of electricity. My legs give out and I can't move my arms. Taser. I remember the feeling from the academy.

I'm not knocked out, but the world goes fuzzy and incoherent. I'm vaguely aware of a man picking me up as bystanders look on. He steps over Bryan's prostrate body, past the preoccupied patrolmen, down the street from the commotion. My head lolls from side to side as we move, but through the haze I realize where I've seen my abductor before. The other gunman from today. Perfect.

My body hasn't rebooted from the shock when he tosses me into the trunk of a Cadillac next to the near-unconscious

Lucy. Before shutting the back, he entwines my hands with riot cuffs at the wrists. In the pitch black, I can feel the car shake to life and pull away. I'm still too out of it to feel fear, but it's coming.

It takes a few minutes but my mind slowly recovers, followed by my body. Hands reach out to me in the darkness. I touch Lucy, tell her not to panic though I can't hear her response as my ears still ring. I do feel her hot, ragged breath on the back of my neck. She's close to panicked judging from her breathing. I'm not too far behind.

When complex thought is possible again, my training takes over. We covered this very scenario at the academy. As I'm telling Lucy to stay calm, that we'll be okay, I kick out the tail light. With the last thrust, dull pain runs across my bare foot. I cut myself, but I barely feel it. When the plastic gives, light streams inside so bright I have to shut my eyes for a moment. This better get someone's attention. Blinking helps and soon I can see. I flip over so I'm facing Lucy. Tears cover her face and I grab her shaking, bound hands with mine, reassuring her until she calms down a little. I try to move, so I can look out the hole but can't. My foot won't fit out either.

I tell Lucy to scoot back as far as she can and then start kicking the top of the trunk as hard as I can, not easy with my injured foot. Each time I hit, a stab of pain shoots through. Great. I don't have much leverage but keep at it. Maybe someone will hear. I think we drive about ten minutes, to where I don't know. The car turns left again and we go down a bumpy incline, the light dimming as we descend on the gravel. Lucy's breath grows ragged again.

"Oh, God," she whimpers.

I'm close to falling apart too. This is bad. This is *so* bad. There's a very good chance I'll throw up at some point, but I'll stave the impulse off as long as possible. "Lucy, listen to me," I say, voice deceptively neutral. "We are going to get through this. You just need to stay calm and do what I say when I say it. Be strong, okay? No matter what."

"O—Okay," she says.

A few more twists and turns, all downhill, before the car pulls to a stop. The car door opens, then a few seconds later a metal door opens outside. We drive through it, then it shuts again. It's pitch black now. We drive another minute on the gravel before stopping again. There's only a little light from the hole. This time both car doors open and the men walk toward us, gravel under their feet signal their approach. My heart is about to leap out of my chest as the trunk opens.

I'm ready for them. I kick the nearest one square in the face, more than satisfied when I hear his nose crack and blood spew from it. As he recoils, leather jacket punches me in the face, stunning me. He grabs my collar and tosses me hard onto the rocks and gravel. It'd hurt more if not for my screaming jaw. As I'm still reeling, leather nicely helps Lucy out of the trunk.

We're underground in the subway, metal tracks crossing over gravel. The only lights are from the portables set up around. There's a nearby subway car parked about twenty yards away near an old station. If I look the way we came, there's nothing but darkness. The other guard stumbles over to me, pissed to hell. "You fucking bitch!" he says as he kicks me in the stomach. I can't breathe. Pain replaces air. I curl into the fetal position to stave off more blows.

"Hey!"

All eyes move to the source. Strolling out of the lit-up subway car onto the platform is the man himself in all his glory. He's dressed in chinos, loafers, white shirt, with his goatee and hair coiffed to perfection. King of the Underground and he knows it. Ryder jumps off the platform, walking toward us. "That's no way to treat a guest."

"She broke my fucking nose and killed Burns today!"

"You did try to kill her as well. I'd break your nose too." He saunters over to me and my nausea returns. My eyes don't leave those wrists. "Hi, Joanna. Nice to formally meet you." He holds out his hand, and I wince. He chuckles, shaking his head. "You try and be nice." Ryder grabs my hands and yanks me up, not easy as my body is reeling from today's torture. The bastard actually puts his arm around my waist to support me as I limp toward the subway car. Whenever I glance at him, he gives me a friendly smile. He really is fucking crazy.

We're led into the car, which is set up like an apartment with a bed, books, a rack of clothes, a hot plate, and a tiny fridge with a power line out to the generator. Better than prison, I guess. He helps me sit on his bed as leather jacket sits a shaking Lucy next to me. Alkaline whispers a few words to the men. I recognize the word "Blitzkrieg," a henchman for hire from Jericho who combines his talent for bombs with his gift of flying. Bastard owes me a samurai sword. When Ryder finishes his instructions the guards walk out, sliding the car door shut behind them. I'm actually more frightened when they leave.

James Ryder. Alkaline. A few feet away from me. And there's not a damn thing I can do to stop what's coming.

He pulls up a chair, casual as hell, and sits facing Lucy and me on the bed. "So. Here we are. At last. Sorry the place is such a mess. I wasn't expecting company so soon. He was just supposed to place the bomb under Ms. Helms' car." He smiles at the lady. "Though when we realized where she was headed, the men had the wherewithal to call and the plan changed, definitely for the better."

"Lucky you," I say.

"It's better to be lucky than smart," he says with another smile. "Though I have been blessed with both, as you know firsthand. That was fun on the bridge that night. Thrilling. I wanted you chasing me from the very beginning, you know. It was all part of the plan. I just didn't know it would be so much fun." Still smiling, he scoots closer to me. I recoil, but that smile doesn't fade. "You know, I remember you from the neighborhood. You were always walking around with that 'don't mess with me' look. Even my dealers knew to leave you alone. It was cute as hell." He reaches across and caresses my chin. I don't react. "Not much has changed."

"Yeah, I'm irresistible," I say sarcastically. I'm powerless, and we both know it. But there is no way in hell I'm going to give this piece of shit the satisfaction of seeing me scared. *None.* "Look, I'm exhausted. I don't want to play any games with you. So I will do whatever you want, okay? I won't fight. Or I will, if that's how you get off. Whatever floats your boat. Just don't hurt Lucy, okay? You raping and murdering me will be more than enough to get your point across."

"How noble. Though, how do you know that's what I intend to do to you?"

"Because you're a fucking cowardly rapist child-killer with no soul whose tried to kill me twice today. So, let her go and just get it over with already."

He leans in closer, apprizing me with that smile that's still growing. "I admire your strength, Joanna. When your friend, the good doctor, found herself facing a similar fate, she crumbled into incoherent sobs and pleas. Yet here you are with your chin up, looking out for a woman who has treated you with disrespect for years." I narrow my eyes. How did he know that? "Your friend is an idiot to have let such a woman as yourself pass him by."

"Well, I don't have a dead mother and child in the next room like Rebecca did."

The smile drops. "I do regret the child. I made sure she didn't suffer. She didn't even know what was happening."

"You're a real humanitarian, Ryder."

"*He's* the one who dragged her into all of this," he says, finally showing some of that famous rage. "He had to have known this would eventually happen. He's destroyed so many lives. One of us was bound to piece together the truth and act on that knowledge. I had a life. Love. He took that away from me. What kind of man would I be if I didn't do the same to him?"

"A chickenshit psycho who has to prey on women and children because he's too gutless to come at him directly," I say, the words almost literally dripping with venom.

He rolls his eyes. "This where I'm supposed to fly into a rage and dispatch you with minimal pain, correct? I'm not one of your usual lowlifes so consumed with anger I can't see straight at a little prodding, so save your breath. I have a very specific plan for you." He looks at Lucy. "*You*, I'll have to think about. I was going to be humane with the bomb—simple, unexpected, tragic—but this might be better. I'd set up a trap where he can save only one of you, but that's rather cliché. Shrieker in New Urbana just did that this week. I'd like to think I have more imagination than that."

"You're insane," Lucy says. "Certifiably."

"Three years locked up alone with no one to talk to. Nothing to do but read. And fantasize. You'd go a little mad too. So…" He stands, smoothing his crisp pants. "I have a few last minute details to take care of. My timeline's been moved up considerably. There's so much to do!"

"Don't let us keep you," I say.

"You might not believe me, but I am sorry you both had to be dragged into this. I really am."

"Go—fuck—yourself," I say, drawing out every word.

He shakes his head. "The things I'm going to do to that mouth."

"Bring it on."

Still shaking his head and smiling, he walks out. He slides the door shut and the man with the broken nose stands guard in front of it. Ryder talks with leather jacket and they walk toward the only door in the station. I breathe a sigh of relief.

Lucy starts biting at her cuffs. "What are we going to do?"

I stand up and start searching for something, *anything* useful. There are a few pens and if these were regular cuffs I'd be out of them in a jiffy. No such luck. I toss the bed but only find a small, lacy bra from La Perla. Jane Smith's been here. Lucy checks the books and fridge. Our shenanigans draw attention. The guard pounds on the door to stop us, brandishing his gun to get the point across. I sit back down with a groan. "Fuck!"

"Justin will find us. Justin will save us," Lucy says.

I take one of Ryder's shirts and wrap up my bleeding foot. "How? A GPS tracking chip doesn't work underground."

"He will! He has to. We just need to buy him some time."

I scoff. "Waiting for rescue is never a viable option. They can move us, or they can just come in and shoot us. No. I need to think." I stand again and walk around the car, looking out the windows for inspiration. Nothing but darkness both ways.

The guard pounds on the door, holding up his gun with a sneer. "Sit the fuck down, bitch!"

Light bulb.

I flip him off with both fingers and mouth, "Fuck you." He glares at me with utter hatred. "Lucy, I'm going to need your help in a second here. Then be ready to run."

The guard pounds again, but I pick up the chair and begin smashing it against the far window. I hear the door open and close. "Bitch, stop!"

I spin around and toss the chair at him. "Fuck you, cocksucker!" I say before I spit at him. "Pussy!"

Too damn easy. He lunges at me, gun pointed right at my head. We fall onto the bed with me underneath him. His free hand clasps around my neck, the other with the gun pushing into my forehead. I can't breathe. "Cunt! I'll fucking—"

Lucy whacks my attacker over the head with the hot plate. He releases me, crying out in pain, and Lucy hits him again. And again. It doesn't knock him out, but he's stunned enough for me to bite his gun hand. He drops the gun as a trembling Lucy backs away. The bastard still won't get off me and now he's even more pissed. I have no choice. Using the palms of my hands, I send his nasal bone straight into his brain with one thrust. He falls off me. Dead. I've never killed anyone before.

There's no time to let this fact sink in. Quickly, I check his pockets and find a small knife and cell, but nothing else. No car keys. I cut off my cuffs and pick up the gun. Lucy barely registers it as I take off her restraints. She can't take her eyes off the dead man. I flip open the phone and almost cry when I see a bar. As I dial Harry, I check out the windows to see if the coast is clear. No one on the platform.

"Hello?" Harry asks.

"Harry, it's me," I whisper.

"Jo!"

"Look, he has us in an abandoned Metro station, I don't know which one. The placard's worn away. Try triangulating the cell, get the tower I'm using. There's two of them, Ryder included. I'll leave the phone on, but we're making a break for it."

"Jo, what—"

I put the phone in my pocket and turn to Lucy. "Stay close and keep quiet."

Lucy and I pry the door open with a piece of the hot plate. I squeeze through first as quietly as possible with Lucy behind me. She runs down the platform as I cover the office door with the gun. When she's halfway there, I sprint after her. So far so good. When my feet hit gravel, my right foot howls in pain from the gash. I wince but keep going, though the limp slows me a little. She reaches the car first, but the doors are locked. Shit. Having no choice, I smash the driver's window with the butt of the gun. It shatters on the second attempt. As I unlock the door and push Lucy in, the office door opens. My heart beats double time. The lower panel with all the wires is already open, so I just have to connect the correct wires. My fucked-up childhood comes in handy sometimes.

"Oh, God, they're coming!" Lucy says.

I just keep rubbing until the car springs to life. When I sit up, a gunshot disintegrates the back window and cracks the front. Lucy shrieks, and I throw the car into gear and hit the gas hard, though I can barely see out through the cracked glass. Ryder and his goon keep shooting, the car jerking as they hit the back tire. Not taking my eyes off the road, I fire a few times out the back. I almost miss the turn and have to cut it too hard. The back of the car skids and hits the wall, shocking us, but I keep going. We both put on our seatbelts after that. I keep driving for a few seconds, the thumps of the flat tire overshadowing our labored breathing. "Harry, we're in the tunnels driving a black Cadillac." I make another turn. "I have no idea where we are, but—"

There's a whooshing sound then movement above us from front to back, but it's too dark for me to make out what it is until it's right in front of the headlights. I know it's a man, but with the fucking window I have to think about who and what. Not good. A second later, about ten feet in front of us, there's another explosion. On instinct, I slam on the breaks and lose control of the car. We slam into the right wall at about fifteen miles an hour. I whack my head on the wheel, dazing myself. Everything becomes fuzzy except for the nausea and Lucy's groans beside me.

As I'm attempting to focus, my door swings opens. A man in his twenties dressed all in black with a gun, utility belt with grenades, and a black bag around his torso unlatches my seatbelt and pulls me out of the car. He lays me on the gravel, and I'm still too out of it to move. I am aware of him looking into the car. "Yeah," he says into his earpiece. "That was me.

They crashed the car. I'll bring the cop now." He pauses, the nudges me with his foot. My eyes shut. "She's out of it." He chuckles. "Yeah, I'll be careful." He presses a button on his Bluetooth before he kneels down and lifts me like a bride. "You don't look so tough."

Good thing I know how to play possum. We lift off the ground and fly. It feels strange gliding through open air. Or that could be the concussion. I count to three before snapping my eyes open. He's surprised, and that gives me a precious second to act. With one hand I grab the pin of the nearest grenade and with the other I stick my thumb into his eye until it pops. He howls in pain, dropping me. I fall about ten feet onto hard gravel, rolling on impact. Now there isn't an inch of me that doesn't hurt.

Blitzkrieg continues howling and flying. I groan and touch my bleeding knee. Shit. My hand is empty. I lost my grip on the pin. I push myself up, and start limping toward the car for the gun. Blitzkrieg roars like an animal and when I dare to glance back, I see he's changing course and charging at me like a phantom bull. He's too fast. My torn legs pump, but not fast enough. He's just about on top of me when Lucy sits up, gun pointed right at me. "Drop!" she shouts. I do. Three gunshots ring out, hitting Blitzkrieg in the chest. He skids to the ground near me. Holy shit. The car door opens, and a trembling Lucy steps out of the car with the gun pointed at the groaning man. One more bullet ends that.

Lucy stares at the man expressionless, gun arm spastic and her other bent and against her chest. It takes effort but I slowly find my feet, walking over to her. I gently take the gun, but she barely notices. "It's okay," I whisper. I think she can't hear me. She's checked out, and rightly so. Wish I had the luxury. Instead, I ransack the corpse for grenades, gun, phone, and a black bag with more bombs. I'm zipping up the bag when I hear voices shouting back the way we came.

I take Lucy's good hand, but she still won't move, won't take her eyes off the man she just killed. "Lucy, move!" I pull her away and she moves, walking behind me as I'm trying to run. She's passed her breaking point. We keep moving but slower than we need to be. This isn't good for either of us. The voices get closer.

When we reach the next junction, we can go straight or right. I lead her straight until I spot a little burrow off to the side which she can fit into. "Harry, follow this to Lucy, okay?" I whisper into the cell phone. "She's in a hole near our car. She has a broken arm. I'm going to lead them away from her. Hurry." I hand her the cell, but have to stick it in her pocket myself. I even have to put the gun in her hand, wrapping her fingers around it. "I don't know if you can hear me, but if anyone but the police comes, you shoot them. I'm going to get help and bring them back. Just be quiet, okay?" I don't want to leave her. She just saved my life, but I have to. Fuck, I have to.

I pull out Blitzkrieg's spare gun, a grenade, and his cell, dialing Cam as I run back the way I came. I see the beams of two flashlights and men coming into focus. "Cam, it's Jo. Trace this!" The phone goes into my pocket seconds before the men open fire at me. I pull the pin and lob a grenade at them. It explodes just as I turn down the tunnel, covering my ears. I pull out Blitzkrieg's flashlight and keep running. On a good day I can run a mile and a half without stopping, but this is uphill on gravel and my body's been through hell, so I'm about to fall after a quarter mile. A bullet whizzes by my head and I spin, returning fire. All I can see is the light from their flashlights coming closer. I'd toss another grenade, but the blast would roll up and incinerate me too.

"The other one's gone! Go find her!" Alkaline shouts.

Shit. Nothing I can do. She has a gun. I keep running. My lungs are about to give out, but my leg beats them to it. My right leg buckles but I keep pressing on. I'm not going to make it. Then I see the next platform and push myself forward. I climb up the rickety ladder onto the dusty platform. Rats squeak and run from the light. I stop dead from fright. Psychos with acid don't scare me as much as rats. I have to force myself up the rest of the way, my breath as sharp as glass in a broken window. At least the station sign is intact here. "Cam, I'm at the old Siegal Street station. Hurry." There are two gunshots far off. Lucy? Did he kill her? Stop it. Keep going.

There's a rusty metal gate with a padlock on it at the exit. I shoot the lock and push the gate apart. It squeals and barely moves, but I squeeze through just as a bullet ricochets off of it.

The bag gets caught and I fall forward, losing my grip on the gun. I wiggle the bag off just as Alkaline runs up. My eyes immediately dart toward that white tube extended from his wrist. It's actually a hollow bone attached to an internal sac of acid, like a snake's venom sac but deadlier. I pick up the gun just as he takes aim. "Joanna, stop running!" he says, more chiding than angry.

As I'm turning to run, a liquid squirts from that bone. It sizzles the metal like a steak on a grill, some landing on my coat. The burning on my upper arm starts instantly and it takes a lot not to drop the flashlight. I run up the wooden ramp, shedding my coat and shooting twice. The bullets ricochet off the metal beams holding up the ceiling in the middle of the ramp, almost hitting me. "Joanna! I have this gun pointed right at your spine. You need to stop or I will paralyze you. *Stop* and drop your gun. Don't make me do this! Please!"

Fuck! Fuck! No. Not fair. Not when I'm so close. I come to a standstill near one of the beams. The boarded-up exit is ten feet away. So fucking close. I feel like crying, but I just don't have the energy. I let the pistol fall and turn around with my hands up, not easy as my burnt arm is covered in my blood. Ryder walks up, gun and acid pointed right at me. "Good girl."

That's when I see him. Just a blur and whoosh of wind. Finally.

Alkaline hears it too, instantly spinning around and firing the gun. Justice slams into him, and they break the metal beam like a toothpick. The roof shakes and cracks, tiles from the walls falling off. I hug the wall as they smack into each other and a huge chunk of ceiling falls. Dust and dirt fill the air, so thick I can barely see through it. Justice tosses him into the wall, roaring like a madman. The entire tunnel lurches. Tiles and chunks of cement fall on and around me. The place is disintegrating. "Justin!" I shriek. "Stop!"

He doesn't listen. He tosses Alkaline through the boards at the end, and then runs him back in here, hitting the villain against the last of the load-bearing beams. That's all it takes. The whole ceiling and room rumbles and crumbles, and there's nowhere to run. I couldn't make it even if I could move. Justice looks at the near-unconscious Alkaline, then at me. I can't see his eyes under the mask, but the fact he quickly looks back at Alkaline tells me all I need to know. Revenge trumps my life.

A horrible pain shoots through the top of my head. I collapse to the ground as the tunnel topples around me. My city is swallowing me up. I'm dying. I'm lifted, transported at an incredible rate. Stomach, limbs, and brain all left behind a few seconds. I fall away from the light into the dark abyss of nothingness.

Twenty years too late. Hope they let me in.

***

Pain. This is how I realize I'm still alive.

My head, my ribs, my legs, my face, my arm, my foot all throb in pain. The rest of me isn't fairing much better. Slowly, I open my eyes. Crap. I'm in the hospital. I hate hospitals. There are tubes and sensors attached in some very intimate places hooked up to machines on either side of me. The room looks like a jungle with all the flowers. Harry's asleep in the chair on my left, his head resting on the edge of my bed. Silly man still has his glasses on. I pet his soft hair and he stirs. He sits up, rubbing his eyes. It takes him a moment to realize I'm awake.

"Jo!" he says with relief.

"Hi," I whisper.

He kisses me with gusto, but even that hurts. I wince and he pulls away. "Sorry. Sorry."

I try to touch my lip to find the source of discomfort, but my upper arm flares with pain as I flex. "Ouch!" My arm is covered in bandages from shoulder to elbow.

"Your arm had a bad chemical burn. Third degree. There might be some scaring."

Oh. Good thing I'm not vain. "What else?"

"Um, you have two cracked ribs but no internal bleeding, a nasty gash on your foot, a bruised jaw," he sighs, "some first and second degree burns, countless cuts and bruises, and two concussions. One minor and one major."

"Shit. Is there any good news?"

"You woke up," he says, voice cracking.

I'm taken aback and a little scared by his response. "How—How long have I been out?"

"Just a day, but…they said if you didn't wake up within forty-eight hours, the chances…" He shakes his head to expel the thought. "You have brain swelling."

I squeeze his hand. "With my hard head? I'm shocked it even made a dent." This garners a smile from us both, though his is strained. He kisses the palm of my hand and holds it up to his scratchy cheek. Then I remember. "Oh, God! Lucy! She—"

"She's okay. She's fine. We found her."

"Is she okay?"

"Mild concussion and a broken arm. They sent her home this morning."

"What happened?"

"I was just parking at the station when I got the call about the bomb. I wasn't even halfway back when Justice came over the police band saying he was tracking you, but lost the signal at the outskirts of the Ward. Every roller was dispatched, and even Lord Nightingale from Independence showed up to help. The GPS on the phones didn't work down there, and I only heard you half the time. We only pinpointed you when Justice heard the explosion. By the time we got down there, he was tending to you and Lucy."

"What about Alkaline?"

"They're still excavating the scene. It's a mess."

"You haven't found him?" I'm surprised by the amount of fear in my voice.

"Jo, there's a sinkhole on Siegel Street. It's completely caved in on both sides of the station, and we combed the surrounding area for half a day. There is no way he survived. None. Justice barely got you out of there in time."

"You'll keep looking, right?"

"We will, but the city engineers don't think we can get to the scene within a week. Not even he can survive without food or water for that long. Don't worry." He kisses my hand again. "I'm going to get the doctor, okay?"

I sigh when he leaves. Lucy's okay, Alkaline's probably dead, and I caught up on some much needed sleep. All in all not a bad day's work. I close my eyes. I think maybe that bump on my head accessed my long-dormant optimistic side. When I get out of here maybe I'll become a clown. Or these drugs they have me on just rock.

The door opens. Poking and prodding time. I open my eyes, and my stomach clenches. He looks terrible. Dark circles under his eyes, hair wild, even his skin has lost its glow. I want to jump out of this bed and throw my arms around him to make us both feel better. I suppress it. Justin makes no move to come closer. He stays by the door, just waiting for me to lead the way. I avert my eyes, giving him nothing.

"O'Hara told me you were awake," he says. "How are you—"

"I'm fine," I say quickly. "How's Lucy?"

"She…um," Justin says, voice quaking, "physically okay. Broken arm. Mentally, um, she hasn't said a word since I found her."

"She'll be okay. It'll just take time." I bunch the covers in my hands, ringing them. Even this hurts. "She saved my life."

"You saved hers."

We don't speak for a few gut-wrenching seconds, the only noise coming from my heavy breathing.

"Jo, I—"

"You're sorry. I know you're sorry. You don't need to say it."

"I wanted to tell you. A hundred million times I did. The words just wouldn't come out. And then…I was just so scared of how'd you react. That I'd lose you, and *that* I could not take. You of all people should know what that's like."

I don't respond for a few seconds, my brain working to find the right words. My supposed gift. "I get why you did what you did," I say, still wringing the sheets with my hands. "I understand the logic of it, I do. You were scared of how I would react. You were scared I'd look down on you, not be able to get past it. That I needed protecting from the dark side of your life. My head gets that. It does. My heart…" I shake my head. "Nope." I wipe the falling tears with my less damaged hand. "You didn't trust me. You *betrayed* me every day by not trusting me when…" I stop the sob from escaping, and take a second to compose myself. "You were my best friend, my confidante, the man I've been in love with for twenty years. You were my world. You were my *hero*. And now…" I shake my head with a wry chuckle. "You let me think I was responsible for Rebecca's death. You kept much needed information from me and the police about a man who just tried to kill me. You didn't say a damn word as I bared my secrets to you, and then turned around and used them to make yourself feel better at my expense. And you chose revenge over my well-being. *You broke my heart.* And for *that* I don't think I can ever forgive you."

I finally look up at him. His eyes are as brimming with tears. He wipes the offenders away and hangs his head. "I never meant to hurt you."

"I know," I whisper. "But you did."

He slowly nods. This is it and we both know it. We've lost each other. We're broken. "Okay," he whispers back. "Okay." He takes a ragged breath and turns around. "Good-bye, Joanna."

In a flash, he's gone.

"Good-bye, rich boy."

CHAPTER SEVENTEEN
SURVIVORS

"Harry, did you remember to buy suntan lotion?"

When he doesn't answer I walk out, or more accurately limp out of the bedroom in search of him. I find him in the living room, phone pressed to his ear and looking none too happy. "Can it wait until after I get back?" He listens, and then sighs. "I don't have…fine. Be there when I can." He slaps the phone shut.

"The office again, dear?"

"We just have to swing by on the way to the airport. It'll take ten minutes, I promise." He kisses my nose. "And I packed plenty of suntan lotion." He kisses me again and walks into the bedroom.

Our first official trip together. Sandals, Jamaica, here we come. Sun, sand, and hopefully lots of sex. Paradise. I follow him into the bedroom to continue packing. I toss the books from my nightstand into the suitcase. As a rule I'm not much of a reader, but in my three conscious days at the hospital I managed to read every magazine ever published. Twice. Not that I plan on doing much reading in Jamaica, wink wink. I may look as if I've been to war but damned if I'll let that stop me from enjoying a tropical island with my awesome boyfriend. I'll just keep the blistering burn on my arm covered. Don't want Harry or the other guests to vomit in the umbrella drinks.

V was kind enough to buy me some clothes while I was in the hospital since everything I own is nothing but ash. Nobody was killed, thank God, but all residents had to move out until it's rebuilt to code. So I'm homeless, clothes less, and recovering from a coma. If ever there was a time for a vacation.

Loose ends first. When we arrive at the station, half the people nod to me with reverence and the other half come up and shake my hand. I could get used to being a hero. The squad room is back to its old self, quiet even. Cam, Mirabelle, and Kowalski aren't at their desks, but the support staff smile when they see me. As Harry goes into his office to sign some incident reports and budget analysis, I plop down at my desk. Well, my old desk. I won't be returning to Priority. When I'm cleared for duty, I'll be working Vice. I've had enough death for the time being. Hookers and gambling are more my speed now.

Mirabelle comes in from the interview area, a bright smile forming when he sees me. "It's the traitor!" We hug and I sit back down. "Thought you and the boss man would be sipping Mai Tai's by now."

"Cam needed him to sign a few things before we left."

"Well, you're looking good. How are you feeling?"

"A lot better. I don't even need the pain pills unless I move my arm too much."

"I'm sure the sun and lots of sweaty sex will help with that."

I smack his arm. "Pig."

He chuckles back. "What? Now you don't have to sneak around in the nursery or locker room anymore."

"I have no idea what you're talking about," I say with horror.

"Come on. We all knew, well at least part of the time. You kept looking at each other and blushing. It felt like we were back in high school."

"And we thought we were being coy."

"Well, I am a superior investigator."

I nod in approval. "So, Harry refuses to tell me anything. How goes it here?"

"Clean-up mostly. We arrested the accomplice in the subway," he says of the goon in the leather jacket. "He talked. Alkaline's old Lieutenant Mike Spencer hired him to watch the Pendergast house. He's been pretending to be paparazzi since the engagement party. He didn't tell us anything we didn't know. The abandoned station he was using was more helpful. We found blueprints of the Thornton house, the Pendergast house, and your apartment, along with surveillance photos of all of you. Still trying to track down the PI who took them. He also had all of your schedules, your financials, psych profiles, basically your whole lives. Our people are still trying to trace his money. This was a well funded revenge plot. Blitzkrieg's fee is reported at close to fifty thousand dollars."

"He won't be collecting it this time," I say. "Anything on Jane Smith yet?"

"Just the bra and condom wrappers. We lifted prints from every surface but no hits. She doesn't have a criminal record. Came up empty on the P.O. Box as well."

"And the search for Ryder?"

For the first time he looks away from me. "They're, uh, calling it off today."

"What?"

"It's been five days and they still haven't made it to the old Siegel station. If he was alive down there, he isn't anymore. When it first happened we combed the tunnels. He couldn't have gotten past us."

"I'd feel better if I could, I don't know, spit on his body or something."

"If it makes you feel any better, he's buried under a ton of rocks and dirt in the Ward. I'm sure every day someone will piss on his grave whether it's intentional or not."

"That does make me feel better," I say with a smile. "Thank you."

He doesn't smile back. His back straightens, and his face turns professional. I spin around. Dobbs escorts the frail Lucy in. She looks horrible. Her forehead has a bandage, she has a black eye and bruising on the right side of her face, and her arm is in a sling. Both are as surprised to see me as I am them. "Miss Joanna!" Dobbs says, as he walks over. He hugs me, something he's never done before. I squeeze back. I try to meet Lucy's eyes, but she gazes down at the floor. Dobbs releases me. "How are you?"

"Good. Fine. No problems."

Mirabelle walks over to Lucy. "Miss Helms, thank you for coming down. We'll try to make this as easy for you as possible."

Her hand clenches into a fist. "Okay," she says quietly. Mirabelle gestures toward the interview rooms, and Lucy slowly walks over. She refuses to look up as she passes me. For some reason this stings.

It must show, because when she's out of earshot Dobbs says, "Don't be upset with her, Miss Joanna. She's just having a difficult time. She didn't start speaking again until this morning."

"Jesus, I'm so sorry."

"An old friend from Independence is flying in to take her back there."

"For how long?"

"Until she wishes to return. If ever," he says, almost haunted by the prospect. My heart goes out to him. He'll have no one to serve in that huge mansion. We were the closest thing to family he has. "Is there somewhere we can talk that's more private?"

I don't like the sound of that. "Okay," I say. I lead him into the nursery and shut the door.

"I don't know who else to speak to about this. I know you're angry and you have every right to be. I wouldn't ask if it wasn't a matter of life or death."

"What happened?"

"It's Master Justin," he says. "I'm frightened for him. He's…I've never seen him like this before."

"Well, what—what's the matter with him?" I've been trying in vain not to think about him the last few days. I'm glad I said what I did, but his expression right before he left plagues me. He might have broken my heart, but I eviscerated his.

"Miss Joanna, he just keeps watching home movies and going through the Alkaline file obsessively. He hasn't slept an hour and refuses to eat. He barely leaves the command center, let alone the house. Every time I suggest he take care of himself, he just walks away without a word. And Miss Lucy, he won't even look at her. I've known that boy everyday of his life. I *know* he's slipping away, and I feel so helpless. It's breaking my heart. Please help us."

"Do you think he'd hurt himself?"

He's unable to talk for a moment, then says, "I honestly don't know. He phoned his attorney to amend his will." Dobbs' look of hopelessness rocks me. "Please, Miss Joanna. I don't know what else to do."

Neither do I. My first impulse is to jump in a car, drive to the mansion, and not leave until I draw out a smile. But the image of him in that tunnel as I'm screaming at him to stop makes my stomach clench. "I'm sorry he's upset, I really am. He's been through a lot, I know that. I just, I can't see him right now. I can't. I don't…have it in me. I don't. He's strong. He'll be fine. I'm sorry."

I rush out of the room from his disbelieving expression like the coward I am.

***

I stare out the window of the taxi at the nearly full moon, willing myself to unknot all my limbs and to push all thoughts of Justin slowly killing himself in that cold mansion away. The words, *"He'll be fine…"* cycle through my head as if repetition will make it so. I'm so deep in thought and wound up that when Harry takes my hand, I jump.

"Sorry," he says, as startled as I am. "Sorry. Are you all right?"

"Sorry," I say with a chuckle. "I was just thinking."

"You've been out of sorts since we left the station."

"I just, I'm fine." I smile and turn back to my window. "I'll be fine."

Fine. What a strange, overused word. We're all always fine, even when we don't mean it, and we rarely mean it. People let us get away with it because they really don't care. Most of the time they're too damn busy dealing with their own fine and don't give a damn about yours, even when you're drowning. One of the reasons I'm falling, if I'm not already in love with Harry is that he never settles for fine.

He puts his arm around me, pulling me toward him. I rest my head on this shoulder. "Tell me."

"Dobbs brought Lucy to the station. She's in a bad way. They all are. Especially…you know. He just sounded so scared."

"What about?"

"He said Justin's not eating. Not sleeping. He's…it's not good."

"Is he a danger to himself?"

"I—I don't know. I mean, of course he's depressed. Anyone would be. But he'll be fine. Just fine."

I don't even convince myself, let alone him. Harry is silent for a moment and I'm afraid to look at him in case I'm greeted by disapproval or disgust. Not that I don't deserve them.

"Driver," Harry finally says, "we've changed our minds. We need to go to 3377 Kane Lane in the Gardens. And please hurry."

The driver nods and turns the car around. I sit up. "What are you doing? We can't go. We'll miss our flight."

"There are other flights."

"No, that's not fair to you."

"I'm not spending my vacation with you like this. You'll spend the entire time worrying instead of relaxing, thinking of him instead of me. Believe me, I'm being selfish."

"No. *No*, Harry," I say, shaking my head, "I can't. I can't face him. I'll be useless. I'm still too furious at him. I'll just make things worse."

"That's bullshit and we both know it."

"I'm not going."

"Then either you're a coward, or you're just cruel."

"What?"

"One bad decision and you're ready to chuck it all in. Twenty years, Joanna. That's longer than most marriages. Does that one bad negate all the good?"

"I…" I have no idea what to say.

"If he harms himself, and you don't at least try to help him, you will never forgive yourself. The guilt will destroy you. Everything he has done, all the sacrifices you both made for the right, will be for nothing." He takes my hand, looking me square in the eyes. "It's your job to save people. You take this job so seriously and are so good at it, you take my breath away. It's what you were put on this earth to do." He smiles and kisses me. "So do it."

Shit. "I hate you."

He caresses my cheek with another smile. "I hate you too."

***

I can feel it the moment I walk in the door. Call it experience or intuition, but I just know there's something off in this house. It may not be the homiest, but the house never felt this oppressive or melancholy. It's as if a shade has been drawn, not allowing any light to filter in. Fear and urgency grip me.

"Justin!" I shout. Harry walks in behind me. "You check upstairs," I tell Harry.

As Harry runs up the stairs, I rush into the kitchen, then the parlor, library, dining room, games room, conservatory, Florida room, study, and finally the living room. Not a trace. Harry meets up with me just as I walk in from the patio. "He's not upstairs, and the staff seems to be gone as well," Harry says. We both glance at the fireplace.

I reach in and trip the switch for the door, and we rush in. There's no sound except for our footsteps as we run down the ramp to the command center. The computers and lights are on and there's a red light flashing overhead, but no Justin. What really catches my eye are the three white envelopes and a large binder sitting on the couch. One each to me, Lucy, and Dobbs. As I rip open mine, Harry checks the binder. "It's an instruction manual for the lab equipment and computer," Harry says, but I barely register his voice because of the pounding in my ears as I read.

"Jo,
You were wrong. You saved my life.
I'm sorry.
Love, Justin"

"Oh, fuck," I say under my breath as I crumple up the note. My head whips over to Harry. "Call the dispatcher. We need an APB out *now*!"

I snatch the instruction manual out of his hands and race over to the computers. He's even provided the password, "RichBoy." Harry makes the call, as I start flipping through the book looking for anything of use. There's just too much information and not enough time. Hell, for all I know he's done it already. I just stare at the monitor, too panicked to think clearly. He won't do it. He *can't*. I couldn't bear it.

"Jo," Harry says, touching my shoulder. I didn't even see him come over. "Think. Where could he have gone?"

"I—I don't know."

"Did he have a favorite spot? The park? His boat? Work?"

"I don't know!"

"You know him better than anyone else. Think!"

Okay. Okay, I can do this. Rebecca's house? Possible. The boat? Not as likely. He'd want as little fuss as possible.

Wouldn't want us to be scarred by finding him looking gruesome. And he has super-healing. A gun wouldn't work unless it was a shotgun to the head. Pills and slitting his wrists are out too, as is hanging, I think. So how the hell… *"You know, that might work."*

"I think I know where he is."

We run for the car. Five of the longest minutes of my life later, I'm proved right. Harry drives along Pendergast Bridge in our borrowed car as slow as he can as I scan both sides. We're about halfway across when I spot a figure in the darkness, almost like a phantom. If I wasn't looking closely, I'd have missed him. Harry pulls the BMW over, and I barely wait for the car to stop before leaping out.

If he notices me approaching, he doesn't let on. He just stares down at the black water, lost in his own personal hell. Cars drive by as if we're not even here, oblivious or not even caring about the man leaning dangerously on the railing. "Do you need help?"

His gaze whips in my direction. At first he's startled, blue eyes wild and frightened, but then I smile and his face falls. He turns back to the abyss, but I keep walking slowly toward him until I'm right beside him, folding my arms on the railing. If I wasn't up close I wouldn't recognize him. He hasn't shaved in a week, his hair is greasy, and dark circles rim his eyes. All the light in him is gone. "You look like hell, rich boy."

He still won't look at me. "How did you find me?" he asks, voice gravelly.

"I just thought, 'If I was going to kill myself, where would I do it?'" I say with a small smile. When I don't get a reaction, I punch him in the shoulder. "Come on, that was a good one."

"What are you doing here, Jo?" he growls.

"Saving you. Thought that was pretty obvious."

"I don't want you to save me."

"Tough."

His face contorts in rage, and he shoves me away. "Get the fuck out of here!"

Out of the corner of my eye I see Harry move forward, but I hold out my hand to stop him. My eyes never leave Justin. "You know there's no way in hell that's happening."

"Why?" he spits out. "You hate me. I—I lied to you. I almost got you killed, for Christ's sake! Everything! Everyone I touch, I destroy. Rebecca! Daisy! Lucy! You! I'm toxic, Jo. I can't," he says, voice cracking, "I can't stand it anymore. I can't. No matter what I do, it's never enough." He turns back to the edge, quivering with emotion. I'm losing him.

"If you do this, Alkaline triumphs. *This* is what he wanted. Don't give him the satisfaction. Don't you dare let him win."

"Jo, I can't…I can't…" He's close to hyperventilating and almost doubles over.

I take a deep breath to calm myself before stepping back over to him. I don't say anything for a moment, just let him get used to my presence again. "You know, people have asked me, rather rudely, through the years why you and I are friends. They assume it was because you were rich and gorgeous, and I was madly in love with you. I didn't blame them because if I was them I'd think the same thing." I shrug. "But actually, I stuck around in spite of that stuff. I hate parties and designer clothes. And you are nice to look at, but I could have done that through magazines. And as for the loving you thing…I *hated* the fact you didn't love me back. There were even a few times when I considered cutting all ties because it just hurt too much." He opens his mouth to respond, but I nod, "I don't hold that against you. I never did."

"I really had no idea," he says. "I am *so* sorry."

"That one's not on you, rich boy. You couldn't help it anymore than I could. So no, I'm not your friend for anything I could get out of you. And I'm not your friend because of what happened right here twenty years ago. I know without a doubt had we met at the movies or at the park or something, we'd still be friends." I catch his gaze and for the first time he meets my eyes. "Because in spite of the lies, the whole unrequited love thing, all of it, I know *you*. I know your heart. I know your soul as well as I know my own." I take his hand. "Because, you see, that's what they don't understand. We're the same. Same heart, same soul. Two halves of the same whole. And nothing, *nothing* will ever change that. I know you're hurting. I know how attractive eternal nothingness is. I do. But I also know you are no coward. You are a fighter. A survivor. A hero. And…a lot of the time that sucks. It's painful, hard. And *not fair*. But what is? You are the Champion of Galilee. The righter of wrongs. Defender of the weak. This city needs you. I need you. Because I know as long as I have you, I can survive anything. And if that's true for me, then it's true for you. I trust you, and I love you." I cup his hand to my cheek as I sniffle. "And shame on you if you throw that away."

He bursts into heart-wracking sobs and falls into my welcoming arms. We cling to each other for dear life, crying on each other's shoulders like we've done a hundred times before, and will continue to do until the day we die. He lets go first, and we wipe each other's tears off, chuckling.

"I love you," he says.

"I love you too." I kiss him chastely on the lips. "Now, let's get off this fucking bridge."

CHAPTER EIGHTEEN
VILLAINS

Why has my life become all about déjà vu?

Here I am at a gala event, dressed to the nines in a black cocktail dress watching the society set walk past me with looks of pity, and my boyfriend is a no show. I've called him twice and no answer. This is getting a little old.

I wait outside the hospital ballroom in the hallway scanning the crowd. Someone is always throwing a charity event for the hospital so they converted a meeting room into a ballroom some years back. I've come to this hospital for parties more than as a patient. The usual suspects are here, hopefully with their checkbooks, looking pleased until they see me. They have no idea how to react, uncomfortable being what they settle on. No eye contact, just half smiles before scurrying into the party. Geez, I survive one little supervillain attack and they act like it's catching. At least most of the bruises and cuts are covered with make-up, otherwise they'd hiss and cover their faces like a vampire confronted by a cross. This is why Harry needs to get his butt here. The only person willing to speak to me is busy with his charity event.

Though never busy enough to neglect me. Justin walks out of the ballroom and through the line of well wishers toward me. "Here you are. I've been looking everywhere for you. I'm about to make my speech."

"Crap," I mutter, not taking my eyes off the end of the hall.

"He'll get here, Jo."

"Well, he doesn't exactly have the best track record." I groan in frustration. "Okay, if he's not here in five minutes, I'm personally going to track him down, Taser him, and drag his butt here and make him spend all night listening to Bitsy talk about her new bathroom tile." Justin chuckles. "What?"

"I pity that man more than words can say."

I smack his chest to stop the laughs. "Shut up."

The chuckles subside. "Seriously, he's a good guy who's probably madly in love with you. He'll be here."

"You think so? I mean about the whole…love thing?"

When he doesn't answer right away, I glance at him. He has the most heartfelt, radiant smile on his face as he gazes down at me. "Oh, Jo," he says, "how could he not be?"

I smile back. "Thanks."

Before he can make me cry, Shannon steps out, harried as usual. "Justin, they're just about ready for you," she says before retreating back in.

Justin sighs. "Oh, goody. Speech time. Why is it I can walk into a warehouse full of men with guns without hesitation, but getting up in front of those people scares the crap out of me?"

"Are you kidding? Those people would wipe the floor with the warehouse goons with just a look. They're vicious." I adjust his bowtie until it's straight. "There. Now get in there, superhero, before I lose all respect for you."

He kisses my cheek. I still get a thrill when he does that. "Thanks, Jo."

I smack his arm. "What are best friends for?"

He grins again, squeezing my good arm before walking away. With a sigh, I turn back to my original position, watching and waiting for Harry. Maybe this is my punishment for postponing our vacation by a week. Or for not staying at his apartment. He said he was okay with both, and we are leaving tomorrow, and I did spend most nights at his place while Justin was out playing superhero, but still. He—No, I'm not doing this. He'll be here. He promised, so he'll be here. He will.

Once again he restores my faith in humanity. My face lights up when I see him running down the hall. "I'm sorry!" he calls to me, almost out of breath. "Sorry. We had a quadruple homicide this afternoon."

"It's okay," I say as I try to tame his disheveled hair. "You're here now." There's applause inside the ballroom. I give him a quick kiss, take his hand, and drag him in. "Come on."

Justin is onstage behind the podium when we sneak in, hanging back by the door. Justin smiles nervously at the crowd, scanning it. He spots me and the nervousness drops, the smile becoming genuine. "I want to thank you all for being here tonight," he begins with confidence, "to support the Dr. Rebecca Thornton Pediatric Recovery Wing." The audience applauds.

"Thank you. Rebecca often spoke of the healing power of family and love. 'I do the easy part,' she said, 'I just put back together their bodies. The parents do all the heavy lifting, repairing their souls. Encouraging their children to fight for life, even when they think they can't do it anymore.'" He meets my eyes and nods. I swell with pride. "This wing, her dream, will aid in that fight. Those children here for long term care, whose parents don't have the means or ability to pay for months in a hotel room, will be able to remain by their child's side for as long as possible to get them well, to be their champion, their strength. So please, dig deep into your pockets and help me heal a few souls. Be a child's hero tonight. Thank you." The audience applauds as Justin walks off the stage, pausing only to glance at the picture of Rebecca behind him.

Harry squeezes my hand. "I'm going to get a drink. You want anything?"

"A diet soda would be great."

He pecks my lips. "You got it." He's about to step away, but I pull him back and plant a wet one on him. He's surprised at first, but kisses me back. "What was that for?" he asks with a laugh.

"Showing up."

"Can't wait to see what my prize is for getting the drinks," he says before walking off.

"Hurry back and find out," I call. Sparkle Cohen, who's been watching the whole exchange, inquisitively stares at me. I raise an eyebrow and shrug. She jots that down with a smile.

As I'm imagining what her blurb will be saying tomorrow, Harry is stopped by the mayor, who smiles and shakes his hand with enthusiasm. A photographer snaps a shot. I roll my eyes. Two weeks ago the mayor was threatening to fire him, now they're best friends. He's even pushing for Harry to become a Major at one of the precincts. I might be dating the future commissioner.

"I didn't know you had a thing for older men," Grace Pickering says as she saddles up to me. I was too busy watching my boyfriend, I didn't notice her approach. We smile at each other. "I thought you liked them tall, blonde, and with cleft chins."

"I do," I say, glancing at Justin who is holding court. "They just don't like me."

"So, is the puppy love over?"

I shrug. "To tell the truth, I think a small part of me will always be a little in love with him. It's just a part of who I am." I sigh. "I've just decided to try requited love for once."

"It's so much better for the skin," Grace says. We chuckle again. "Well, happiness suits you."

"Thank you. You look exquisite tonight as well." She does. She's gained a few pounds and has this glow. She must be getting some.

"You must feel a lot better knowing all the drama's over."

"You too. Must be a weight off knowing he's not coming back."

"I suppose," she says, sipping her champagne. She gazes at the crowd while people keep glancing at us and whispering to each other. Grace and I exchange a look. "I feel like some fresh air. Keep me company?"

Harry is still being fussed over by the mayor, and Justin is drumming up donations. "Love to."

I follow Grace into the hall. "Mind if we stop by the bathroom first?" she asks.

I shrug. "Sure."

"I hate these people," she says as we walk. "I always have. They're so stuffy and selfish. They have the depth of a puddle. I will not miss them."

We walk into the bathroom as two women walk out. "You're leaving?" I ask.

She goes into the stall. "Tonight. I'm sick of this town. There's nothing for us here now."

"Where are you going?" I ask, applying more lipstick.

"Brazil," she says inside the stall. "Rio, more specifically."

My back straightens and a feeling of dread runs down my spine. Oh, shit. No way. No way in hell. Just in case, I start reaching for the gun strapped to my thigh. "Why there?"

Before I can get it, the stall door flies open. Grace holds a small gun with silencer right at me. "You know. No extradition treaty." She gestures up. "Hands behind your head, please."

Shit. I do as she says, lacing my fingers behind my head. "Jane Smith, I presume."

She smiles. "I hear you've been looking for me."

I stare at her, eyes bulging out of my head. "What the fuck, Grace? The man kidnapped and raped you. He killed your fiancée."

She laughs, shaking her head. "You know, I'm not surprised you never knew about Justin. You are really a moron, Joanna."

"Enlighten me."

She considers it, walking over to the bathroom door and locking it before resuming her position right in front of me. "I fell in love with James the moment I saw him and him me. Chad was…dull. He was like every other man I had ever dated. No fight, no vim or vigor. No imagination. James had fire in his eyes. Ambition. A devil-may-care attitude that drove me wild. After that first night, we met up wherever we could. The gym, the opera, it was thrilling. The sex was…" She shakes in ecstasy at the memory. "Intense. Passionate. Then one night we misjudged time, and Chad almost caught us. I made up the mugging story."

"Why didn't you just dump Chad?"

"I needed his money. Pickering was in the red. Daddy overextended before he died, and left me with a dead company. I knew Chad always had a thing for me, and I wanted to keep my legacy afloat. He was a billionaire, and I was fond of him. Marriages have been built on less. Then James came into my life and showed me what was really important. But I couldn't let my company go under. I couldn't let Daddy be right about me. James didn't have enough to cover it all, so we came up with a plan. Chad and I changed our wills to make each other the beneficiary, and James was supposed to kill him at the AIDS gala. Justin ruined that. So we came up with a new plan."

"You staged your own kidnapping to cover up the murder?"

"Exactly. Then it all went to shit once again because of Justin. For years he'd been looking for Alkaline's identity and he chose *then* to put it all together. James went mad. I couldn't be released after the ransom drop and then go on to be comforted and courted by James Ryder if he was the man who kidnapped me. So we plotted, and planned, trying to find a way out of it without getting suspicion thrown on me."

"You were never a prisoner."

"Nope. I went out when I wanted, in disguise of course. In spite of all that was happening, it was the happiest time of my life. We made love all day, we cooked each other meals, played chess. It was bliss." She scowls. "But he just wouldn't listen. I begged him to just leave it all. Chad, the money, Justice didn't matter anymore, only we did. James couldn't let Justice win. He was obsessed. The confrontation at the library was the final straw. He came home so enraged even *I* was afraid of him." She scoffs. "The one time I went out without a disguise, I was spotted. I told them the story James said for me to tell if either of us was ever caught. See? He went to jail to protect *me*."

"And so you helped him murder people?"

"We have both been living in *hell* these past few years because of Justice. He deserves everything he got."

"You bankrolled this whole thing. You hired the P.I. to stalk us. You lured me and Cam to the prison that night. You gave him the invitation to get into the engagement party. You used your Cayman account to frame Stu Moore."

"And a million other things I don't regret."

"He *raped* a woman, Grace. He killed a child."

"In a war, there is always collateral damage."

"You really are insane, you know that right?"

She closes her eyes, shaking her head sadly. I push the panic button on my bracelet. "You wouldn't make that statement if you ever knew true, unabiding love like I have. I would do *anything* for him, as he would me."

"So, what? You're going to shoot me to avenge him?"

"Oh, honey," she chuckles. "You wish."

That's when it dawns on me. "He's still alive, isn't he?"

"And *so* looking forward to seeing you again."

Someone crashes through the door, jolting us both. Justin rushes in. "Grace—"

Without missing a beat she points and fires the gun twice, hitting Justin in the forehead. I scream as he crumples to the floor. I'm too shocked to move, but she isn't. "That should buy us about five minutes," she says, gazing down at my lifeless friend. She holds her huge diamond ring up to her mouth. "My love, plan fucking B." She grabs me, gun pressed right at my head. She pushes me forward. "Move it." We step over Justin's body into his blood and I get a chill. I know he'll heal, but this is still a bit much. "Open the door," she says. "Then put your hands back up."

More guns greet us when we step out. Harry, Geoff, and three other officers dressed in tuxes wait outside the door. Other officers try to corral the rubbernecking party goers, attempting to get them out of the line of fire. "Drop the gun, Grace," Harry says. "You're surrounded."

Grace presses the hot muzzle even harder into my temple. "Don't think so. You're going to let me and your dear Joanna make our appointment."

"Or we could just shoot you right here," Harry says.

"I wouldn't advise that. You see, if you touch one hair on my head, James will blow this hospital sky high." All the men's faces fall. "Oh, yeah. We've planted charges all over. We both do so love a party with a *bang*!" she shouts that last word and we all flinch. Grace chuckles, causing a shiver down my spine. "So, you have two options. Well, really only one. Joanna comes with me, and you don't follow. If we see even one cop or Justice in there, kaboom. Got me there, handsome?"

Harry stares at her with utter contempt, gun shaking in his hand. He wants to shoot her, and I think he might. "It's okay, Harry," I say. He looks at me now, fear overshadowing his eyes. "Let us go."

"Listen to your girlfriend, Harry," Grace says. "For once, an intelligent comment has escaped her lips."

He looks at me again, eyes begging. There's nothing he can do and we both know it. He lowers his gun and the others follow suit. "Fine."

"Got yourself a smart one, Joanna," she says. "Now back off and we'll be on our merry way." She pulls me back and the men part. We walk backwards down the hall past frightened bystanders hugging the walls. Bitsy yelps and crouches down, covering her head as we pass. "Hello, Bitsy. Love to the family." Bitsy squeals in fright, and Grace chuckles. We reach the elevator and she pushes the button with her elbow. Harry takes a step toward us, but Grace cocks the gun for effect. "Don't worry, Harry. I promise you'll get her back." I feel her body move when she shrugs. "Might be in pieces, but still." The elevator doors open and she moves us in. "Remember, gents. *Kaboom!*"

The door shuts. She pushes me away and I spin around, hands still up. With her free hand, she presses the button for the top floor. "Well, that got complicated," she says with annoyance. She holds up her ring. "Honey, I'm in the elevator. Hope you're in position." She looks back at me. "You. You have five seconds to lose any weapons or bugs on you. If I search and find one, I'll replace it with a bullet, get me? So where are they?"

I glare at her. "Gun, right thigh. Necklace, panic button and tracking device."

"Good girl." She rips the cameo right off my neck, then stomps on it before lifting up my dress and pulling off my .38. She tosses it on the floor too. "Knew we were coming?"

"Knew if he was, it'd be tonight."

"Didn't see me coming, though," she says with pride. "Or this." She pulls the emergency button on the panel and we jerk to a stop between the twenty-second and twenty-third floors. Before I can even register this, there's a thump on the roof. Grace stays as calm as ever, gun never leaving me. The hatch on top opens, and one of the guards from Grace's apartment peers down. "Up you go, Jo." Having no choice, I take the man's outstretched hand. He pulls me up into the elevator shaft with little effort, then Grace. She points the gun again. "Up the ladder. *Now.*"

I climb with Grace right behind me. I'd kick her, but I can't risk the gun going off. About three floors up, I'm greeted by another guard, the former Independence linebacker, half in and out of the open door on the floor above us. He yanks me up the rest of the way. The twenty-sixth floor is the future site of the recovery wing. It's deserted, just a storage area that used to be a research lab. A familiar face greets me. Alkaline, without a scratch on him, is dressed in his old dark green costume and trench coat. He holds out his hand to help me up. "Nice to see you again, Joanna."

I bat his hand away and stand on my own. "Fuck you. How the hell did you survive?"

"Ran like the wind and was fortunate enough to find a sewer hole. Disgusting, but it saved my life. I was so happy to hear you made it as well. Touch and go there for a moment."

Grace is hoisted up by the linebacker, who then pulls out his gun and points it at me. Grace brushes the dust off her dress. "Did you hear what I told them? About the bombs?"

Alkaline takes her in his arms and kisses her deeply. "Convincing as always, darling."

"There are no bombs?" I ask.

"Of course not," Grace says as if I'm a dunce.

"We're not *monsters*, Joanna," Alkaline says.

"Matter of opinion," I say with my best shit-eating grin.

Alkaline shakes his head at my insolence. He and Grace spin around when the second guard pushes himself out of the shaft. He pulls out a little black box with a switch on it. "All breaks disabled, sir, and the charges are set."

"Good. Everyone step back," Alkaline orders. The bomber pulls out the door jam and the elevator door closes. I'm yanked by the linebacker a few feet as the other guard presses the button.

"Kaboom," Grace says with a smile as the explosion rings out.

The metal door crumples from the blast and smoke spews from the cracks. I can hear the elevator fall, the screeching of twisted metal like nails on a chalkboard making me cringe. A second later there's another boom as the elevator crashes to the ground.

"That should keep them busy," Alkaline says with a satisfied smile. "Let's go. Rio awaits."

The linebacker and bomber exchange guns, so now the linebacker has the pistol and bomber the shotgun he then roughly pulls me along with the small crowd. The bomber leads the way, gun at the ready. Alkaline and Grace walk hand in hand behind him like they're strolling in the park, with me at the back. "So, that's your plan? Take me on vacation?" I ask.

The bomber opens the stairwell door, going in first while we wait. "Oh, you're coming with us," Alkaline says. "Though I doubt you'll enjoy yourself that much." The guard waves us in. We run up the stairs, all the bad guys looking up, down, and sideways for bogies. "You see," he says as we go, "I don't plan to kill you."

"Not unless you make him," Grace adds.

"But I am going to melt off as many of your appendages as I can and mail them to your friend. You should be able to survive to return to him, so for the rest of his life he can look at you and know he's failed."

"Don't worry, though. We'll keep you so doped up you won't know what's going on," Grace says.

"How thoughtful," I say through the rising bile.

We keep running up the stairs, and the panic rises with each footfall. I don't know what to do. He must have a helicopter waiting up there to whisk me off to visit Dr. Mengele in South America. I only know one thing. There is no way in hell I'm getting on that chopper. They'll have to shoot me first.

The bomber opens the door at the top and a gust of cold wind bursts in. I get goose bumps and shiver, but not from the weather. I'm dragged outside, the wind whipping my hair around. The angled chain-link fence surrounding the perimeter of the rooftop vibrates and rattles in the wind. We gaze up at the empty raised helipad. "Where the hell is it?" Grace asks. They scan the horizon and spot it in the distance, descending like the angel of death. There's just one more flight of stairs, well a ramp, between me and pure hell. I always wanted to go out fighting.

The linebacker's attention, like all the others', is on the approaching helicopter. Now or never. With every inch of my strength, I spin at the waist and cold-cock my captor square in the nose. Involuntarily, he releases me to touch his nose. Not missing a beat, I knee him in the groin while grabbing the gun. I take aim at the others as they spin around. Grace fires first, but I'm too fast for her. I leap behind the stunned linebacker, and she hits him instead. As I sprint back toward the door, and I fire back. Their bullets miss me by centimeters. I leap through the open door, and push it closed just as two slugs hit it, leaving indentations on my side of it. Better it than me.

There's no way in hell they'll let me get away that easily. With no way to lock the door, I race down the stairs, reach the landing, duck under the corner of the railing and taking aim back up at the door crouching low. The moment it opens again, I fire. The door shuts just as I hear Grace shriek, "Just leave her!" Guess she's had enough.

I wait a second. No storming down, just the faint sound of the whirly bird. Another second passes and I can breathe again. I can't just stay here. No matter how much I want to, I can't run away. He'll keep coming after me until he has me. I'll be looking over my shoulder, we all will, for the rest of our days. I have seven bullets left. He'll get on that chopper over my dead body.

I'm about to storm up the steps when I hear a noise below. Without thinking, I swing the gun toward it. The moment I do, there's a flash of movement on the stairs below. Before I can register this, Justin appears in front of me, blood on his cheeks and shirt from the now healed bullet wounds. He throws his arms up. "Don't shoot!"

I lower the gun and throw myself down the two steps into his arms. "About time."

We squeeze each other tight, but only for a moment. "Are you okay?"

"Fine. He's out there."

"How many?"

"Three at least."

"Bombs?"

"A lie."

He nods. "Thought so."

"Plan?"

"You cover me from the door."

"No way. We go out together."

"I work alone."

"Fight together, or die alone. I know which one I choose."

He hesitates for a split second, but knows me well enough for it to last only that split second. "Alkaline's mine."

I nod in agreement. "Let's go be heroes."

I start up the stairs with him one pace behind me. We stop at the door, listening. The sound of the helicopter is loud, which means it's landed. I look into my best friend's blue eyes and he into mine. We give each other a thrilling smile. "It's an honor to fight by your side, Justice."

He grabs the back of my head, pulling me into a quick kiss. "The honor is mine, Detective." The smile doesn't leave either of our faces as he turns the handle.

This is it. What we were put on this earth to do.

And God do we love it.

The door flies open, and he's off. I take one step outside and begin shooting. Grace and the bomber have no idea where to look, the source of the gunfire or the superhero rushing up the ramp like a freight train. My shots hit the guard square in the head, exploding it just as Justice grabs Alkaline. He runs the villain through the open door of the helicopter and out the other side. The copter jolts as the door breaks off with a creek, the two men and the door all tumbling over the side of the platform out of sight.

"James!" Grace shrieks.

I take cover behind one of the air conditioning vents. I get her in my sights, firing once and missing her head, but hitting the helicopter. Realizing she's a sitting duck she fires back, getting too close for comfort. I duck again, and the next time I peer out she's leaping off the side of the ramp for protection. The helicopter pilot wises up, taking off. "No!" Grace shouts after it. She fires at me again. "Bitch!"

I poke my head out and she fires, this time the spark of the bullet on metal striking close enough to feel. "Guess that trip into the sunset is cancelled, huh Grace?" I call out. "You know, if he really loved you, you two would be gone by now. How does it feel playing second fiddle to a superhero?"

"Shut up!"

I check around the corner again, and she fires. I can still see her, so I fire back. And that's it. I'm out. Shit. "You know what I think," I say after a chuckle, "and the GFPD, as well as our psychologist shares this theory. We've been laughing about it all the time. We think it's not you he loves. We think when he's

on top of you, whispering promises of love, it's really Justice
he's thinking of. How about it, Grace? In the heat of passion, has
he ever called out, 'Justice, oh Justice,'" I say in my best porn
voice. "Huh? Has he?"

"You fucking bitch!"

I peek again and she fires twice. I step back, chuckling.
"Hit a nerve, did I Grace?" She has one more bullet left now.
She—

A bleeding and battered Alkaline stumbles into view, the
trench coat gone and his costume ripped. With a roar he runs
back behind the helipad out of view. Judging from the state of
him, I think we're winning. "Just saw your boyfriend, Grace," I
shout, "and he is getting his ass kicked. What—"

I spy around the corner, but this time I'm greeted by a
gun right in my face. Training takes over. Using the barrel, I pull
the gun toward me to break her finger while bending her wrist
down with one fluid moment. It works. She screams in pain and I
retrieve the gun. But I underestimate crazy strength. Before I can
re-position the gun, she's on me, knocking us both onto the
concrete, hitting my still tender head. She bites my hand, and I
drop her gun. As she reaches for it, I smack her in the nose with
my forehead. We're both stunned, but she more so. I grab her
arms and roll her onto her back, retrieving the gun and pointing it
right at her face. "Don't move."

She just sniggers. "Ward trash."

With one good swipe of the gun to her head, she's out.
"And proud of it."

I tear a piece of fabric from my dress and knot her hands
behind her back, and race off to help my friend. I run up the
ramp to get a better view and grab the dead guard's shotgun. Five
shots left. It'll have to do. At least I have the high ground. I dash
over to the side of the heliport. It's a mess down there. The roof
is smoking and melting from where Alkaline's shot. The twisted
metal of the helicopter door lies in a heap directly below. About
ten yards away, I see them. Justin rests against the rattling chain-
link protector, unconscious. Alkaline looms over him, laughing
manically as he punches Justin's chest over and over again,
blood blooming with each hit. The bones coming out of
Alkaline's wrists barely have time to drip blood before they're

plunged back into Justin's chest. Justin doesn't move, doesn't even register the blows anymore. I think he's dead.

"Ryder!" I shout. The madman looks up, blood caking his face. "It's over. Get off him or I'll blow your brains out. Pretty sure you can't regenerate a new head." I cock the shotgun.

"Do that and I'll stop being nice. I'm right near his heart, Joanna. Shoot me and it gets a nice dose of acid. Think he can grow an entire heart? Because I don't."

"You're bluffing. You would have done it already if you hadn't blown your wad."

"Think so?" With the bone not inside my friend, he shoots a small amount of liquid right by Justin's head, disintegrating the chain-link behind. "Drop the gun, Detective, or be responsible for the death of the city's champion."

I don't know what to do. If I shoot him, he might obliterate Justin's heart. I don't, there's a tiny chance he'll let Justin go. Justin makes the choice for me. His eye opens, and a wave of relief washes over me. "Okay," I say. "We go at the same time." I start bending down as he begins pulling out the bone at the same pace.

Justin comes alive. As Alkaline keeps his eyes on me, Justin grabs both his wrists. The bone in his chest breaks in half, acid spilling onto Justin, but Alkaline is howling in pain. I spring up again, firing into his back. His body jerks from the impact. He falls off Justin onto the chain-link, blood, the acid spewing from his wrist. Smiling, I expel the shell. "I think we win."

I run down the ramp, past the still unconscious Grace, and around the corner. Alkaline is whimpering and Justin is still leaning against the fence when I reach them. Both look like hell, but Justin's face and chest are covered in blood, burns, and gaping holes. Even with regeneration I think he's going to need a doctor. I lean beside him. "Are you okay?" He doesn't register my presence. His eyes remain glued to the man beside him. I shake him. "Justin?"

His face contorts in bestial fury. He knocks me away onto my butt as he lunges at Alkaline. I barely see the blows, just the aftermath as Justin hits and hits, cracking his jaw, nose, teeth until he's unrecognizable. Pulp. He's going to kill him, no question. "Justin, stop!" He can't hear me. I leap up and try to grab his arm, but he swats me away so hard I skid a few feet, the shotgun gliding away. I'm dazed again with the wind knocked out of me, and when I shake my head to recover Justin grabs Alkaline by the shirt, positioning him over the fence. The acid from Alkaline's damaged wrist drips onto the metal. "No!" I shriek.

Justin's gaze whips toward me, madness and rage filling those blue eyes. "What?"

"Justin, put him down." I slowly find my feet. "Don't do this."

"Why? He killed them!" he roars, taking another step. "He killed them! He…burned her alive. He raped her!" He turns back to Alkaline, who hangs there like a rag doll with his eyes closed. "He ruined my life! He's a monster!"

"He is, he is," I say desperately as I take another step. "He will pay for his crimes. He will. We'll make sure of it."

"No," Justin says, voice quaking. "He'll just escape again. I know he will. I have to protect you. I have to protect everyone!" Alkaline's now suspended only by Justin with nothing but the river thirty stories below. The fence barely supports them both, the metal bending and rippling with each movement.

"This is not the way to do it," I say with another step. "Justin, look at me. *Look at me!*" His tear filled eyes meet mine. "I know what he's taken from you. I do. But if you do this, that is cold blooded murder. You will be a murderer, Justin. Everything you have worked for, everything you stand for will be meaningless. It is not up to you to be judge, jury, and executioner. Justice isn't about people killing the dregs that need killing. That's why we have a system. Our society is based on laws and due process. It takes time, it isn't perfect, but it's better than every individual meting out whatever justice he feels is right. If Justice, Champion of Galilee, succumbs to the base instinct of vengeance by killing Alkaline, it would do more than just kill him. It would kill the trust in the system you and I have worked so hard to uphold. This is bigger than your hatred. Do this and you will lose your soul. Then where will the citizens of Galilee be?"

His arms quiver and he turns back to Alkaline's lifeless, pathetic, broken body. He looks at him, emotions running the gamut from revulsion to hate and finally to shame. "Oh, God," he says before tossing the body back on the roof. "Oh, God."

I run over to him as he steps off the fence, throwing my arms around him, his blood soaking me. "It's okay," I whisper as I stroke his bloody hair. "It's okay. It's over. It's over."

I don't know how long we stay locked in each other's arms. He cups the back of my head, pulling me into him even closer and kissing the top of my head. "Thank you. Thank you."

"You'd do the same for me. I—" His body grows tense. I look up at him, fear gripping me when I see the look of shock on his face.

It all happens so fast. I feel him spin me around just as the sound of the shotgun explodes through the air. Justin lurches as the pellets smash into him, and then him into me. Spots of blood bursts onto my face. We stumble back into the chain-link as another blast rocks us. Then another. We topple onto the metal, rolling. Justin releases me, and I only catch a glimpse of Alkaline holding the shotgun on us before I realize I'm right at the edge and can't stop moving. I see the darkness below me and The Falls off in the distance before I roll once more onto nothing. I'm too shocked to scream.

My body is weightless for a moment, but then something warm grabs my wrist to stop my descent. My arm almost comes out of its socket, but I swing to the side. I grab the metal bar at the top of the fence and the hand releases me. I turn and see Justin dangling a few feet away. My shoes slip off and like an idiot I look down. I can make out the lights on the outdoor patio thirty stories down and the river beside it. My arms begin shaking from terror and weakness. "Hold on!" Justin says beside me.

The fence shakes and bends even further down. I barely hold on as we drop two feet, moving my hands to the rungs instead of the bar, curling my toes and fingers in them for dear life. I look up to my left. Alkaline smiles like a maniac above us, especially with his jaw out of whack. He cracks it back into place and walks closer, spilling his acid along the length of the fence where it meets the roof. It sizzles and twangs as it melts. "You know," he says, sounding odd because of the injuries, "you used to be better at this, Justin. In the old days, you never would have let your guard down like that. Love and domesticity have made you complacent. I'm not having nearly as much fun as I thought I would."

One of the metal rods holding the fence splits and falls. As do we, I scream as we drop and swing at least four feet so we're almost vertical. My arms and legs shake from fatigue. We're too heavy. It's going to keep breaking.

"Stop it," Justin shouts from above me. He tries to climb but Alkaline fires. Justin's outstretched left hand disintegrates all over my face. He falls a foot, almost on top of me. We both cry out.

"Don't tell me what to do, Justin." Alkaline bends down, swinging the shotgun over his shoulder. "See, that's why I had to knock you down a peg. There's nothing I hate more than the high and mighty. You're not perfect. You're not God. You don't get to decide other people's fates. You're just a man, capable of both good and evil. Just showed you that, didn't I? You like scales. It's all about balance, right? Now, I'll admit mine is definitely tipped in the favor of evil."

I hear more sizzling as he dissolves the fence directly above us. The first of it snaps, then another bit. I can't move, I'm so terrified. "The thing I learned early on, though," he continues as if he's at the pulpit, "is that it really doesn't matter," he says with a chuckle. "Here you are! You saved countless lives, and what do you have to show for it? Your good deeds caused the death of all of those you hold dear. That's what I'm trying to teach you, Justin! There is no justice in the world!" Another two melt. "You can save a hundred thousand people, and it wouldn't matter a bit. There is no point to your self-sacrifice. People will always be selfish. People will always kill each other over money, or drugs, or just for the sheer fun of it. Your life and everything you stand for is *meaningless*. You're obsolete. Ineffectual." He sprinkles more acid. "Redundant. The bad will always outweigh the good. You really can't save anyone. This is not a world for heroes."

Then we hear and see it, a helicopter gliding in behind Alkaline. He turns to view it. GFPD is embossed on it. I've never seen anything so beautiful. It circles toward us. "Police! Put your hands up!" The spotlight shines on him, and he smiles as he raises his arms. Inside there are four men with assault rifles pointed at him. The chopper moves toward the helipad.

Alkaline gazes down at us, triumph still on his face. "Too late."

He's right. Two more links rip and a third pops a second later. Only four left. We drop another few inches. It can't hold us anymore. I look up at Justin, and he down at me, and I know it. My best friend smiles down at me with such love it's as brilliant as the sunrise.

And my stomach free falls. "You're wrong, Ryder. *So* wrong," Justin says calmly.

"Justin…" I say through the panic.

"I love you."

He lets go.

Both Alkaline and I shout, "No!" as he plummets down and down and down for what feels like an eternity, thirty stories into the black river. I can't even see or hear the splash.

He's gone. He's gone.

I hang here, unable to even blink. Anguish like nothing I have ever felt envelops me. The world disappears. There is nothing. I gaze at my quivering fingers. It'd be so easy. Just open them and plunge. The ultimate freedom. I'm tired. So tired. Just open. Open! They won't. If I do this, Alkaline wins. The ultimate selfish act. It'd all be for nothing. He'd win. *No.*

My gaze whips up to his stunned and angry one. For the thirty seconds it takes for the helicopter to land and SWAT to run up to Alkaline, we don't break the silent battle. Not even when I climb up or they push him to the ground and handcuff him. We are the only two people in the world. Never breaking eye contact, Alkaline is yanked up, a small smile on his face.

"What he did doesn't prove a thing," he says with a smug smile before they begin leading him away. He knows what's in store for him. Three meals a day. Fan mail. More time to plot his escape. We're both aware of it. Not fair.

"Wait!"

With one fluid moment I pick up the shotgun at my feet and point it at him. The sound of my cocking it makes him and

Alvarez, the SWAT officer, turn. I briefly glance at Alvarez, something in my eyes making him relax. He knows me. Brothers in blue always. He'll cover for me, no question. He even steps away when I gesture for him to. Ryder's smile falters, but doesn't disappear.

My best friend just died before my eyes because of him.

He's terrorized the city for years.

Killed dozens.

Tortured.

Maimed.

Destroyed my life.

It's not fair.

My finger puts pressure on the trigger as Alkaline watches, captivated yet horrified. A slight twitch of the finger and it's all over. Something visceral inside me longs to see his head explode right here, right now. It's feel so fucking sweet. He deserves to die, and I have every reason to kill him. He knows it.

"But this does." I lower the barrel and toss the gun to Alvarez. Both men are shocked, Alkaline's smile turning into a scowl. "The good guys win, even when they lose."

"Come on," Alvarez says as he yanks the livid Alkaline away. I wait until he's out of sight before I turn back to the night sky and waterfall in the distance, hugging myself and shaking until Harry wraps me into his warm arms. I burst into tears.

Chapter Nineteen
Justified

Fifty thousand people from all walks of life have come together in Stan Lee Park to honor my best friend, the largest gathering in the city's history. I insisted it be called a celebration of life instead of a memorial, just the way Justin would have wanted it. There's even a Ferris wheel, games, and clowns around with all proceeds going to the hospital. Justin and Rebecca would approve.

I do wish he could have been interred in the Pendergast crypt with his parents and grandparents, or had a proper funeral, but this is better. His body never washed up. They dragged the river for days, but not even a shoe surfaced. For those days I clung to the hope he made it, that he could survive, but I know that's not the case. He would have made contact by now. Not even Justice could survive a thirty story fall into water without being knocked out and subsequently drowning. He was officially declared dead a week later.

The media went into an orgasmic frenzy over the whole thing. The public couldn't get enough of the whole story. Galilee's captain of industry and upholder of justice, protector of the weak, all melded into one handsome package gives his life for his best friend. The news stations rehashed both his lives until he was practically canonized for sainthood. I don't disagree.

I lean against a tree near the stage, a small smile on my face as a twenty-something girl tells the story of the time Justice saved her from being raped. The man was convicted and tried, and she became a rape crisis counselor, to help others like her. This type of story, coupled with anecdotes about the men behind the mask, have been going on for almost two hours. I especially loved Bitsy's retelling of their dinner in New Urbana when she looked across the table and just *knew* he was Justice. So never happened. The girl finishes to applause and steps off the stage, replaced by an elderly gentleman who recounts the time Justice saved him from a mugging twenty years ago.

After a dozen police and bystanders saw Justin recover in a few minutes from two shots to the head, the Pendergast secret was out of the bag. I didn't deny it. They deserve to be recognized for all they've done for this city. Good deeds should be acknowledged, and fifty thousand people here agree with me.

Harry worms his way through the crowd with my water. "Sorry. There was a line." He gives me a kiss before handing me my drink. "Hey, you'll never guess who is here. Captain Moonlight. I used to have his poster over my bed when I was a kid." He slides his hand around my waist and I rest my head on his shoulder. "I got his autograph." I smile at him. Don't know if I love him yet, but I sure as hell need him.

The old man finishes and we all applaud. Shannon, an absolute god-send these last two weeks, rushes over. "The press is getting restless. You should go on next."

"Okay," I say. She nods and runs off to put out more fires.

Harry looks at me full of concern. "You know you don't have to do this. If you don't want to or aren't ready—"

I press my finger to his well meaning lips. "Of course I do. Think a little thing like fifty thousand people is going to scare me? I think not." But it does. It *so* does.

"What if they ask you about Alkaline? Or Grace?"

"I tell the truth."

Ryder and Grace were both taken into custody and charged, but only Grace pleaded not guilty. I have a trial to look forward to in the coming months, but right now she's in solitary under close scrutiny. As for Alkaline, even I don't know where they took him. It's rumored he's in the underground bowel of the prison, completely cut off from humanity and doped to the gills where he will remain until the end of his days. They won't make the same mistake twice. I just pray they don't make any new ones.

There are times when the weight of regret crushes me. When I walked into Justin's bedroom and smelled his scent. When I had to tell Lucy that her nephew was dead. When I wake in a cold sweat from a nightmare as I just watch him fall over and over again is almost unbearable. Pretty much every second of the day because Alkaline's out there breathing when my best friend isn't. But it's not about what's fair, it's about what's right.

I get that now. It's not about dying for Justice, it's about maintaining justice. Much harder.

The speaker, an old friend of J.T.'s, finishes his tale and the audience applauds. The mayor steps onto the stage to introduce me. I hand Harry my water and fluff my hair. "How do I look?"

"Beautiful," Harry says with a proud smile. "Absolutely beautiful."

I give him a quick kiss before walking toward the stage. The photographers go nuts and reporters shout questions. V waves and I wave back. She's been getting scoops and exclusives from me for two weeks. I take care of my friends.

"...the woman who put this day together, Joanna Fallon."

The audience roars with applause. I smile graciously as I step onto the stage, waving. "Thank you!" I say into the microphone. "Thank you everyone!" The applause continues for a few more seconds then dies down. "I want to, um, thank you all for being here today. This is an amazing turn out. And I want to thank all the people who shared their stories today. It really...means a lot." The audience applauds again and I nod. Harry beams up at me as Dobbs joins him. I smile back before continuing.

"We're all here today to honor a man, well rather a family of men, who gave their lives for this city. By now you are all aware of who I am speaking of. J.J., J.T., and Justin Pendergast IV, Justice." They go wild again. "Now, I never had the honor of meeting the others, but they touched my life regardless, as they have all of yours. Like many of you, I grew up worshiping the man who called himself Justice. I'm sure I'm not alone in having an old box filled with t-shirts, posters, and action figures of Justice tucked away in my closet. You know who you are." The people chuckle with me. "I wish I had known them. They were honorable, brave, and helped make this great city what it is today."

I hold for applause again, and then take a deep breath. I have one goal today. To get through this without crying. "Like all of the other speakers today, I have a story about our hero to share. When I was twelve and he was just thirteen, Justin Pendergast saved my life. He didn't do it with brute force or super-speed or any type of superpower. You see, my father had just been murdered. My father was my best friend, my protector, the best man I've ever known. And his death, the unfairness of it, the hole it left in my life was just…too much. I found myself alone in the dead of winter, icicles forming on my cheeks from my tears, looking over the side of Pendergast Bridge willing myself to jump." I meet Harry's eyes and give a small smile. I've never told him this story. His visage is pained, but he garners a reassuring smile. I can continue now. "I didn't hear him approach. I was too busy working the odds of breaking through the ice versus crashing onto it like concrete.

"'Do you need help?' was the first thing he said to me. I turned around, not all together happy with the presence of another human being, and more than willing to let him know this. But the moment I set eyes on him, I was speechless. For those of you who don't know me, I should tell you this was an unprecedented occurrence." The audience laughs along with me. "Here was this gorgeous thirteen-year-old boy coming to my rescue, in a limo no less. It took me a moment, but I reminded myself what I was there to do. No raging hormones or angelic boy was going to stop Joanna Fallon from doing what she wanted to do. I told him to go away in a not very nice way. He just stood there and said, 'I can't do that.' That…did not go over well with me. I will not repeat the litany of abuse that followed because it would make a sailor blush." More laughs.

I gaze at the audience and shrug my shoulders. "He still wouldn't go. 'What kind of person would I be if I left you here?' he asked me. So he didn't leave. He stood on that bridge with a total stranger freezing his butt off, shivering next to me, for an hour just talking. That was it, he just talked to me…until there was nothing left to say. He took my hand and we walked off that bridge together. You're looking at the first person Justin Pendergast IV saved, and he did it with a smile, some conversation, and just—showing—up," I say, my voice cracking.

I pause to collect myself. I'm going to cry, I know it. I can't do this without breaking down. I can't. An errant tear leaks out and slides down my cheek. I don't have the strength. The audience murmurs about me. I'm about to step off the stage when I see him. Off in the distance, standing alone underneath a tree, I see a tall man, hair rimmed gold by the sun, smiling at me with such love and pride. All fear vanishes and grace washes through my soul. I smile back before he gallantly nods, tipping his imaginary hat, and vanishes before my eyes. I look down at the podium, breathless. A newfound strength settles into my bones, and I look up at the concerned audience, and hold my head held high.

"'All that is necessary for the triumph of evil is that good men do nothing.' These are the words Justin Pendergast lived by. Words he took to heart, and practiced every day. He didn't have to don the costume his ancestors did. He didn't have to go out there every night, getting shot and stabbed to stop the muggers, rapists, and crazies with superpowers. He did it because he felt it was the right thing to do. The just thing. He did it…because this city is worth it. People are worth it." I look at the audience, catching the eyes of as many people as I can.

"And don't a single one of you forget it."

I step off the stage to uproarious applause. Thank you, Justin.

The press shouts questions at me and city government members congratulate me as I scan the crowd for Harry. A patrol woman is speaking to him, both very intense. He tells her something and she runs off. I push my way to him. The woman comes back with her partner, just as I reach them. "What's going on?"

"Hexen's enchanted some trees," Harry says with a sigh. "They're coming this way, threatening everyone. It's a mess." He shakes his head. "Just another day in Galilee Falls."

A woman screams in the distance. The stomping begins a second later as the tops of trees sway and part as the monster approaches. The crowd panics, dispersing every which way in pandemonium. "Oh, hell," I say as I pull out my gun and badge from my purse. A hero's work is never done. "Let's go get him." And we run into the fray.

God, I love this city.

Joanna Fallon will return in Book Two coming soon…

Acknowledgements

First, to my agent Sandy Lu at the Lori Perkins Literary Agency. She stuck with this book until the bitter end, and it was a bitter end. We tried, *they* failed.

To my cover artist Damonza. It turned out so good, better than I imagined. You were worth every penny. Visit him at www.damonza.com.

To my Beta readers Susan Dowis, Jill Kardell, Ginny Dowis, Lydia Vigna for helping shape the book. And to all the editors who gave their suggestions and fought for the book. I appreciated your time and lovely rejection letters.

To Alan Orloff who once again answered all my questions and guided me through this process. You're a mensch.

To Newport Beach Library, Huntington Beach Library, Fairfax County Library System, and Prince William County Library Systems for giving me lovely places to write. I miss you first two, and the cute boys within your walls.

And finally, to anyone past, present, and future who has taken a chance on my books. I hope never to disappoint you.

ABOUT THE AUTHOR

Jennifer Harlow spent her restless childhood fighting with her three brothers and scaring the heck out of herself with horror movies and books. She grew up to earn a degree at the University of Virginia which she put to use as a radio DJ, crisis hotline volunteer, bookseller, lab assistant, wedding coordinator, and government investigator. Currently she calls Northern Virginia home but that restless itch is ever present. In her free time, she continues to scare the crap out of herself watching scary movies and opening her credit card bills. She is the author of the Amazon Best Selling F.R.E.A.K.S. Squad and Midnight Magic Mystery Series. For more information and the **soundtrack** to this and her other books visit www.jenniferharlowbooks.com or follow her on Twitter @jenharlowbooks.

www.ingramcontent.com/pod-product-compliance
Lightning Source LLC
Chambersburg PA
CBHW070843250626
47159CB00003B/906